THE Only ONE

NECIE NAVONE

Brothers OF Camelot

The Only One

by Necie Navone
Copyright 2017 by Necie Navone
Cover Design & Formatting by:
RMGraphX
Editor with an enhancing eye:
Michelle Luxembourger

ISBN: 978-0-9997235-0-0

Michelle Cook, Kaila Duff, and Sandy Schmidt. You ladies ROCK. I don't know what I'd do without you. Your love and support compares to no other and means the world to me.

Andrea Jee, for all your grammar edits of all my books. You really had your work cut out for you. Warning: more is coming. I owe you greatly. Thank you.

Michelle Luxembourger, girlie, this book would have never made it this far without your help, support, encouragement and creative editing, and for enhancing my work and making it come to life even more. Thank you from the bottom of my heart.

To all my other Facebook friends, there are too many to name, I say a huge THANK YOU! And last but not least, I need to thank my hubs who also had to listen to my storylines and crazy ideas. I thank you for your love and understanding, support and for allowing me to pursue this crazy dream.

DEDICATION

I'd like to thank one of my sons, Joel, even if he never reads this book completely. (Which I hope he doesn't!) He's provided constant support and encouragement to me in pursuing my dreams of being a writer. Even though I suffer from severe dyslexia, he would tell me to try harder and never give up. After he ripped my work apart, he'd never take 'no' or 'I can't' for an answer, and would give me time to lick my wounds before he'd ask again,
"Are you writing yet, Mom?"
Thank you for all those late nights of answering my storyline questions, letting me bounce ideas off you, and for spending last Christmas vacation helping me rip apart and re-write 'My Hidden Life' over and over again. I'd also like to thank you for teaching me not to give up on that trilogy, which will also be coming out very soon. None of this would've ever happened without you.
Joel knew, with the right friends supporting and encouraging me, I could actually do this.

I'd also like to thank my 'Wenches of Camelot': Anissa Beatty,

CONTENTS

THE BROTHERS OF CAMELOT

CHARACTER GLOSSARY

Drake Allen Gregory-Fitzpatrick, "Fitz": Camelot Security, brother of Brenden Gregory

Grayson Riggs: Former Special Forces, Head of Camelot Security

Noah Stevens: Former Special Forces, Camelot Security

Brenden Gregory: ER and Camelot doctor, brother of Fitz

Nicolas Hawkins: Head of IT for Camelot Enterprises

Asher Clausen: CEO of Camelot Enterprises

Blake Spencer: Lawyer of Camelot Enterprises

Samson Carpenter: Camelot Construction

Gabriel Jackson: Camelot Security and Accountant for Camelot Enterprises

Liam Bishop: Operations Manager for Camelot Enterprises

Zachary Hunter: Manager Camelot Bar and Clubs

Cameron Clay: Lead Architect for Camelot Construction

FAMILY AND FRIENDS

Isabella Ivy Anderson, "Bella": Owner of Rainbows and Unicorns Daycare Centers

Dr. Monica Gregory: Doctor, Pediatric Specialty, mother of Fitz, Gregory, and Britney

Allen Drake Gregory: Lawyer, father of Fitz, Gregory, and Britney

Britney Gregory: Sister of Fitz and Gregory

Dr. Diana Riggs: Doctor, Obstetrics, and Gynecology Specialty, mother to Grayson Riggs

Nurse Barbara Stevens: Nurse, mother to Noah Stevens

THE BROTHERS OF CAMELOT
ORIGINS

These twelve boys were inseparable as they grew up, always together and causing a ruckus. To keep them out of trouble, Mom Gregory had the perfect playground built in her backyard, including a massive tree house. She included a large wooden round table, telling them the story of the Knights of the Round Table. They played knights every chance they could, at first with cardboard shields and swords and then with plastic costume pieces. The neighbors grew accustomed to seeing the boys running through the neighborhood, fighting enemies and for their honor.

The boys adopted a knightly code to always be honest with each other, no matter what, and that all decisions are to be made by unanimous vote. They pledged always to be there when one of them in need. Pricking their fingers and sealing the pact with a blood oath, they kept their promise from childhood into adulthood. If anyone messed with one of them, the other eleven had his back.

As the older boys came closer to graduating high school, they realized that some would be going to college or into the military, while others wouldn't. Once again, The Brothers gathered around their round table, where it all began, and pledged that no matter where life took them, they would one day come back together and join forces.

Years later, they kept that pledge. They pooled their money together; it didn't matter if some of them only had a few hundred dollars while others had large trust funds, they saw each other as equals. This is how they formed Camelot Enterprises. Each Brother found the role that fit them, from Camelot Security to Camelot Bar and Club, Camelot Construction to Camelot Law Firm.

The Brothers have maintained their promise to each other and are just as close as when they were boys playing knights. The round table may have gotten larger, but the pact they made as boys still stands.

Join me and meet these amazing men, starting with Fitz.

CHAPTER ONE

FITZ: ONE AND DONE

*M*y eyes pop open, my body tense. *Fuck, I dozed off.* Glancing around a room I don't recognize, it all comes flooding back. The chick in the bed beside me… Man, she was fun and flexible. When I picked her up at the club after ladies night, I thought it'd be a quick in and out, no pun intended, but my body must have given out after round four.

Trying to find my clothes in this pigsty is like finding the red and white striped shirt in a *Where's Waldo* book. There are mountains of clothes, shoes, and junk *everywhere*. Heading to the bathroom, dodging her junk like an obstacle course, is almost as much exercise as I just had in her bed. I've got to get the fuck out of here and fast.

Slowly closing the bathroom door, I turn the light on. *Damn, the bathroom is even worse than her bedroom, if that's possible.* Makeup and hair shit covers every inch of the bathroom counter, even the trashcan is overflowing. This place is downright nasty.

After I piss and wash off my cock, I give a few towels the smell test. Deciding I'll have to let Henry air dry, my lips twitch in amusement, remembering when my eleven friends and I all named our cocks, back in junior high.

Come on, a lot of girls name their bits and tits. Right? I'm proud of his name, Henry Peter Longfellow. He must have a mind of his own, or I wouldn't be in this biohazard of an apartment just so he could fuck a girl with ginormous, fake tits. It's hard to find a real girl these days.

"Hey, hurry up! I wanna go for another ride on that big, fine cock of yours," I hear through the door. Fuck, I hope this chick remembers what I told her before agreeing to take her home.

Opening the door, I begin the hunt for my shoes. "I gotta bounce. I need sleep for tomorrow. I gave you several satisfying rides on my fine cock," I wave my hands in front of Henry, like I'm Vanna fucking White, "giving you multiple orgasms, I might add. Now, we both go our own ways. I don't do second nights."

Dropping the sheet, she tries to look sexy, flipping her hair and rubbing her tits. "You said you wanted to fuck me in the ass. I'll let you if you stay."

There's no response from Henry, not even a twitch. After all the acrobatics he just performed, he doesn't care either. "Sorry Jugs, I've got breakfast plans in the morning," I respond while slipping into my jeans and then my shoes as quickly as possible. I'm getting the fuck out of here, and now.

Walking out of her bedroom and spotting the front door, I make a bee-line for it as she calls out, "Here, take my phone number, just in case you change your mind and want seconds. I know I want to ride that big boy again. You sure know how to use that thing."

Glancing back, she's striking a pose in the doorway to her bedroom, trying to look sexy while holding out a business card. Well, I tried to let her down nicely. Now I have to be an ass.

"Look, thanks for giving Henry the compliment and the fun night, but it doesn't change anything, toots. I don't do seconds. Have a good life."

"Fuck you, asshole! I can get laid easy, I don't have to beg! Lots of men want me!" she screams from the doorway, still naked.

Ecstatic to make my escape, but I can't help chuckling. *No more picking up girls after ladies night.* I'm always upfront, promising them multiple orgasms and an enjoyable time, but only the one night. My philosophy has always been *one and done.*

The longest time I've ever fucked the same girl was three days in a row. Ah, Frenchie. She was fun. She came up to me and said she wanted nothing more than to fuck like rabbits for three days before she went back to Paris. Who was I to turn down that offer? When she started texting, saying she missed me and wanted me to call her if I found myself in Paris, she got blocked real quick. Attachments give me the shivers.

Opening the door to my cream-colored Aston Martin One-77, I sink into the plush bucket seat, relieved to be sitting on the oh so soft brown leather that cradles my ass to perfection and take a deep cleansing breath as I close my eyes before letting it out slowly. I fucking love this car, there's nothing like the sound of her starting up. Putting her into gear, I finally get the fuck outta here and head home.

Hitting the freeway, my mind takes me back to how pissed my father was when I showed up at his birthday dinner with this car. I paid well over a million bucks for it with my inheritance. It's a twisted sort of pleasure, reminding him it was my money and I could do as I damn well pleased with it. He's so easy to tick off. I have no idea how Moms put up with his shit all these years.

Tomorrow morning is my monthly breakfast with Mom. I'm sure she'll be grilling me on my dating life, hoping there'll be someone special. She'll be consumed with talking about my twenty-sixth birthday and the big celebration at the country club. It's this Friday, and I'm fucking dreading it.

Mom always makes a huge deal about birthdays, saying *"Honey, birthdays are our chance to celebrate your life and show you we love you. Just you wait until your engagement party and rehearsal dinner… when you finally find a woman to give me grandbabies."*

Mom wants to marry off me and Brenden, my older brother, so badly. She's dying for some grandbabies. Honestly, I've got the best mom anyone could ever ask for. She has the biggest heart and loves me just as much as if she'd given birth to me.

Thinking back on how horribly it all started, the realization of how damn lucky I truly am hits me. Mom didn't have to take me as her own son and adopt me, but she did. She's been my mom for twenty years now, and I love her just as much as she loves me.

FORTY-FIVE MINUTES LATER, I pull up to my estate. Hawkins, the technical guru of Camelot Security who I've known since I was a kid, is an insane computer genius. He'd installed some cool recognition chip on my license plate, which causes the entrance gate to open automatically once it senses my car. It's just a short drive around and up the hill toward my house, which has the same recognition equipment that opens the garage doors for me without me touching a thing.

After pulling into the garage, I get out of my car and look around. Seeing my bad-ass Harley with the custom flames, warms me. That custom paint job was worth every penny. I smile, just a boy with his toys, as I proudly gaze upon at my other toys; Lincoln Navigator, with a click of my key fob, the dim lights underneath turn on, making it glow. My bad ass lifted Dodge Ram 2500 Hemi, to name a few. What do you expect when a twenty-one-year-old guy inherits a half a billion dollars, but to buy a sprawling estate with an eight-car garage? There's still plenty of room for more toys if I want.

As I walk in the house from the garage, the sensor lighting illuminates as I pass then slowly dims and turn off when I leave the room. Hawkins also set up everyone's home security, from mine to The Brother's and our families, as well as the security and monitoring at our club. I have no idea how he does this shit, he just does, and it's magic.

Glancing out the back window, I spot Stevens' old truck by the guest house. He's one of my Camelot Brothers and has a heart of gold. He lives here most of the time because he's saving his money to pay off his mom's house but refuses any help. I've tried more than once, and it just turns into a fight. He said if I wanted to help him out, I'd let him stay in my guest house. It's easier for him here because of some family drama. I'll steer clear until Stevens asks for help.

He's like my household manager, making sure the house staff and groundskeepers have everything running smoothly, even though I hired the best before he came to live here. Stevens knows how important it is to me to have things clean and organized. I'll keep letting him think he's doing something to help me out.

Mom and my sister Britney decorated my new abode, adding all kinds of family pictures and personal touches. But it still feels empty, not warm and homey, nor even a bit welcoming. It seems to lack heart and feels a bit cold. Maybe it's just me.

Heading upstairs to my room, the first thing I do is grab my room controller. There's nothing better for a man than a huge ass tablet that can control every fucking thing in his room, from the TV and music to the AC and more. My favorite thing about this controller is that with the push of a couple of buttons, the curtains part and my floor to ceiling windows slide open, affording me a view that made the exorbitant price tag on this house worth every penny.

Hearing the ocean in the distance gives me some comfort, a moment of peace. Seeing the sheer curtains blowing in the breeze calms me. Sleeping like this is paradise. Hawkins programmed the controller to close the windows and curtains at four o'clock in the morning. We can't have the bright, morning sun interrupting my sleep.

Stripping off my clothes, I walk into my closet and toss everything into the hamper. The shower beckons me. I really need to get the remains of that chick off of me. I'm someone who can't sleep without feeling fresh and clean, the feeling that only comes from a long hot shower. After a few minutes of some much-needed scrubbing, and a quick hand job for Henry, I'm finally ready for bed.

As I lie in bed listening to the soothing sounds of the ocean as the silk curtains gently sway in the breeze, I decide it's time to cut back on the impulsive hookups. Recently, I've felt like crap afterwards and I don't know why. It's not like I've grown a conscience or anything. It just doesn't feel right anymore.

Honestly, sex without the complications is getting a bit tough to find. I may not feel anything for the chick other than a sexual release but finding a chick that feels the same way isn't an easy task. They always seem to want more which I cannot, and will not, give them.

Sex with a random hookup isn't that much better than a good old-fashioned hand job anymore, which has become a part of my everyday routine. Henry's far from neglected, at least with my morning and evening showers that is.

With just a sheet to cover my naked body, I see the time from the clock that projects onto my ceiling mirror. I've got about seven hours before it's time to meet Mom for breakfast. Thankfully, she likes to have breakfast at the club.

Closing my eyes, I feel the day and my increasingly hectic life catch up with me. I subconsciously trace the scar on my left side lightly. It's about seven inches long, and it's where Mom had sewn me back together again the night we first met. She'd done an excellent job, it's barely even noticeable but it will never completely go away.

Some wounds physically heal while others leave you damaged and scarred on the inside for life. That's me, damaged, forever.

CHAPTER TWO

FITZ: MY REOCCURRING NIGHTMARE

20 years earlier

*G*randma and I are in our secret room, the one hidden in the back of Ma's big walk-in closet. One of Ma's man friends built it when I was a baby. We have a fully stocked fridge, food and a microwave. Grandma has her big rocking recliner, and I have a bed to myself with a roll-away for Grandma. All my best books and toys are in here too.

When Ma has a man friend visit, we spend a lot of time in here. Grandma always puts headphones on me when we first come in here. She says it's because Ma and her friend are talking about adult stuff. I don't care because I get to listen to my books while following along or watch movies. Sometimes, we're in here very late, and I fall asleep listening to music.

Tonight, we've been in here for a long time, I've already read my books, and I'm now sitting on my bed playing with my Power Ranger Deluxe Double Morphing Rescue Megazord while listening to my music. Suddenly, I feel a large sharp pain in my side. I look down and see blood.

Grandma jumps up from her recliner and pulls me down to the floor, almost laying on top of me. The movement knocks my headphones off, and I hear loud yelling from a man. Ma is yelling, "No!" and then *Bang! Bang! Bang!* Just as quickly as it began, the noise suddenly stops, and the only thing I hear is Grandma crying and praying in Spanish.

Slowly Grandma gets up, putting her finger to my lips. She quietly tells me to stay where I am and not to follow her. Once she walks out the door, I shift and look down at my side, it hurts so bad. Seeing a lot of blood soaking through my shirt, I lift my Spider-Man t-shirt and notice a large, deep cut. How did I get cut sitting on my bed? Grandma cries out and starts speaking in Spanish. Bracing myself, I try to sit up a little bit more, but it hurts too bad to move. I look at the door, wanting to see my Ma so she can make me better.

Grandma rushes into our little room and sees my side. "Ay no, *mi niño!*" she yells, then grabs the blanket off my bed and wraps it around me, even covering my head. Grandma picks me up and carries me, telling me, "Drake, it is going to be okay. I'm going to get you help real soon. I am so sorry, my sweet *niño pequeño*, I will take good care of you. I promise we will be okay."

I hear Grandma sniffle like she's crying. Why is Grandma sad? I don't like it, she's always happy.

She carries me outside and carefully sets me down on

the bench in front of our townhouse and gingerly unwraps me, trying to find my booboo. "How did I get cut? Why are you crying? And where is my ma? I heard her yelling, where is she?"

Grandma wiped her eyes, saying, "I will not lie to you, something terrible has happened to your ma. She won't be coming back. She went home to be with Jesus."

Staring at her, I shake my head. Looking at the front door of our townhouse, I try to get up. "No, I heard her, she was still in there. I'll go get her."

Grandma carefully puts her arms around me, pressing the corner of the blanket in to my side, making it hurt more. "No, no *mi hijo*. Be still and stay here with me."

Hearing sirens, people gather on our street to find out what happened. Touching my side, I feel the blanket is sticky and soaked through with blood. Several police cars, an ambulance, and a fire truck pull up in front of us.

Why do we need a fire truck? I wonder, but I'm too scared to ask. Grandma is crying a lot while talking to an officer in Spanish rapidly. The officer calls to the man and lady getting out of the ambulance, "Get over to the boy, he's been shot."

I've been shot? Who shot me? Feeling confused, I look at the officer wondering when could have been shot. I call to Grandma, "Where's Ma? Where's Ma? I want my ma!" By the end, I'm screaming.

Grandma and the officer ran over to me and she wraps her arms around me trying to explain, "Oh *mi pobre hijo*, it will be okay *beb*. Your ma has gone to be with

Jesus in Heaven. She will not be coming back. But we will find your papa, I promise."

The lady from the ambulance kneels next to me and removes my blanket to look at my side. There's a lot of blood, and I can see my booboo open and close, my blood seeping out of it. The man carefully picks me up and puts me on a bed with wheels. Wiggling, I try to get away from him. Grandma puts her hand on my shoulder and says softly, "Be still sweetie, they are going to help make you better."

"Grandma, don't leave me! Please don't leave me," I cry, grabbing her arm.

She grabs my hand and holds it tightly. I guess these people trying to take care of me are like doctors. The man talks into his walkie-talkie while the lady tells me, "You are going to be okay, but we need to cut off this cool Spider-Man shirt so that we can take care of your booboo, okay honey?"

Nodding my head at her, I hold Grandma's hand tightly. Suddenly, I feel a poke in my arm. I try to pull away but can't. She tapes a needle to my arm and hangs what looks like a water bottle to a pole sticking up from the bed I am laying on. Then she puts sticky things on my chest. I realize I don't like this at all. I just want it all to go away. I want my ma.

Looking towards our front door again, I see more police officers going into our home. As they are rolling the bed I'm on and putting me into the back of the ambulance, one of the police officers stops Grandma before she climbs in after me.

"We are sending a couple of officers to follow you to

the hospital. They have more questions for you. There are no survivors inside, I'm sorry."

I blink my eyes and think, *no survivors inside*. That means my ma is dead. She's gone forever.

AT THE HOSPITAL, several nurses and doctors are running around me. They push Grandma away from me before counting to three and lifting me up to put me on a different bed. Shaking, I look at Grandma and reach out for her. She walks back over to me and takes my hand, squeezing it. She leans down and whispers in my ear, "You be still and do what the doctors say. I promise I will not leave you. You will be okay. I love you, *mi hijo*," then she kisses me on the forehead.

One of the nurses stands next to Grandma and places a hand on her back.

"We promise to take really good care of your grandson, but we need you to come outside and answer some questions, so we can get the information we need to take better care of him and evaluate his injuries."

Grandma nods and kisses my hand. "I'll be right back, I promise. Okay?" I just nod my head and watch her walk out with the nurse.

Looking up, I see a large bright light shining on me. The nurses are attaching all sorts of cords and stuff to machines. I'm even more scared than before. A lady doctor comes in and places her hand on my arm while talking to all the nurses around me. They are telling her numbers and said something about giving me blood once they know my type or something.

The doctor lady looks at me with soft, light brown eyes and says with a smile, "Hi there. It looks like you got yourself a big booboo here. I'm going to need to take a closer look at it, and you'll need some stitches to put you back together again. Is there anything else that hurts?"

I shake my head no. She then asks me, "Do you know how old you are, and your full name, Drake? Your Grandma only told us you were called Drake."

Blinking my eyes, I whisper, "Yes Ma'am. I'm almost six years old, and my name is Drake Allen Gregory-Fitzpatrick."

Her face looks surprised, and she's the one blinking now. Clearing her throat, she says, "Wow, my last name is Gregory, too."

I look at her coat and see her name tag says, "Doctor Monica Gregory." She looks kind of upset now, demanding, "Look at me for a minute, Drake."

Turning my head toward her, she waves a little flashlight in my eyes.

"Do you know what your daddy's name is?" she asks.

I shake my head no. She gives me a small smile. Pushing my black hair out of my face, she inspects my face.

"I'm going to get you fixed up, but you are going to go to sleep for a little bit while I do that, okay honey?" She turns to the nurses, "Get him ready for sedation, we need to evaluate this wound better. I also want full blood work ASAP."

When she turns back to me, I ask, "Where is Grandma? I want her with me."

She smiles again and says, "She is outside talking to a police officer. She'll be in your room with you when you wake up, okay?"

I look at the doctor and wonder why she is looking at me so oddly. Beginning to feel sleepy, my eyes close as I hear her say, "You know Drake, I've only seen one other person with those same dark green eyes and his name is Allen Drake Gregory, very similar to your name."

As I fall asleep, I wonder if she knows who my daddy is because my ma said the same thing, "*I've only known one other man who has those dark green eyes, and that's your daddy. I'm sure one day, when you are a lot older, you'll probably bump into him and you'll recognize him because you both look so much alike.*" Except I have my ma's black hair and my daddy has blonde hair.

CHAPTER THREE

FITZ: MY PERSONAL STRUGGLE

*B*olting upright and breathing heavy, the realization hits me and I sigh. *Fuck, another flashback dream.* Rubbing the center of my chest, nothing sucks more for me than starting the day off like this. After a quick shower, my mind is still not letting it go. Pulling on some jeans and buttoning up a nice dress shirt, I'm still mentally struggling with the dream. *Why now?*

Shaking my head and trying my best to clear it, I head straight to the kitchen to grab a cup of coffee. The espresso machine is always programmed to automatically make coffee at this time because I'm too damned impatient for my morning fix of Joe, and the hot cup full of the dark brew soothes me a touch.

Leaning against the counter while enjoying my nice, strong cup of coffee, in walks Stevens, barefoot and wearing loose basketball shorts.

"What the hell are you doing in here?" I growl, knowing I'm being an ass. "I saw your truck in front of the guest house last night, so I thought you crashed out there."

"As always man, your casa, my casa. But I also knew you had fresh coffee ready for me in here. You know I'm not worth shit until I have my first cup," he says while making himself right at home, grabbing a mug and pouring himself some.

"You do know that you have your very own coffee pot out there, don't you?" I remind him.

"Yeah, I know. But I'm not as anal nor as organized as you are. And it's not like you're gonna drink the whole pot yourself. I know its Sunday and you have breakfast with Mom Gregory." He snickers. "Are you ready for the usual grilling about your dating life, or should I say, lack thereof?"

I flip him off. "Fuck you, it isn't any worse than what I'm sure Mom Stevens gives you. Because you're two years older than me, I'm sure she's also counting down the days, just waiting for you to give her some grandbabies. Mom knows I don't do relationships.

"It's just another birthday, and *twenty-six* is way too young to even be thinking about marriage in my books. I just don't think that will ever be a part of my life. But hey, I can see you married, with a couple of rug rats running around in no time, *Noah*." I call him by his first name, knowing how much he hates it.

"Don't make me kick your ass this early in the morning. Noah, shit, no one calls me that, except Mom, and that's only when I'm in trouble. So, watch it, I wouldn't want to mess up this spotless house of yours," he adds with half a smile.

"Keep dreaming, Stevens. We both know that kicking my ass is not something you can do without some backup. And you don't even have that evil, demon-possessed ferret of yours with you today. Which reminds me, *shit*, please tell me you didn't leave it in my guest house unattended? I know you don't bring chicks here, so if he messes anything up, you will fix it or I *will* kick your ass," I said, firmly.

"He isn't going to do anything. When I left, Freddy was asleep in his cage with Morris sleeping on top of it, on guard. Morris is a good ferret sitter," he shrugs.

"You have got to be kidding me. You brought that mini mountain lion and that evil ferret over here? Dude, the next time I'm out there, I better not smell animal piss. You got me?"

Stevens sighs and pours himself another cup of coffee, "Come on Fitz, you know Morris is potty-trained. As long as I leave the toilet seat up, he's never had an accident. You better hurry up, or you'll be late for break-fast with Mommy," he reprimands with a boyish smile.

I quickly rinse out my cup and put it in the dish-washer, shouting over my shoulder, "You better not leave that dirty mug in the sink! You rinse it out like a big boy and put it in the dishwasher, just like you saw me do. Got it? Or when I get home, I will drag your ass back in here by the ear to do it."

Stevens laughs as he yells out in mock little boy's

voice, "Yes, Mommy!" Returning to his normal, deep voice he says, "I'll see you in a couple of hours at the club to see how you survived breakfast. And hey, you need to buy some real food for your friends to eat. You don't have shit in this house."

Walking out to the truck, I yell back, "Last time I looked, you are more than capable of doing your own shopping!"

DRIVING DOWN THE ROAD, I realize that I'm going to be in a funk for days because of that fuckin' dream of Ma's death. It always feels so real, like I'm reliving every horrifying moment. I need to make myself think happy thoughts before bed tonight. *Happy thoughts* makes me think I'm five years old again.

God, this sucks. Trying to clear my thoughts, I crank up my music, hoping to redirect my mind and steer clear from my personal shit.

The beauty that surrounds me as I drive helps settle a few nerves. Santa Monica is like no other place, and to me, its paradise. We have the best weather, always a nice breeze, never too hot, nor too cold. Even in winter, it isn't that bad. We get enough rain, but not too much. If I want snow, it's just a few hours' drive to Big Bear or a short flight to Tahoe. Yeah, there's the possibility of earthquakes, but come on, that's very rare.

My mind flashes to the moment I first saw my father's face when he walked into my hospital room.

Shit, even when I'm purposely trying not to think of my past, to distract myself with mindless crap, it just comes rushing back. I give in while driving, taking that horrible walk down memory lane.

Waking up the morning after my surgery, I found Dr. Monica waiting for me to wake up. This time it wasn't as my doctor though. She brought my father with her. I knew he was my father at first glance because of our resemblance and she told me she was married to him. Dr. Monica was what I used to call my mom. She told me that day in my hospital room that she knew I was his son the moment I said my full name and she looked into my emerald green eyes, the same eye color as my father.

Lucky me, my ma named me after him, a bit tough to deny him as my father after that. Thankfully, at least my ma attached her last name, Fitzpatrick, to his, which meant I've got one long ass full name.

Dr. Monica sat on the corner of my bed as she told me, with the biggest smile on her face, that we were going to all be family now, and that I should call her Mom now. Both Grandma and I would be coming to live with her and my father forever. I realized then, Grandma must have told her the truth about herself, and everything she knew about me and my ma. I couldn't believe then it was all happening so fast. My life would never be the same, and it wasn't.

Grandma had been best friends with my ma's mom, who had passed away when my ma was very young. Naturally, Grandma took over and helped to raise my ma, but Grandma was an illegal immigrant. Dr. Monica wasn't going to let me lose the only family I knew. So, she worked her magic and made it possible for Grandma to stay in this country and move in with me and be a part of the Gregory family forever.

Dr. Monica, or 'Mom' now, also informed me that I had an older brother, Brenden, and a younger sister, Britney. She looked so happy sharing all about her family with me. My father just sat there, not saying a word, letting Mom do all the talking.

I remember so well how he didn't smile, not even after meeting a son he didn't even know he had. The way he looked at me was like I was a problem he didn't know how to solve. I felt no warmth, nothing from him. He was just a man that resembled me.

Mom thought she would help us bond by leaving us together in my hospital room while she and Grandma went to get me some of our things from the townhouse I grew up in. Not more than fifteen minutes after she turned my world upside down, she left my father and me alone.

At first, he tried to talk to me, showing me how to page the nurse and control my bed and TV with the controller attached to my bed. My father showed me pictures in his wallet of my brother and sister.

One of the pictures he showed me was of him and Brenden, dressed exactly alike. Wearing tan Dockers and light blue polo shirts, they had similar short haircuts, styled with gel. He kept repeating how nice and clean cut my brother looked with a proper haircut while looking at my hair like it was dirty.

I don't recall him looking at my face even once. I know now that it was my resemblance to him. But my father made it clear he didn't like my long hair. Mom decided my curls were precious and didn't let him chop off all my hair. I knew that didn't make him happy, either. My hair is still long, past my shoulders now. The number one reason I have it this long is to spite my father. I know he hates it and well, it makes me happy to piss him off.

He also told me that I didn't act like a normal five-year-old kid. He was distant and cold, completely without feeling or concern that I was recovering from being shot. I felt like a specimen for him to study and nothing more. I don't think he even touched me or asked once how I was doing.

Sure, I wasn't a typical five-year-old. Being gifted, I was already in first grade when he found out I was his second son. The other parents at the private school I attended must have known my mother was an escort. There were no party invites, let alone friends. The only time I saw other kids was during school and they avoided me.

The few people I knew outside of Ma and Grandma were all adults, either escorts like Ma or occasionally one of her decent johns. Sometimes they even took me to the park or played video games with me. I knew from the moment I met my father that he wouldn't allow that to continue.

It didn't take me long to settle in with my new family. By the time I was seven, Brenden and I had bonded as brothers, even if he was a brat most of the time. Even Britney was okay, well, once she outgrew the whining phase. Mom was active in my life and with school, even introducing me to two of my best friends. Riggs' and Stevens' moms' both grew up with my new mom, so the four of us boys ran rampant while the moms had lunch.

It didn't take long for my friends to notice that my father treated me differently than Brenden. They saw how he would look at me with disdain. When something went wrong, or if someone left a toy out, I was the first one he sought out to yell at, always assuming it was my fault.

Many times, they saw him smack me on the side of the head and tell me to put something away. They knew I wasn't the one to leave it out. Even as a kid, I was always organized and clean, but I'd give my father an evil look and put it away myself.

I would never turn on a friend. There were a couple of times someone would stand up for me. Usually it was Bella, but only when she was around. *God, Bella.* She actually kicked him in the shin once when he accused me of leaving the bike out. It was Brenden who left it out, it wasn't even mine. But Bella, she always took up for me. God, how I miss that girl.

When I was almost eight, all my friends loved playing Camelot and the Knights of the Round Table. We formed our own group, or maybe 'club' was a better term. We called ourselves "The Brothers of Camelot."

We had a huge two-story treehouse that Mom had Carpenter Construction build for us as kids. One of the rooms had a round table in it. We made all our plans in that little room. If we all didn't agree on something, it didn't happen. We made a solemn pledge to never lie to one another and to always be there for each other, no matter what. Heck, we even all poked our fingers and made it a blood pact. The twelve of us were inseparable.

One day, in fifth grade, we had a substitute teacher who called out my full name, Drake Allen Gregory-Fitzpatrick. That got the attention of Jackson and Hawkins, who asked me about it after school. I knew I had to tell them the truth. I'd never lie to one of the Brothers. The story spilled out about Ma being an escort and that Fitzpatrick was her last name, and about her murder and discovering Mom and my father.

I told them how my father wanted me known as a Gregory, so I'd have the same last name as my brother and sister in school. That was the reason everyone thought Gregory was my real last name, when, in actuality, it was hyphenated: Gregory-Fitzpatrick.

Immediately, they all began to call me 'Fitz,' including Brenden. Honestly, it felt great knowing they knew my past and understood me not wanting to lose my connection to my ma. They couldn't care less what my father thought of my new nickname.

I felt complete with them. I always knew, even as a kid, that those eleven friends were my brothers. They had my back as they still do to this day. If I ever needed anything at all, I knew of eleven guys that would move heaven or hell to make it happen, and I would do the same for any of them.

Throughout my life, Mom has always been my

sunshine, support, and strength. With my father, it was always an argument or fight and he was never happy with the choices I made. So yeah, it bothered me, but I gave up trying many years ago. Maybe that's why I still get these nightmares. I laugh at the thought, knowing nothing between us will ever change.

CHAPTER FOUR

FITZ: BREAKFAST WITH MOM

*A*s I pulled into the parking lot of the club, I see Mom's white BMW parked near the front. My clock shows eight minutes till ten, which means, as always, she's early. She's probably in there giving one of my Brothers a tough time. Or, more likely, chatting with the girls in there, interviewing them so she could suggest to me which one she thinks I should ask out on a date.

Before I move to get out of the truck, all that we've accomplished here sets in. Formerly a condemned warehouse, Camelot Construction salvaged it, turning it into "The Brothers of Camelot Bar and Club." Hunter manages this place like it's his baby. It's a restaurant during the day and the hottest nightclub in town at night, complete with our private apartments and satellite offices upstairs.

I've got no idea how he does it, but he keeps this place hoppin' with a karaoke night, throwback (80's and 90's) nights, heck even twice weekly, just shy of illegal, stripper nights, featuring both males and females. No one is fully exposed, but it gets super close.

Getting out of my truck I head to the door, imagining what my mom has been up to. Sally, the hostess, looks up from her seating chart and smiles at me as I walk in.

"Your mom is in the back corner booth, chatting with Bonnie, your waitress. I'm pretty sure she's already ordered breakfast for you."

One corner of my mouth kicks up. "How long has she been here? And has she been interviewing anyone?"

Sally laughs, "Come on Fitz, she's Mrs. Gregory. When is she not questioning all the girls in here for you *or* Brenden? Today she's inviting any of the girls who aren't working Friday night to your birthday party. She even promised each of us at least one dance with you or Brenden."

"I'm so sorry, Sally, please forgive my mother's bluntness."

Sally just giggles as she leads me towards Mom. Sally glances at me with a smirk.

"Hey, that's at least one way to make you dance with me. I'll just resort to siccing your Mom on you."

I don't have a response to her comment. I'm beginning to regret not canceling this breakfast, now that I'm fully aware of my Mom's mission. If only I could get a message to one of my Camelot Brothers to plan a rescue mission. Dammit, we need a bat signal.

Nothing lifts my spirits or makes me smile more than seeing Mom smiling back at me. Jumping up, she rushes toward me and throws her arms around me.

"Good morning son. Don't you look handsome today?" She turns to include Sally and Bonnie, "Doesn't he, girls? With that black hair, dark jade green eyes, and big strong, broad shoulders, I know he's a heartbreaker." The girls giggle in response.

"Okay Mom, let them get back to work," I say, walking Mom back to her side of the booth. Once she's settled, I take my seat across from her. Mom's wearing her signature clothes, light pink short sleeved sweater with a matching cardigan. Best of all, she's wearing the mother of pearl cameo locket I gave her almost fifteen years ago. She doesn't know how much I love her for that.

Ma and Mom were as different as night and day, in style and personality and both are beautiful in their own way. Comparing my Mom to my birth mother would be like comparing June Cleaver to Peggy Bundy. Ma's clothes were a bit higher quality than Peg's, but everything she wore was tight, short and very revealing.

Mom leans closer, patting my hand. "Well honey, Friday is your big day. Some of the Brothers have already RSVP'd and said they were bringing a date. I was hoping you'd tell me today you're doing the same? Because that would make me so very happy if you have a date. There are plenty of nice girls here that I've met."

"Okay, Mom." *I need my Brothers to read my mind!* "First, if you met them here, they work for me. I don't date girls that work for me. That could easily turn into a sexual harassment lawsuit, and Spencer would have my ass. You know he's a good lawyer, but he doesn't tolerate sexual harassment suits. And you wouldn't want that now, would you?" I add, with a chuckle.

Releasing my hand, Mom leans back in the booth. "Well, naturally I wouldn't want that. Your father would hear about it, and we all know that wouldn't be good." Sighing, she continues plotting. "Okay, so not a girl from the club. But, you're good-looking so you shouldn't have any trouble finding a date. If you are, let me know. I know several beautiful young ladies who would be thrilled to accompany you."

"Fine, Mom," I sigh, knowing it's pointless to dissuade her, "Since it means so much to you, I'll bring a date. Let me tell you now before you ask. No, I do not have a girlfriend. I still don't do relationships, and you know that. I have absolutely no desire to get serious with anyone. If you want to play cupid, start with Brenden. He's older, in case you forgot."

She winks, a mischievous smile playing on her lips. "Oh, I've already started being a bit more aggressive with your brother about this. He did tell me he was planning on bringing a date, a Ginger Summers. Have you met her?"

Choking on my coffee, I try to hold back a laugh. Ginger is a highly paid escort that we, or rather Camelot Security, provides protection for, as well as provide background checks on all her johns. Shit, is Brenden dating her, or is he paying her for this date? Oh, my birthday party just got a bit more interesting. But I'm not about to pop Mom's bubble and throw Brenden under the bus.

"Honey, are you okay?"

"Yeah, Mom, I'm fine. The coffee just went down

the wrong pipe. Did you already order us brunch?" I ask, changing the subject so I wouldn't have to answer questions about Ginger. Mom loves ordering for me, and I'm glad for it. It's her way of showing she cares for me. To be honest, I like it.

"Yes, honey, I did. I ordered myself an egg white omelet, and I ordered you your regular ham, bacon, sausage with extra cheese omelet, along with two pieces of French toast lightly sprinkled with powdered sugar and a large glass of orange juice."

"Mom, you know me and my uncontrollable appetite so well. That sounds perfect. Since this is my third cup of coffee and I've had no food yet, I'm starving."

As I finish my statement, Bonnie brings out our food. As she places my plate in front of me, she gives me a wink and a smile.

"Fitz, I'm looking forward to Friday night. Mrs. Gregory promised me a dance with you."

Raising an eyebrow at Mom, I turn to Bonnie. Trying to be as delicate as possible, I attempt to pull myself out of the path of a harassment suit.

"Well, Bonnie, it all depends on if my date will give me up. There'll be plenty of men there that would enjoy dancing with you. That I promise."

Bonnie's happy smile morphs into a sad one.

"Oh, okay then. Still sounds like fun." As she walked off with slouched shoulders, I knew I'd hurt her feelings. Still, there's no way in hell that I'd let any of these girls believe they have a chance with me. That's not happening.

Turning back to the table, I shoot Mom a look.

"Now see, I've already had to let her down gently. I'm hoping you didn't promise I would be dancing with a lot of the girls who work here. You know I don't want to lead any of them on or give them hope. Come on, Mom."

"Well, maybe I told about three of the nice young ladies here you'd dance with them. It's been a very long time since I've seen you dance with anyone. You know, it wouldn't kill you to get out on the dance floor. We all know you can dance." Continuing to eat her omelet, Mom watches me for my response.

I refuse to answer her, knowing she is like a dog with a bone when it comes to getting Brenden, Britney and I married off. I keep eating, shuddering on the inside at the thought of providing her with grandbabies.

Mom leans against the table looking at me oddly. Taking a deep breath, she continues to stare at me. I know something important is about to come out because she usually doesn't take a break in our conversations just to admire me. She's always talking.

Not able to take the staring any longer, I finally ask, "Okay, Mom, out with it. I know you are dying to say something so go ahead and spill. Tell me whatever it is that's eating at you."

"Oh, sweetheart, nothing's eating at me, not in a bad way." She giggles as she smiles. "I'm just so proud of you. Well, in all honesty, I'm proud of all of you. The twelve of you boys, and the pact you made with one another as kids. We honestly didn't think you kids would stick with it, but you did. You've turned that backyard little boys club into very successful multi-business ventures, worth millions. The Brothers of Camelot are known almost everywhere."

Nodding to the mural of the twelve of us, she continues. "Just look at the success of this club alone, and soon you'll be opening other locations. And what mother wouldn't be proud of her sons in that beautiful painting?"

We love our mural, it was expensive too. From the costumes to the makeup, it looks like we stepped right out of the Middle Ages. Spencer, Hawkins, and Clausen were in full armor complete with helmets and swords.

The rest of us were in our own mix of Viking and Knight gear. Jackson and Carpenter had leather pants tucked into their boots and were shirtless and holding battle axes. Their long hair was a mess and had dirt smudged on them. Everyone thought they looked quite scary, and they both loved that reaction.

Clay and Hunter had on those blousy, lace-up style shirts, holding maces and flails. Bishop had his car guys turn his Segway into something that looked like a chariot. It was great, and he enjoys riding it around the Camelot Security building to this day. He wore a navy tunic and breast plate, with a crossbow and a quiver of arrows strapped to his back. He pulled the look off perfectly.

Riggs, Stevens, Gregory and I were wearing burgundy tunics and breastplates with tassets. Riggs and Stevens both held shields with our Brother of Camelot logo on them and halberds in their other hand. Gregory was holding his sword up ready for combat. I had one hand on the grip of my sword in its sheath while holding the head of my Beast costume with the other.

Seeing that Beast costume reminds me of Isabella. She was my best friend and the only girl I ever gave my heart to. She was always my Bella, and I was her Beast. I had to hold the Beast's head in the portrait as a symbol of my hope that one day she would see it, and maybe, if I was lucky, she would contact me again.

There's individual portraits hanging in different areas of the bar, painted by the same artist, with our last name on a brass plaque beneath them as well. We have billboards across town with our pictures, depending on what we're advertising. We're quite vain about these, knowing we look damn good in them.

"Thank you, Mom. We're damn proud of ourselves too. I know my father isn't thrilled, but as you can tell, I don't give a rat's ass what he thinks anymore."

"Drake, your father, well, he's just afraid that with the security firm, you guys sometimes come awfully close to breaking the law. But don't give up hope. I'm still working on him. I've told him, more than once, you guys are not pimps to those escorts, and none of you are having sex with them either. You only provide them with a service, protection and background checks for their johns, and nothing more. I'm correct, am I not?"

"Yes, ma'am, you are." I chuckle. "Camelot Security does a lot more than just 'helping escorts', like providing protection for celebrities and their children, to rescuing kidnap victims. Hell, a couple of years ago, we even helped rescue an ambassador's daughter from being taken as a sex slave. Let's not forget all the times we've helped the police with their harder cases.

"Let's not forget the domestic side of Camelot Security, we're also the best home security money can buy. The guys even set up yours and my father's home. So, come on, there are a lot of good things our company does. Feel free to tell my father to get over it. His opinion is not now, nor has it ever been, important to me. Yours, however, means the world to me. As long as I have your love and support, I'm good." I reach across the table and squeeze her hand.

"You do, honey. I love you more than life itself. I just want you happy, healthy and to find love one day," Mom said with a wink. "You do a lot of good, no matter what your father says."

"Okay, Mom, you know I consider us all just Brothers of Camelot. This is only possible because of our promise to each other as brothers. I don't give a flip about who put in what money, just that we're all dedicated to each other's success. You and I both know I inherited enough money to last me, and everyone else I know, a lifetime. If I can help Camelot and my friends out with this blood money, I'm okay with that.

"I bet Phil Gibson is rolling over in his grave, leaving all his money to Ma. I know he was a long-time john of hers. Grandma told me he was in love with her and thought that by putting everything in her name it would prove his love for her. He believed she'd leave the escort business and travel the world with him. But when Ma laughed and said no, he lost his shit, killing her and himself.

"What a stupid man, not to investigate Ma before changing his will and making her his single heir. If he had done his research, he would have discovered me," I ground out in disgust.

"Let's not talk about that or him. Because as much as I wish he hadn't murdered your mother, I feel I've been very blessed with a wonderful son from that tragedy. I would have never known you otherwise. So, let's change the subject and talk about something a bit happier, like your birthday!"

Laughing, I look up to find the appearance of Stevens has saved me. He sits down by Mom and gives her a sideways hug. "Good afternoon, Mom Gregory. Have you tortured your son enough, uh, I mean, uh, shared your love and admiration with him today? Or should I give you more time before I steal him away from you, so we can go rescue some damsel in distress?"

Mom swats Stevens on the leg. "Stop teasing me young man, or I will tell your mother on you. She's still one of my best friends. And we work together at the hospital, don't forget. We see each other daily. In fact, I probably see her more than you do."

Stevens jumps up and salutes Mom, saying, "Yes, ma'am. Since you're pulling the Mom card, I'll just go and check on Hunter at the bar and see if he needs any help." Bowing to Mom, he teases, "I'll just leave you two to continue your visit and bonding."

"Dude, I'll catch up with you later," he says to me, with a wink before trotting off to the bar where Hunter's pouring drinks and chatting with three women.

Mom looks at me a bit nervously, "Drake, I only have

one more thing I feel I need to say, and I'd like you to hear me out."

"Mom, I'll always listen to you. I might not agree, but I'll always hear you out. Feel free to tell me anything," I reply, looking into her light brown eyes.

"Drake, I've had many years to try to figure out why your father doesn't treat you properly. I'm aware of it and can see it myself. I've asked him so many times, and even he doesn't know why he does it. But I think I've figured it out.

"I know every time he looks at you, he's reminded of his lies to me - not only about your ma, but also about you. He tried for years to deny he ever really had feelings for your mother. I know he loved me more, and he chose to come back to me and Brenden. But I've seen those pictures, just as you have, of when they were together those six months. He was attracted to her and did care for her. Even if he started out paying her, it became more. I've accepted that, but I think the guilt plagues him."

Mom lets out a deep breath before continuing, "I need to be honest with you. I'm the one who made your father take you and Grandma in to live with us. I didn't give him a choice. With her being your adoptive grandma, she was the only family you knew at the time. But when I found out she was an illegal immigrant, there was no way I'd allow them to send her back to Mexico.

"I knew we'd need her help, and you loved her so much. It took no time for us all to blend as a family. She was such a wonderful woman. She ended up being everyone's grandma. It's been three years since she passed away, but not a day goes by when Grandma isn't missed. I'm so glad we got to have her as a part of our family as well.

"But when I discovered you, I flat out told Allen it was either going to be all of us as a family, or he could move out. I'd have no problem going after custody of all of you children. I'm sorry, but it's true. I was hoping he would get on board once he saw you and fall in love with you as much as I did.

"I'm sorry he's hurt you all these years, trying to make you something you're not. But I don't regret taking you in, or any of it. Not for a minute. I love your father and always will, but you are just as much my son as Brenden is." Finally, she gets up and walks over to me as I stand and hug her.

Kissing the top of her head, I whisper into her hair, "Thanks, Mom, I know you love me, and I love you too. I'm glad you took Grandma and me in. You made my life wonderful, even better than it was with Ma. She tried, but people always judged her and judged me for being her son. You made me normal."

Stepping away from Mom, I look her in the eye. "Now, no more gloom, I've got to handle some business things. We'll have breakfast again next month. But I'll see you with a date on my arm Friday night." I kiss her forehead one last time. "Mom, let me escort you to your car."

She smiles up at me as we link our arms together. "Thank you that would be nice. And don't give up on your father. One day, I'm hoping he'll realize all the time he's lost with you and will see the good in you and make

things right. But if he doesn't, you'll always have me."
She gets on her tippy toes and kisses my cheek.

"Oh, one last thing, I promise." She pauses for a
second before she continues. "I know why you don't
want to date or have a relationship with anyone. Your
heart still belongs to Isabella. Why don't you reach out
and call her? You might be surprised by her response.
You shouldn't have given up on her, nor believed for a
moment you weren't good enough for her. You're her
Beast, and she's your Beauty. Make your move before it's
too late. Otherwise, you'll regret it for the rest of your
life. Now, I won't say another word about it, but you
know how I feel."

We finally make it to her car. I don't respond to her
comments about Bella. That subject is too painful. I was
a real asshole to her a few years ago, not responding to
her texts as I should have. But Mom is right, my heart
still belongs to Bella.

Watching Mom sitting in her car, I notice her move
the cameo locket back and forth on the chain around her
neck, a nervous habit of hers when she's thinking. It's
something that always makes me feel good inside, reas-
sured by how much the necklace means to her.

To be honest, I feel a bit relieved after finally talking
to Mom about my past, laying it all on the table and
finally clearing the air. I'm sure she feels better clearing
her head now too. But as for me, shit, my head is scram-
bled learning all this.

Waving goodbye one more time, she finally drives
away. Once back inside the club, I walk right up to
the bar.

"Hey Hunter," I call out; "give me a couple of beers. I'm taking them up to the apartment. Gonna relax before doing some work in the security office." *And try to clear my head…*

Grabbing the beer, he states, "Here you go, dude. Breakfast that bad with your mom, huh?"

"No, Mom was great, just got a lot on my mind. I need to sort a few things out is all." Raising the beers up to him, I say, "But these will help with that, thanks."

Not looking at anyone hoping to avoid any idle chat, I head straight to our private entrance to the upstairs apartment, with my head down. I'm hoping to push all thoughts of my conversation about my father out of my head, and I'd much rather not dwell on Bella all day either.

Walking into the living room of the apartment, I flop down on the overstuffed, leather couch and put my feet up. After taking a sip of my beer, I close my eyes and reminisce about my childhood and about the Christmas when I was ten when Bella made me see the light, and I started calling Monica, Mom.

TWO DAYS BEFORE CHRISTMAS, we had a sleepover with all our friends. With sleeping bags scattered across the living room, Bella and I made sure we were next to each other in front of the fireplace. Britney and Brenden always stole the couches.

That night, like every other sleepover, Monica walked around with Grandma and made sure to kiss each one of us goodnight. I was the last one to get my kiss goodnight from Monica before she said, "I love you, kids, sleep tight little ones and don't let the bed bugs bite," then she and Grandma would head up to bed.

I remember Bella looking at me, whispering, "Why do you call your Mom 'Monica'?"

Blinking, a bit surprised at the question, "Well, she isn't my real mom. I thought you knew that?"

"She kisses you goodnight every night, doesn't she?" Bella asks, with one eyebrow raised, making me smile.

"Yes."

"And she makes you your favorite breakfast sometimes, doesn't she?"

"Yes," I answer, wondering what she's up to now.

"And when you are sick, she stays up and takes care of you, doesn't she?"

"Yes," I replied, chuckling. I'm still confused by her questions.

"Then why don't you call her Mom? Like I call my Mom 'Mom'? Because you didn't call your Ma 'Mom', you called her Ma. So, 'Mom' is a different name, and I think Mom Gregory is a good mom to you, and you need to start calling her 'Mom'."

Looking at her with surprise, I realize she's right. "When I first came to live with her and my father, she told me not to call her Dr. Gregory anymore. She told me I could call her Monica, so I did.

"It was around the time Grandma talked to me, telling me that at school and stuff I'd be going by Gregory and not by my full last name. Since Brenden and Britney's last name is Gregory, the same as my father, that's what was proper, but my birth certificate would always say Gregory-Fitzpatrick."

Bella tilts her head, watching me with those big dark chocolate brown eyes. "That still doesn't tell me why you don't call her 'Mom' now. Do you love her like a mom?"

"Yeah, I think she's the greatest. And I know she loves me too."

"Then why not call her 'Mom'? I know it would make her very happy if you did. Do it on Christmas, make it an extra special Christmas for her."

I think about it for a minute, and deep down I know Bella's right. I really should start calling her 'Mom'. That's what Brenden and Britney called her, and she is married to my father, so that makes her my stepmom. And the only mother I have left.

"Okay, you're right. I'll make her something extra special and give it to her for Christmas, and from Christmas Day on I'll call her 'Mom'."

I lean over and kiss Bella on the cheek. Looking around the room, I notice everyone else is asleep. "Bella, once again, we're the only ones awake." We always get so involved in our talking, we forget about everyone else.

Bella giggles and asks, "Do you want to put lipstick on all our friends?"

We both quietly giggle as I joke, "No, I don't want them to get it all over Mom's stuff. Besides, they'd have a baby fit tomorrow because it'd be smeared all over their faces, never mind Mom's pillows. We'll do it next time. I'll tell them to bring their pillows from home."

We laugh again, snuggling deeper into our sleeping bags.

"You do know you're my bestest friend in the whole wide world. No one will ever come between us."

I laugh at her, shoving her a bit while rolling my eyes, "You're so funny. Bestest isn't a word, and you are my best friend too. Let's promise to stay this way forever, okay?"

"Okay. Best friends forever. Pinky-swear." She sticks her little pinky out to me, which I promptly link with mine.

We both snicker as I inform her, "You know, boys don't really pinky swear, that's what girls do."

Bella looked at me with surprise and inquired, "Well then, what do boys do?"

"We spit in our hand and shake. Or we prick our fingers and rub our fingers together, making us blood brothers."

"Eww, I'm not ready to cut myself and bleed. That would hurt. I don't like blood, it makes me want to throw up. And I don't want to throw up tonight." She pushes up and spits in her hand and sticks it out to me. I do the same, spitting in my hand then shaking her hand.

"Now we're best friends for life, even though it's gross."

I quickly respond, "Yeah, we are. Now you can never get rid of me."

After a few minutes, I look over to see Bella's long dark eyelashes sweep her cheeks in the light of the fire. I lean over and kiss her on the forehead, whispering "Sweet dreams, Bella. I'll always love you."

~

I SIT up and rub my eyes from my daydream. Oh God, how I miss that girl. A day doesn't go by when I don't think of her. What little good is left in me was all created by having her in my life.

Fuck, I knew that damn dream was going to mess me up. I'm going to need something a lot stronger than this beer. Standing up, I run my fingers through my hair. Gotta get out of here and get my head on straight. The security office should have something else for me to focus on for a few hours, and luckily, it's just across the hall.

CHAPTER FIVE

ISABELLA: BUMPING INTO OLD FRIENDS

*S*itting at my regular table at the Farmshop, my favorite restaurant, I ignore the menu on the table in front of me. I gaze out the big picture window beside me and see a flower vendor across the street. My eyes can't leave the Circus roses, those long stemmed bright yellow roses with the red tips. Oh, I love those roses and the memories they bring back. My mind keeps wandering, thinking about my past and the people I miss the most. I've been feeling strange recently, it's not like I'm sick, or anything. *Well, maybe a bit mental at times.*

For some insane reason, I can't stop thinking about my childhood, and my first love, Drake. Naturally, those roses would trigger memories of him. If I'm honest with myself, he's the only man I've ever truly loved. Most of my friends think I'm nuts to even still think about Drake, but we just clicked. From day one, there was always something special between us.

All week I've been having dreams about him, as well

as seeing and smelling those roses. I'm tempted to text him again, but the fear of him ignoring me or getting his curt responses stops me. Doesn't matter, I'll text him this Friday on his birthday.

He'll probably be drunk with his Camelot Brothers, and some flavor of the night. I hope he gets past this stage soon. I know guys are different, they can have sex with random strangers without feeling anything for them. Drake explained it to me several times when we were growing up, but that doesn't mean it didn't bother me.

And it is not like Drake and I are anything anymore. But thinking back to eight years ago, even when we had our moments... Was I anything more to him back then, other than his best friend with *some* benefits? We never had sex. I was only fifteen, and he would always stop us from going too far. Even if, deep down, I wish he hadn't stopped.

He never said I was his girlfriend back then, either. He would promise, "You are my Bella, my best friend. There will never be another you. No one can ever take your place." He repeated it to me often. So many times, I wanted to beat myself for not asking him to explain the meaning behind that statement.

I was young and insecure. I wanted Drake any way I could have him. Gosh, I could drive myself nuts like this. I've grown up since then. I would never stand for any of that now, but I still can't get past him in my life. It makes me wonder, does he even think of me anymore, as I do him?

My mind takes me back to those sweet memories. I

loved the way he'd call me "babe." He had three different situation when he'd call me 'babe', and they all meant different things. When he grabbed my hand and cried, 'babe!' with a slight whine, I stopped in my tracks. That was his 'stop' sound. Just a quick 'babe' would make me smile. Then there was his guttural, growly, drawn-out 'babe.' That one melted my heart, causing it to race. I think it still would. It was my favorite of his "babe's."

I was 'his Bella' in front of people, but I was "babe" when we were alone. I knew I was special to him. I could see it in the way he looked at me, and when his dark green eyes would light up when he spotted me from across the room. I miss it... I miss him.

Gosh, all my internal battles over my love for him. It isn't like I haven't tried to get over him. I have, but I can't get past the memory of him, the way he made me feel. I've never had *that*, not with any other man.

I've dated, I've even had a few boyfriends that got pretty serious, but they wanted more than I was willing to give. And every last one of them had screwed around on me. None of them set my body and soul on fire the way Drake had.

Paul, the last jerk I dated, is a two faced, lowlife, cheating piece of dog crap. I'm not getting involved with any man for a very long time. I'll just live in my fantasy world of memories with Drake. It's safer there, anyway.

Thinking back on Drake, he had boinked half the girls in school, some of them my supposed friends. Drake would put both his hands on my cheeks and look me in the eye, saying, "Babe, it means nothing to me, *they* mean nothing to me. But I'm a man, I need the release. You gotta believe me."

I don't think Drake understood how much it hurt me, but I never let him know. He was the strong alpha bad boy that every girl wanted. Many of them were jealous of my friendship with Drake. But deep down, I was jealous of them for being able to have sex with him when I couldn't, or rather, he wouldn't.

Golly, he was my first kiss, my first everything. I remember lying on his bed lightly caressing his chest, counting every chest hair. At seventeen, he had exactly 37 hairs in the center of his chest.

His body, even back then, was a girl's wet dream. He weighed about 200 pounds and was six one of solid muscle. His jet-black hair was barely past his shoulders, with just the slightest curl. It was made for running your fingers through and made those dark green eyes stand out even more.

My mom always called him a man-child, with the hormones of a horny dog chasing a female dog in heat. If she knew about all the times Drake and I spent making out, she would have killed us both. Mom threatened him, holding her fabric shears.

"Look here, you overgrown man-child," she said, pointing the shears at him. "You touch my daughter, and I will cut off that thing between your legs. Then I'll hang it from my rearview mirror as a warning for the next young man who thinks of touching my daughter inappropriately."

Drake always answered, "Yes ma'am. I'd never do any such thing to Bella. I respect her completely, as well as your rules." Mom would continue waving the scissors around at him as she walked away.

Mom preferred Hawkins for me. He was a nice boy in her mind, clean cut with blonde hair and blue eyes. He was one of Drake's Camelot Brothers. He was the swimmer in the bunch and a computer geek.

I think Mom liked him because he was always polite and knew how to behave in front of parents. She never heard him swear like I did. She also didn't know he slept around almost as much as Drake.

Hawkins and I were just good friends and could talk about anything. I never liked him that way, even if at times I thought he might like me. He never did anything about it though. Hawkins knew I was Drake's and would never cross that line. The Brothers just didn't do that.

Over the last several years, so much had happened in my life. I'm sure Mr. Gregory, Drake's dad, never mentioned the reasons why I left, just like he never mentioned one word about the other three women my dad was involved with, or the fact that I had two half-brothers and a half-sister.

Dad died of a heart attack five years ago, still trying to get my mom back. I learned about it all and met my half-brothers Asher and Ashton, and my half-sister Arielle, when Mr. Gregory read my father's will. Mom hates them both for not telling her years ago.

Mom was furious and did not want me to befriend them. I refused to listen to her. I wasn't an only child any longer, and they knew my father even better than I did. I wanted to know them and have a family. I became very close to them. My father named me as the executor of his estate.

That's when I finally learned why Mom literally ripped me out of Drake's arms and forced me into the cab to live in New York. She refused to explain anything to me back then, other than saying she was done. This is yet another reason why I'm back home in Santa Monica and she is still in New York.

Drake's father had always been a jerk, but over these last few years I've seen him regularly since my father's death. He was the one handling my fathers will. I could never get a word out of him about Drake, or any of the Brothers, for that matter.

He would only say, "Isabella, Drake knows your number. If he wanted to contact you, he would. Let's leave it at that." I'd only asked him to say hi to Drake and the rest of the Brothers for me.

He was just a rude, mean, cranky-pants of a man in my book. He never told us anything, not even after my father passed. I wonder if he ever told Mom Gregory. How she chose to stay with this man, I never understood.

A squeal pierces my reverie.

"Oh. My. God. Isabella! Is it really you!?" Looking up, I come face to face with my past. Getting up from my chair and squealing myself, I run over and tackle-hug Britney, Drake's sister.

Stepping back, I notice Britney's other brother behind her.

"Look at you, Brenden. Aren't you going to give me

a hug?'"

Opening my arms towards him, he scoops me up and lifts me off the ground, spinning me around. I know people are staring, but I don't give a flip.

"You two have to join me! I would love to catch up, see what you're all doing, you know, and ask why no one has called me. Yeah, I still suffer from foot-in-mouth. No filter with me. I think it, I say it. Sorry," I mumble while leading them back to my table.

"Golly, so fortuitous! I've been thinking about all of you so much lately," I say as we take our seats.

"I can't believe we bumped into you! What are you doing in Santa Monica? Last I knew, you were living in New York. Drake is going to have a shit fit when he finds out," Brit says with a huge grin.

"Well, I've kind of been living here or at least in SoCal for over six years. I had to come home to California. I've been back since I was seventeen when I started Cal Poly, San Luis Obispo. My senior year in college, I opened my first Rainbow and Unicorn Day Care Center. They took off after I graduated with my bachelor's degree in Childhood Development and Business Administration, so I decided to open more locations south of San Luis."

"What the fuck, Isabella? You've lived this close all these years and you never called any of us? How could you not stop by the club to say hi?" Brenden demands, sounding pissed.

"Uh, well, yeah. I did stop by the club. I didn't see

anyone I recognized, so I left. But you did it, you guys fulfilled your childhood dream, Brothers of Camelot is real. Oh, my goodness, that portrait of you all is downright sinful." I can't help but bat my eyes at him, fanning myself.

No way was I going to tell them I saw Drake flirting with some beautiful Amazon woman I'm sure he hooked up with later. Nope, I'm keeping that heart crushing moment to myself.

"You've been to Camelot? And you didn't say hello to any of us? Are you shitting me?! I know we teased you a lot growing up, but I didn't realize you didn't like us," Brenden mumbles, a breath of pain in his voice.

"Didn't like you?! Me?! Oh, no. That's not it at all. I adore all of you. I just thought you might not remember me. Besides, the last thing I thought any of you would want was an old friend coming out of the woodwork, wanting your time. You guys are hugely successful now, and way too busy for me."

They both chortle, then Britney sets me straight, "You should have called. Mom would have been thrilled to see you. And so would Drake, not to mention the rest of us."

"Oh! Did you see it? The mural? He's holding the Beast head in it, just for you. Hell, he even has a Beauty and the Beast tattoo right over his heart."

I gasp, "No, really? I saw the Beast head, but all of you called him that too. I just thought... I didn't think it was about me!"

"Isabella, come on, don't you remember the day you met all of us? You sat beside Fitz on that piano as the two of you sang not one, but two songs from Beauty and the Beast. That's when we started calling him Beast, and he started calling you his Bella," Brenden informs me, with a cocky grin.

I blush, looking down. "I know. I was scared, to be honest with you. I've texted Drake a couple of times, and well, he's just so short in his replies. I thought... I thought..." I stammered. "I thought he didn't want to talk to me. You all had my number too. It's never changed. I still have the same number I've always had."

Britney laughs, holding her hand out, "Give me your phone girl, because this ends today. None of us, except Drake, has the same number. I'd get into a fight with a boyfriend and then change my number. You two are perfect for each other, anal as anal can be."

I hand over my phone, and Brit turns it to me to swipe it open. She opens the contact list in her own phone and begins correcting everyone's numbers. Brenden watches her for a minute then turns his gaze to me.

"Now, young lady, you have no excuse."

Smiling, I nod, "That goes both ways, you know. You two have no excuse not to call me either. We live and work pretty close to each other."

While Britney continues updating my phone, she starts in with her twenty questions. "Okay, now tell me about you. What are you doing here? I don't see a ring, so I'm guessing you're still single? Do you live close by? We have to hang out. I can't wait to tell Brenda and Sarah I bumped into you!"

When she takes a breath, I interrupt, "Okay, first.

No, I'm not dating anyone. Right now, all men are on my poop-head list. No offense, Brenden. Men are super lying, two faced, cheating, dirtball, maggot eating, scumbag, suck the life right out of you, heartless, pieces of stinking foul smelling poop!"

I realize I've opened my blabbing hole when they both crack up, laughing uncontrollably, holding their sides. I'm sure they realize I haven't changed a bit. Lack of a filter always embarrasses me.

It takes a few minutes for them to compose themselves, wiping tears from their eyes. Brit gives me a sad smile, "I completely understand where you're coming from, girl. I've been involved with a couple of those scum bag jackasses myself. I guess you had a bad break up?"

Giving Brit a stern look with one eyebrow raised, "Bad break up!? Well, if you mean after three months of him begging me to make a commitment to him and take our relationship to the next level, then once I decided what the hey, why not, I find out what a true lowlife he really is, let me tell you.

"Paul gave me a key to his place, but I hadn't used it yet. I wanted to surprise him, so I got all dolled up and drove to his place. I didn't want to show the world, so I took a page from the old romantic movies and wore a trench coat, then drove over to his house on our three-month anniversary to surprise him.

"I open the door and walk in, but I was the one who got the surprise. I found my now ex-best friend, *and accountant*, bent over the back of his couch, naked. Her fake boobs were bouncing as he was boinking her from behind. Worse, he was pulling her hair and screaming, 'Give it to Big Daddy!'

"Well, I listened to him and threw his keys at him, nailing him upside his head. When he stopped boinking Susan, I opened my trench coat, showing him what he just lost. I yelled, 'See all of this? You could've had it all! But you couldn't keep your wee willy in your pants! Now you'll never see it, never touch it. No second chances!'

"I'm not the forgiving type. After telling Paul we were done, I turned my anger on Susan and fired her. Demanding that she return all my records to me by morning, or I'd destroy her reputation.

"I couldn't help myself, I was beyond ticked. I took off both of my pink stilettos and threw one at each of them, hitting them, naturally. You boys did wonders for my aim," I wave at Brenden. "Then I exited as fast as I could. I slammed the door and took off running to my car.

"Once I got home and changed, I poured myself a huge glass of wine, took off my sexy outfit, and went outside to my fire pit and burned it all, even the trench coat. I polished off that bottle while watching it all go up in smoke. Then I had every single thing he gave me couriered to him.

"PAUL, well, he's a bit of a slow learner about it. Both he and his parents have been kissing my behind ever since. They keep trying anything they can think of to get me to forgive him, to take him back. But this girl... Oh no, I *do not* do sloppy seconds."

By the time I finished, they could have caught flies with their mouths hanging open.

After a time, Brenden finally asks, "Are you kidding me? You really did all of that? Screw Drake! Marry me." We all crack up at that.

"I promise you, I did and said all of it. I haven't seen or spoken to Susan since then, other than her returning all my files via courier the next day. I still haven't seen Paul either. In my book, he's the scum of the earth and not worthy of my time. I'm sick and tired of men who can't keep it in their pants."

"Isabella, you're real. I'm so glad you haven't changed a bit! The Brothers will be thrilled to have you back in their lives. We've all missed you!" Brit exclaims.

"As for this Paul asshole," interrupts Brenden, "he needs his ass kicked in a big way. If he ever gives you trouble again, you just let us know. We'll handle him for you."

"Thank you, that's awfully sweet. But I'm not worried about Paul, I can handle him. In fact, he might have finally given up. I haven't spoken to him in over a month. I've got this handled. I'm just not giving any man a chance for a long while." I can only pray they believe the forced confidence in my voice.

Chuckling, Brenden relents, "Okay, if you say so. What else have you been up to?"

My eyes sparkled with sass, "Well, since the last time you've seen me, I've grown a whole three and a half inches. I am now five foot three and a half inches tall."

Brenden whoops a laugh, "Well, look at you, big girl!

You're still a foot shorter than Fitz. You're still our little *Shrimpy*, but we love you all the same."

"Are you kidding me? He's grown two and a half more inches since I saw him last? Wow, he's gotta be huge!" I exclaim with surprise.

"Yeah, Isabella, he's a big boy, but not as big as Riggs, Jackson or Carpenter. They've got at least two inches on him, and a good twenty or more pounds too."

I cross my arms under my ta-tas, getting defensive. "I'll have you know, I still don't like that nickname, *Shrimpy*. And for your information the average woman in the US is five four. That only makes me a tiny bit shorter than average."

"Well, in all honesty," Brenden responds with a laugh, "we probably won't call you *Shrimpy* anymore." Clearing his throat, Brenden's face becomes more serious. "You know, Brit was telling you the truth. Drake holds that Beast head in the mural hoping you'll see it, maybe contact him. It's his way of reaching out to you."

Surprise and shock take my breath for a minute, finding that hard to believe. At a loss for words, I try to organize my thoughts. If he's been carrying around this Beast head, gotten a tattoo for me, why hasn't he called me? Why hasn't he even texted? He could have done either over the years.

"Let's order lunch, and we can tell you what you're doing Friday night," Brit announces, pulling me out of my trance.

Brenden waves for the waitress, asking, "Is salmon okay with everyone? My treat, I can't remember the last time I've had so much fun at lunch."

We both nod as we watch Brenden order. "We'll have three butternut squash soups, and the seared Scottish salmon, followed by the cinnamon raisin pain perdu for dessert, and you can pick the best bottle of wine for this. Thanks, sweetheart," he flirts, winking at her. The waitress smiles before walking away.

When Brenden finally peels his eyes off her retreating bum and turns back to us, both Brit and I are giggling like school girls. Brenden tries to hide that he was flirting and checking out her bum.

"What?" he asks, trying to look innocent.

"Oh, lordy! Do you flirt with all the girls like that?" I ask, trying to keep the smirk off my face.

"Hey, I wasn't flirting! I was just being nice." Brenden tries to look shocked and indignant, but he fails.

Brit winks at me. "Oh... okay. Whatever you say," she fires back with sarcasm.

"I wasn't, that's just how I am. Now, I'm changing the subject. Isabella, you cannot tell me that you don't know what Friday is?" Brenden blurts.

"Yes, I know what Friday is," I retort. "It's Drake's birthday. He'll be twenty-six. And where's the party going to be? Oh, let me guess... The country club, he'll hate it." Drake hates these parties his mom insists on throwing every year.

"Yup, you guessed it right, and he *will* hate it. But you could make it better if you come with us and surprise him."

Nervous, I shake my head. "I don't know, he might not want to see me. I don't want to make his birthday awkward for him or anything. Even though I would love to see all of you again, he might not feel the same way."

Brenden reaches over the table, resting his hand on mine. "Believe me, Isabella; Drake will be beyond ecstatic to see you again."

"Look, I'll be completely honest with you." Brit pauses, taking a deep breath. "Drake has the reputation of being a total man whore. But he's still carrying a torch for you and you alone. He's told Mom more than once that he'll never marry. He's flat out said he let the best thing he ever knew get away from him. He was talking about you.

"I'm serious here. I'm not telling you to marry Drake tomorrow or anything. God, I'd be the first one to tell you *not* to marry him anytime soon. But, I'm begging you. Give him a chance and let him make it up to you. Come on, you two were best friends forever. I know it's still there for you too. I can see it in your eyes. You have to give my brother a chance to make up for being an asshole all these years."

Blinking my eyes to clear the sudden tears, I'm more nervous than I've been in a long while. Finally, in a tremulous voice, I respond. "Okay, if you're sure." My voice grows stronger. "But check with your mom first, make sure it's okay."

Brenden's face looks like a little boy's on Christmas morning, jubilant and elated. He shoots from his chair, walks around the table and picks me up in a bear hug. "Thank you! You just made my brother the happiest man alive, and he doesn't even know it yet. After he shits himself, he's going to snatch you up and never let go.

Hell, it wouldn't surprise me if he throws you over his shoulder and takes off with you to his estate and keeps you forever."

As the waitress brings our soup, Brit and I giggle. Brenden continues to flirt with her with yet another wink. He checks her out with a long head-to-toe look as she smiles at him. Oh yeah, Brenden scored with her, barely saying a word. I'm sure he'll end up getting her number before we leave.

"Guess who Brenden and I are having lunch with right now?" Brit exclaims into her phone, drawing my attention. "No, I'll give you a hint. We have *the best* birthday surprise for Drake, ever! He's gonna love me for the rest of his life! I mean, yeah, he loves me, but this will put me at the top of his list."

Hearing Mom Gregory's voice telling Brit to knock it off and just tell her brings a smile to my face. Brit relents, whispering "Isabella."

The squeal from Brit's phone hurts my ears across the table, I don't know how Brit withstood it. She shoves her phone in my hand as Mom Gregory demands *"Oh, my God! Is it you, Isabella? Really? When did you get into town? Oh, sweetheart, I've missed you so much."*

"Hi, Mom Gregory! Gosh, I've missed you too," I echo, joy lifting my heart.

Brit interrupts us loudly, making sure she's heard. "Mom, I'll tell you everything over dinner tonight. Isabella just wants to make sure that it's okay for her to come Friday night to surprise Drake."

"Well, of course it is honey. I think that would be the best gift ever. I look forward to catching up and seeing how much

you've grown into a beautiful young lady. I can't wait to see Drake's face when he sees you!" Mom Gregory says with a sniffle. I hear a page in the background, meaning she's at work.

Brit has to comment again, not letting me get another word in, "Mom, she is only a little younger than me. Naturally, she's grown up a bit since you last saw her at fifteen."

Realizing I wouldn't be able to get a word into this conversation, I hand Brit back her phone when Mom Gregory replies, *"Young lady, watch your tone with me. I'm still your mother and don't need your smart mouth. I'm just speechless trying to talk to Isabella. Now give Isabella back the phone for a second."*

Brit rolls her eyes and hands me back her cell phone, *"Isabella, you be there early so we can hide you and surprise him, okay sweetheart? I'll be talking to you again real soon, and we can catch up."*

I'm so elated at having this woman back in my life that it takes me a moment to respond. "Yes ma'am, I will. I can't wait to see you too, Mom Gregory. We have to do lunch or breakfast real soon, okay?"

Brit takes her phone back and says, "Mom, I'll see you tonight. I'm sure Isabella has plans for this evening. We'll talk later. Love you. Bye for now."

Brit hangs up her phone and looks at me with that mischievous grin on her face and says, "Do you have something sexy to wear? If not, the two of us are going shopping."

I smile, "I might have a few things. But, I'm as nervous as a prostitute in church on Sunday morning after a long night working the corner, but I think I got this."

Peals of laughter burst from Brit and Brenden as the waitress brings the rest of our meal. We spend the next thirty minutes eating, recalling funny childhood moments and catching up. Brenden insists on paying the bill, and I watch as he gets our waitress' name and number.

Giggling to myself because Brenden insists on walking me to my minivan, Brit asks, "Why in the hell do you have a minivan? Come on, girlie. Maybe an SUV, but never a minivan! You're only twenty-three, for crying out loud."

Grinning, I explain, "Well, I love it, it's low to the ground for Mojo, my doggie, to get in. Any kiddos I need to drive around for my business can get in and out easily. This van is the most practical thing I could've gotten. It's so cool, look, I have dual sunroofs, a cooler to keep drinks cold. I have an awesome system in here for movies and music, and more."

Brit shakes her head, "Whatever. Call me later, girlie." We hug again and say our goodbyes.

Turning to Brenden, he lifts me off the ground and spins me around as if I weigh no more than a feather.

"I can't wait to tell the rest of the Brothers I had lunch with you today. Don't be surprised if your phone starts ringing off the hook. They're gonna yell at you for not letting us know you lived here all this time. But I'm so glad you're back. See you Friday night. You'll make Fitz the happiest man alive." He kisses my cheek then shuts my door for me.

I watch them get into Brenden's BMW. *Lord help me.* I'm seeing Drake. No, I'm seeing all my old friends again. Not in a million years would I have thought a few hours ago I'd be bumping into two old friends like this. Now I have to figure out how to not have a panic attack *and* find something sexy to wear that'll knock Drake's socks off.

CHAPTER SIX

FITZ: PAINFULLY REMEMBERING ISABELLA

*A*fter spending some time in the office, FaceTiming with Hawkins to make sure the club's security is perfect and the cameras are angled properly, I decide it's time to up my drinking game. Making my way from the security offices, I head towards the bar on the third floor. This floor is off limits to everyone except family and very elite clientele for private parties and such.

The lower floors are getting full, judging by the noise level. Once the bar comes into view, I'm surprised to see so many of the Brothers are here on a Sunday evening. Only Clausen and Hawkins aren't here. Before the night is over, someone'll have Hawkins' iPad stand set up, I'm sure of it.

I grab a seat at the bar and look toward the stage to see Britney, Sarah, Brenda, several of their friends, and six Brothers doing the dance from "Thriller." Jesus, it's been a long time since they pulled this out, but throwback night brings out everyone's best moves.

"Hunter, give me a Black Russian and keep'em coming. And use top shelf, man, none of that cheap shit. Don't be stingy with the vodka, either." Chuckling, I grab a handful of the nut and pretzel mix in front of me.

Hunter starts making my drink, inquiring, "Look at them, how many years ago did they do that dance number? Was it, nine or ten?"

I shake my head as he finishes preparing my drink, "No Brother, it was only eight years ago."

"Yeah, I knew you'd remember. You kicked your sister's ass in the dance competition that night," Hunter says chuckling while filling several glasses with beer.

Once the song finishes, the group from the stage runs up and grabs the beers Hunter just placed on the bar for them. Everyone starts chatting and laughing.

Riggs walks up and pounds me on the back. "Did you enjoy the walk down memory lane?"

Slack jawed, I'm about to respond when Britney interrupts, "Oh my God, you have to pick someone and do your "Time of My Life" routine. You'll make the panties melt off every girl here, well, except mine. That would just be gross. Anyway, you're way hotter than Patrick Swayze, and that dance number is every girl's wet dream. Come on, we can still do the backup part for you."

Shaking my head, I finish off my drink. Britney barely takes a breath and keeps going. "I still watch you and Isabella dancing in Mom's old home movies. I can't believe I never found out about it, with how much you two had to have practiced. God, you guys had the outfits and everything. Who would have thought you could have shocked us all and beat me!? Well, we did help you with the finale when we all joined in with you. That's the only reason you won, you know."

I wave my glass in the direction of Hunter, needing a refill. Britney is going to give me heart failure. There was no way in hell I would be doing that dance number. Not tonight, or any other night.

As I pick up my fresh drink, Britney starts up again. "Fitz, we have a bet, and I know I can win this one. During that dance, that was the first time you kissed Isabella, wasn't it?"

Busting up, I cock an eyebrow at my sister. "You really think that was our first kiss? In front of everyone? If you do have a bet on it, you just lost big time. Our first kiss was way before that." Everyone, the Brothers, and Brit's friends are hanging on my every word.

"Remember that birthday party, when you were thirteen, and you got several of the Brothers to play old school spin the bottle, and seven minutes in heaven? Which meant you, dear sister, would be stuck in a closet with one of the Brothers getting cheap kisses and probably them trying to cop a feel? Yeah, you remember.

"Well, Bella didn't want her first kiss to be like that, or with one of them. She came up to my room and said just that. Knowing how she felt and reading her meaning, she really wanted me to be her first kiss.

"What's a boy to do, but to fulfill her dream? And I wanted to be her first kiss as much as she did." I close my eyes for a second and remember that moment, that soul defining moment that rocked my world for life.

Several people howl with laughter when Brit exclaims, "Are you shitting me?! I just lost twenty bucks on that one. Grayson, rather *Riggs,* was the only one that thought she snuck up there with you. I thought she got scared and went and told Mom. Not more than fifteen minutes after she disappeared, Mom came down all pissed and sent everyone home." Walking away she mumbles, "Why you all insist on calling each other by your last names is beyond me."

Sarah, Riggs' younger sister, lays her head on my shoulder, pleading, "Come on Drake, it's been years since you've danced with anyone. Isabella moved away ages ago, it's time to move on. Come on, do that dance with me. I'd love to be your partner, let's do this." She begs as she tugs on my hand.

"Sorry Sarah, that's not gonna happen. I don't want to hurt your feelings or anyone else's, but the answer *no.*" Finishing my drink, I survey my Brothers and the rapidly filling bar area.

"Okay, I'm only going to say this once, so listen up and remember these words. That dance I did eight years ago was a one-time deal. I'm not doing that dance with anyone else, not now and not ever. I'm not messing up that memory, it's too important to me. Now, Hunter get me another goddamn drink and make it a double."

"If anyone understands, dude, it's me," Riggs throws an arm around me and reaches to grab the pitcher of beer sitting in front of me to refill his mug.

"Thanks, bro. Bella's memories are too precious to me," I respond, knowing he sympathizes.

Riggs leaves, giving me space to decide what to do in retaliation with Brit. That was low, even for her. I know she just wants what's best for me, but... *Fuck, speak of the devil.*

Britney bounds up, asking, "So, big brother, are you telling me that after all this time, you're still carrying a torch for Isabella? If you are, why don't you just look her up and call her? Isn't that one of the things Camelot Security does? Find lost loved ones?"

Like I suspected, someone has already Facetimed Hawkins, because I hear him from the iPad at the end of the bar.

"Fitz I could find her easily, in a matter of minutes. Give you a full report, what she's been doing since she left, if you want."

Whipping my head toward him, I exclaim, "No! Don't do that. Bella's probably just graduated college, and I'm sure her mom has picked out some country club, stuffed shirt asshole for her to marry next summer. I'd rather just keep her memory as is, no update. Thanks but no thanks, man."

Catching the sudden lack of noise, I find all my friends staring at me like I grew a second head.

"Fuck! Okay, stop with the creepy stares. You all know what she meant to me. We were best friends since I was six. When she had to move, I thought it was best to set her free. Let's just remember the fun and laughs we had, okay? Hunter! Pour some shots and let's get this party started!"

Riggs backs my play, "Yeah! Everyone get a shot and let's drink to Isabella. I know she was a pain in my ass most of the time. She'd try pulling any body hair she could latch her paws onto, and that shit hurt like a motherfucker! But damn, she always made us laugh."

Raising his glass, Riggs put his hand on my shoulder and toasts our lost friend, "To Isabella, may you come back to us one day, so we can finally hear you swear."

After a few snorts of laughter and a smattering of "here, here," we throw back our shots. Thanks to Riggs' toast, everyone begins telling stories about Bella. Stevens asks, "She would be what, twenty-three, right? She must have started swearing by now. How could anyone make it through college saying, 'fudge buckets'? No one can make it through life without saying 'fuck it.'"

Everyone guffaws at Stevens when Bishop rolls up on his Segway, commenting, "I don't know man, she was pretty creative with her very own personal way of swearing. I got into a big argument with her one day when she called me a 'no good, corn filled, poop eater.'" Laughter follows his announcement.

"Yeah, I told her she might be saying 'poop,' but she was thinking 'shit,' and it was just as bad. We spent a good hour bickering back and forth about how those words didn't even enter her mind. Wow, I miss the girl, she was really funny when you got her mad."

Jackson stands up next. "Come on guys, that little girl was the biggest cock block ever. Do you remember when she caught Fitz just about to fuck that cheerleader, the one with the big apple ass? Fitz, what'd Bella say again?"

With tears in my eyes from laughing so hard, I respond, "Oh shit that was funny. I never lost a hard on so fast in my life. She looked at Apple Ass, sorry ladies, you know I don't remember any girls name ever." I quip to more peals of laughter. "Bella told her, in her wonderful, smart ass way 'You know, you don't mean anything to him. You're just an easy screw when he should be using his hand. He doesn't love you, and never will. He's mine.' Then she gave me a dirty look and stomped her proud little ass out of my room. Apple Ass left right behind her because when she asked if that is all she was to me, I didn't deny it. Bella was only thirteen, then. Good God, I miss that girl."

I realize it's been years since I'd thought about all these wonderful childhood memories of Bella. Damn, they make my chest hurt. I'm gonna need another drink if we're going to keep talking about her.

Waving to Hunter to signal my need for another drink, I know I'm about to get hammered. Mom's little speech, my walks down memory lane and now this. It's too much.

Stevens adds his two cents to the conversation. "Let's talk about chicks with good aim. Remember when we were battling to see who would rule the treehouse, and the little brat snuck up there somehow with a bucket of water and dozens of mud pies? She dunked them into the water and threw them at us, defending the treehouse and helping Fitz get up there first. Man, some of those bad boys hurt like a motherfucker. I still think she laced some of them with dog shit. What was she then, seven maybe eight?"

As they continue telling stories and laughing, I sit with a fake smile on my face, feeling my heart being ripped to shreds all over again. I'm trying to keep my shit together, but I feel the alcohol hitting me.

Shouting at Stevens, "Bella was eight, and you're all just jealous because I always had someone helping me, watching my back. She had those mud pies on that roof for days, just waiting for you to try and claim it. And yeah, knowing her, they probably were laced with dog shit. She always knew what we were thinking. Those were the good old days. Man, I wish I could go back and relive them."

Reaching over, I grab the half empty bottle of Absolut and my shot glass. "You guys enjoy your conversation, while me and my new best friend go to my favorite booth over there to drown in my memories."

Turning, I stumble to the booth in the far corner marked *Reserved for The Brothers of Camelot.* Behind a red velvet rope, it's where we can escape the club for privacy if needed. Hearing several offers for company, I hug my bottle tight and focus on the booth. I'm getting shitfaced tonight.

CHAPTER SEVEN

FITZ: DROWN MY SORROW

I've been sitting in this booth for over an hour now, drowning my sorrows. I've almost finished off the bottle of vodka, and I'm debating on grabbing another one, or just call it a night. Looking over at the bar, I see everyone having a good time. Most of the guys have girls by their side, a couple even have girls on their laps.

Yeah, the Brothers of Camelot never have trouble getting laid. None of us are in a committed relationship. Most of us have never even tried to have one, either. I chuckle at the thought.

If I were to bet who'd be the first one to get hitched, it'd be Grayson Riggs. He's the only Brother who's ever felt anything like I have.

Closing my eyes for a brief minute and just remembering Bella. Damn, I miss her. Her laughter, just an innocent little giggle, filled my heart with bliss. I remember the first day we met, she was almost four. I smile thinking of her in that outfit she wore. She twirled up to me, exclaiming "I'm a princess ballerina showgirl! I love to sing and dance!" She was all that and more to me.

Fresh wounds shred my chest, recalling the day she moved away. I rub my chest, right over my heart, like that would help ease the pain.

Hearing someone slide into the booth across from me, I open one eye to find Riggs. He pushes a plate closer to me and hands me a glass of water. *Oh man, my weakness*, a French dip sandwich and fries. Finally, he slides another large Black Russian, my favorite drink, as well as a Coke towards me.

Cocking an eyebrow, I wonder when the hell he turned into a girl.

"Hey, I didn't know if you were done with your pity party yet or not, but I think you shouldn't be alone. Stevens told me he didn't think you'd eaten since breakfast with Mom Gregory.

"Anyway, I brought over a variety of things for you. Food, because you need it, and I know how much you like the French dips here, and a Coke with that sandwich is a must. But if you want to sober up a bit, you need to start drinking plenty of water. Then again, if you still want to continue to drown your sorrows, I brought you a refill," Riggs explains.

"Thanks, man. Food sounds good, but first things first." I pick up my Black Russian and drink half of it before I put it down. "As you can see, I'm not finished drinking yet, but I do need some food. Thanks again, Brother."

Riggs continues to stare, concern marking his face, "You wanna talk about it?"

"What's there to say? I remember what you told me over eight years ago. You were right. 'If you love something set it free. If it comes back, it's yours. If not, it was never meant to be.' Well, I left it in the hands of fate.

"Bella and I are probably the only two people you know who still have their first cell phone numbers. I never changed mine in case she ever wanted to reach out to me. But I'll tell you now, at this moment, I feel like hunting her down and making her mine. Screw fate."

Riggs chuckles, "Hand me your phone, dude. With the mood you're in right now, it's not good for you to have it. The last thing you need to do is drunk text her. By the way, when was the last time the two of you texted each other, or, hell, even spoken?"

I put down the sandwich I'd already taken two big bites of, then reach into my back pocket and pull out my phone. "You're probably right about that one. I was re-reading all our texts earlier. I don't blame her for not texting me more. I always answered her, but my replies were short and didn't give her an opening.

"I've been a dick. She deserves better than me, anyway. I know her mom probably hates me. Come on, I'm the son of a whore in her eyes. And just look at who my father is, the man who never told her that her husband was living a double life with three other women. I'm probably the last person she wants her daughter to be with. But goddamn, it hurts like a moth-erfucker. Bella was it for me. That I know for damn sure."

I pick up my drink and down the rest then holler across the club. "Stevens, bring me another bottle of Absolut, now."

Several people turn and look at me, including a few Brothers. It's so loud in here, I don't know if Stevens heard me. I hold up my empty bottle, giving it a wiggle and finally get a head nod from Stevens. He gets up from his stool and heads around the bar to grab me another bottle.

Proud of myself, I announce, "Shit, it actually worked, he's coming."

"Look, if anyone knows what you are going through and battling with, it's me. Remember, at least you know Isabella's full name and could find her if you seriously wanted too, unlike me. You just need to get off your ass and do something about it. If you feel in your heart, soul, and mind that she's it, your real soulmate, go and find her, damn it. Claim her, before someone takes her away from you forever. I don't want to hear this shit about you not being good enough for Isabella either."

Stevens strides up, carrying my bottle of Absolut and two glasses. I take the bottle and glasses from him, offering the second glass to Riggs. I put the other one in front of me and fill it with vodka, then I pour one for Riggs. I'm pretty shitfaced because I feel myself swaying. I'm gonna regret this tomorrow, but right now I don't give a flying fuck.

Focusing back on Stevens, I slur, "You're cut off ash-hole. No more jrink-ing for you, bro. Jou're my driber tanight. I can't dribe jlike dis. No pussy either. Because pussy ain't welcome in my house! Sure as fuck not in that bed. Never fucked anyone in my house or my bed, and jou're gonna make damn sure I don't. You got me? Cause you're in charge of babysitting my sorry ass.

"As for you Grayson, good buddy, jou're right. Can't do it now, jou took ma phone... But after my fuckin birthday party, when I'm not shit-faced, I'm gonna call Bella, 'pologize for being such a dick-faced, asshole, motherfucker to her, and for not shtayin' in touch with her. Wish me luck." I lift my glass in the air and chug it down.

I'VE no idea how I got home. I don't even remember leaving the club, but I just landed on my bed, face down. The whole room is spinning while Stevens and Riggs talk above me. I try to say something, but it just comes out as a moan. Straining to hear them, I feel someone take my shoes off.

"I don't think I've ever seen him this trashed. Luckily, he threw up outside the club and not in that truck of his. He'd be beyond pissed in the morning, having to clean that shit up," Stevens says.

"You got that right. Why don't you find a trash can, just in case he gets sick again? Are you planning on staying in the house to make sure he's okay? I think he probably drank a bottle of vodka straight and only had that sandwich to eat. I thought his head was gonna start spinning with how much he threw up. Luckily, I jumped out of the way. When'd you get so damn slow?" Riggs laughs.

"Yeah, man I'm planning on it. Let me get my shit and take a quick shower before you bounce. Gotta get Morris and bring Freddy's cage too. Fitz gets nervous around Freddy since he tried to play hide and go seek up his sweatpants a few weeks ago. He's convinced Freddy wants to eat his junk." They both chuckle.

"Um, that would freak me out too. If that thing crawled up my pants leg, it'd be lucky to still be alive. You go get your shit, I'll get Fitz some aspirin and water and put it on his nightstand for tomorrow. He's gonna feel like shit in the morning. Here, you take his phone and put it somewhere until he sobers up. I don't want him calling or drunk texting Isabella, screwing up his chance of getting her back."

Stevens chuckles, "I got this. I'll be back in a few."

After a few minutes, everything quiets down. On the backs of my eyelids, all I see is adorable little Bella, when she's not quite four. Her dancing around makes me smile. I refuse to open my eyes for fear of losing her again. Drifting off to sleep, I know I've found my happy thoughts.

Monica's super excited, one of her best friends from childhood is moving in next door. She told us Ivy is coming over for lunch and is bringing her daughter. They're hoping the two girls can be good friends just like they were growing up.

Sitting on the huge couch in our massive family

room, I hear the doorbell. Monica squeals louder than Britney and races for the door.

While she's squealing and laughing with her friend, this cute little girl with long, curly, reddish-blonde hair and oval shaped, chocolate brown eyes walks in. For some reason, she makes me smile.

Looking like a dress up box exploded, she's wearing a purple t-shirt that says "Sparkle" in silver glitter, a neon rainbow tutu, a red feather thing around her neck, a tiara on her head, bright pink tights and plastic high heel shoes. They click-clack as she walks across the floor. She stops and looks around.

Britney, in her light pink ballet tutu, leotard, and soft shoes, jumps off the couch and runs over to the girl, grabbing her hand. "Hi! I'm Britney, and we're going to be best friends. Just like our moms!"

The little girl beams, "Hi! My name's Isabella. I'm a princess ballerina showgirl, and I sing and dance."

Britney laughs, "You can't be all those things. You look so silly."

Isabella huffs and walks away from her, saying over her shoulder, "I like to be silly, it's a lot more fun." Stepping up to Brenden, she greets him. "Hello."

"You're funny." Brenden laughs. "How old are you? I'm eight years old and going into the third grade. My brother, Drake, he's in second grade, and he's six. Britney's going to pre-kindergarten this week, and she's four."

"I'm having a Beauty and the Beast birthday party next week," Isabella says as she moves toward me. "I'm gonna be four!" Climbing on the couch, she kneels next to me and lightly grabs my face, turning my head so she can examine me. "Your eyes are green. I've never seen anyone with green eyes before. They're very pretty." Moving to my hair, she states, "You have really, really pretty hair. It's black and soft. You have curls, but not curly like my hair."

I smile, "I've never seen red hair before. You have the biggest, darkest brown eyes I've ever seen. And I think you make a wonderful princess ballerina show-girl. I bet you can sing and dance just as wonderful, too."

Her smile widens, causing huge dimples to pop on each cheek. Moving from her knees to her butt, she grabs my hand with her little chubby one and whispers loudly, "*I like you best. You're going to be my new best friend. When we grow up, we're going to get married and have lots of green eyed babies.*"

Grandma, Monica and her friend Ivy all start giggling. Brenden, being overly dramatic rolling around on the couch, suddenly stops and sits up. "Drake can be your Prince Charming! He can play the piano while you sing him love songs."

Britney follows his lead, as usual, teasing, "Drake's got a girlfriend, Drake's got a girlfriend."

Isabella's eyes light up, "You can pway the piano? Will you pway for me pwease? Then I can sing for you."

I smile, loving the way she said 'pwease'. There's something special about this little girl. Glancing at Grandma, she smiles and nods, "Go on, *Nieto*. We haven't heard you play in a while."

Monica is also smiling, "Go ahead, Drake, you may

go in the living room. We'll all come with you and watch."

I stand and take Isabella by the hand. "Come with me Princess Isabella, and I'll play you a special song." I've always been able to play any song I've ever heard. Ma used to tell me I was gifted. Once Monica found out, she got me real lessons.

Isabella jumps down from the couch, holding my hand on our way to the living room. Listening to her plastic high heels click-clacking on the floor makes me smile.

Once in the living room, I help her up on the piano bench, sitting her to one side. Once I'm seated next to her, I say, "Sing along, okay?"

Her smile is beautiful. "Oh yes, my Pwrince. I will sing to you."

I begin playing "Beauty and the Beast," the theme song from the movie. She squeals, leaning into me, singing a bit off key. It's still beautiful. We get lost in the song, but I can hear them chuckling behind us. Monica grabs her camcorder to tape us.

Once I finish that song, I move straight into "Something There." I sing the Beast parts while Isabella sings Belle's part. This time, everyone is quiet while Monica continues to tape us.

When I stop, Isabella gets up on her knees and kisses me on the cheek. Turning to her mom, she announces, "Mommy, I think I'm in love."

Everyone laughs as her mom replies, "I'm so excited for you, Isabella. Sometimes, first loves can last a lifetime."

~

MY HEAD'S POUNDING, and there's this roaring noise along with something heavy vibrating on my chest. I lift my hand and place it on top of my chest, feeling hair, soft and smooth. My eyes snap open, and I look down praying. *Dear Jesus, don't let it be some random chick I brought home last night.* I'm relieved to discover Morris, Stevens' monster of a cat, asleep, purring away on my chest. My laugh makes me realize I'm hungover because my head throbs in pain.

Slowly, I slide out from under Morris as my dream of Bella stirs in my memory. It felt so good. God, I have to figure out how to win her back. Spotting the water and aspirin on my nightstand, I know I have Riggs to thank for it.

After chugging the water and the aspirin, I head to the bathroom to take a much-needed leak. Still dizzy, I decided to lay down with Morris. Damn, he's a huge, furry beast. Lazy as hell too, and hasn't moved an inch. I wonder if there are dogs like this, ones that just lie around and wait for their master to come and love on them. I need one of those.

As I lightly pet Morris, my eyelids feel heavy. Hoping to dream more about Bella, I give in to sleep, knowing that after this weekend, I'm going to hunt her down to claim her as mine.

Screw fate and waiting for shit to just happen. I'm taking over.

CHAPTER EIGHT

ISABELLA: THE DAY OF THE PARTY

*S*itting at the computer in my office at Rainbows and Unicorns Daycare Center, trying to get a few more things done before lunch. My door is ajar when Tory pushes the door open with her foot and comes in, carrying a monstrous bouquet of dark red roses. There must be at least three dozen in there, mixed with baby's breath and twigs sticking out in all directions. I'm surprised Tory can even carry it or see around them, it's so massive.

"How much do you want to bet I can guess who these are from?" Tory asks from behind those godforsaken flowers.

"I hope you're wrong. But since I have a good idea who they're from, I'm going to have to pass on that bet. Sorry to disappoint," I respond with a chuckle. I walk over and help her place them on the large window sill. I grab the card and open it.

My Dearest Isa,

How long must you ignore me? How long must you torture me? I am truly sorry that you saw what you did, my love. You know I love you and cannot live without you. Haven't I suffered enough? I need to see your beautiful face. I need to hear your sweet, calming voice.

Please accept these roses as a token of my apology. I picked them out just for you. Stop refusing my gifts of love and admiration. I'll allow you some more time to cool off but call me. I feel lost without you. I must hear your voice. Stop torturing me by leaving me.

Loving you always,
Paul

"YOU HAVE GOT to be freaking kidding me! Paul is such a stubborn dimwit. How many times do I have to tell him it's over? Gosh, it just makes me want to throat punch him, and I'm usually not a violent girl."

Laughing, Tory says, "Just admit it, that dude is whack. I used to love red roses and dream of someone sending them to me one day, but this nut job has ruined that for me.

"How many times a week is he going to keep sending them? He knows you don't keep them. The idiot must have told the florist to leave them by the door since we stopped accepting them. When was the last time you actually spoke to him? Three months ago?"

"I haven't said one word to him. I refuse to answer the phone when he calls. He does text, but I don't read them. I give him a three-word response, 'It's over. Stop!'

but he just ignores it. At some point, he'll move on. He just has to," I reply in exasperation.

Tory is obviously upset that Paul keeps harassing me. "What the hell is up with that twisted note? I think this whack job is turning full-on stalker. He had to go to the florist to give them that card. He wouldn't want anyone to see what he said. You might want to make sure to keep these delusional letters and a record of all the shit he sends in case you need them one day for the police."

"Come on, Paul is harmless. He's as wimpy as they come. He'd be too worried about his family's political career and his future to ever really do anything. His parents have him on a short leash. That's why he only sends things instead of showing up here. He'll get bored, eventually. Paul's spoiled, that little boy who always gets his way. He thinks if he keeps pestering me, I'll give into him, but that will never happen. Paul's not used to the word no." I'm trying to convince her, but I secretly wonder what it will take to make him stop.

"I don't know, I still don't trust the guy. He gives me the creeps now. I mean come on, what normal man would keep this up for three months, without getting anything in return? That's creepy," Tory demands.

"Just ignore him. Do you mind calling the nursing home to see if they want this monstrosity?" I wave my hand in the direction of the flowers, "These things are *not* staying here."

"Okay boss, I'll call around to see who wants them. I'll have them gone before you get back from lunch," Tory promises as she walks out of my office.

Looking at the note again, I wonder if I should send

the whack-a-doodle yet another text, telling him to stop. I've got too much going on to deal with his idiocy right now. Drake's party is in less than eight hours.

Sitting down at my desk, I put the note in a file, adding it to the others. I'm one step ahead of Tory's suggestion, already compiling evidence, just in case. I don't think anyone could ever make him stop. He's not really breaking any laws by sending gifts... is he?

Not wanting to share all this drama with Tory, or anyone, I try to minimize it. I'm not scared of Paul, but I'm not stupid either. I have a log of every gift he sent.

Trying to refocus on my work is difficult. Hopefully, I have a big weekend full of happy times ahead. I'm nervous about seeing the whole gang tonight, but even more so about seeing Drake.

"Oh, Isabella!" Tory calls from the daycare center. "You have another surprise coming your way."

"Oh, bugger. It might be time to get a voodoo doll of this jerk-faced dweeb!" I shout as I get up and walk to my door, wondering what the heck Paul has sent now.

"I sure hope it isn't my brother or one of the Camelot boys you're making a voodoo doll of," Britney inquires as she and Mom Gregory walk into my office.

Squealing so loud that the kids in the center must have heard me, I run past Britney and throw my arms around Mom Gregory.

"Oh, my goodness! I'm so happy to see you! What are you doing here? I didn't think I'd see you till tonight."

"Sweetie, I'm happy to see you too." Stepping away, she takes hold of both my hands, holding them out.

"Isabella, you look beautiful, even in your cute little glittery rainbow t-shirt. You're too adorable. Drake is going to eat you up."

Thrilled to my core, I simply beam at her for a moment.

"Now, tell me what you're doing here when Drake's party is in less than eight hours?" I ask.

"Honey, Brit and I are here to take you to lunch. I'm sure you'll be too nervous tonight to eat. Besides, once Drake gets his hands on you, I won't get the chance to catch up with you."

Brit interrupts, spotting the monstrosity Paul sent earlier, "Wow, who sent you these beautiful roses? And who do you want a voodoo doll for, I ask again?"

"Brit, it's the same lowlife I told you about at lunch the other day. I must be one of the few women in the world that doesn't like red roses. I'm on the verge of hating all roses, except for one. If I never see another red rose again, I'd be ecstatic. Stupid, whack-a-doodle Paul keeps sending them to me.

"Sorry, Mom Gregory," I say, turning to her, explaining. "Paul is my ex-boyfriend. I dumped him three months ago and for some insane reason, he thinks I should take him back after catching him in the act with my ex-best friend. Don't worry, I'm not taking him back, nor am I ever speaking to him. He's just a spoiled little boy that's not getting his way. He'll eventually give up." My face is red with embarrassment at even having to explain this.

It's time to change the subject.

"Okay, where do you want to grab lunch?" I ask.

"There's a steak house right down the street. It's a beautiful day, we could walk there and chat on our way. How does that sound? My treat."

"Isabella, you should know me better than that, young lady. I'll be the one picking up the tab for this lunch. Now, let's get out of here and tell me all about your daycare business.

"And by the way, that was a nice change of subject. But if he doesn't stop, I know twelve very big men that love you dearly, who'd love to help you out. And one, in particular, that will have a royal fit if he saw those roses." Mom Gregory winks as she links her arm with mine, perhaps fearing I'll disappear again.

We all laugh as I reply, "I'll keep that in mind, thanks. But really, I've got this under control. I've dealt with plenty of spoiled bratty little boys in my line of work. Paul's older, but still as stubborn and bratty. He'll learn I won't give in. Now, let me give you a tour of the center before we head to lunch." Keeping my arm linked with Mom Gregory, I lead them toward the center and away from those disgusting roses. I only hope Tory can get rid of them before I come back from lunch.

As I PUT the finishing touches on my makeup, I recall the wonderful lunch I had with Mom Gregory and Brit. I've missed them both so much. Mom Gregory is much more down to earth than my mom. While I love her dearly, Mom is too enraptured with the high society lifestyle. I couldn't care less, much to her dismay. Mom is cold and formal, but Mom Gregory? She makes you comfortable, and she's real.

Mom always judges people based on their clothes and their jobs, especially me. If you know the right people, speak properly and have an acceptable job, she'll love you. She never understood my desire to work with children, to help them grow and be safe. She wants me to be a part of high society with her, and I can't. It's just not me. Those people are snobs who care more about what the other person's connections can do for them than for the person themselves. Maybe that's why I ran away over six years ago, back to California where my soul is complete.

Moving to my mirror, I only hope I didn't overdo it with this ensemble. The sparkling, dark yellow and gold formal dress is fitted from my neckline to my hips, making my boobs look enormous. I could give Dolly Parton a run for her money. It clings in all the right places, making my waist look smaller than it is, and adds a bit more curve to my tush too.

Glancing at my reflection, I do a twirl, watching the satin skirt. With two slits starting mid-thigh, my legs peek out with each step. When I stand still, it hangs straight to the floor. This dress is smokin' hot.

Not that long ago, I thought I might have a future with Paul, the king of poop-faces. Knowing that he's destined to be a DA, I'd procured several formal dresses for black-tie affairs. Thankfully, I hadn't thrown the baby out with the bathwater. I had these dresses custom-made for my figure. Golly, the seamstress I used is amazing. She's a true miracle worker when it comes to accenting the right stuff and minimizing my flaws. With my chest, I can never find anything off the rack that doesn't need major alterations.

Remembering how much Drake used to love my hair, I decide to wear it down in loose waves. Long and thick, almost to my bum, it's one of my favorite features. I love the way it changes colors in different lighting, from a light auburn at night to a strawberry blonde in the sun.

Drake could never resist playing with my hair. Whenever he sat next to me, he'd subconsciously pick up a lock to twirl around his fingers. For some strange reason, that little touch would soothe us both.

With a glance at the clock, I take a deep breath. *Time to go.* Squatting to talk to my 265-pound English Mastiff, I say, "Okay Mojo, Mommy is going to be out late tonight. Wish me luck, big guy. I might need it."

Bending closer, I kiss the top of his soft, velvet head. As usual, he looks up at me and decides I'm not worth the effort to get up. Within seconds, he's sound asleep and snoring away. He makes me smile, that big, lovable bear of a dog. Grabbing my clutch, I head for the door.

ONCE I GET to the country club, I park my minivan in the back, not saying anything to anybody, just as I was instructed by Brit and Mom Gregory. I head straight towards the kitchen, not making eye contact with anyone. My mind and my memories take control over me. I just pray this goes well.

Thinking back, the memory of Drake's final game in

his senior year of college floods my brain. He intercepted the ball and after running it back for fifteen yards, he was held up. Fighting for more yards, someone came from the side, tackling him at the knees, shredding his ACL and MCL. It was a dirty hit. It turned out to be a blessing, Drake said in an interview a few days before the NFL Draft, because now he could devote the attention he wanted to the company he'd started with friends, which I knew was The Brothers of Camelot.

I knew Mr. Gregory had to have been madder than a wet hornet. He'd been pushing Drake all his life to get into the NFL and suddenly that opportunity was gone. I don't think he'll ever accept Drake's dreams and wishes.

Pushing through the double swinging doors to the kitchen, Brit squeals.

"Holy shit! Look at you!" She runs up and grabs me in a hug. "You're beautiful! Drake's gonna have a shit fit when he sees you."

Stepping back, she holds me at arm's length and looks me up and down. "Dayum, girl. I know I told you to dress hot, but I didn't mean for you to give every guy here an instant hard on!"

Giggling, I give her a gentle shove. "I'm going to make several swear jars for my foster kid's care fund. You already owe two dollars!"

Several men start laughing as four huge guys in dark suits turn around and stare at me. Jackson's the first to find his voice. "Fuck, she hasn't changed one bit. Goddamn, look at that body! Shit, Fitz's gonna have a fucking heart attack. Damn!" he says, discreetly adjusting his junk.

"Damn, poor bastard's gonna cream his suit when she pops out of that cake," Stevens chimes in.

"He's one lucky motherfucker, that's for damn sure," Carpenter adds, checking me out.

Brenden saunters up to us and whispers, "Keep it down. We don't want anyone to find out until we roll her out. I already told you guys, other than gaining three inches in height, she grew a nice set of tits."

After giving Brenden a shoulder punch, I smile my hello to the other boys. "I'm right here, you know. I can hear every nasty, vulgar word you're spewing out of your gross pie-holes. My foster kid's care fund is going to grow ginormously with all your potty mouths. I'm setting up a ton of swear jars, you guys will love them.

"That'll be nine dollars from you, Jackson, and only two dollars for Stevens and three from you, Carpenter." Jackson picks me up, like a rag doll, and hugs me before passing me off to Stevens, who does the same before handing me off to Carpenter.

"I'm going to enjoy being around you giants. You make me feel small. And that's saying a lot," I quip.

Carpenter looks down at me, scolding, "Darling, none of that shit. You are one helluva hot little cupcake. Fitz is gonna eat you up. If one of us doesn't steal you from him first, that is." He winks, ever the flirt. "Now, come with me so I can show you where you're, uh, sitting." Taking me by the hand, he leads me to the other side of the big kitchen where a huge, fake cake on wheels is waiting.

Stupefied, I glance at each of them in turn. "You

have *got* to be kidding me. You want me to pop out of a birthday cake? How cliché is that?"

Brit stops next to me. "This was Mom's idea. She called Carpenter the moment I left her house on Monday night and asked him to create a cake you could sit in as they roll you out while we sing "Happy Birthday" to Drake. Once we're finished, Carpenter and Brenden will pull it open. You'll be stuffed in there with a bunch of balloons, and when they open the doors, the balloons will fly up and away, then you can come out and say happy birthday. Or hell, with that dress you're wearing, we should just give you a mic. You can sing like Marilyn Monroe. *Happy Birthday, Mr. President,* she sings, in a deep throaty voice.

I swat at her, hitting her in the arm as I exclaim, "Not going to happen! I'm too freaking nervous to sing!"

Mom Gregory saunters into the kitchen, wearing a navy sequin gown and the cameo Drake gave her the Christmas he called her Mom for the first time. It's so sweet to see she still wears it.

Taking both my hands, her eyes take me in. "Oh, sweet girl. You look stunning in that gorgeous dress. It's perfect for your first dance with Drake."

"What first dance?" I ask, confused.

She waves her hand, turning me toward the cake. "Well, let's help you sit in here, and I'll tell you."

Following her lead, I step up into the beautiful white with navy trim cake. It looks so real, it even has fake LED candles. Placing my bum on the little stool, Mom Gregory leans into me for a quick hug and air kisses.

"Honey, I'm more nervous than you are right now,

believe me," she assures me. "In a couple of minutes, these young men will close you up with the balloons. I'll call Drake to the dance floor, and I'll say a few words. When I'm finished, they'll roll you out. We'll sing "Happy Birthday" to Drake, and when we finish, Brenden and Carpenter will open the doors for you. When the doors are all the way open, you release the balloons, revealing you, just like Britney already explained. Do what comes natural, wish Drake a happy birthday, or give him a hug. By the way, we'll be playing the video from when you and Drake first met."

Oh, goodness, what have I gotten myself into? I'm shaking like a leaf when Brit hands me the huge bouquet of navy and yellow balloons. They shake and rattle right along with me.

"Hold on tight, they're not tied together," Brit whispers. "Thank you for this. You've made Drake's birthday wish come true. He still loves you. I only hope one day someone will love me the way he loves you."

The guys shove the balloons in wherever they can fit them. I try to help, but I'm still in shock from Brit's bombshell. Finally, the guys finagle the doors closed. Blinking my eyes, I try to keep the tears at bay. The guys put little spotlights in here, aimed at my face. Two on the floor, one from the top.

Jackson's deep voice comes through the crack of the doors.

"Relax in there, sweetie. You have nothing to worry about. You just made our boy's life complete."

"Don't go passing out in there either, you hear me?

Take slow breaths, you'll be in Drake's arms in just a few minutes," Stevens adds, trying to help me relax.

My mind races, this all has happened so fast. Am I really going to see Drake? After all this time? Does he truly love me? As more than a friend? Would all my dreams finally come true?

Oh God, I might faint. I slow my breathing as I feel the cake moving. *This is it.* What was the last thing Mom Gregory said, something about a video from when we first met? *Oh, no!* Our song is going to play? What have I gotten myself in to?

CHAPTER NINE

FITZ: THE BEST BIRTHDAY OF MY LIFE

*S*itting at my table with all my Camelot Brothers, I'm wearing the ridiculous navy suit and gold tie my mom insisted upon. My Brothers are the best, considering they gave up a Friday night to go to some snobbish party. Unfortunately, Tonya, my date, is right next to me.

I'd rather not be here at all tonight. This country club ballroom is getting packed, and I've always detested birthday parties. My only wish is that time would speed up, ending this horror sooner.

There's five empty chairs at this table. Clausen takes a seat directly across from me. He's sporting a nasty black eye, and it looks like he's been sparring with someone. *What the hell?* He's not one who normally gets into fights.

"Hey, what the fuck happened to your face?" I interrogate.

Clausen shrugs. Fine, he can be cagey if he wants.

"Have you seen my brother and sister tonight?" Another shrug. "How about Stevens, Jackson, and Carpenter? I haven't seen any of them in over thirty minutes. They *cannot* flake on me tonight."

Clausen shakes his head, a tight flex in his jaw. "Dude, be patient, you'll find out that, and more, in a matter of minutes."

Now that pisses me off. Something is going on with the Brothers, and they're keeping me in the dark. We don't keep secrets from each other. Come to think about it, they've been acting strange all fuckin' week.

Glancing around the table, I notice every single one of the Brothers present staring at me and whispering like chicks. Right as I'm about to say something, Mom calls for everyone's attention.

Standing in the middle of the dance floor, a big screen slowly lowers behind Mom. *Holy shit*, she's gonna play old family movies. Motherfucker, this night *could not* get any worse. She motions me over, beaming from ear to ear.

Slowly, I climb from my seat and approach her. Putting my arm around her, I whisper, "Please tell me you're not about to embarrass the shit out of me with home movies."

Winking, she ignores me in favor of the mic. "Good evening, everyone. I want to thank you all for joining us to celebrate Drake's twenty-sixth birthday."

Everyone applauds, and there's some whoops and wolf-whistles from my Brothers.

"I'd like to share a little story with all of you. When Drake came into our lives a little over twenty years ago, he wasn't used to parties. He's never been a huge fan of birthday parties for himself at all. No matter how hard I tried, he just went through the motions to make me happy. But as his mom, I knew he hated every minute of it.

"But tonight, I decided to switch things up. With some major help from his sister, brother, and the Brothers of Camelot, I think tonight's party will be his best ever!"

Cheers and cat calls spread through the room.

"Let's all sing "Happy Birthday" to Drake so that he can have his dessert before dinner!"

As the music begins, everyone gets to their feet and moves onto the dance floor. Oh, fuck, what is going on?

From the back of the room, Stevens, Jackson, Carpenter, and Brenden are pulling in a huge birthday cake by long navy ropes. Holy shit, if there's a stripper in that thing, in front of Mom, I will physically have to kill them.

Once the cake is directly in front of me, they stop. Brit runs around the cake to Mom, who steps back and puts her arm around her. What the hell is going on? What has my bratty sister done now?

The rest of the Brothers have joined the group who pulled the cake out. Carpenter and Brenden slowly open the doors, causing a shit ton of navy and yellow balloons to float to the ceiling. My eyes snap back to the cake when I see movement out of the corner of my eye. There, standing in the middle of that cake, is the most breathtaking sight.

"Happy birthday, Dray…"

Her words are cut off when I fly to her, snapping my arms around her. Holding her tight, I lift her off her feet and spin her around. Is this really happening? Is my Bella here in my arms? I kiss her on the top of her head, inhaling her scent. God, I've missed her!

The party around us penetrates my nice little bubble with Bella. Flashes are going off, and Brit's sniffling. The video on the screen is us singing "Beauty and the Beast" when we first met. Keeping my arms around Bella, I lower her to her feet. We watch the video, swaying gently. My smile rivals the sun, I'm over the moon that Bella is in my arms.

Feeling Bella tremble, I turn her face to mine. Unshed tears pool in her eyes, but her smile is radiant.

"Okay?" I mouth.

"Perfect," she whispers.

Yeah. Perfect. Bella is perfect in my arms.

"*No. No fucking way*," Clausen growls from my left. My head turns, trying to will him to shut up and not ruin this. "I cannot accept that his *Bella* is *my* sister. *Isabella*? I cannot allow this shit to happen."

Stevens and Riggs maneuver him toward the doors, while I'm left in confusion. What the fuck did he just say? Isabella's his sister? No fucking way. I squeeze my girl, hoping she didn't hear that.

Turning her around, I tip her chin up. I could get lost in those big almond shaped eyes that are the color of dark milk-chocolate forever.

"Is it really you, Bella? Tell me I'm not dreaming."

"Yes, you big doofus. It's truly me," she promises.

Laughing, I gather her in my arms and start spinning. I whisper in her ear, "You are never leaving me again. You're mine. You're the only person who brings me happiness. I want to throw you over my shoulder and lock you away. Think Mom would be okay with that?"

Her giggles fill my heart. Oh, how I've missed that beautiful, little laugh of hers. It makes me whole when she's in my arms. I haven't felt like this in years. I'm complete, and I'm never letting her go.

The opening chords to the theatrical version of "Beauty and the Beast" interrupt my complete absorption of Bella. Angela Lansbury's voice is my cue to give a bow. Bella curtsies right along with me. Perfect timing.

Everyone's cleared the dance floor, allowing me to sweep Bella into a dance. With my left hand grasping her right, I wrap my right hand around her waist and pull her close. Bella's left-hand rests just below my shoulder. Gazing into her eyes as we twirl around the dance floor, it's still unbelievable that she's here, in my arms.

When my eyes have had their fill, my ears want to hear her voice. "Who found you? Who brought you out here for my birthday? I meant what I said, you know that, right? I am *not* letting you go back to New York, not without me. I don't care what your mother has to say this time."

She giggles again, "Well, I bumped into Brenden and Brit on Sunday by accident at a place I've gone to for brunch for a while. What can I say? They begged and pleaded for me to come to your birthday. How could I turn them down?"

Something in her answer strikes me. "Did you just

say the same place you've been having brunch for a while? How long is a while?"

She looks away on a blush. "Well, um, I've kind of been living in California for um, a little over six years. I went to college in San Luis Obispo, and then moved to Santa Monica around nine months ago."

"Babe, why didn't you call me or even text?" I ask.

"Why haven't you?" she challenges.

She was right, so I tell her the truth. "Because you deserve better than me. I'm an asshole and a bastard. For that, I'm profoundly sorry. I will do everything within my power to make it up to you. I promise."

Slowing our motion around the floor, I slide the hand at her waist to her neck. I need to kiss her, just one brief taste of her lips. Bending, I hear the hitch in her breath as I close in on those beautiful lips. Heaven. Her lips are heaven under mine. Reluctantly, I pull away and wrap my arms around her, tucking her head under my chin.

After a few seconds, she slides her arms up to the back of my neck. Her fingers entwine in my hair, sending a shiver through me. I slide one hand along her arm to hold it in place as I lift my head. The other hand moves to her chin, tilting her head up and back so I can have her eyes on mine again.

"Look at me. I need your eyes," I sigh. "Honest to God, I was going to have Hawkins track you down on Monday. I wanted to find out if I still had a chance with you. But you're here now, in my arms, my Beauty. I'm never letting you go."

With tears in her eyes, she gifts me with her glorious

smile. I'm hoping they're happy tears, but she steps back, thrusting her hand out.

"Okay, you big dork. Let's start at square one. I'm Isabella Anderson."

Laughing, I grab her hand, pulling her back into my arms, demanding, "Fuck that, babe. That 'square one' shit ain't gonna work for us. We've known each other almost twenty years. We are *way* past square one."

Mom taps my shoulder, bringing me back to the room. *Fuck, when did the song change?*

"Okay, I know you two have a lot of catching up to do, but it's time for dinner. Show her to your table like a gentleman, Drake, so that everyone can eat. The night is young, we have plenty of time for catching up." Mom winks.

"Yes, ma'am." Sliding my arm around Bella's waist, I lead her back to my table where all the Brothers are sitting with shit eating grins on their faces. That's when I remember Tonya. She's standing by my chair, her arms crossed over her chest, and not looking too happy. Man, if looks could kill, both Bella and I would be ashes. Fuck, this is *not* gonna be fun.

Leaning down, I whisper in Bella's ear, "Umm, forgive me a second. Mom insisted I bring a date and now I have to be a dick to her. No way in hell am I sharing tonight with anyone but you."

She gasps as I step up to Tonya. "Sorry Tonya, but our date is over. I really didn't want to bring anyone with me tonight anyway, but my mother insisted. I'm sure it was before she knew about Bella. I can call you a car if you want? Or you're more than welcome to stay. But, hey, I let you know up front. This was nothing more than a one-time date."

Brenden pipes in, "Tonya, sweetheart, I'm this asshole's older brother, Brenden. I'm a trauma doctor. My date had something come up this evening. I'd gladly be your date if you'd like to join me. I promise you a night of fun and dancing, and if you want more, I'm your guy." His charm wins her over.

"Thanks, Brother. It looks like I owe you for a lot tonight."

Tonya smiles as she unfolds her arms and sashays over to Brenden. "Hey, it's your loss," she announces. "She doesn't look like the putting out type."

Bella's back snaps straight, bringing out her sass. Damn, I missed her sass.

"Oh, bless your heart. I'm not easy at all, but I *am* the one he wants to keep around for a lot longer than one night. Now, move along. That's my chair."

Oh, man, that smart-ass mouth. Fuck, Henry's taken notice and is stirring in my pants, which all of a sudden feel two sizes too small. When several of us start laughing, Tonya tries to save face.

"Wow, I never knew you liked bitches, Fitz," she retorts.

More guffaws precede Bella's come back. "A bitch is a female dog, but if you ever tick off a female dog and try to take what's theirs, don't be surprised if they bite your head off." Damn, this woman amazes me. In a honeyed voice, she continues, "Consider yourself warned, sweetheart. Drake is mine. You can't have him tonight, or any other night. Enjoy your evening. I know I'll enjoy mine."

Bella slides her arm around my waist, leaning into me. I lead her to our chairs and get her settled. If Henry keeps this up, I'm going to have trouble walking later.

Smiling like a dumb ass, I sling my arm over Bella's shoulders and twirl a strand of her hair. The Brothers are still wearing those shit eating grins, and some of them flat out laugh when they catch my eye. I know I look like a love-struck fool, but I don't give a shit what they think. I *am* a love-struck fool. I have Bella next to me, and both Henry and I are thrilled. I can't remember the last time I was this happy.

Finally, everyone settles down, and the chatter rises. I get an occasional chin lift from some of the Brothers. They know I'm over the moon.

Bella innocently places her hand on my leg. Sparks fly from that one spot right to my cock. Poor Henry, hard as stone, and I can't help him out.

Looking at her, she's more beautiful than the last time I saw her. She's finally right where she belongs, by my side. So much time has passed, but it feels like yesterday. Fuck, it's like I'm in some sappy chick flick.

Her hair is still long, thank fuck. I can only imagine wrapping it in my fist as I thrust into her. Henry jerks behind the fly of my pants. Fuck, moving on from that subject...

Bella's face has matured and is thinner than the last time I saw her. Her high cheekbones are more pronounced, and the smile lines around her eyes show her joy in life. And her eyes... those almond shaped eyes with those killer lashes. She smiles, and damn, those dimples pop out, causing me to inhale sharply. Bella giggles at me and it's music to my ears.

Lowering my gaze, I take in her body. Holy fucking shit, what a body. Her tits are glorious, satin smooth skin waiting for my mouth. Her skin flushes under my heated gaze. I can't wait to find out what turns her on and explore every inch of her.

Dragging my eyes from her chest, I return to her hair. *When did I grab a strand to play with it?* Soft as silk, smooth as satin, her hair has always been a balm to my soul. Recalling the countless times I've done this, I close my eyes, relishing every second.

This is paradise, this very moment. Having Bella in my grasp is my dream come true. Now, I just have to keep from fucking this up.

CHAPTER TEN

FITZ: FINDING OUT SECRETS

*A*fter everyone has enjoyed their dinner, but still are chatting and teasing each other, I pull Bella into my lap, causing her to release that adorable giggle again. The servers give me a slice of Mom's traditional white birthday cake with cream cheese icing, decorated with navy and yellow flowers. Mom always keeps the color scheme consistent.

I know Bella's sweet tooth and how much she loves cream cheese icing. Oh, the things I could do, using some of that in the bedroom with her. I feed Bella bite after bite, watching her eyes flutter in ecstasy. Damn, her lips wrapping around the fork as I slowly pull it out is hot as shit. Trying to keep a leash on Henry is futile.

After everyone finished their dessert and the servers clear our plates, the DJ starts with some soft rock and moves on to suitable dance music. The Brothers hit the dance floor and don't waste any time trying to steal my girl. I'd scowl and growl at each of them, and tell them,

"Get your own date." Bella giggles each and every time, filling my soul.

Finally, with great reluctance, because I'd rather keep her in my lap forever, I lift her to her feet. Taking her hand in mine, I lead her to the dance floor and gather her into my arms, holding her tight to me. She's a perfect fit in my arms. I'm lost to her, song after song plays as we dance, not sharing her with anyone.

"Drake, my feet are about to fall off. Let's sit for a while and chat," Bella implores. Wrapping an arm around her waist and kissing the top of her head, I lead her to the couches. She tries to sit next to me, but I pull her right where she belongs, in my arms and onto my lap.

Slowly, my Brothers make their way over and burst our little bubble. Kicking back, I allow the peace to wash over me, listening to the stories and laughter of my friends. Clausen finally makes an appearance, looking like he's had a few drinks. I'm still wondering who beat the shit out of him.

"Isabella, why didn't you tell me this idiot was your childhood flame? Did you think I wouldn't approve?" Clausen demands, sitting down across from Bella and looking her in the eye.

Silence reigns and everyone watches Bella. She straightens her spine and grabs my hand. "I never kept anything hidden. I always called him Drake. Heck, why didn't you tell them about *me* when we met? I know all about the Camelot pledge. I'd also like to know why you never even mentioned you worked for Camelot. I would have figured it out myself if you had. And what the heck happened to your face?"

Clausen's eyebrows snap down, but he better watch how he talks to Bella. I'm still in shock that he never told us he's her half-brother. Fuck, now I want to kick his ass myself. He and I'll be having a little talk later.

"Fuck, Isabella. I've been friends with these assholes forever. Sorry for not wanting to talk about the family drama," Clausen argues with heavy sarcasm. "I've known Drake since before I turned four. If you've been friends with them as long as you say, you knew me back then too. I played and fought with all of these guys growing up," she retorts.

Brenden adds his two cents, "Dude, you're the oldest out of us, but you went to some of Fitz's little league games. She went to every one of them. She wore that cheerleading outfit, making up cheers for Fitz."

Clausen cocks his head to the side like he's trying to remember. As if the clouds clear, his eyes light with understanding.

"Fuck! You're that pesky, chubby little girl who followed Fitz around like a lost puppy? You're *Shrimpy*? You're the one who helped Fitz claim the treehouse by nailing us with dog shit filled mud pies?"

Shifting Bella to the side, I'm preparing to punch this fucker in the face. Bella was adorable, not chubby or pesky. Bella giggles and squeezes my hand.

"Yeah, that was me. And, yes, I did lace those mud pies with dog doo from the neighborhood. You guys always made fun of me for being thicker and short. I had to get you back somehow, and you deserved every one of them. And P.S. I don't care what you think about who I see, and maybe date. You were on Team Paul when I first started dating him. I caught that two-timing, slimebag, man-hussy boinking my best friend. That alone disqualifies you from commenting on my love life!

"Not to mention your choice in bed partners sucks, those so-called *women* I've had the pleasure of meeting. You know, the ones who try to dash out the door when I come over for breakfast. Their outfits scream *professional*."

We all crack up. Brenden wheezes, bent at the waist and holding his sides because he's laughing so hard. Jackson whoops as he smacks Clausen's back.

Clausen shrugs Jackson off. Leaning closer, he almost gets right in Bella's face. "Fuck, listen to me. Yeah, I'm your big brother who doesn't approve, but I know this guy a lot better than you do now. He doesn't do relationships. He's *one and done.* He fucks and bails. He doesn't even know their name half the time. You damn well deserve better than that, little sister."

Trying to get up to beat the shit outta of him, I move to slide Bella off my lap, but she beats me to it, shooting to her feet. Shoving her finger in Clausen's chest, "I don't give a flying flip of dog turds what you think you know about Drake! I knew his motto back in high school, and I doubt it has changed over the last eight years. I don't spread for anyone until I have complete trust and devotion from them. I've never been easy, and I'm not about to start now just because I'm right where I want to be. I learned a lot from that dirtbag, I'll *not* be making the same mistake twice.

"Don't worry about my panties. They're staying put.

Thanks, big brother, for your concern, but from now on, watch your mouth when it comes to Drake. I'll not tolerate you bad mouthing him, or I'll kick your self-righteous butt myself."

Grabbing her hand, I tug her into my lap as the group hollers and cheers, applauding Bella. Several shouts of 'Preach it!' 'You tell him, girl!' and 'Hand him his ass!' sound out. Wrapping my arms around her, I kiss her forehead as I flip Clausen off behind her back.

"Looks like you got your attack dog back, too," Riggs says from behind me, causing me to snort. "No one can mess with you without answering to her wrath. We all remember her years ago. I sure as hell don't want any more dog shit thrown at me."

"Fitz, I'm calling it now," Carpenter calls out, "If you fuck this up, I'm moving in. Damn, that rant of hers just gave me a stiffy."

My head snaps to his, glaring daggers. "Dude, say that one more fucking time and I will cock punch that *little* stiffy of yours."

After the laughter dies down, Hawkins calls from his iPad stand, "Hey, Isabella, I want to hear more from you about Paul Edwards, your ex."

"What about him?" Bella inquires.

"You caught him fucking your best friend, and Clausen didn't kick his ass? He should have shared that kind of information with us. We don't let anyone fuck with family."

My head swings to Clausen. "Why didn't you come to us?"

Silence reigns, as eyes bounce between Clausen,

Hawkins and me. Finally, Clausen responds. "Isabella was angry and embarrassed. She didn't want me to do or say anything about him. She was afraid with him being the assistant DA that he'd get me in trouble, creating lies about me. I respected her wishes. I told her if he kept pushing her, trying to get back together, to let me know and I would handle it for her."

"Did she fill you in, Clausen? Did she tell you about the gifts and texts?" Hawkins demands.

"Fuck!" I explode. Grabbing her shoulders, I turn her to face me. "Woman, talk to me. Now. Right now."

"Drake, my gosh, I haven't seen Paul since the day I walked in on him and that floosy. Sure, he's sent me gifts and texts, but I just ignore him. He's harmless. His parents are worse, they cornered me one night when I was out to dinner. They want us back together, but that will never, ever happen. The last time I talked to him, I reiterated that it was over. He said he'd give me time to cool off like that's what was wrong. Yeah, he still sends me flowers and such, but I refuse to sign for them, making the florist take them to the nursing home or Veteran's Center."

Hawkins interrupts, "Sweetheart, you're moving in with me. This fucker is showing signs of a textbook stalker."

"The fuck you say?" I bellow.

Bella rests her hands on my chest. "Guys, calm down. I live in a gated community, I told the guards not to allow him access. I've added a new security system to my house. Besides, he's scared of my puppy, Mojo, anyway. I don't think I have anything to worry about."

Hawkins gives a small chuckle, "Never mind that. This is shit *we* should have been informed of months ago. Don't worry your pretty little head, though. We won't touch him...*yet*.

"Clausen, you should have told us your sister's full name. We could have figured this out and handled it. I'm checking out this asshole, along with his family, in depth. They'll never know cuz that's what I do. Guys, mandatory meeting at my house. Sunday. Noon. No fucking excuses unless I find something out sooner.

"Clausen!" Hawkins shouts, "prepare for another ass kicking. You brought this on yourself. Fuck, not telling us about Isabella is a cardinal sin, never mind that Edwards was fucking with her."

"Wait," Bella pleads, "is he serious? I told you, I have this handled. Paul's a wimp. I can kick his butt if I have to. Believe me, I've already slapped him for being too aggressive. I put him in his place."

All my Brothers collectively suck in a breath as my blood boils.

"Excuse me," I demand. "What the fuck do you mean 'a bit too aggressive?'"

"Come on, Drake," Bella chuckles, "you know I'm not the easy kind of girl. When we first started dating, he tried to feel me up. I pushed his hand away, firmly saying 'no'. Well, he wasn't very happy with that. He got the crap knocked out of him and a knee to the family jewels when he tried again."

"Hawkins, get me this fucker's address. Now!" I command.

"Drake, calm down," Bella begs. "He told me he

respected me more for not being easy. He spent weeks apologizing and begged me to forgive him. He accepted my boundaries after that."

I'm so far beyond fucking pissed, I'm close to nuclear. The only reason I haven't hunted down this Paul asshole is because Bella's still on my lap.

"So, Isabella," Jackson inquires, "you're telling us that this asshole tried to force himself on you, grabbed those luscious tits and, all five foot three of you slapped the shit out of him and kneed him in the nuts? But you still kept him around, and after three months, you still didn't put out? Then you found him fucking your best friend and cut ties, and now he's trying to get you back?"

"First, I'm five three and a half, and guys, listen to me. I'm done with him. I'm not taking him back. He just wanted arm candy for his DA chance. He just hasn't figured out that he needs to find a new woman to be his arm candy. The only reason he keeps calling is because I flashed him the night I dumped him. I wanted him to have a good look at what he missed out on. That's the only reason he hasn't given up yet."

"Isabella," Jackson begins sternly, "I promise that asshole has not forgotten you flashing him the goods. Probably whacks off regularly just thinking about your tits. He just proves what a real asshole he is by not being loyal to you. However, we'd feel a little better if we could come over and check out your security, just to make sure you're safe."

"Jackson, I hired pros to install it. I think I'm fine," she replies.

"Isabella, you don't have a choice. We'll be checking

out your place tomorrow. Okay, sweet cheeks?" Jackson says with a wink

"Fine, if you must," Bella consents while rolling her eyes.

Needing to lighten the mood and to make myself feel better, I snag Bella's attention.

"Babe, you know you're not going home tonight, right? You're coming home with me. It's time for one of our sleepovers. We need to catch up without everyone listening in."

She blushes slightly, biting her lip. "Okay, but we have to get Mojo. He can't be home all night by himself."

"Are you two making plans to escape?" Clausen butts in. "I need in on these plans."

"Dude, back off," Brenden says, knowing I'm already on a short fuse with Clausen. "You're gonna have to get used to this. They're meant to be together. If he fucks it up, the rest of us will hand him his ass, then try to steal her heart ourselves."

His teasing is pissing me off. I reach over and smack Brenden upside his head, tucking Bella deeper into my hold.

"Shit, Bella's fuckin' mine. *No one* is gonna lay a finger on her. You hear me?" I announce loud enough to ensure all the Brothers hear me. I know they'd never really go after her...would they?

"Planning an escape so soon, huh?" Jackson asks, "You must have some *intimate* catching up to do," he jokes with a crooked grin, waggling his eyebrows.

"Yeah, Fitz wants to help her *work out*," Carpenter adds.

Clay rises, shoving his cowboy hat on his head. "Nah, boys. Fitz just wants to teach her to *ride*," he says mimicking riding a horse. "Isabella wants to ride his *pony!*"

Fuck, these guys are ridiculous. I just hope Bella's not embarrassed.

Bella snaps her little finger in the air, getting everyone's attention. "First off, let me clear the air. I know exactly what you're implying with your nasty comments. We have a lot of catching up to do before any of *that* happens. This man respects me completely and has never pushed me into anything.

"Second, if you'd have listened earlier, I don't put out on the first date," Bella states, much to their amusement. She leans up and kisses my cheek. "But, come on, we haven't even had a first date yet." The guys roar with laughter. "Stop with the horny toad looks, winks, nods and innuendos. It's not happening tonight." Fuck, that smart mouth of hers is making me hard again.

Damn, I can't wait to cuddle with her. I hope I can convince Henry that he's not getting access until she's ready. Knowing how she feels doesn't put a damper on my desire to consume every inch of her. I damn well plan on making her mine, and very soon.

I want to be her lover. If I had my way, we wouldn't have made it through dinner. I'd have dragged her from that big ass cake straight to my car, driven to my place and ripped off her clothes. I would spend an hour on her magnificent breasts, sucking, kissing and fondling them, just to see how long it would take for her to come from that, then I would move on to…

Bella shifts in my lap, causing my teen fantasy to come true. My cock is pressed right along the seam of her ass. Ho-ly shit, she feels amazing. Fuck, she's got to feel Henry jerking, trying to get closer to her. Slowing my breathing, I try to think of anything to get my boner to relax… cantaloupes, no…wrong thought. Oh damn, Mrs. Carmichael, the high school librarian. She had to have been ninety-three. Oh yeah, that works just like it did when Bella would get me all riled up in high school.

Clay pulls out his wallet and throws a twenty on the table. "Well, take it Stevens, and add it to the pot. We just heard Fitz ain't gettin' puddin-tang tonight!"

Bella shoots to her feet. "I just told you NO BETTING. You guys are incorrigible, you're all turd face dweebs!" Bella snatches the twenty, crumples it and throws it at Clay.

We're all howling now. *Turd face dweebs,* holy shit. Stevens retrieves the twenty from Clay and pulls an envelope from his jacket pocket to put it in.

"Dude," I call to Stevens. "Go by Bella's house, get her puppy and bring it home, will ya?"

Clausen just about falls out of his chair in laughter.

"*Mojo?* A puppy?! Oh, this is classic. Hey Stevens, you gonna drive Isabella's minivan to get him? I'm gonna need pictures of this shit."

Stevens brow wrinkles in confusion as shock hits me hard.

"Babe, a minivan?" I ask, disbelieving.

"What are you, Isabella, some thirty-year-old soccer mom? Tell us Brit was kidding earlier," Stevens calls out.

Brit jumps in, waving her hands in the air. "Oh, no! She *loves* her minivan. It's all decked out in Rainbow and Unicorn decals, of her daycare center logo. Brenden and I saw it in all its glory. It's right out the back entrance."

Bella huffs with each insult toward her minivan. Seeing how proud she is of that thing, I'm having a hard time keeping from laughing right along with them.

Turning, she gives me the most adorable look of annoyance before she turns back to them.

"Look, you inconsiderate imbeciles," she says to the group, "my minivan is brand new. It's great for my daycare business. There's a video system so I can play movies for the kids. Besides, Mojo can get in and out easily. It has dual sunroofs and a cooler to keep my drinks cold."

Her defense of that damn minivan causes us all to crack up.

Jackson joins in, "Isabella, I don't care about all those bells and whistles. You need an SUV upgrade, decked out with a dog ramp. Your fine little ass does not need to be driving a dorky, mommy minivan. Not with those tits."

Bella leans over and with her middle knuckle sticking out, she punches Jackson as hard as she can in the soft underside of his arm.

He pulls away, rubbing his arm. "Fuck! That hurts like a son of a bitch. You are going to leave a bruise on me with those skinny ass knuckle punches. Didn't your mother teach you not to hit people? Fitz, can't you control that little woman of yours?"

Bella leans into me, a smug smile on her face. "My mother taught me to defend myself. That's all I did. Now, stop making fun of my minivan. And, FYI, Drake is *not* the boss of me."

Clausen is still laughing for some odd reason. Bella grabs Stevens' hand. "Mojo's a true sweetie. You'll just adore him. If you pick him up and bring over his food and bedding, I'll make you breakfast in the morning. Your favorite, cinnamon French toast with cream cheese icing and an omelet."

"Damn woman, I'll gladly bring your puppy over. You know I love animals. But for your French toast and an omelet… I'll even drive your fucking minivan for that shit!"

Just the thought of Stevens driving Bella's minivan with Rainbows and Unicorn Daycare decals has everyone cracking up again.

"Damn, Fitz," Stevens says "you and the little woman are gonna have to hit the store for provisions. There ain't jack shit in that fine ass kitchen besides coffee. Hell, the only cooking I've ever seen in there is reheating a pizza."

"Hold up, I've made eggs and protein shakes in my kitchen," I defend.

"Oh, such cuisine expertise," Stevens chuckles, "dropping fruit into a Vitamix and pushing the power button. Well, aren't you special?"

"If that's all you have in your kitchen Drake, then we have to stop at the store before we go to your place, for sure. We can't have an old-fashioned sleepover without all the treats and the things I'll need to make breakfast in the morning," Bella says.

"Anything for you babe, as long as I have you in my house tonight, I'm all good."

Riggs and Brenden yell, almost in unison, "Hey, if it is an old-fashioned sleepover, we get to come!"

Clausen adds his two cents, "If my sister is sleeping at your place, I say we all get to come. Especially if she's cooking goodies and breakfast in the morning. I'll even watch chick flicks for that shit."

"Oh, *hell no.*" I need to head this off. Fuck. "If you guys want to come for breakfast, fine. No earlier than ten, fuckers. We need time to ourselves. This is not open for discussion."

Having stated my intentions, I decide enough is enough. It's my fuckin' birthday, and it's over. Gathering Bella in my arms, I drag her towards the coat room.

"Babe, do you want to wear my jacket?" I ask, getting it from the coat check. "It might be a bit chilly out there."

Her smile is radiant. "Have I ever turned down wearing anything of yours? You do know within seconds of walking into your house, this tie is coming off and I'm getting that shirt. Everything I've stolen of yours over the years has lost your scent. I need to start a new collection."

"Babe, you can take it all off if you want. I'm never turning you down again." I chuckle as a blush spreads across her cheeks.

Bella swats me, "None of that, young man. This is difficult for me. We need to talk later when we're alone."

I nod my head, glad to hear it's difficult for her. Maybe I won't have to wait three fucking months like dick-face did.

"Give Stevens your keys, and he'll meet us at the house with your puppy," I instruct her.

Bella reaches into her little handbag, and I take a peek, being nosy. She only has a cell phone, credit card, lip gloss, and a key fob. She's so practical, it makes me smile.

Passing the key fob to Stevens, she explains about getting her dog.

"Mojo's a big boy, but I think he'll know you're my friend. You might want to hit a drive-thru and get him a plain cheeseburger. He'll be your friend for life if you do."

"You feed your dog cheeseburgers?" Stevens inquires, unbelieving. "Damn Fitz, you treat this woman right, or I'm stealing her. She feeds her dog cheeseburgers," he repeats on a wistful sigh.

"We will see you at the house," I answer, eager to get going.

I help Bella into my jacket as we say our goodbyes to everyone. Mom is the last one waiting to say goodbye. She looks as joyous as I feel. Mom holds onto Bella, hugging and whispering to her.

My father doesn't even smile. He shakes his head and wishes me a happy birthday with a hearty slap on my shoulder.

When Mom and Bella finally separate, Dad turns to

Bella. "I guess some people never learn," he says, enigmatically.

"Nope," Bella retorts. "Once a poop face butt hole, always a poop face butt hole." She steps around him, reaching back for me. Knowing there's more to that exchange, I decide to place it on the back burner for now. More imminent things require my attention. Plus, I'm sure it'll only piss me off.

As we walk to the car, I chuckle as I see Mom grilling my father about Bella's reaction to him. It gives me the warm fuzzies knowing he probably won't be getting any tonight. My mind snaps back to being alone with my Bella, to have her in my arms, to taste her lips. I've waited so fucking long to have her back. I only hope I can control myself.

CHAPTER ELEVEN

ISABELLA DISCOVERS PASSION

*R*ushing through the store, I try to remember all the ingredients I need for breakfast. The cart is loaded with all the necessary ingredients: eggs, bacon, sausage, bread, milk, butter, cream cheese and orange juice. I also grab vanilla, cinnamon, confection sugar, and flour. If Drake's kitchen is empty, he probably doesn't have these staples. I quickly add several more basics, for safety's sake.

At the last second, I dash back for Rice Krispies and marshmallows. Those are Drake's favorites, especially when I add extra butter and marshmallows. Surveying the cart, I decide we have enough staples. Even if all the Brothers show tomorrow morning, I'll be ready for one heck of a breakfast.

"See, I knew we should have driven my minivan and just picked up Mojo ourselves. Stevens would have enjoyed driving this car much more," I tease Drake.

"Nope, shoulda brought the Nav," Drake mutters,

trying to stuff groceries in every nook and cranny of his little Aston Martin.

"Wait, you have another vehicle?" I question, thinking this car had to have cost a mint.

"Yeah. Aside from this, I have a Lincoln Navigator, a Dodge Ram 2500 and a Harley," he chuckles, placing the last bag on my lap. Surrounded by bags, I can only gape in astonishment as Drake rounds the hood.

On the ride to his house, it's quiet. With my nerves getting the better of me, my mind is bouncing around, going over the last several hours. I can't stay focused on anything. Drake, however, looks eager to get home. His smile is dazzling.

Drake takes a right onto a small street. Huge gates part without Drake's hands leaving the wheel. *Holy moly, is this his driveway?* Trees line each side of the road, spotlights highlighting them from the ground.

His house appears at the rise of a small hill, and golly, it's exquisite and huge. A cream façade with wood beams outline huge, beautiful windows. And those balconies! Are any of them Drake's bedroom? We round the house to the garage, the *eight*-car garage. Now I know why everyone calls it an estate.

Once Drake parks the car, we load our arms with the bags of supplies. He leads me into my dream kitchen. Standing there, slack-jawed, I take in the glory that is Drake's kitchen. I set my bags down on the largest island I've ever seen.

Making my way to the double oven, I pull one door open. Geez Louise, the instruction manual is still sitting in there. My eyes roam the massive room, as my breath catches at the sight of a rotisserie oven. The manual hangs from the spit too. Reheated pizza, protein shakes and eggs, *GAH!* Such a shame this master kitchen has gone to waste. I can't wait to cook breakfast tomorrow.

Biting my tongue, I hold back a million questions bouncing around in my head. Why would he buy a family home at such a young age? Did he have someone in mind when he bought it?

Just as I set the milk in the formerly empty fridge, Drake grabs me from behind, turning me to face him. There's a twinkle in his eye as he lifts me into his arms. Spinning, he sets me on the huge island as if I weigh nothing at all.

Even as high as the counter is, he's still just a tiny bit taller than me. At least we're closer to eye level. Grabbing his tie, I pull him closer, getting lost for a moment in those forest green eyes. I've dreamt about being with him like this forever.

"And just what are you doing, putting me up here?"

"You have no idea what you do to me," he growls. *Yes, growls.* "I want to taste you so much, Bella. I can't wait to see you in my shirt and in my bed, to hold you in my arms.

"So many nights I've spent in that bed, *alone,* thinking of calling you, imagining hunting you down and dragging you back to me. But stupidly, I decided to wait, to give you the chance to call me, to come back to me," Drake confesses.

At a loss for words, I continue to gaze into his eyes. Drake leans forward and slides my hair over my shoulder. My breath hitches as he trails kisses from my shoulder, up my neck, to behind my ear.

"What were the last words I said to you when your mother took you from me over eight years ago?" he asks in a husky voice. Feeling his breath on my ear sends shivers all over.

Trying to control my breathing, I close my eyes and recall that day. Mom was calling me from the cab while Drake passionately kissed me goodbye on my front porch. When he pulled away, tears cascaded from my eyes. I didn't give a flying flip that everyone could see us.

Drake cradled my face in both hands, brushing away my tears with his thumb vowing, "Don't ever forget me. I'll always love you, Isabella Anderson. You're the only one for me. I'll be waiting for you to come back to me." He sealed his vow with a kiss.

Mom dragged me from his arms as Drake shoved past Mom Gregory and took off running. I kept calling for Drake as my mom dragged me into the cab, crying uncontrollably.

Opening my eyes, I feel fresh tears at the painful memory. On a shaky voice, I reply, "You told me never to forget you, and to come back to you one day... I never forgot you, and I'm here now. I would have been back a lot sooner, but... but, I was scared that you had changed your mind."

"Babe, I could *never* forget you. I've missed everything about you. Your smell, your laugh, our late-night talks... You're still the only woman I've ever fallen asleep with and stayed next to all night." His eyes grow more hooded with each word.

My heart melts in anticipation of what's to come. That voice, *sigh*. Slowly, I loosen his tie and pull it from his neck. Tossing it aside, my eyes focus on the top two buttons of his shirt. Sliding my hands up his chest in a quest for those buttons, I bite my lip, feeling his warm firm muscles beneath his shirt. Oh Lord, I could get into so much trouble with this man.

With one finger, he pulls my lip from my teeth.

"Don't bite that lip," reprimands in a gruff, sexy voice. "It makes me want to suck on it. I know you want to take this slow, but, babe, I don't do slow real well. You have to help me out some, by not doing things that make me hard."

Blinking my eyes, I try to remember how to breathe.

"Do you trust me, babe?" he whispers.

Nodding my head, I watch a smirk appear on his lips as he places his hands on my knees. Thanks to the slits in the dress, his warm hands find my stocking covered skin. Drake leans back, watching as he slides my dress up, exposing the tops of my stockings and my garter. His breath hitches at the sight.

Continuing his exploration, he runs his hands up my thighs under the fabric of my dress. I gasp when his finger traces my panties at my hip. Reversing course, he drags his hands down my legs to my feet, gathering my left one and removing my shoe, dropping it to the floor.

Pressing a kiss to the top of my foot, he rests it against his chest. Lifting his eyes to mine, he confesses in a deep voice, "I'll never do anything you don't want, but I will push you. All you have to do is say no or stop and I will. I'll push your limits, waiting to hear those words from your lips. If you don't say it, I *will not* stop."

The rest of my body joins my heart screaming in anticipation, flashes of heat race along my skin. My core contracts and flutters. My mind races, I can't believe this is happening. I can only pray he doesn't know what's going on inside my body.

Thanking my dress designer mentally, I feel the fabric of the center piece fall between my legs, covering my panties. Then, with his eyes still locked on mine, he raises my foot and presses it against his chest. He turns his head, licks along the top of my thigh, right above my stocking.

Drake pulls away from my thigh and runs his finger along the top lace of my stockings, following it around to the back of my thigh, sending shivers along my spine. Leaning my head back, I inhale deeply, trying to control all the new emotions and desires that are racing through me.

"Fuck, babe," he shudders. "I'm gonna finish removing your shoes, then I'm gonna peel these sexy as fuck stockings from your magnificent legs. I'll give you my shirt like you asked, and then you're gonna go change. Stevens should be here soon with your puppy, and I don't want him interrupting me."

My breath whooshes out of me. My goodness, am I dreaming? Is this really happening? How am I going to make it through tonight if he keeps talking like this? Am I strong enough to tell him to stop? Or do I even want to? Oh man, I'm in trouble.

Tapping my chin, Drake brings my attention back to

him. "When I send you upstairs, go get comfortable. I'm gonna try to take care of a little problem I've developed. Once I feel your skin under my fingers, it'll be a much bigger problem. I need to do something to maintain control around you."

Sliding his hand on my left leg along my garter, he follows the strap to the clasp. He unsnaps it, then slides his index finger under my stocking. Glancing at my face, he follows the lace to the back clasp, which he unsnaps with the same ease as the front one. His pupils dilate as he slowly peels my stocking down my leg. His hands on my skin are hot, sending spikes of pleasure to my core. He licks his bottom lip, causing me to sigh.

Once he finally removes my stocking, he presses his thumbs into the arch of my foot, massaging the pain of my high heels away. He runs one hand up to my calf, squeezing and kneading the tension there before returning to my foot. Heaven. His hands are heaven.

Boneless, I fall back on my elbows, my head lax on my shoulders. Biting my lip so as not to moan, I feel my core pulse in need. His hands are like magic after dancing in heels all night. Golly, I might just combust from this.

Drake lowers my leg before moving to my right one. He repeats his moves from my first leg, removing my shoe, letting it fall to the floor with a smack. This time though, he slides his hand further up my dress past my garter. With a feather light touch, he traces the edge of my panties near my core. I shudder, falling flat on my back.

Drake quickly reverses course, continuing back down

to my stocking. He efficiently unsnaps it before rolling it down my leg. I can feel his eyes following his hot hands. Finally, blessedly, he has it off and massages my foot, just like he did the other one.

My eyes roll back, and I feel like I'm about to burst from pleasure. I never thought the mere act of removing shoes could be this hot. I feel like I'm about to explode, but I'm clueless what to do about it.

Lowering my leg, he slides his left hand to my thigh, leaving it there. I lift myself back up to my elbows, feeling the heat radiating from his hand. With his right hand, he pulls his shirt from his pants. I watch in awe as he unbuttons his shirt single handedly. *Holy moly, what a talented hand!* This is the sexiest thing I've ever witnessed. With every button, he reveals more and more of his chest. I hope I'm not drooling.

Drake's hand flexes on my thigh, drawing my attention. It inches up my leg, moving dangerously close to my core. Lightly, he traces the edge of my panties again, causing goosebumps to rush down my arms. His thumb sweeps out, delicately passing over my core. Sucking in a breath, my head falls back from the sensation. A soft moan escapes me as a groan rumbles from Drake.

Suddenly, his hand disappears. My head snaps up to see his shirt open. Quickly sitting up, I lean forward and push it further apart to his shoulders, watching his muscles twitch with the touch of my hand, revealing a chest chiseled from stone, with a light dusting of black hair across it. I let my eyes roam downward to his happy trail as it thickens and disappears into his slacks. Oh, how I long to see more. I look back up just a bit and admire those abs of his. The urge blooms inside me to trace the lines defining his eight-pack abs with my tongue.

Not able to look away from his gorgeous body, my eyes slide back to the tattoo on his left pec, the one Brit told me about. It's a perfect replication of the picture I have on my nightstand, the one where we're dressed as Beauty and the Beast.

My hand is shaky as I reach out to trace it. Drake's breathing is ragged, similar to mine. His eyes fall closed when my hand makes full contact with his chest. He sighs when my finger traces the words below, '*The Only One.*' As I lightly touch his tattoo, goosebumps spread across his chest. Bigger than my entire hand, the tattoo is a work of art.

Looking up, I feel his eyes on me, watching me closely. "What does it mean to you?" I whisper.

Drake takes my hand in his and kisses it. He finally removes his shirt completely, revealing his defined arms. I sigh again, imagining being held by those powerful arms. Drake has an incredible body. Taking it all in, I'm amazed by his masculine beauty. I reign in my urge to explore him with my hands, knowing it would be too much for him and me right now.

Heat hits my cheeks when Drake clears his throat, knowing he caught me ogling his body all this time. Slowly, I lift my eyes to his sparkling green ones. Embarrassed, I mutter, "Sorry, I couldn't help myself. You've always been hot, but dang, Drake. I'm speechless."

"Football helped a lot, babe. I keep fit now because it helps with my job. Now I have another reason to maintain this. You. Gotta keep that look in your eyes." He tucks a strand of hair behind my ear, trailing his fingers along my neck.

"Drake, what does '*The Only One*' mean to you?" I ask again.

"You sure you don't already know? A long time ago, we promised to never lie to each other or keep secrets, that we would only ask something if we wanted the truth." Drake replies looking at me intently.

"The question is do we still have that now, after all these years? I know what I want, but what about you?"

My heart stutters. What do I want? Before I can come to a conclusion, Drake continues.

"We're not teenagers anymore. We're adults. I want more than what we had as kids. I want it all."

His hands drift up my legs to my hips. He tugs me to the edge of the counter, wrapping my legs around his waist. Drake's erection presses against my core, sending shivers along my spine.

Leaning forward, he cradles my head in one hand and braces himself with the other. He kisses me lightly before pulling back slightly. He groans, then crashes his lips to mine. His tongue sweeps along the seam of my lips, prodding me to open and I oblige. He plunders my mouth, tangling his tongue with mine.

Unable to stop myself, my hands sweep up his chest, to his neck, and into his hair. Tangling my fingers, I try to anchor him to me, returning his passion. I can't get close enough.

Drake adjusts his position a bit, the hand bracing himself slides underneath me and grasps my bum, pulling me more snuggly against him. His hips rock into me, sending shocks of pleasure through my veins. The only thing separating us are the clothes we're wearing. I curse these clothes. Curse them! I've never felt like this, oh gosh, I don't want him to stop.

The peal of his cell phone shocks me from my moment of strumpet-ness. His house phone rings a second later. Drake pulls back reluctantly, resting his head on my chest. We try to catch our breath, but it takes a bit.

"Fuck. I gotta get that, babe. It's Hawkins. He wouldn't be calling right now unless it's urgent."

Drake helps me up into a sitting position and slowly caresses my back. He doesn't move to answer the phone, so I snuggle into him, thinking. Well, I'm in a heap of trouble. There is no way I could tell this man no or to stop.

He pulls me from the island, setting me on my feet. I wobble a bit when he reaches for his jacket. Drake steadies me as he sends a quick text, causing the house phone to fall silent.

"I'm gonna call Hawkins back. You're gonna go upstairs, change into my shirt and get comfy in my bed. Think about what I just said, about what you want, and we'll talk when I get up there, after I shower and take care of... things. Okay?"

I'm so turned on that I can't make sense of his words. Every cell in my body is screaming for his touch. No one has ever been able to get me to this point, and I can't focus on anything but my pulsing core as I stand here like a dork.

"Babe, upstairs, at the end of the hall, is my bedroom. Go on, get changed, I'll meet you in my bed." Drake swats my behind, jolting me from my reverie.

Handing me his shirt, he bends and gives me a quick peck. His lips on mine remind me of what just happened, cementing my feet to the floor. Oh man, I'm in a big pile of trouble. Drake chuckles.

"Okay, change of plans. Go change real quick and then make me some of those amazing Rice Krispy treats. Then we'll talk while I devour your amazing delicacies."

"Yes, yes... I'll make treats, and we'll talk," I mumble.

"That's right, now move that cute little ass of yours." Drake delivers another swat, this one harder than the first.

Rubbing my bum, I scowl at him, trying to appear mad. "What was that for?"

"Nothing," he answers on a shrug. "I just wanted to. There'll be more of that later." He winks and heads down the hallway.

My jaw is hanging open as he whistles on the way to his office.

"This better be fucking important, calling me tonight of all nights. Fuck, Hawkins!" Drake's voice carries, telling me he didn't close the door.

Hmm, I pause. Do I eavesdrop and see what's so urgent? Or do I go poke around Drake's bedroom? My body responds before my mind decides. Sprinting up the stairs, I'm smiling like a maniac.

CHAPTER TWELVE

ISABELLA: GETTING CAUGHT

*B*y the time I reach the door to Drake's bedroom, I've regained my composure. Opening the door, I'm shocked by the sight that greets me. Taking center stage in his massive bedroom is a huge, four-poster bed in dark wood with navy and burgundy sheers tied back to the pillars. His bed is perfectly made, making me wonder if he made the bed himself or if he has a maid service.

Unable to resist its call, I cross the expanse of his bedroom. Running my hand along his comforter, I'm greeted by the softest velvet I've ever laid my hands on. Catching my eye, I glance up to the ceiling and find a mirror as big as his bed. What in the heck does he need a mirror on his ceiling for? He said he's always alone in his bed, so what's it for? Does he lay there and admire himself? My mind dives into the gutter. *Does he watch as he takes care of himself?* Lordy.

Getting hot again, I recall how he kissed me. My

hand lifts, touching my swollen lips. I can still taste him, still feel his hands roaming my legs. My thighs squeeze together as my core contracts, needing *something*. Waves of heat flash across my skin when I remember how he rocked his erection into me. I was so very close to something, something I've only read about. Gosh, what am I going to do? I need a clear mind. Maybe I should follow Drake's plan and take a cold shower.

Shaking my head, I drift toward the windows. Peering out the beautiful matching sheers, I find an amazing view. Rolling hills, covered in green thanks to the late fall rains, stretch for miles to my left. To the right, I can see the ocean in the distance. I wonder if he can hear the waves crashing at night. I'll have to explore the balcony another time.

This room must have been inspired by his love for Camelot. It looks as if it would fit right into a castle in England. I run my eyes over the room again, looking at it anew. A frame on the nightstand catches my attention. Picking it up, I'm pleased to find the same picture that I have next to my bed, the inspiration for Drake's tattoo.

Finally finished exploring, I move to the bathroom, ready to climb into Drake's shirt. Flipping on the light, I enter a bathroom made for a couple. Stepping up to the vanity, I pull the zipper down on my dress under my arm. I slide the sleeves from my shoulders and shimmy out of my dress and lay it over the chair next to me.

Removing my garter belt, I turn to lay it on the counter, catching sight of myself in the vanity mirror. Gosh, was I responsible for that beast Drake had pressed against me? I'm on the short side, at least compared to his massive six four frame. Sure, I've got huge boobs and a trim waist, but my hips are narrow, and I'm not a fan of my rear. I think it's on the small side.

"Well," I announce to the mirror, "he sure seemed interested in something on that kitchen island. Maybe I'm just too self-conscious."

Lifting his shirt, I bring it to my face, inhaling deeply. A flood of memories, of hormone- filled teen desires, rush through me. Dang, how will I be able to control this? What am I going to do? How can I ever bring myself to deny him when I want nothing more than to have my dirty way with him? Squeezing my thighs together, I try to relieve some of the pressure I feel. Drake has been the only person ever to get me this worked up.

Pulling the shirt on I recall Drake's instructions from earlier, thinking about what he said and Rice Krispies treats. Checking myself out, I find the shirt falls to mid-thigh covering all the essentials, but if I get cold, it offers no barrier to Drake's eyes. With a mischievous grin, I decide to leave the top two buttons undone, showing some extra cleavage.

FINISHING up the huge batch of Rice Krispies treats, I'm thinking it's been over half an hour since Drake and I separated. Hmm, maybe I should try my hand at eaves-dropping. He's been in that office of his forever. Tip-toeing my way down the hall, I don't hear any voices.

Drake's office door isn't closed completely, so I slowly

push it open, listening for any clue that he's in there. The sound of a running shower greets me as I cross the threshold. Oh, man, I should flush the toilet and freeze him like we did when we were kids. A deep moan echoes from the bathroom, freezing me in place. What's he doing in there?

Curiosity peaked, I make my way to the bathroom door on quiet feet. The door's cracked open, probably so the room doesn't fog up. Lifting my eyes to the mirror, the most glorious sight greets me. Standing in a glass encased shower, Drake's back, glistening with water, is in full, Technicolor display. Oh, my. Those muscles have to be carved from granite.

Following the path of the water, my eyes trail down the valley of his spine. His firm backside is stunning. Full globes, with a muscular dip on each side. I suck in a breath at the sight. Tight and firm, I'd probably be able to bounce a quarter off of that rear.

Continuing my perusal of his body, his thighs are enormous, thick and strong as water cascades down their length. His calves are just as muscled as his thighs. There isn't an ounce of fat anywhere on his body.

My eyes sweep up to find Drake's head thrown back, his long, black hair reaching the bottom of his shoulder blades. This is so naughty, so wrong of me, but I can't bring myself to leave. It's flipping hot.

Noticing movement, my gaze finds his arm, slowly drifting up and down. Realization dawns. He mentioned taking care of a little, soon-to-be big problem in the shower. Oh, gosh. Is he taking *care* of himself? Biting my knuckle to stifle a moan, I keep watching.

Drake's breathing gets heavier as his arm moves faster. He pumps rhythmically, causing his rear to flex with each forward thrust. I'm finding it hard to control my breathing. I barely manage, not wanting to give my peeping away. I watch, transfixed.

Suddenly, he freezes, moaning my name, a deep and guttural moan. My eyes fly to his head, thinking he's caught me. Thankfully, he's looking down as a shudder overtakes his body. With one last, long look, I decide it's time to return to the kitchen.

Holy crap-a-doodle, thank God, he didn't catch me. Turning, I take off running. In my hurry, I misjudge the door jamb, slamming my foot into it. Grabbing my foot, I mouth, "Fudge boogers!"

I can't stop, so I hobble to the kitchen as fast as I can. Pain radiates from my foot, and I pray it isn't broken. Rushing to the freezer, I shove my whole foot inside. Finally inspecting my poor, battered foot, I find a bruise spreading across the top of it. Lord, have mercy. How am I going to explain this?

When we were young, we promised to always be honest with each other, no matter how embarrassing. What the heck am I going to say? *Well Drake, you see, I jammed my toe in the door as I ran out of your office. You know, after you 'took care of yourself.'* Yeah, like that would happen.

Still standing with my foot in the freezer, mentally arguing with myself, a throat clearing causes me to jump.

"Um, babe? What in the world are you doing with your foot in the freezer?" Drake inquires.

"Oh, I'm, uhh, getting ice for, uhh, a Coke," I mumble, grabbing a handful. "I could really use an ice-cold Coke. You know, some people keep a mug in their freezer, for beer and such. I can see you don't do that, so I'll just have to settle for ice, I guess. Do you want one, too? Oh, I made the Rice Krispies treats you asked for. I could add ice to your milk if you need something ice cold. You just let me know." I babble, hobbling to the cabinets for a glass for a stupid Coke I do not want.

"Why are you limping?" Drake asks, with laughter in his voice.

"Oh," I mutter, slamming my second cabinet. *Where are the glasses?* "I, uh, I, umm, the dancing really hurt, umm. Yeah, the dancing and my shoes. Yup."

"Babe, nice try. You've never been good at lying, and you're even worse now." A cheeky smile spreads across his face. "Next time you want to watch, all you need to do is ask. I'd love to have you watch. No need to sneak around and risk hurting yourself."

I'm beet red, and he finds my embarrassment amusing. His chuckles reach my ears, spurring me into motion. Forgetting my quest for a glass, I turn to face him. Grabbing the front of his sweats with my empty hand, I shove the ice right into them.

Drake jumps back, trying to avoid the ice, but it's too late. Pulling at the crotch of his pants, he shakes one leg trying to dislodge the ice. Laughing, I hobble off to the living room, screaming, "You deserve that for teasing me!"

"Oh, babe. You're in trouble now," he teases, getting more ice from the freezer. "I think you might need to cool off too. You must be hot and bothered from watching me handle Henry."

"No, don't you touch me with that!" I squeal, trying to hide behind the couch.

"Woman, payback's a bitch," he says, dodging to one side.

"No! Don't! I'm sorry!" I yell, trying to keep the couch between us.

Bang bang bang! "Police! Open up!"

CHAPTER THIRTEEN

ISABELLA: LIFE'S MOST EMBARRASSING MOMENT

"*M*r. Fitzpatrick, open the door!" a voice booms.

Drake flies into motion, grabbing a blanket and wrapping it around me. The door shudders with a loud bang.

"Stay here and keep covered. Your nipples are hard, and those are for my eyes only," he says before turning toward the door.

"Give me a damn minute! Let me shut off the alarm, and I'll open it. No need to bust it down!" he shouts.

Moving to the alarm panel, he types in his code. The light flashes green, and he moves to unlock and open the door.

Four uniformed officers barge in, holding a battering ram. Dropping it to the floor with a thud, they quickly draw their side-arms, aiming at Drake. He raises his hands in the air, standing stock still, his glorious chest on display. Goodness, he's bigger than the officers. My mouth falls open in shock. *What is happening?*

Two detectives follow in behind the officers. One looks at Drake, swallowing hard. The other approaches me.

"Are you Isabella Anderson?" At my nod, he continues, "Are you okay, ma'am?"

"What?" I ask in confusion.

"Are you okay?" he repeats.

"Yes, yes. I'm totally fine. We were just playing around. Will you put those guns away before someone gets hurt? There's no need for you to aim at Drake."

The officers do as I ask, looking bewildered.

"What the hell is going on here?" Drake bellows.

Weaving through the officers, I make my way to Drake, sliding an arm around his waist. I make sure to hold the blanket tight, covering my chest. Drake wraps his arm around my shoulder.

The detectives and officers share glances, communicating their confusion. Well, I'm freaking confused too.

"Mojo! Come back here!" Stevens yells, as my beautiful 265-pound puppy comes barreling through the door.

Squatting down, I wrap my arms around Mojo's neck, giving him loves and getting sloppy kisses on my neck in return.

"Don't shoot him!" Drake yells.

Looking up, I find a wall of muscle between Mojo and myself and the officers. Were they going to shoot my puppy?

"Why would you point a gun at my sweetie?" I cry.

"Will someone please tell me what the *fuck* is going on here?" Drake demands, again.

"Officers, holster your weapons," one of the detectives instructs. "I know these men. Let's hear his story before jumping to any conclusions."

"Fitz, Stevens," he greets. "Mind telling me what's going on? Why is ADA Edwards' girlfriend here? Why could I hear her screaming 'No! Don't!' right before we demanded entrance?"

"Excuse me!" I interrupt, standing up. "What did you just say?" I ask, peeved.

He peers between Drake and Stevens' massive shoulders trying to see my face. I'm trying to squeeze between them, but they're immovable.

"Ma'am, this evening your boyfriend called sounding very distressed and requested a welfare check for you. According to him, your phone was turned off, which is out of the norm for you. He stated that you were at the Paradise Country Club, then a grocery store before arriving here at the Fitzpatrick Estate, where it was then shut off. He also informed us that your minivan, which only you are allowed to drive, left the country club, and stopped at a Burger King before continuing to your residence, and then stopped at a park about five miles from here.

"Your boyfriend stated he had been trying to call you all night, thinking you might be in some sort of trouble, as this is very much out of your usual routine. He feared you might have been taken against your will."

Flabbergasted at what I'm hearing, I just stare at the detective.

"Boyfriend, my ass," Stevens mutters, jolting me from my shock. I shove my way through Drake and Stevens, beyond angry. I could tell they were angry, too. Drake has a tight rein on his body, holding himself stock still, the tension vibrating off him.

"Let me clear up some of the misunderstandings you're under," I explain, pointing a finger at the detective. "First off, Paul Edwards is *not* my boyfriend. He has not been my boyfriend since I caught him boinking my ex-best friend *three* months ago. I have not seen his face since the night I stormed out of his house.

"How did he even know where I was, or where my van was? That's super creepy, isn't it?" I ask, looking back at Drake.

"Yeah, babe," he says, pulling me into his arms.

"Why don't we move this conversation somewhere more comfortable than the entryway? Perhaps your living room?" the detective suggests.

Drake turns with me in his arms, moving to his living room. "Come on in," he says before planting me on one of the big black leather couches. He tugs the blanket closed, drawing my attention to the fact that it slipped, revealing my still hard nipples to the officers.

"Let's not give these assholes any more of a show than you already have." He winks, before turning serious. "Be careful of what you say. I need to get as much information from them as possible."

I nod in understanding, feeling their eyes on me. A shiver crawls down my spine as Mojo saunters in, planting himself at my feet. Such a good boy he is, protecting me from these officers. His hackles rise, showing he's in full protector mode.

"Is that beast going to attack us? He doesn't look like he's very happy right now," one of the officers inquires.

Smiling, I pat Mojo's velvet-soft head. "He's just protective of his pack. As long as you don't touch me, Drake or Stevens, you'll be fine."

I'm not totally sure about what I just told the officer. Other than a warning growl, I've never heard him bark. I don't think Mojo would bite anyone, but I'd rather keep the officers away than have to find out the hard way.

The officer looks a bit scared as he backs up towards the doorway. Drake settles next to me, tucking me into his chest. Stevens sits on my other side, petting and praising Mojo for looking out for me.

The detective who said he knows Drake and Stevens plants himself on the couch across from us. The other sits in the recliner near the end of the couch.

"Ms. Anderson," the detective across from us begins, studying Drake's arm around me. "First, let me introduce myself. I'm Detective Jerkins, and this is my partner, Detective Franks," he waves his hand towards his partner. Franks gives me a nod before looking down at his notepad.

"Now if Assistant District Attorney Paul Edwards isn't your boyfriend, why would he go to such great lengths to find you? Why would he request a welfare check on you?"

"Maybe because he's a whack-a-doodle nut-job?" I

retort, crossing my arms. "And a jealous creeper, obviously. If you need proof, I have it."

"Dray, honey," I ask, looking up at him. "Could you please grab my phone? It's on the kitchen counter, in my purse."

"Sure thing, babe," he replies. Oh, hearing him call me 'babe' again is the most gorgeous sound. My stomach flips every time he calls me that. Before he gets up, he kisses my forehead. *Oh, swoon.*

A few seconds later, Drake returns with my iPhone. The screen lights up, meaning Drake powered it on after retrieving it from my clutch. Unlocking my phone, I ignore the alerts of missed messages and phone calls, going straight to my contacts.

"Here," I say, showing my phone to Detective Jerkins. "You can contact Susan Berg, my former accountant and former best friend. She's the one Paul was boinking the night I broke up with him."

"Oh, if you contact my courier," I continue, showing him the number, "and ask for Chuck, he'll tell you about the three boxes he delivered to Paul that night, containing every teeny, tiny gift that low-life, two-faced cheating jerk-hole ever gave me. I have a list that Chuck witnessed, stating everything in those boxes."

Detective Jerkins copies all the information down on his notepad. Several of the officer's snicker at my speech. Detective Franks has kicked back, lounging in the recliner while typing on his phone.

"Oh, and it seems to me that Paul is somehow tracking me. I need you guys to get to the bottom of that. That's just icky. He's been incessantly calling and texting. Do you want to see those? He's also sent gifts. I got this ugly display of red roses earlier today. We gave them away, but I still have the card and previous letters. They're in a file at my office in case something like this happened. I think I need a restraining order," I huff.

The poor detective tries to keep up with my rambling. Jerkins gives me a sad smile before turning his attention to Drake.

"That doesn't explain why Ms. Anderson was screaming 'No' when my officers approached the door. Do you want to explain that?"

"I can answer that!" I yell, placing my hand on Drake's knee. His body shakes as I start blabbering. "You see, that's completely my fault. Drake caught me in a little fib and was teasing me, so I took a handful of ice and dropped it down the front of his pants. Then he grabbed a handful and was going to retaliate, which made me scream and beg him not to. That's all, just some harmless fun. No big thing." Moving his hand to his mouth, Drake tries to muffle his snort but totally fails.

Mojo shifts, moving to lie down. I quickly lift my throbbing foot and place it on the table, fearing he'd lie on it. All eyes narrow on my now purple and blue foot. The swelling has spread to my ankle. Now that I can see it, maybe it is broken.

"Fuck me, babe. I didn't know it was that bad," Drake mutters.

"Dude, what the hell happened to her foot?" Stevens asks, getting up and moving to the kitchen. "That has to hurt like a son of a bitch."

"Please explain the injury to Ms. Anderson's foot, Mr. Fitzpatrick," Detective Jerkins states firmly.

"So not to further embarrass my girlfriend," Drake starts, causing a blush to spread along my cheeks. "Let's just say she saw something happening in my office and took off running because she didn't want to get caught and jammed her own toe on the door frame."

"What do you mean she saw something happening in your office?" Jerkins grills. "This is a major injury, not a stubbed toe. What exactly did she see in your office that made her run so fast she caused such a bad injury to herself?"

Stevens returns from the kitchen, carrying a bag of ice as Drake chuckles. I'm so embarrassed, I wish a hole would open up and swallow me. I cannot believe this.

"Dude, this isn't funny, it might be broken." Stevens grabs a burgundy pillow, one of many, from the couch and carefully places my foot on it. Slowly, he lowers the bag of ice.

Jerkins turns to me, "Ma'am, are you sure you feel safe here? I can have one of the officers take you and your dog home if you'd like. Was what you saw criminal in any way?"

Oh man, once this is over, I'm going to give Paul a piece of my mind... No, I am just going throat punch the wastard. I'm so embarrassed, and it's all Paul's fault!

"Ma'am?"

Dying from embarrassment and just wanting this to end, I mutter, "Someone shoot me, now PLEASE!"

Taking a deep breath, I try to figure out what to say. "Gah, fine. I'll tell you. But then you guys are leaving. I'll

146

come down to the station tomorrow to file the restraining order."

"Babe," Drake says, sitting forward, "you don't have to tell these officers shit. It's none of their goddamn business what we do in *our* fucking home."

"I beg to differ, Mr. Fitzpatrick," Franks interferes. "With the way that toe is swelling, I think she broke her foot too. I have no problem separating you and taking you down to the station. We can question you there if you prefer."

"May I call you Isabella, ma'am?" Jerkins asks. I nod, trying to figure a way out of this mess. I do not want to go downtown, this is ridiculous.

"Your foot looks pretty bad. It's a gruesome shade of purple, and with that swelling you should get it checked out. Why don't you let one of us take you to the hospital? Once you're away from Fitz, you might feel more comfortable telling us what caused such a reaction. You seem stressed, and you're flushed," Jerkins finishes with a warm smile.

Son of a biscuit, they aren't going to let this go. They're determined to find something bad about Drake, and I will *not* allow that to happen. Well, there goes my dignity.

"Fine," I yell a bit too loudly. "I'll tell you already!"

"Babe, you don't have to tell them anything. I'll call Spencer right now," Drake says, resting his hand on my knee.

"We don't need a lawyer, honey," I respond, getting lost in his forest green eyes. I can't believe this is where we are right now. After all that's happened in the last seven hours, I can't believe I'm about to explain to the cops that I watched Drake pleasure himself. "I will not allow them to think poorly of you."

"Before I explain what happened," I declare, returning my attention to Jerkins, "listen up. If you broke Drake's gate, you need to fix it and send the bill to Paul for filing a false police report. You should charge him with that too. Now, I'm only going to explain this once. Y'all can put your little notepads away, they're not necessary."

Taking a deep breath, I can't believe what I'm about to admit. It's bad enough I've got to tell these two detectives, but the four officers have all gotten closer as well. Never mind Stevens sitting next to me. *Gah!*

"Okay, earlier Drake took a phone call in his office. It'd been a while since I'd seen him, so I went looking for him. Fine, I was being nosy. I wanted to listen in to Drake's conversation with one of his Camelot Brothers. When I got to the door, I didn't hear any voices, so I peeked in. But, uh… But I heard, umm, the shower…"

"Damn it. Guys, she watched me take a shower, okay? I startled her, and she ran from the room. Fuck! Can we move on?" Drake demands from my side.

"Come on, look at him. He's pretty hot." I say sheepishly, waving my hand at Drake like he's some prize on a game show. "Tell me you wouldn't want to see all that."

Several officers chuckle, there's even a few snorts. The loudest one is from Stevens.

"Wait, wait a minute," Stevens gasps. "What exactly startled you, Isabella? I think you saw more than just Fitz taking a shower."

148

Stevens cackles like a buffoon. Drake reaches around me and smacks the back of his head.

"Knock it off, asshole," Drake reprimands.

Several of the officers must have completed the puzzle Stevens laid out for them, as they either chuckle or leave the room red faced. I face-plant into Drake's chest, trying to burrow in to him.

Drake gathers me into his arms, pulling me onto his lap. "Babe, it's okay. Don't be embarrassed. I loved having you watch me," he whispers into my hair.

My foot throbs when Drake changed my position, drawing my focus back to it. Lifting the bag of ice, I find it's worse than before. The bruise spreads across all my toes and has inched up my foot. The swelling is worse, despite the ice Stevens put on it.

"Okay Stevens, show these officers to the fucking door," Drake commands. "This interrogation is over. We'll bring Bella down to the station in the morning, along with our own lawyer, Blake Spencer. Make sure you have the paperwork to file a restraining order against Paul Edwards ready and waiting. This doesn't end here, that's for goddamn sure."

"Jerkins take her minivan, so your boys can look for any tracking devices on it. I want everything done by the book. This is beyond simple harassment. I want to protect Bella, so you guys need to do your jobs right. Also, have your computer guys ready to look at her phone, figure out how the fuck this asshole is tracking her.

"If you need help with any of this, let me know. We can handle this ourselves, but with this fucker being an

ADA, we would appreciate you taking the lead. However, if you fuck up, we'll handle this in house, at Camelot Security."

Feeling the couch move, I peek out from under my hair to see Stevens lead the officers to the door. Once the door slams, I whisper to Drake, "Can you shoot me now? Put an end to my embarrassment and the pain in my foot?

"I'm so sorry," I wail, looking up to Drake's face. "That idiot ruined our night. Ugh! I could just strangle him."

"Babe," Drake laughs under me, sending vibrations through me. "I'm not gonna shoot you. I just got you back. Don't be embarrassed. Hell, I'm getting turned on imagining your face as you watched me. Damn.

"But hear me now," he says, sweeping the hair from my eyes. "If the cops don't handle Paul properly, my Brothers and I will. The asshole won't stand a chance against us," he vows. Drake kisses the top of my head, sliding out from under me. Carefully, he arranges me on the couch, propping my foot up on several navy and burgundy pillows. He lightly kisses my ankle then sets the ice back on it. Finally, he throws the blanket over me.

"And FYI, your puppy ain't no puppy. That's a damn horse. But, fuck, I was relieved to see how he positioned himself in front of you. That grumble in his chest was impressive. I thought some of those cops were gonna piss themselves. Now you stay right there. I'm gonna call Brenden and get his ass over here to look at your foot. He'll know if we have to make a trip to the ER tonight, or if it's something he can handle himself."

Drake leaves as Stevens returns with Mojo's things. "I'll just go put these in Fitz's bedroom. That's where Fitz wants you, and I'm sure that is where Mojo will be sleeping from now on too." Stevens chuckles, turning toward the stairs.

"Oh, Isabella," he calls out, over his shoulder. "I've got a nice set of binoculars out in the guest house. Just in case, you want to borrow them to watch Fitz *shower* with Henry again."

Reaching for the coffee table, I quickly grab the TV remote and hurl it at him, nailing him dead center in the middle of his back.

"Ow, Isabella," he affects a whine. "I'm only trying to help you, no need for violence." His laughter trails up the stairs.

Laying back down, an uncontrollable smile spreads on my face. This could only happen to me. I can only hope they're not as big of gossips as they were back in the day. The torture will never end if they still gossip like hens. Who am I kidding? I'm in so much trouble.

CHAPTER FOURTEEN

FITZ: HANDLING THE ASS AND BELLA'S FOOT

*P*ropped up on the couch, I take a long sip of the ice-cold Coke Drake just delivered. My foot throbs like a cartoon character with a mallet pounding on it. With the ugly bruising spreading the way it is, I really hope it's not broken. I'd never live it down with Stevens. Drake had just informed me Brenden's on his way before he returned to the kitchen, so I guess I'll find out soon enough. The wonderful perks of having a trauma doctor for a brother, I guess.

My phone buzzes on the table and I lean over to grab it. Assuming it's another text, I'm unprepared for the rage when I check the screen. Paul has the nerve to call me now? Answering it, I unleash my anger before he even has the chance to speak.

"Listen, you low-life, no good piece of fermented dog crap. How *dare* you call me? What the ever-loving heck, Paul? I am *not* your girlfriend. Do you understand me? *We. Are. Done.* Now and forever. Do I need to spell it out for you? D-O-N-E. *Done.* Calling the police for a welfare check on me? I *cannot* believe you!"

Through my entire rant, Paul calls out my name, but I ignore him. I'm so mad at him. How could he think this is okay?

"Isabella, Isabella! Listen to me for a minute. Just shut the fuck up for one goddamned minute and Listen. To. Me."

Shocked, my mouth falls open. "What did you just say? You just swore at me! Did you just tell me to shut up? You track my phone and my van, and *you* tell *me* to shut up? As a D.A., you do know that's illegal, right? And stop sending me stuff. I'm sure the nursing home and Veteran's Center appreciate them, but I. Do. Not. I *hate* red roses. How many times do I have to tell you that! You have never listened to me."

"Please, Isabella," Paul yells again. *"Please just give me one MINUTE!"*

"Fine, you have one minute," I reply, taking a deep breath.

Paul inhales. *"Thank you. The flowers and gifts are because I love you. And yes, I've been watching you, but only to protect you. It's my job. You belong to me. You don't have anyone but me to take care of you. You need me. Those guys you are hanging out with are criminals. I wouldn't lie to you about that. Fitzpatrick is a pimp. That is a fact."*

Oh, no he didn't. Paul did not just bad mouth Drake. "Listen here, you butt muncher. I have known Drake all my life. He is *not* a pimp, and his Brothers are *not* criminals. I will not listen to you speak ill of my friends, my family. Enough, Paul. We. Are. Done."

"Isabella," he pleads. *"I swear I'm not lying. He hasn't*

been arrested, but he and several of those scumbags are under inves-
tigation. You have to believe me.

"*And what the fuck are you doing at his house at two o'clock in*
the morning? Damn it, Isabella, you never stay out past midnight.
And never with a man!. How was I to know he didn't kidnap you?
You turned off your phone, and I couldn't get a hold of you!"

Shock holds my voice hostage. What is wrong
with him?

"*You belong to me. We could easily move on if you'd just let it*
go. Now, you need to leave there. You aren't safe. Come to my
place." The plea in his voice is insane. Like he truly
believes what he's saying.

"Paul, stop. Do you even hear yourself? Paul, I am
D-O-N-E, done. This is over. There is no more us, and
there hasn't been for a very long time. You cheated on
me, I don't give second chances after a betrayal. I don't
love you that way. I doubt I ever did. You didn't love me
either, or you wouldn't have been boinking Susan, or the
others. Yeah, I know about them. You need to move on.
I never want to see you again."

"*Well, Isa, I don't know how eager some parents will be to*
leave their children with someone who is mixed up with criminals."
Paul's voice is heavy with sarcasm. "*Are you fucking him,*
Isabella? The police said you're at his house, wearing his shirt, that
his hands were all over you and you were in his lap, like some cheap
whore."

Mad as a mule chewing bumblebees, I scream into
the phone. "Do. Not. Even *think* about messing with my
daycare centers. I will sue you for slander. And I will win.
You spread one single lie about Drake, and I will tell the
world how you're a no good, dirty, cheating stalker!

"You can kiss your DA job goodbye, as well as any future as a senator. I'm filing a restraining order against you first thing tomorrow morning, you scum bag of regurgitated of cow dung!"

Fitz

FILLING THE DISHWASHER, I'm kicking myself for not noticing how bad her foot was. How did I miss that when she was limping around the kitchen? Jesus. Bella screaming from the living room snaps me from my self-recriminations. Dropping a bowl, I turn and rush to the living room.

Catching the end of her tirade, I enter the living room to see that she's on the phone. Snagging it from her hand, I look at the screen, seeing Paul's name on the screen. Oh, this fucker has balls. He's screaming, calling my Bella a bitch and a whore.

"Listen up, dickless," I shout into the phone. "You don't *ever* call Bella that again. You lose her number and forget about her, or you *will* answer to me."

"*Are you threatening me, asshole?*" God, he sounds like a crybaby pussy.

"No, you cock-sucking, pussy-assed, motherfucker. That was a fucking promise." I end the call and power down her phone.

"You *do not* talk to him again," I instruct, putting Bella's phone in my back pocket. "If he tries to contact you again, you tell me instantly. You'll get your phone back when Hawkins removes all the spyware that's probably on it. Jackson will bring it to Hawkins after we visit the station tomorrow. Do you have any computers Hawkins needs to check?"

"Geez Louise, you don't have to be such a Mr. Bossy Pants," Bella whines. "I have no problem letting Hawkins look at my stuff. I appreciate his help. And don't worry, I never want to see that pathetic, malignant tumor again. I don't think I have anything to worry about, he's all talk. A real pansy."

Leaning over the back of the couch, I cup her jaw. "Babe, *you* are my world. I may be a 'Mr. Bossy Pants,' but you need to deal with it. I will *always* be that way when it comes to you and your safety. Nobody messes with you. You're mine now," I vow.

Unable to resist myself, I bend and capture her lips with mine. Sucking her lower lip, she gasps, allowing me to explore her mouth with my tongue. Passionately, I make love to her mouth.

The front door slams open, causing Bella to jump. I don't stop kissing her, though. Goddamn, I can't get enough of her taste, It's fucking heaven on Earth.

"Knock it off, Fitz!" Hunter yells. "Step away from the patient. I heard she already broke her foot because of you."

With one last kiss, I reluctantly pull away, shooting Hunter a look that I hope would set him on fire. Jackson and Hunter enter, carrying Brenden's medical bags. Brenden brings up the rear, rolling a little cart.

Parking the cart, Brenden sits on the coffee table, probing Bella's foot. She winces when he lifts it for a deeper examination. My heart hurts, seeing her in any kind of pain.

"How in the hell did you do this?" Brenden grills. "How the fuck did you let her get hurt?" he asks me.

"Oh, dude!" Stevens comes in, eating one of *my* Rice Krispies treats. The asshole. "She was spying on Drake whacking off in the shower."

Bella hides her face under a pillow and screams into it. She's so fucking adorable.

"No fucking way!" Hunter shouts.

Jackson chimes in, "You're shitting me!"

"Noah Stevens!" Bella yells from behind the pillow. "If it's the last thing I do, I *will* make you pay for this. Oh, revenge will be mine, you jerk-hole!"

"Knock it off, guys," I scold them, "or I won't share my Krispies treats… and no breakfast for you, either!"

"Well Bella," Brenden announces. "I don't think your foot is broken. But I'm going to look at it with a portable ultrasound to make sure. I'll put some cold gel on your foot before I start."

He leans down and whispers something to Bella, and I barely catch his words, "Tell them you enjoyed watching. That'll shut them up so fucking fast. They'll be even more jealous of the two of you than they already are."

Brenden pulls the cart closer and fishes the gel out from a drawer. Bella's still hiding under the pillow, the goof. As Brenden performs an ultrasound on her foot, then he asks, "How are you with needles, Bella?"

Feeling Bella jump, Oh, shit. Is she still scared of needles?

"Why?" Bella asks, removing the pillow from her face to shoot daggers at Brenden. "It's just an ultrasound. You don't need needles for an ultrasound, do you? I don't like needles. Nope. No thank you. You can keep your needles and shove 'em where the sun don't shine, you sadist!"

A laugh escapes me before I can stop it. She's too fucking funny.

"Fitz," Brenden calls, "why don't you have a seat and put Bella's head in your lap?"

"Don't you worry, Brenden. Drake's on my side. He knows I don't do needles. Nope. He even helped me get out of that tetanus shot when I was twelve. He was a true gentleman and took it for me. Nope, I do not do needles. Not at all."

"Maybe we should take her to the ER?" I say, trying to ignore Bella's rant about needles. "Is it broken? Stevens, go start up the SUV and open the garage door. She can lay in the backseat."

"Jesus, Fitz," Brenden exclaims. "Calm down, or I'll have to sedate you. She doesn't need a hospital. I just need you to keep calm so you can calm down Bella, got it?"

"Brenden, if I don't have to go to the hospital, what's the needle for? I don't want a needle." Bella inches her way up the couch, and I smile.

Approaching her, I lift Bella's head and maneuver under her. I put her head in my lap, and her eyes find mine. They're wide and scared, as I cup her jaw with my left hand as I play with her hair with my right.

"Babe, take a breath and calm down. Brenden's got this. I trust him." Her eyes drift closed with every word out of my mouth.

Pulling her closer, I tip a nod at Brenden. Sweeping my left thumb over her cheek, I run the fingers of my right hand through her luxurious hair. She relaxes into me, snuggling close.

"Okay this is what's going to happen," Brenden whispers. "Stevens, sit near Bella and hold one of her hands. Fitz, you keep on doing what you're doing. That seems to be keeping her calm.

"Hunter, you get down here next to me. If she kicks, I need you to hold her leg still. I'm gonna have to use this," he says, holding up a syringe. "She definitely broke her fourth toe, but she also dislocated her pinky toe, which explains all the bruising and swelling. I need to put her pinky toe back in place, but first I have to numb the area."

"What?" Bella mumbles. "I missed some of what you said. Drake's hypnotizing me with his magic fingers. No fair."

"Isabella," Stevens says, taking her hand. "You just keep making goo-goo eyes with Drake and focus on those magic fingers. Hold my hand as tight as you want, but don't look down at your foot. Drake's gonna keep on playing with your hair and whispering sappy shit to you. You just lay still."

Ignoring Stevens' dumbass-ness, I keep my focus on Bella. "Babe, Brenden needs to set your toe. He's gonna rub a cold wipe on it. You shouldn't feel a thing, but you need to stay still, okay?"

Brenden swabs her foot with an alcohol wipe and Bella jolts in my arms. Hunter braces her leg with both hands, above and below her knee, pinning it to the couch.

"You got this, Isabella," Jackson calls out from behind me.

Brenden grips her ankle, being careful of the swelling and lines up the needle. Quickly and smoothly, he injects her with the numbing solution.

"Mother fucking shit!" Stevens yells. Bella must have squeezed his hand hard. That's my tough girl.

Bella yells, "Brenden, that was a needle! You lying, toe jam eating, smelly dog turd! That hurt!"

Bella's insults are so cute that I lean down and kiss her. Sucking her lower lip, I nibble it. Between kisses, I whisper encouragements to her.

"You got this, babe." *Kiss.* "Just give it a minute." *Kiss.* "You can handle the pain." *Kiss.* "You're my brave girl." *Kiss.* "It'll be over in a second." *Kiss.* "You're strong." *Kiss.*

She takes a deep breath as I pull away. Her face is now relaxed, no longer scrunched in pain. The meds must be kicking in.

"You're right, honey," Bella murmurs. "The pain is over."

Her eyes hold astonishment. I'm not sure if it's from taking the shot or because I just kissed her in front of the guys. She'd better get used to it, I'm gonna kiss her every damn chance I get.

"Girlie," Brenden chuckles, "with the injection I just gave you, I could cut your toe off, and you wouldn't feel a thing. Let's give it a few minutes before I put your toe back in place, and make sure that your foot is completely numb.

"The swelling should be gone in less than a week. However, you need to stay off that foot as much as possible. No running or too much walking. You listen to me, or I'll have Fitz spank that cute, little ass of yours. I'll bring a walking boot tomorrow morning so you can still make breakfast."

"Fine, fine," Bella grumbles. "But I'm wounded. Drake won't spank me in the condition I'm in. Oh! I can wheel around in my office chair. I'm a fast healer, you'll see." Her enthusiasm makes me chuckle.

Stevens shoves his hand at Brenden, "Did she break it? I think it's broken! She sliced me with those damn dragon claws. I'm bleeding in four places!"

Hunter and Jackson laugh at him while Brenden shoves his hand away.

"Stop being a pussy, Stevens," Jackson says. "You deserved it with how you teased her earlier. Hell, she probably did it on purpose!"

Brenden hands Bella a pill and her Coke. "Can you take this, or does Fitz need to hold your nose like he did when you were a kid?"

I lift her up a bit as she gives him an evil look.

"I'm a big girl," Bella retorts. She pops the pill in her mouth and chases it down with the Coke. Bella gags, choking on the pill. Taking another long swallow, she jerks her head back and swallows hard.

"Gah!" she gasps. "Did you rifle through that doctor bag trying to find the biggest pill on earth? I hate taking pills!" Bella sticks her tongue out at Brenden.

"Good to know," Brenden chuckles. "I'll make sure

to reserve the big pills for you if I ever have to take care of you again, oh, and I'll bring lots of my biggest needles too.

"Now, while we're waiting for your foot to numb up, I'm going to go get one of your famous Rice Krispie treats as payment for putting up with your nagging ass."

Hunter and Jackson are still giving Stevens shit, and normally I'd join in but those beautiful, dark brown eyes of Bella's capture my attention. Gazing into her eyes, I twirl her hair in my fingers.

"It seems like I've waited a lifetime for you to come back to me," I whisper. "I'm never gonna let you go. We have a lot to relearn about each other, but we'll do it together. I'll always be here, and I'll never lie to you. Never. You are the air I need to breathe."

Kissing her lightly, she melts and slides her hand up my shoulder. With my hand, I cradle her head, devouring her mouth. With effort, I pull away and whisper, "Rest, babe. Let the medicine do its work."

"Dray, I feel the same way," she murmurs as I cradle her to my chest. "We'll do it together. You and me, forever."

She drifts off in my arms, and I couldn't be more content.

CHAPTER FIFTEEN

FITZ: PLANNING OUR ATTACK ON PAUL EDWARDS

When Brenden returns from the kitchen, Bella's fast asleep. Enjoying the feel of her cuddled up to me, I continue running my fingers through her strawberry blonde hair. I know, without a doubt, that this is true love.

"You're the luckiest bastard I know," Brenden says quietly. "You have something special in your arms. Don't fuck this up. We all love her, too."

"Yeah, I know," I reply. "She's my world. I'm done fucking around. She's it for me."

"Duh, dumbass," he smiles. "I knew that when we were kids. You were such a moron back then. Anyway, let me set and wrap her foot, then you can take her up to bed. Hopefully, she won't wake up until morning. With that shot and the pill I gave her, she should be out for a while.

"Hawkins wants to chat, he's waiting for us to Face-

Time him. Stevens went to get his iPad so we can include Spencer in on this too. It doesn't sound good."

My only response is a nod. I'm lost in what little Hawkins told me while Bella was changing. What he'd discovered had pissed me off, making me want to kick Paul's ass. Hawkins said he was working to hack into Edwards' computer and I'm hoping he's succeeded.

Relief washed over me when I overheard Bella tell him she never loved him. She'd messed up taking that call, but it felt good hearing what she thought of him. Bella's mine now, and that's all that matters.

With ease, Brenden pops her pinky toe in place then uses tape to strap it to her foot. My poor baby had fucked up her foot good, I think as I watch Brenden also strap her fourth toe.

"Why don't you just tape them together?" I ask, thinking that's what they did in football.

"Because she dislocated her pinky toe, I need to immobilize it while it heals, so I strapped it to her foot." He indicates the pieces of tape running the length of Bella's foot. "And because she broke her fourth toe, I can't tape it to her third toe. That would cause pulling and make it heal incorrectly."

Satisfied with his answer, I nod, and the reason why she broke it flashes in my mind's eye. God, knowing she was watching me causes Henry to stir again. I wonder how much she could see from the angle of the mirror. She had to have heard me moan her name when I came. I wish I could have seen her face. The image of us watching each other touch ourselves makes me hard as steel. I'd love to watch her, see her explore herself. Fuck, now is not the time for these thoughts. I've more pressing issues to deal with first.

Brenden starts packing up his shit as I get up slowly, shifting Bella in my arms. Carrying her to my room, no, *our* room, brings me comfort. I've waited for this for so long. She's never sleeping anywhere else but by my side from now on.

Mojo's right behind me, his steps thudding up my stairs. He's the biggest damn dog I've ever seen. He's also the most loyal. Mojo hasn't left Bella's side since he arrived. Thankfully, Stevens already took him outside and put some water in a bowl in my bathroom for him. Knowing how important he is to Bella, I gotta do right by her beast.

Holding Bella with one arm, I pull back the covers. I lay her down and pull her hair out from under her head, remembering how she would complain about feeling restricted in her sleep. I prop her foot on two pillows, then cover her up with the sheet and blanket, leaving that poor foot exposed.

"Watch your momma," I instruct Mojo, patting his head, "and come get me if she needs anything." He promptly flops on the floor with a grunt and is soon snoring away. Bending down to Bella, I lightly kiss her lips. Unable to resist, I kiss her again, more firmly. She moans, responding even in her drug induced sleep. Fuck yeah, she wants me just as much as I want her.

After tucking her in, I turn to leave but not before looking back at my dream come true. The first woman to sleep in my bed is the one I wished for. My heart tumbles at the sight.

"Sleep well, my love. I'll be back in a few," I whisper and blow her a kiss. Yeah, I know she's passed out for the night, but I've turned into a sap. I can't wait to have her back in my arms, so I hurry to the door and head for the kitchen. Impatient to sleep beside her, I can only pray this meeting is short.

Thank God Brit and Brenden ran into Bella. I shudder to think what that asshole could do. Shaking the disturbing thought from my mind, I remind myself that she's safe now.

The smell of freshly brewed coffee greets me as I walk into the kitchen. Not a good sign. This meeting may take longer than I'd hoped. Spencer and Hawkins are chatting away. Glancing around, there's more iPads than I'd expect. From the screens on the propped-up devices, I can see that Jackson's at the Camelot Security offices and Clausen is somewhere I don't recognize, but it might be Bella's house. Brenden and Stevens are chatting by the sink.

"Alright, catch me up," I say while pouring myself a cup of coffee. "What the fuck's going on?"

"I'd rather wait until you are sitting down," Hawkins says.

"Fuck, this doesn't sound good at all," I mumble as I take a seat at the table.

"It's not good, Brother," Hawkins announces from his iPad. "Since I talked to you a couple of hours ago, I was successful getting into Edwards's computer, and what I found is definitely criminal.

"That's why I asked Spencer to join us. This asshole's been stalking your woman for a while, months before he persuaded her to date him. I guess Edwards thought Isabella would be a great piece of arm candy and a good senator's wife. He thought she would be easy to control and docile." Chuckling he continues, "Obviously, he doesn't know our Isabella.

"Anyway, there are pictures time-stamped from up to nine months ago of her at work, eating lunch and even with Mojo. While they were dating, he placed several micro cameras in her home. Most of the footage is of her friends, leading me to think he never got into her bedroom."

"Stop right there. What the fuck did you say?" I explode. "He's been taping her? In her home? Have you watched these tapes? I'm gonna kill this fucker with my bare hands." She better not be nude in any of these fucking tapes.

"Give me a minute to explain. The moment I found the pictures and tapes I realized what he'd done. I sent Carpenter and Clausen to her house. Since Clausen had keys and was on the security list at her gated community, getting in was no problem."

"Once they did a sweep, they called in the PD and advised them of what they discovered. Everything is being handled within the law so this asshole can be locked up." Hawkins informs us.

"Hawkins, man, what the fuck is on these tapes and pictures?" I plead, about to lose my ever-loving mind. "So help me God, if it's her naked, the man is fucking dead. There will be no trial for anyone to see these pictures. Period."

"Hold on there, Brother. He has thousands of

pictures of her. Mostly taken from the videos he recorded. Nothing worse than what you would see on a Victoria's Secret model. She said something to Gregory about her dog not liking the douche-bag. I'm thinking Mojo saved her from the worst of it, as well as her modesty. Unlike most people, she never leaves her bedroom without at least underwear on.

"I bet she had to lock Mojo in her room whenever that asshole was over. He never had the chance to put cameras in her bedroom or bathroom. Not true for the rest of her house. Every angle was covered. These are high tech ones, too. They only record if there's movement and they fucking follow the movement. Since he couldn't put them in her room, he planted them in her guest bedroom and bathroom. There's a ton of footage of her friends who've stayed the night. The sick fuck planted one with a line of sight to the toilet, giving him full frontal shots.

"Many of the shots don't show the faces, thankfully, but still, man. This is sick. Thank God he didn't get any in her bedroom."

"Are you fucking kidding me? If you can't see their heads, how do you know none of them are Bella?" I demand.

"Dude, let me put it this way. The skin and hair color don't match her. But you still need to ask if she ever used that bathroom. The police are at her house now, with Clausen, collecting all the evidence. I'm sure they will have enough to get this perverted DA locked up in a matter of hours. That is why Spencer's here. Spencer, take over."

Running my fingers through my hair, I'm ready to scream and kick some ass. I cannot believe what I'm hearing. Goddamnit, the need to beat the life out of something overwhelms me.

What could have happened to her, if not for that accidental meeting with Brit and Brenden? Fuck, I put her in this danger, wasting time and not going after her. At least she's safe right now, in my bed. I just need to make sure she stays that way.

"Fitz!" Spencer calls. "Don't zone out on us now."

"Yeah, sorry," I nod at the iPad, breathing heavy.

"We got this, dude. Trust us," Spencer vows.

"Fuck, I was just thinking that I let this happen, by waiting. What if Brit and Brenden hadn't bumped into her? Fuck, I'm an idiot."

"First off," Hawkins chimes in. "You're fucking welcome," he says with a shit-eating grin.

"What? What are you talking about?" I demand.

"Dude, two weeks ago, we had a vote. You've been fucking miserable since she left, but it's been getting worse lately. We've had enough of your shit, and that was before your sorry-assed pity party last week.

"Riggs proposed we find her for you, even though Brit's been begging me for years to do it. The vote was unanimous. You deserve to be happy."

Flabbergasted, I just stare at Hawkins on the screen. They decided to find her, without telling me? That fucker knew where she was last Saturday when I told him not to find her. Damn, my Brothers are awesome.

"I traced her from here to New York, and then back here for college. That's how Clausen ended up with a black eye. I called him out when I discovered Isabella is his half-sister. That moron never figured it out. I had to connect the dots for him.

"Your woman is a creature of habit. I sent Brenden and Brit to that restaurant last Saturday, knowing they'd be the best to pull this off. It worked perfectly. You're welcome, dumbass. Now, listen to Spencer. We have a lot of work ahead of us."

"Damn," I murmur. "I owe you guys huge for this. Thank you."

Turning my attention to Spencer, I say, "Okay, Brother, tell me what's up."

"First and foremost," he says seriously, "you need to keep your shit tight. Over the next day or so, you're going to be tested. Thank God Hawkins sent a crew over and made it look like we stumbled on this tonight, doing improvements to her security system, because none of his hacking would have been admissible otherwise. Wonder Boy made it look like he traced the camera link-ups.

"You dumbasses are finally making my job easier. The law demands a chain of custody, so when the crew asked, I told them to call the P.D. That's why everything they pull out of Isabella's house is admissible. I had Jackson bring her minivan to the station. So far, they've pulled two trackers, the camera in the AC vent, and three bugs. He even had someone add a virus to her navigation system that sent him notifications when her van moved.

"I just got off the phone with Judge Peterson. He wasn't too happy with being woken up, but he signed the protective order I faxed him. It covers not only Isabella, her house, and her work but also all of us, our homes and the club. Camelot Security just got a new client, boys. Judge Peterson said he'd sign the search warrant as soon as he received it from the P.D. Should be in a few hours, with the amount of evidence already found against Edwards. I'm confident he'll be behind bars by dinner tomorrow night.

"He must have seen the cops on his video feed because Hawkins is pretty sure he's in the process of backing up his little porn collection and wiping his hard drive. The P.D. permitted Hawkins to clone his computer to salvage the evidence and to log Edwards' actions tonight. He needs to remain in the dark about the warrants and what we've uncovered so far. Isabella is not allowed to talk to him again. He'll try to talk her out of a restraining order. That's it for right now. We'll meet up at your place, Fitz, tomorrow morning for breakfast. We'll game plan, and then head to the station."

My head swims under the flood of information I just received. Fuck, I need something stronger than coffee. I can't believe how much danger my Bella is in. *Was in.* She's safe now, thanks to my Brothers.

"There shouldn't be anything new tonight, but keep your phone close in case, Fitz," Hawkins instructs. "I'll call during breakfast. I gotta keep an eye on this fucker's disgusting computer. Later dudes." The iPad goes black.

Spencer follows with, "Peace out."

I sigh, turning to Stevens. "Can you stick around tonight? Maybe call Carpenter and have him get some guys to come repair my gate? The P.D. will take weeks to get around to it, and I need Bella safe *now*."

Stevens nods, "No problem. I'll walk the property before I head to bed. Your house is safer than Fort Knox. I already called Carpenter and he said he'd have a full crew here by first light. We won't let anything happen to Isabella."

Feeling relieved and thankful for Stevens, I nod and head upstairs. Stevens can lock up on his way out.

Killing the lights in the hallway, I make my way in the dark to my bedroom by memory. The ugly image of that sick bastard whacking off to my Bella as she innocently moves through her house turns my stomach. I just need five minutes alone with the twisted fuck. For now, I need to keep it together for Bella.

Entering my room, I ignore the room control tablet, deciding to keep the windows and curtains closed tonight. I mentally debate for a second but sleeping in the nude tonight is not an option. Walking into my closet and open several drawers to find my Chewbacca pajama pants that Brit gave me two years ago for Christmas. I never thought I'd be wearing these, but I don't want to make Bella uncomfortable. Climbing into bed and pulling her into my arms, I breathe a sigh of relief. This is where she belongs.

CHAPTER SIXTEEN

FITZ: BELLA'S ENLIGHTENMENT

*N*othing in my life prepared me for what I'm feeling right now. Bella is snuggled up to me, her head on my chest, arm slung around my waist and her leg entwined with mine. I thought I'd gone to Heaven when I woke up a few moments ago. It's like she's trying to burrow into me.

Gathering her thick mane in my hand, I move it out of my way. I slide my hand along her back, then under the bottom of my shirt, which had, thank Christ, ridden up during the night. Caressing her back, the feel of her smooth skin under my rough fingers is like nothing I've ever felt before. This is how I want to wake up for the rest of my life.

Henry stirs, reminding me of how hard last night was for me. *Heh, how hard.* We both wanted her so fucking bad that I thought for a while I'd have to whack off with Bella lying beside me. But after reminding myself that Bella was hurt, I calmed down enough to fall asleep.

Shit, I just realized at some point during the night I kicked off my pajama pants, but at least I still have on my boxers. That's what I get for always sleeping naked and feeling free. I just hope Bella is okay with it.

Right now, though, there's no calming me, or Henry, down. My usual morning wood combined with Bella wrapped around me like a vine makes that impossible. The feel of her warm, soft breasts pressed against me causes Henry to jerk. Fuck, I need to get into the shower to get a handle on this. Maybe I can whack off right here. She did watch me last night…

Bella stirs, breaking my inner conflict. I watch her long eyelashes flutter as she slowly opens her eyes, then lifts her head and tilts it back to look up at me. A soft smile forms on those exquisite lips.

"Oh, thank God! I thought it was all a dream. Good morning, Dray," she murmurs softly, snuggling back into my chest.

"Good morning to you too, babe. I hope you slept as well as I did."

"If you mean, did I experience paradise last night cuddled up to you?" She tilts her head, her almond shaped eyes finding mine. "Then the answer is yes. I don't ever want to move."

Bella shifts her leg, sliding it right over my rock-hard cock. Henry jerks, thumping against her thigh.

Her face is comical when she realizes what she just felt.

"Babe, Henry can't help it," I chuckle, "especially in the morning. He really wants you. I keep telling him he has to wait. Unless…?"

A beautiful blush spreads across her cheeks.

"Oh my gosh, you still call him Henry? What was his full name again? Give me a sec, I know this. Oh! *Henry Peter Longfellow*! Jeez, the name fits, judging by what I just felt."

"I can't believe you remember that."

"Psh, of course I remember. You were, what, thirteen? Please tell me you guys still don't talk about them with each other, like they're more than just your wee willies?"

"Well," I smile, "about five years ago, Stevens got them all stockings with their names on them for Christmas. They're huge stockings too. We hang them up every year," I inform her with pride. Those things are awesome.

"No, tell me he didn't!" she gasps between laughs. "You do not literally hang them up each year. You don't, you wouldn't!"

"Babe, we do hang them up," I reply, giving her a squeeze. "We even have a gift exchange for them. Some of the gifts are hilarious. One year Stevens got us shirts with their names printed on them. Some of the gifts are super nice, too. Another year, Spencer got us awesome pens with their names engraved on them. It's my favorite pen. It's a lot of fun."

"You… give… gifts…" she's laughing so hard I can barely make out the words. She takes a deep breath, shouting "To each other's willies!" Gasping for breath, Bella waves her hand in front of her face.

"Oh... can't... breathe," she gasps. Finally collecting herself, she declares, "I'm coming this year. I need to see this in person."

"You can come anywhere you damn well please," I say, shifting, so we lay facing each other and push her hair out of her face. God, I love her hair. There's so much of it, I can't wait to wrap it in my fist as I fuck her. Staring into her eyes, I try to gauge her pain level.

"How does your foot feel this morning?" I ask softly.

"Oh, it doesn't even hurt. That might change when I try to walk on it. Brenden did a wonderful job, but don't tell him I said that."

Bella's big chocolate eyes wander over my face, traveling from my eyes to my mouth and back again.

Slowly, I roll her over, pushing her to her back as I lower my mouth to hers. She wraps her arms around me, her fingers finding my hair. I lick the seam of her lips, requesting entrance. Our tongues entwine when she grants me access.

Bella is so responsive, its mind-blowing. Reaching down, I slide my hand behind the knee of her injured leg and lift it to wrap her leg around my waist. Damn, the way her hips cradle my pelvis is perfection. Through the barrier of my boxers and her thin panties, I slide Henry along her folds, feeling the heat of her pussy.

"Oh, Dray, that... that..."

Thrusting my hips forward while my lips slide along her jaw to her neck, a shiver wracks her, making me determined to see her climax. She needs this. I need this. Neither of us is leaving this bed until I make her come.

Pulling away from her neck, I stare down at her gorgeous face, watching for any sign to stop. Her eyes close as she releases a soft moan as I rotate my hips, pressing Henry more firmly against her. Her hips jerk tentatively as if she's unsure. Fuck, this feels amazing. I'm not gonna last long like this.

"Oh Dray," she cries out.

"I know babe, I know. Let me take care of you. I want to see you come. I won't go any further, but I need to love you, to touch you right now. I just have to see you come."

"Dray... Dray... I, I don't know if I can," Bella cries, with a wrinkle in her brow. She needs this release as much as I want to give it to her.

"Yeah you can, babe. Oh, yeah you can. You're gettin' close, I can feel it."

Sliding my hand under her luscious ass, I command her, "Move with me."

Isabella

My mind is racing from thought to thought as my body trembles. What is Drake doing to me?

Drake's hand grips my bum, rotating my hips in time with his. My core contracts, over and over again. I feel myself getting wet between my legs. His erection, long and thick, feels incredible. The way he wrapped my leg around him has opened me up to him. If not for his boxers and my panties, he'd be inside of me.

Oh, God. I don't know if I can take this. I've never felt like this. My core flutters, sending waves of pleasure rippling along my skin. This is so frustrating yet utterly amazing at the same time.

Returning to his assault on my neck, Drake's hand finds the buttons of his shirt that I'm wearing. With his talented fingers, he swiftly unbuttons and parts it, revealing my breasts. He kisses and nibbles a path down my neck, his hand sliding to my breast. A moan escapes me as he squeezes it gently. Oh, God, I feel like I'm going to combust from the sensations coursing through my body.

Drake lifts his head and looks at me hungrily, devouring the sight of my breasts.

"Fuck," he murmurs. His head descends, his mouth capturing my nipple. I suck in a breath as he licks and nibbles my breast. Capturing my nipple with his teeth, he gently pulls it. *Oh my*, I think, as sparks dance along my skin.

He lifts his head, moving to my other breast, but I intercept him. With both hands, I grab his face and pull it to mine, kissing him deeply. Desire and something instinctive spurs me into action. Wrapping my other leg around his waist, I rock my hips, chasing something, a need I can't quite put my finger on.

Panting, my head falls back. Drake takes advantage, licking and sucking my neck. His tongue plays with my earlobe, causing me to shiver. I shove my fingers into his hair, my nails scratching his scalp. He groans as I kiss and nibble his neck, tasting the salty flavor of his skin. He thrusts harder against me, hitting something that causes lights to flash behind my closed eyes. I moan loudly, not caring about being embarrassed.

Every muscle in my body contracts as stars flash before my eyes. Great waves of pleasure burst free, taking over my body as I shudder, shaking me down to my soul. I bite Drake's neck, unable to control my reaction.

"Dray…" I moan, feeling boneless.

"Bella," he groans, his voice gravelly. He thrusts his pelvis one final time, pressing hard against my core. His erection jerks as I feel a new wetness between us.

We lay there, panting into each other's necks. Shivers still run through my body. Words cannot express what I'm feeling. Oh my, is this what I've been missing all these years?

He slowly rolls over and sits up, rearranging pillows to prop himself up at an angle. Then he pulls me into his arms so I'm straddling him. He carefully wraps my feet behind him, making sure to protect my booboo foot from touching anything.

My whole core is open to him in this position and I can feel the residual pulses from his thick penis, causing my core to flutter. I wrap my arms around him and collapse onto his chest, unable to hold myself up. Drake caresses my back, sweeping my hair to the side.

"Babe, that was amazing. I'll admit I've never come like that, but *damn*. I dreamt of doing that when we were younger, but it far exceeded my imagination. That was better than anything I've ever done."

I lift my head, resting my chin on his chest. "Dray, that... That was... I have no words. That was a first for me. I've never felt that before," I say, watching his face.

He looks confused like he doesn't understand what I'm saying. Drake leans me back a bit, arranging us so he can still see my face. My bum drops between his legs, making my core rub more firmly across his naturally thick semi-erection.

"What do you mean, 'That was a first for me?' Have you never come, never orgasmed before?" he questions, his voice incredulous.

"I mean, I've gotten worked up before, but never experienced what I just did."

"Fuck, no man has ever made you come?" he asks, shocked.

"Well, they never got as far as you did. No one's ever made me lose my mind like that." Hoping he gets what I'm trying to say without having to say it outright.

I can practically see the gears turning in his mind as he thinks carefully about what I just said. I'm pretty certain he gets it when his eyes pop open.

"Babe," he says in that deep, sexy as sin voice of his, "are you telling me you're... you're still a virgin?"

I bite my lip, as my cheeks heat. Nodding slightly, I get lost in those dark jade eyes of his. My stomach flips, the excitement he made me feel returning. *Is that even possible?* I wonder, *after what I just experienced, to feel it again so quickly?*

"Holy fucking shit. You're serious? Babe," he groans, gathering me in his arms and shoving his face into my neck.

"Well, I, umm, never really met a guy I trusted enough. I wouldn't let them get that far. I mean, you know how it is. Well, maybe not you since you're a guy. Brit would probably get it. She's a girl."

I turn my head away, knowing I'm babbling nervously. My face is probably bright red. I don't want to explain why I'm still a virgin at twenty-three. *How am I getting turned on again?*

His hand grasps the back of my head, his fingers wrapping in my hair. Drake turns my face back to his and kisses me passionately. His erection jumps between my folds as I feel it getting hard again. *Oh man, this is so hot.*

"Babe, it's okay. It means you're all mine. You'll be the first woman I ever make love with, the only woman I'll *ever* make love with. Not today, but soon."

Kissing me again, he grabs my butt and moves my hips. Through the barrier of our clothes, I feel his rock-hard erection sliding between my folds. I never knew men could get hard again so quickly. His penis, thick and wide, gets bigger as he moves with me, turning me on that much faster.

Once Drake shows me the rhythm, he leans back with me on his lap.

"Babe, is your foot okay? I don't want to hurt it, but damn I want you to ride me," he growls. "I want to see your face this time when you come."

"Yeah, it's fine like this, but… but…" I can't finish my sentence because of this new feeling, this *need* filling me. I'm trying to move like he is. Gosh, it feels so good, I'm speechless.

Drake slides his hands from my hips, up my torso to my shoulders. Slowly, he pulls his shirt from my arms. Instinctively, I lean back, pressing my palms into his muscular thighs. My breasts bounce with my every movement, sending spikes of pleasure straight to my core.

His warm fingers fall from my shoulders, cupping my breasts. He caresses and squeezes them. He captures my nipple in his rough fingertips, giving it a light pinch with a twist. My hips jerk in response.

With his mouth, he lavishes my other breast, biting and nibbling my tingling flesh. He catches my nipple with his teeth and bites me softly. My head falls back, my hair sweeping his thighs, as an embarrassingly loud moan leaves my mouth, echoing throughout the room.

I push him back away from my breast to get more pressure and friction, and this new position gives me room to grind my hips, rocking on Drake's penis. He is so big, he hits me in all the right spots. But like this, it really gets that one spot that making me feel like I'm going to combust to the point I can barely catch my breath. I can't believe the size of him. I need to feel him inside of me.

"Oh, God. Dray, I can't!"

Drake's hand drifts down my stomach, slipping into my panties. The heel of his hand presses in perfect motion against my clit. I feel a finger enter me, just a little, up to the first knuckle. Drake moves it back and forth, sending stars into my vision. I lean back more now, giving him better access. Oh God, what is he doing to me?

That is all I need, it's perfect. I throw my head back and moan as I continue to ride his hand and just enjoy the experience. The pressure builds, I'm close. I feel Drake watching me. He licks his lips, his eyes hooded with desire. He taps that spot rhythmically, as I grab his head, sliding my fingers into his hair.

"Dray, oh! I'm going to come," I cry out

"Come for me, babe. Come with me. *Now.*"

Peaking ever higher, I let go. Fireworks light off in my vision. My forehead meets Drake's as waves crash over me. Every muscle trembles as Drake's body stiffens. His hips jerk, and he groans.

"Goddamn, woman. That was the most beautiful thing I've ever witnessed. Just watching you come, seeing you explode for me." Slowly, he pulls his hand from my panties. I'm flooded with embarrassment.

Drake brings his fingers up to his mouth, sucking and licking them. My mouth falls open in shock.

"Babe, that's just the beginning. There's a hell of a lot more that you'll experience, and soon. I'll taste every inch of you, discover what turns you on, hear your gasps and cries. So fucking hot, I cannot wait."

He grabs the back of my head, winding his fingers through my hair. Pulling me close, he plunders my mouth, swirling his tongue with mine. I taste myself on his lips, turning me on again.

"This has been the best morning of my life. I'm not just giving you a line, babe. I've never come that hard in my life...and twice. Now, though, we need to get up. As much as I'd love to stay in bed with you all day, the

Brothers will be descending on my house soon because *someone* promised them breakfast."

I'm still reeling from my orgasms, my *first* orgasms. Drake shifts so he's facing me and tucks a strand of hair behind my ear. His eyes roam my face then lock onto my eyes. A little smile plays at the corner of his mouth.

"Now you have to make a decision. We can either shower together, which is my vote, or I can try to be a gentleman and I'll go use the shower in my office while you use this one. Either way, you're wearing something from my closet. When those assholes get here, they'll see you're all mine."

Kissing him quickly, I smile. "Dray, honey... I've had quite a few firsts this morning." My cheeks flush with heat. "I'll need to take you up on your offer to be a gentleman. I would like to wait for our first shower together. Let's not rush this, okay?"

"Sure thing, babe," he sighs, before kissing the tip of my nose. "I'll see you downstairs. The coffee should be ready."

Drake climbs from the bed and I admire his retreating bum, which is quite fabulous. He bends down and grabs some pajama bottoms from the floor, giving me an even more sinful view. He pulls them on and heads for the door. To my surprise, Mojo gets up and follows him. Oh, crap, how'd I forget about my poor puppy? Good thing he's a sound sleeper. He and Drake look adorable leaving the room together.

"Hey, Dray," I call out. "Chewy's my favorite, too," I giggle at him, referring to his comical pajama bottoms. "Also, could you please let Mojo out to go potty?"

"Brit knows Chewy's my favorite. It was a gift from her several Christmas's ago," Drake says, with a boyish smirk on his face. "And sure thing, babe, I'll make sure Mojo gets out. You know, he's pretty damn awesome,"

"Thanks, honey. I'll be downstairs before you know it."

Sliding my still quivering legs to the edge of the bed, I slowly put pressure on my foot. The pain from my toes isn't as bad as I would have thought. Maybe it's because of the orgasms Drake gave me. Lord have mercy, that man is talented.

Heading to the shower, I know I need to find the strength within myself. No sex. I'm not ready for that. Gosh darn it, I need the strength to tell Drake so I don't get lost in the passion. I'm not stupid. There's no way I could tell him to stop in the heat of the moment.

While the water is heating up, I rummage around the cupboard beneath the sink and find a small plastic garbage bag and wrap my foot in it so it won't get wet. Everything that happened last night comes rushing back. Peeping on Drake in the shower, breaking my toe, the police, Paul's threats about my daycare center, and, oh man, Stevens making fun of me for peeping on Drake. Ugh! Why couldn't our reunion just go smoothly? Stupid, idiotic, stalker-boy Paul.

But I won't let that doofus hamper my mood. I just experienced the most passionate moments of my life. I've had not just one but *two* orgasms. Drake has enlightened me to a whole new world of passion. Gosh, am I in trouble.

∽

Breakfast was a smash. The boys descended, en masse, falling on the French toast and eggs like they hadn't seen food in months. Smiling to myself, I stand and grab my empty plate and rise to place it in the dishwasher. Stevens takes it from my hands.

"You relax. Brit and I will clean." Shocked, I gape at him.

"Fine, I'll just go get some more juice," I retort.

Leaning against the counter, I take in the sight of all of my old friends, laughing. I'm beyond thrilled to have them back in my life. Thankfully, Stevens didn't mention my Peeping Tammy moment. I think Drake's threat of no breakfast held him back.

Drake gets up from the table and approaches me. He slides his arms around my waist, pulling me close. A private smile plays on his lips, making me smile as I wrap my arms around him.

"Thank you for making everyone breakfast, babe," he whispers in a husky voice. "You've made quite a few of my dreams come true. I'm looking forward to tonight where more of those dreams can come true."

Ignoring the fact that the kitchen is full of people, Drake captures my mouth. I'm swept away, lost in mind blowing passion. Stretching up on my toes of my good foot while lifting my booboo foot up like an old fashion movie, I slide my hands into his hair, tugging it as my excitement builds.

"Fuck, Fitz. Your room's right upstairs!" someone

shouts, slamming me back into reality. Embarrassment rides me hard as I hide in Drake's chest.

"Dude, you gonna piss on her leg to mark your territory too?" Jackson asks.

"I'm surprised he didn't give her a hickey," Stevens says. "Didja see the one he's sportin'?"

"You go, girl!" Brit exclaims.

Drake turns us, so he's leaning against the counter. He raises a hand, probably to flip them off. I can't lift my head. How did I forget we weren't alone?

"Y'all are a bunch of jealous assholes. I got the love of my life back and you pieces of shit are whining cuz you don't have what I do."

The love of his life? Shock barrels through me. Does he feel the same way I do? Could all of my dreams be coming true?

"Obviously, the two of you hooked up last night—" Clay starts.

"Eww! That's my brother!" Brit interrupts.

"I need to know, did I win the pot? Was it last night or was it this morning? Cuz, Hunter wins if it was this morning. I didn't think you could make it past three hours."

"I'm not stupid, I took the first twenty-four hours. Hand it over Stevens," Hunter demands with a smirk.

My mouth gapes open. Quickly shutting it, I whip my head around to glare at Hunter. Drake takes a breath like he's gearing up to yell at his friends.

"Let me clear this up for you, boys," Stevens announces, holding up his hand. "Drake didn't attack the pink fortress last night. He strolled downstairs, wearing Chewy pajamas, demanded I take Mojo potty, then sauntered off to shower in his office. If he'd scaled those walls, do you think they'd shower separately?"

Brit calls out, "Woohoo! See, I told you you'd need those Chewy jammies one day, and I was correct, once again." She dances around. "You're welcome. But I agree. If Fitz was wearing those pants that he swore no one would ever see on his body, he didn't get any last night." She and Stevens high five each other.

"However, he wasn't sportin' morning wood, so he did get a little sumthin' sumthin.' But it wasn't her lady box. Pot's still open, people," Stevens announces.

Everyone cackles. Turning to face everyone, I slam my hands on my hips, the universal stance of a pissed off woman. I'm just about to tear into Stevens when Drake beats me to it.

"What the fuck, dude? Why were you checking out my dick?"

"Confirmation, Fitz. We got a bet going here!"

"Fuck that. What Bella and I do, in *our room*, is our own mother fucking business. Knock this shit off. All you assholes do not need to be in the know of when Bella and I make love."

"And there you have it, folks," Stevens announces. "He didn't get any puddin-tang last night *or* this morning."

Marching up to Stevens, I smack his shoulder. "I know I told you this last night, but it appears I need to repeat myself. No. Freaking. Betting. On. This. It's perverted. It's low, even for you degenerates. There is no need to be that disgusting. Don't spoil this for us,"

I plead.

"Oh, sweetheart, you've known us almost your whole life. You know we bet on everything. It's because we love you so much that you're open season." Jackson declares. I turn my attack on him, smacking his shoulders and chest.

Hawkins yells for quiet from his iPad. He hadn't joined us physically, which surprised me since he adores my cooking. He had eaten Cinnamon Pop Tarts while everyone teased him, going on and on about how good my French toast was. I remind myself to find out what's up with Hawkins later. There has to be some reason why he isn't here, but he doesn't look sick or anything.

"I hate to break up the party, boys. However, Isabella cannot go to the police station dressed in one of Drake's shirts and a belt, as hot as she looks in it. She needs to go home to change. Fitz, have her help you cover up that hickey. I can see it all the way over here. Most importantly, Isabella needs to be informed of what was found at her place last night then we need to get this ball rolling."

My head swivels from Hawkins to Drake and back again.

"What do you mean, Nicholas? What did you find at my home? Please tell me that douche-canoe, fart sniffer didn't put something on my laptop. Did he?" I plead, my concern mounting.

Drake pulls me close, ready to answer, but Hawkins interrupts him. "I'm gonna let Fitz fill you in, Isabella, but you guys need to get moving. I've got more hacking to do, and I've got to continue deleting some of the shit

Paul did. Just remember, darling, you're one of us. We will not let this asshole get away with shit. Gotta go."

The iPad goes black, causing me to turn to Drake with a million questions on the tip of my tongue. There's a few shuffling feet, which tells me that everyone knows what's going on but me. I'm not happy that everyone in this room knows more about what's going on in my life than I do.

Asher and Jackson come over to me. Jackson leans in and kisses my temple.

"We'll see you in a bit, Isabella. We got your back. No one messes with someone we've claimed." He grabs his motorcycle half helmet and heads for the door.

"Yeah, little sis. We got a few things to handle, but we'll see you soon." Asher gives me a side hug and kisses my temple too. He's gone just as quickly as Jackson. I'm gaping like a fish at their quick departure.

Drake takes charge.

"Stevens, mind staying here and babysitting Mojo?"

"No problem, bro. Me and the big guy will hang out. I need to introduce him to Morris and Freddy since he'll be staying here for a while. I'm sure he'd love to go for a ride in my truck and get another cheeseburger too. I'll take real good care of him, Isabella," Stevens answers with a wink.

"Spencer and I will take Bella home to get dressed and fill her in on everything that we found last night. As Hawkins said, we need to get down to the station to get this asshole locked up."

Drake looks down at me, cupping my cheek in his strong hand.

"I'll be back babe. Gotta grab a turtleneck."

I know once we get in that car, not only would I be demanding answers about that dirtball ex of mine, but I'll be questioning Drake about Hawkins too.

CHAPTER SEVENTEEN

ISABELLA: SOMETIMES HONESTY CAN BE PAINFUL

*O*nce we're in the car and headed to my house, I find I can't hold my tongue any longer. My mind is racing with questions. Taking a deep breath, I brace myself for the answers.

"Okay, guys. What in the world is going on? I know you aren't telling me something and it doesn't make me happy. I hate secrets."

"You're right, babe. What I'm about to tell you is gonna piss you off. It'll probably hurt too. But, we'll deal. We have your back." Drake takes a breath like he's preparing for my reaction.

"Some of the guys have been at your house since last night. That's why Jackson and Clausen took off so fast, to get back there. Paul's been up to some bad shit."

My head might just explode from the anger building in me. I want to cause him some serious bodily harm. He needs a good throat punch or a swift kick in the family jewels...or both!

I sigh, hanging my head. Staring at my hands in my lap, I ask "What did he do? Did he try to break into my house or something?"

"Babe, I promise you," Drake swears, lifting my chin with his index finger. "We will deal. Let's go over everything at your house so you won't be in for any major surprises when you talk to the police. The police were there last night collecting evidence too, so you don't have to worry about that part."

Fine. He wants to wait to fill me in on Paul. I'll move on to the other issue running around my brain.

"Okay, honey. I'll wait until we get to my house. But tell me about Nicholas. Why isn't he around? Why do I only see him on an iPad? Did he move somewhere?"

Drake groans, his head falls back to the headrest as he pinches the bridge of his nose.

"I know you love Hawkins and want to know what's going on. No, he didn't move, but this is his story to tell. Can you just stay focused on this situation with Paul for now?"

"Honey, please," I beg. "We were so close, and I would love to see him in person."

I find Spencer's eyes in the rearview mirror. He shakes his head. Great, no help there. I turn back to Drake, grasping his knee.

"It's a heartbreaking story, babe. I'll tell you this. Hawkins has PTSD and doesn't leave his house much. He feels safer there."

My hand flies to my heart on a gasp. "What happened, Drake?"

"You'll see Hawkins soon and in person. But for now,

let's get past this shit with Paul first. I promise, once that asshole is dealt with, I'll fill you in if Hawkins doesn't. Okay?"

"It had to have been something horrific to keep him away from everyone like this," I mumble. "But I'll leave it for now."

"He doesn't keep away from us, Hawkins just doesn't go out into the world much. He definitely doesn't do crowds. Sometimes, he'll shock the shit out of us and show up at one of our homes when we get together. We leave it up to him, though."

I'm lost in my thoughts of Nicholas as the car stops in front of my house. Drake opens the door, bringing me back to the present. Jackson's motorcycle is in my drive-way, and he and Asher are standing on my porch with the front door wide open.

This is not going to be good. I hope I can keep it together and not go King Kong crazy on them. Getting out of the car, Drake grabs me and tucks me to his side. Asher and Jackson give me a small, sad smile as my brother says, "Sorry, sis."

Crossing the threshold, I'm ready to scream. My place looks like it's been ransacked. Drawers open, stuff strewn about, cushions overturned, even furniture moved. I'm far from Miss Clean and Tidy, but this is a disaster.

A sob works its way up my throat and my breath hitches. Drake's arm around my waist gives me a little squeeze, reminding me I'm not alone. Closing my eyes, I take a deep breath to compose myself.

"Start explaining this mess, *now!*" I exclaim, my eyes bouncing between my brother and Jackson.

"Isabella," Asher starts, "we tried to get the cops to respect your place. But what can I say? They were only interested in the evidence. I can call Brit, Sarah, and Brenda. I'm sure they'd be more than happy to come help you."

"The freaking police did this? *Why?*" I cry.

"Last night, we came over to check out your security system. We found cameras, lots of 'em. A shit-ton of micro-cameras were hidden all over your house. Paul's been watching you, taping you for quite a while."

My voice is shaky in my reply. "He *what?*"

"Isabella," Spencer says. "Look at me, sweetheart."

Slowly, I raise my eyes to his face. I'm shaking, trying to control the bile rising in my throat. *Paul was watching me.* Oh, my God.

"I need you to listen to me. I know you're scared right now. I told them to call the police. This needs to be handled to the letter of the law, to protect you. Paul's an Assistant DA. He can fuck this up for us if we don't do everything by the books.

"When Hawkins started looking for you, he found your connection to Edwards. He already knew some not so good stuff about him, but once he saw you linked to the asshole, he dug deeper."

Drake then interrupts Spencer and fills me in about the photos and videos Hawkins found, even one of me saying goodbye to Mojo. With each word out of his mouth, my shoulders slump further and further. I shrug off Drake's hold and walk to my favorite chair. It's big and comfy, perfect for reading in. I plop down, curling in on myself. *He was watching me.* Drake picks me up and sits with me on his lap. I burrow into him, wanting to disappear. Trying to pull myself together, I take several deep breaths.

"Bella, babe, the only saving grace is there were ZERO cameras in your bedroom or bathroom," Drake finishes.

"Don't lie to me," I plead. "Who's seen these pictures? Am I in my underwear? How many cameras? Where were they? Did you guys see the pictures? Oh, God. Have the police seen them?"

Questions fly from my mouth, cracking through the silence of the room.

"Sweetie," Spencer's voice is gentle, "no one here has seen the videos or pictures. Hawkins is the only one who has. He fast forwarded through most of them but did look at some of it. He had to turn some of them over as evidence. He's madder than hell, and even wants to put a hit out on Edwards.

"Any moment now, Edwards is going to be arrested. Hawkins is scouring the internet, trying to pull any images of you that he can. The sick bastard posted some of the pictures of you on a porn trading site. At least the asshole blurred your face or cropped it out completely."

Terror floods my body as I imagine some disgusting pervert staring at my picture on some gross porn trading site. I want to cry and hide from the world. I feel so violated. But more importantly, right now all that is on my mind is the evil things I want to do to Paul.

"Okay babe," Drake says, hugging me tight, "here comes the really bad part."

"How could it possibly get worse?" The fear is evident in my small voice.

"Babe, the evil, dick-less, pussy is a major sicko. He put cameras everywhere. *Everywhere.* We're assuming you put Mojo in your room because there were no cameras in there, but there were cameras in your guest bedroom and bathroom. He got some very sick, majorly perverted footage of your friends. The police will probably want their names. I'm so sorry, babe."

Tears cascade from my eyes. I try to wipe them, but more replace them.

Drake holds me tighter and slowly rocks me a little as I cry uncontrollably. I need to get it out of my system. I knew this was going to be hard, but I never thought it would be this hard. Thank God Hawkins found me. I kind of owe him my life.

"What kind of pictures? Are they in the shower? Are they naked?"

"We'll talk about that later, babe," Drake says, ticking me off. "It's gonna be okay."

"I need to pack. I'm moving right now. I feel so dirty, so gross. I *cannot* stay here another night," I wail.

"We can have you packed and out of here in a few hours. You can move into the guest house or our home. But until he's in prison, you need the protection of my place. None of your friends have the security that I do."

Did he just say *our home*?

"Naturally, I want to stay with you, but it's just too soon, Dray. That house is plenty big, but I'm not going to kick Stevens out of your guest house either. Maybe I should move in with my brother."

"Babe, listen to me. My house is the safest place for you. If you're not comfortable with that, Hawkins is your only other option. His house is a literal fortress."

I nod. Drake only wants me to be safe. I need to listen to them. This is what they do, keep people safe.

Spencer squats in front of me and takes my hand, "Isabella, we need you to help us put him away. I just got word that they arrested him. They're executing warrants, searching his house and office. They'll confiscate all of his computers, tablets, phones, everything. But you need to help us. Talk to your friends and give their names to police. The news and media were alerted and have footage of the police putting him in the back of a police car in handcuffs. I know this is tough, but you need to be strong."

The reminder of my friends being victims of Paul's twisted perversion sparks my anger. I cannot believe he did this to me, to them. My tears dry as anger and resolve take their place.

"I'll do whatever I have to. It can only be three girls from work. I haven't had anyone else over. They're going to be pissed but will do whatever they need to lock Paul the Perv up. I only hope they don't hate me after this.

"Right now, I am so mad, I want to kick Paul so hard in his family nuggets they pop into his mouth for him to swallow. Then when he has to poop them out, I want to stomp on them until there is nothing but a pile of digesting, foul goo. That's what he is to me, disgusting, foul goo."

"That goddamn motherfucker, cum sucking pussy," Jackson yells, startling me. "I want to rip off his goddamn pencil dick and feed it to him. Then, I'm gonna stick my arm up his ass and pull it out. Finally, I'm gonna stomp on it with my boots and scoop the dick-less goo up and feed it to him again. Fuck! I gotta get the hell out of here before I do something stupid. I'm sorry, Isabella, we'll take care of this motherfucker for you. That I promise you." He slams his way through the front door with Asher following, calling his name.

The roar of the pipes on Jackson's Harley shakes my windows. He peels out of my driveway. A few seconds later, Asher returns.

"Uh, Jackson had to go deal with some family shit. Tell 'em to stand down, that we'll be doing this legal-like."

Asher sits on the end of my coffee table in front of Drake and me. He takes my hand, looking like he's trying to brace himself.

"I guess I'm the one that has to suck it up and be brave. I'm the one who found that sick fuck's camera in the bathroom." His eyes close on a grimace. A vein throbs in his temple and he looks like he's barely in control.

Wanting to relieve the tension, I try to crack a joke. "I'm keeping a running tab of what you and Jackson owe to my foster kid's care fund. You guys have very bad potty mouths. Heck, Jackson's gonna need a small loan to pay off his tab."

Spencer walks over and leans down kissing my forehead as Asher cracks up. "You're handling this great, sweetie."

"Stop hittin' on my girl, dammit,"Drake growls behind me.

Spencer and Asher both hoot with laughter.

"Dude, calm down. I'm not makin a move on your girl," Spencer says. "Just thanking her. Don't worry, Isabella. We'll make sure everyone pays up, or I'll personally kick their goddamned asses. What's that, four bucks?" he laughs.

"You remembered," I say in surprise. I take a deep breath, mentally pull up my big girl panties and brace myself. "Okay, sweetie, I'm ready. Where did you find the cameras in the bathroom? Were the cameras in the shower? Did he get full nude shots of them?"

Asher scrubs his hand over his face. Oh, no. It's a lot worse than full nude shower pictures. Oh, God.

"No. That sick fucker hid cameras in the vent across from the toilet. He got shots of their private parts. None of their faces are in the shots, he was aiming lower. Hawkins is confident none of them were you because the skin tone doesn't match yours. Your friends will have to identify the pictures themselves, based on if they're waxed or trimmed, or, um, well, you get the idea. I didn't want you to be shocked when the cops ask you about your, uh, grooming habits."

Angry tears pour from my eyes. My breath comes in pants. I force broken and disjointed words from my mouth.

"I have… never," I hitch, "*hated*… someone more… in my… entire… *life!*" My words vibrate with hatred. "I want… him to… *suffer*. How could… he do… something… something so… *vile*? To… me? To… my friends? He's… sick and… and perverted. Oh, God. He is so evil. I want to hurt him."

I break down, the tears, anger, and fear overwhelming me. It ticks me off more because I'm not a crier. But this *hurts*. Drake pulls me back into his arms, tucking me tight under his chin.

"Why don't you guys go get some coffee from Starbucks or something?" Drake suggests. "Just give us about thirty minutes. Bring us back something. Coffee, black for me, and Bella would like a skinny mocha latte. Oh, and a chocolate croissant too. My girl needs some chocolate."

My heart feels a little lighter when Drake tells Asher and Spencer my coffee drink of choice, and, *chocolate*. He still remembers? Holding me in his lap, he caresses my back and occasionally runs his fingers through my hair.

"Babe, listen to me. Can you hear me?" he asks, his voice gentle.

I nod into his chest, wiping my tears on his long sleeve Henley.

"We will deal, babe. I'll be right by your side every step of the way. Hawkins is moving Heaven and Hell to uncover everything he can about Edwards. But right now, we need to get to the police station and get the ball rolling. We gotta press charges and get that restraining order. Why don't you go wash your face and get dressed, okay? Let me know what you need, babe. I'll be right here with you."

"You're right," I nod, finding some reserve of

strength. "It's time to get my rear in gear… pull myself together. I'm not letting Paul break me. We gotta kick his butt and get as many charges as possible to stick. Let's go make his namby-pamby butt someone's boy toy in jail."

Drake's chuckle vibrates through me. "That's the strong, fearless woman I fell in love with years ago. You got this, babe. Let's go kick some ass."

Shocking myself, I grab his face and give him a quick kiss before I climb from his lap. My legs are wobbly, probably from being curled into a ball. At least the boot Brenden brought over for my busted foot at breakfast kept me from causing further damage.

As I turn to go to my room, I realize I have one more thing to say. Freezing in place, I watch as Drake puts his hand over his head and grabs the back of his Henley, pulling it off. Completely mesmerized by every flex and movement in his muscular back, I forget what I was going to say. He grabs a black turtle-neck off the back of the couch he put there when we walked in. Watching that action pulls me from my ogling moment, I have to get ready.

Making my way to my bathroom, I think about how I want to do my makeup and hair. Subtle makeup, nothing too over the top. French twist for my hair. Yes, that should do it. Sweet innocence is the look I'm going for.

CHAPTER EIGHTEEN

ISABELLA: MY SCENE AT THE POLICE STATION

Seven and a half hours. Seven and a half freaking hours of questions, pictures of myself in my underwear and a ton of embarrassment I'm not sure I'll ever get over. Drake and Spencer were right by my side, witnessing my utter humiliation. With each picture the detectives revealed, Drake's anger ratcheted up another notch. His body was statue still while his fury pulsed off of him in waves. I wouldn't have been shocked if he exploded.

I, however, vowed to burn every piece of underwear I owned. No one would ever see me in those again. In addition to being humiliated, I feel dirty, gross, and so used. I need a shower. I have never felt so dirty in my life.

By the time the detectives started wrapping things up, resolve had begun to take the place of my embarrassment. I will not allow Paul to get away with this. For the safety of womankind, he needs to be locked away for a very long time. Knowing I have my dreams of a life with Drake within reach only further adds to my determination to see this through.

Walking out of the police station I find myself surrounded by the boys. Spencer is leading us, Drake by my side and Asher bringing up the rear. They know I'm fuming, so they remain silent. A familiar voice stops me dead in my tracks. Spencer, noticing I've stopped, turns around.

"Isabella, are you okay?" he asks.

With the barest shake of my head, my eyes find Paul's parents to our right, talking with a reporter.

"We'll get this straightened out very quickly," his mother says.

"This is just a jealous ex-girlfriend," Paul's father chimes in. "She's upset he broke up with her after six months and is trying to destroy his political future. She thought she had it made with him."

"Paul didn't like that she wanted an open relationship," his mother adds. "I warned my Paul about how young she is. She's causing trouble because she tried to pervert my boy and he wasn't having it. She wants to make our son look bad, to ruin his life."

Rage and bitterness pound through my mind. Shrugging out of Drake's hold, I march up to Paul's mother. The cameras, the reporter, have disappeared and my focus is solely on this evil wench who spawned such a perverted degenerate who is bad-mouthing me, spewing lies and hatred.

"Excuse me?! What did you just say?" I whisper in a fury.

"Babe," Drake says, drawing me back to his side. "Let us handle this."

Paul's mother turns and takes me in. She eyes Drake, Asher, and Spencer. Obviously not too bright, she continues to spew her vitriol.

"Here she is now, Isabella Anderson. Look at her, surrounded by three thugs. Everyone knows those Camelot boys are trouble. They're trying to protect themselves because they're under investigation by my son. As Assistant DA, Paul Edwards, my son and the police have been trying to bring down their prostitution ring for years," she huffs haughtily.

The gall of this woman steals my breath. How *dare* she speak of my friends, my family, this way? I'm about to interrupt her, but she continues.

"My Paul tried to warn her last night because he cares about her. She was at one of their houses in the wee hours of the morning, probably living out her sexual perversion. He was worried that they would force Isabella into prostitution. It's only a matter of time before their racket is brought down and they're all behind bars where they belong. She's trying to destroy my son's life, so she can continue with her disgusting ways."

Leaning forward, against Drake's hold, "I beg your pardon?" I shout. "How dare you! Don't you say anything bad about the Camelot Brothers. They help people, keep them safe. Never mind all the people they employ through their various companies, *none of which* is a prostitution ring. I will not stand here and let you tarnish their good name. I've known these men all my

life. They are good men who I would entrust with
my life.

"As for the perverted one, why would a judge so
quickly issue warrants against your *precious* son? Should I
inform you of how sick and twisted your son truly is? He
was never faithful during our very short, *three*-month
relationship. I broke up with him three months ago when
I walked in on him cheating on me.

"You both knew this because you both cornered me
one night when I was out with friends two-and-a-half
months ago, *begging* me to take him back. After I
caught him with my *best friend.* Open relationship?
You've lost your mind. I never let him touch me more
than a kiss. I had to defend myself a few times when
he got too aggressive. Do you understand that? Don't
even get me started on the lies you two have spouted to
my face.

"Here's the problem: I have evidence, facts and truth
to back up my words. What do you have? I have a paper
trail a mile-high showing how sadistic and vulgar your
son is. The police have other witnesses besides me. Your
son is a vile, repugnant excuse of a human being. He
planted cameras all over my home, violating not just me,
but my friends, without our knowledge or consent. Not
only is that sick and demented, but it's also illegal. Your
Assistant DA son is about to be *former* Assistant DA
Pervert Edwards.

"You and Senator Edwards might want to think
about whose side you're standing on during this trial. If
you value your political career, you might just want to
leave this alone. You should get in your car and drive

away right now. Your son is going down, and if you're not careful, your political career will go down with his."

Mrs. Edwards' spine snaps straight after my long tirade, and she shoots me a look full of malice.

"You little whore," she grates out between clenched teeth. "You're nothing but a cheap piece of trash, just like your father. You're not good enough for my son. You're just a gold digger who was after his money and lavish gifts. You must have learned from your father. He was a whore who had three women on the side. He was a disgusting sexual deviant who had children with women who were not his wife, and your mother looked the other way. It looks like the apple doesn't fall far from the tree, you slut."

Out of the corner of my eye, I spot Spencer and Asher grabbing Drake to hold him back. They chose the wrong person because her crude remarks were my last straw. Vibrating with outrage, I step into her space.

"You evil witch! I returned every minuscule thing your son ever gave me the night I broke up with him. The police have a receipt that he signed listing every item, along with the pictures. I don't need his money.

"How crass of you to bring up my *deceased* father! A man who isn't here to defend himself? That's just disgraceful. But, since you brought up sexual deviance, let's talk about that. Where did your son learn his sexual perversion? Is it you, Mrs. Edwards? Or you, Senator? Which one of you likes to peep on people in the privacy of their own home? Which one of you is the voyeur?

By all means, if you insist the sins of the father befall the child, well, lady, then one of you two is a sick deviant, too. I just might need to inform your voters about that. What do you think?"

Finished with my ranting, I turn, shocked to find several cameras aimed at our huddle, as well as a microphone boom. Holy crap-a-doodle. Every second of our exchange is going to be on the six o'clock news.

Pain lances through my scalp as Mrs. Edwards grabs my French twist, pulling me back. Reaching up, I try to capture her wrist to keep her from pulling out my hair, but she jerks my head side to the side.

Trying to weaken her hold, I throw my hurt foot back, hoping to catch her with the massive boot. My foot makes contact with her shin, but it only raises her fury. Swearing worse than Jackson, she jerks my head even harder.

Twisting in her hold, I turn to face my attacker. I reach up trying to grab her hands, but she's taller than me. Grabbing her wrist is easier now, so I hold it to try to control her. Beyond furious, I claw at her arm causing her to yelp. Bugger, this has turned into an all-out cat fight.

Blood rushes through my ears, but I faintly hear officers yelling at the reporter and camera crew to back up. Drake's hand wraps around mine on Mrs. Edwards' wrist, his fingers trying to pry hers from my hair.

"Valerie, darling, stop this nonsense now! We need to leave!" Senator Edwards yells at his wife. It doesn't affect her.

This nasty, vile woman is still swearing, calling me all manner of vulgar names. Now I know where her son got such a colorful vocabulary. Drake is bracing me on one side, trying to minimize the damage Mrs. Edwards can inflict. I feel someone on my other side, but I don't take my eyes off Mrs. Edwards' crazed expression.

Out of nowhere, she reaches up and backhands me. My head snaps to the side as I feel more hair ripped from their roots. Agony sparks across my face, filling my eyes with tears. Finding a new avenue, she scratches at my face, trying to draw blood.

Oh, that is the last straw. I didn't grow up with twelve rough and tumble guys and not learn how to defend myself. Time to put this nasty woman in her place.

Releasing her wrist, I capture her free hand and hold it tight. Shock lights in her eyes as she sees my change from defense to offense. I pull my arm back and let fly. A satisfying crunch resounds as my fist connects with her nose, causing her to release my hair as she covers her face.

"You bitch!" she screams behind her hands. "I'm pressing charges! You're going to jail for this! You broke my nose, you cunt!"

Oh man, I think, shaking out my hand, that stings. God, I hope I didn't break it. That's just what I need, her trying to file charges. Then it hits me.

"Oh, no you don't, you evil wench. Just in case you forgot, this whole thing was caught on camera. There's video proof that you attacked me first! If you ever say another bad word about me or mine, including the Brothers of Camelot, be prepared for the consequences. Do you understand, you pathetic sack of sludge and sewage?"

Drake grabs my hips and spins me away from Mrs.

Edwards. He throws me over his shoulder, *squee!* and marches toward the parking lot. Holy macaroons, I can't believe I just got into a knock-down, drag-out catfight on the steps of the police station.

"I want that slut arrested for assault!" Mrs. Edwards screams. "She attacked me, kicked me and broke my nose."

Grabbing a handful of Drake's muscular backside, I push myself up to see officers trying to usher Senator and Mrs. Edwards into the station. No one's paying us any mind as we make our departure. Seeing the cameraman packing his gear, I need to make sure it was caught on tape.

"Hey, camera dude! Did you get her attacking me on film?"

"Best thing I've seen all year," he replies with a thumbs-up. "Got the whole thing on tape, and the station aired it all live."

A smile breaks out on my face, and I yell to the officers.

"I want to press charges on her for assault! She started it, and the camera guy has the whole thing on tape! You can shove that up your broken nose, Mrs. Edwards!"

"All right, you little badass," Drake says as he swats my bum. "You need to hush, woman."

"Why are you hitting me? She started it! You were right there." I reach down and swat the round globe of his bum. The magnificent view from my position hits me, and I sigh.

Drake ignores me, laughing with Asher as they

continue to the car. Spencer must have beaten us there because the door is already open.

"Get that little hellion in the car. We've had enough press for one day. Let's get out of here before both of those wildcats are locked in a cell facing assault charges."

Drake playfully tosses me into the car, and I slide over to my side. Asher gets in the front, and they slam the doors, laughing. Spencer starts the car and tries to navigate the sea of photographers that showed up somewhere in the middle of my cat fight.

"Isabella, shit!" Asher says, turning to me. His eyes are alight with humor. "Did you forget about the cameras? Your entire tirade and that awesome cat fight are gonna be all over the news. And not just the local news, that shit's going national."

I take a deep breath and let out a sigh, leaning my head back. "She started it."

"That was the funniest thing I've seen in a long time," my brother's trying not to laugh. "That bitch was cursing left and right, but you didn't swear once. Almost everything she said will be bleeped out, but your words will ring loud and clear."

Drake's eyes crinkle at the corners, but he's holding back his mirth. Even Mr. Always Serious Spencer is chuckling. Asher, seeing his friend's faces, loses it and busts up.

"You're right, she's going to look like a vile hag. Come on, guys, what was I supposed to do? She ticked me off, pushed all my buttons saying nasty things about you guys and my father. I have an explosive temper, you all know that."

"I just hope for your sake," Spencer says, looking in the rearview mirror, "that none of your daycare students caught your catfight on the steps of a police station on the news. Violence is not the answer," he tisks on a laugh.

Oh no! What kind of example am I setting for my kids? Damage control, I need to do damage control. Pulling my iPad out of my bag, I turn it on and log into my work email. How do I explain this to the parents? I can only hope I don't lose clients over this. No parent would want their kids being taken care of by someone who gets in fights in front of a police station.

"Babe, what are you doing?" Drake asks, his voice serious.

"I'm drafting an apology to the parents," I reply, not looking up from the screen. "No parent will want their kid to see their favorite preschool teacher on the six o'clock news in a catfight. I'm hoping to warn them about it and to tell them how horribly embarrassed I am about my behavior and my lack of control."

Drake smiles and slings his arm around me. "Bella, when they see that, they'll see just how in control you were. That bitch said nasty things, called you some fucked up names and not once did you swear. And besides, you didn't start the fight. She did. You just ended it. I think it'll be okay."

He leans over and kisses the top of my head. I ignore him, finishing my letter to the parents. Deep down, I'm praying Drake is right. Once I finish, I send a quick note to my staff to give them a heads up that there may be a lot of calls tonight and Sunday. I fear what awaits me Monday morning.

Gosh, what in the world has gotten into me? A week ago, I had no clue I'd be back within the fold of the Brothers of Camelot and in Drake's arms. This is all happening so fast, my world is spinning out of control. But thank God I have the guys. Lord knows where I'd be when it comes to Paul, that demented pervert.

But what happens now? What happens next with Drake? He said he's looking forward to tonight. What does that mean? Oh man, oh man. My mind is all over the place.

CHAPTER NINETEEN

FITZ: BELLA LAYS DOWN THE GROUND RULES

As we pull into my driveway, Bella notices the moving trucks full of her furniture and spots the guys carrying boxes into the house. It's comical the way her head swivels from her stuff to me and back again.

"What? How did you do that? When? Did you text them when I wasn't looking?" she inquires, looking adorably confused.

Spencer stops the car and looks in the rear-view mirror at me. "We'll give you two some privacy. It's going to be okay Isabella, I swear. But you need to stay with Drake or Hawkins. It isn't safe anywhere else." With a small smile and wink at Bella, both Clausen and Spencer exit the car.

"No, babe. When you broke down in my arms, I knew I had to bring you home. To *our* home, where you belong. You'll be safer here with me.

"Brit, Brenda, and my mom are unpacking your

things in my room unless you'd rather be somewhere else. It's your call, babe."

"That's sweet of you Dray… but I can't live with you, honey. Not right now. This is all happening too fast," she says, her voice soft with concern.

She rests her hand on my leg and gives it a squeeze, probably hoping to reassure me. But seriously, fuck that. Where the fuck is she going to go? She's not going to some friend's house, that's for damn sure.

Seeing me about to blow, she continues. "I'll stay here tonight, but tomorrow I should probably stay with Nicholas for a while. I'll pack a few things and stay with him. You understand, don't you? I'm just not ready to live with you just yet."

Deafening silence reigns in the car. I'm not at all pleased by her words. I kind of understand… she's nervous. This *is* happening fast, she's only been back in my life for a little over twenty-four hours. But dammit, this feels so right. I need her by my side.

Looking out the window, I take a deep breath, trying to keep control. "Bella, babe, I want you with me. I know you're scared, but I need to know you're safe. The only way I can do that is if you're here, with me. Look, you can take my bedroom. There are five other rooms I can sleep in if this is too fast for you."

Turning to face her, I grab her hand. "I'll slow things down if that's what has you running from me. But babe, I need you here with me."

She lifts her free hand to my face and strokes my cheek with her thumb. She stares into my eyes for a few heart-stopping moments.

"Dray, honey, I want to be with you just as much as you want me to, but I just can't go from not seeing you for over eight years to living with you. When was the last time you... you... um, had sex with some nameless girl?"

"Isabella, what the fuck?" I growl. Where is she going with this? "That has nothing to do with us. You are it for me, I only want to be with you. I never want to touch another woman again. You're the only person I want to make love to, but I will wait for you. I'm not in high school anymore, I don't need some random fuck. All I need is you. You have to believe me."

"What's with the *Isabella* nonsense? You haven't called me that, *ever.* Never mind that, you're avoiding the question. When was the last time you had sex with someone?"

Fuck, she's serious. She wants me to answer. I run my fingers through my hair, sighing.

"Fuck, Bella. Fine. It was just over a week ago. But I decided after that I was done with random hook-ups. It wasn't worth my time or energy, it was getting complicated, it didn't feel right anymore. I swear. Please believe me."

She leans over and tries to give me a quick peck. I don't let her pull back, grasping the back of her head. I pour my love into the kiss, licking the crease of her lips, requesting access. Sighing, she lets me in.

Her response ignites my heart. I lean into her, pushing her back against the door. Sliding my lips from her luscious mouth, to that spot behind her ear, the one that makes her shiver.

"Dray... God... wait a second," she pants. In defeat,

I rest my head on her neck and breathe her in. Damn, she's always smelled amazing.

"Honey, yes, you're right. Neither of us is the same as we were in high school. But, please, listen to me. If you want this to work, I need some time and space. I need to know I can trust you. You have the power to destroy me, which you very nearly did when you were humping everything with a pulse in high school. When you hooked up with my friends, I almost broke. I *need* to know I can trust you. If you cheat on me, it's not only the end of us, but it will completely break me."

Fuck, I'm willing to do anything for this woman. God, I should have called her instead of being such a pussy. She's mine, I would never do anything to hurt her. It rips my heart that I caused her such anguish. Son of a bitch, I was such an asshole to her in high school. Those days are done and over, though. How do I get her to believe me?

"That means no hookups, zero sex, with anyone. You need to handle Henry yourself. But, umm, maybe sometimes, umm, *we* can handle him, like we did this morning." A gorgeous blush spreads across her cheeks.

"But I want to date you too. I want you to pick me up and take me out on a real date, and drop me back off at the front door and kiss me good night."

What in the actual fuck? She's moving us back to fucking square one?

"You're serious? You don't trust me? Come on Bella, I'm not a horny teenager anymore. I can control this shit. You genuinely want to date? You want me to pull out my old lettermen's jacket for you? I'm sure Mom has it somewhere. Damn, though. Parking would be fun with you, making out in the car." My sarcasm is biting, but seriously, what the fuck?

"Drake, don't do that. That's not what I mean. We need to learn about each other again. It's been eight flipping years. I can't go from not having you in my life to living with you within twenty-four hours! And I don't mean that we can't make out a little, but I would like to date you, go to the movies, have fun, dine out and more. Work with me here."

Her voice is strong, clear. She slapped down my attitude, reminding me of why I fell in love with her when I was too stupid to realize what she was offering me. She doesn't put up with my shit.

Sitting up, I scrub my face with my hands. I'm seriously struggling with this, wanting to control her and this fucked up situation. Considering what she's going through, I'm right. I will not give in to her demands completely. Glancing out the window, my Brothers are still unloading Bella's things. Thank God for the window tinting, those assholes are worse than chicks always up in my business.

Bella grabs my attention, whispering "Look, since you've all determined I can't live by myself or even with my friends, that means I'll have to move in with Nicholas. Can you please try to understand why this is important to me? I need to know I can trust you when we aren't together under the same roof. How about I stay with Nicholas, umm, Hawkins," she rolls her eyes, "during the week, and I'll stay some weekends with you? You can still see me every day if you come over. But at night, you go home. By yourself. I can't just move in with you right way. Please give this time to me."

She leans in to me, resting her hand on my chest. Her kiss is tentative like she's afraid. I can't have that. Wrapping my arms around her, I drag her against me and slowly make love to her mouth.

It sucks, but it finally dawns on me that I have to accept this. I was a dick in high school and need to regain her trust, to prove to her that she is it for me. It hurts like hell that she doesn't trust me, but I only have myself to blame.

With a final sweet kiss, she pulls away and rests her head on my chest. I take a deep breath and continue to run my fingers through her hair.

"I really don't like this babe, but I do understand. I'll wait until you're ready for more. Because, babe, listen to me, hear me. You. Are. It. For. Me. I never want to touch another woman again. Only you. And thank you for at least taking the next best option. You're right, your friends' places aren't safe enough. If you're not in our home, then you need to be at Hawkins'. But I'm telling you now if he makes one fucking move on you, I'll kick his ass. Straight up."

"Really, you're going there?" she asks with a giggle. "Nicholas and I are just friends. He never did anything inappropriate growing up. You need to quit that line of thinking right now." She gives me a little shove. Her face turns serious, and I know I'm in trouble.

"Drake, after I left, umm… How long did it take for you to move on? I ask because this is relevant. Do you know how long it took me to get close to someone enough to kiss them? It took me over two years because I was still hurting from leaving you. How long did it take you to find some bimbo to soothe *your* hurts? I don't want anyone but you, Drake."

"Okay, okay point taken," I return, a dumb ass smile on my face. "I'll figure out some way to deal with my jealousy. Sometimes it surprises the shit out of me, the rage I feel about you choosing Hawkins over me. But, I want to talk with you before bed every night and I want to hear your soft snores like you're still in my bed. Okay?"

"First," she swats at me, "I do *not* snore. And if I did, it's rude of you to mention it. But I like that idea." Her smile turns mischievous. "Besides, I've never had phone sex. Can we do that?"

"Holy Christ, woman," I rub my hand over Henry, shifting him to relieve the pressure I'm feeling. "Fuck yeah, we can have phone sex."

My voice is rough and gravelly as I continue. "I can tell you all the things I want to do to you while you play with yourself. Hearing your soft sighs and sweet moans will be enough to make me come. I look forward to the day you're in our home for good."

I give her a quick kiss. Impishness lights her eyes, but nothing can prepare me for the next words out of her mouth.

"Umm, about that… instead of telling me what *you* want to do to me, would you tell me what you want *me* to do to myself? You're better at making me fall apart than I've ever been."

"Fuck," I groan, throwing my head back. "Shit yeah,

babe. I'll gladly tell you how to touch yourself. You're here with me tonight though, right? I'm gonna need a little help with Henry."

"Yes, Dray, I'm here with you tonight. But first, I need to burn every piece of underthings I have. Then I'll go get new cute bra and panty sets for your eyes only. I'll go to Nicholas's Monday after work. We'll check with him to make sure it's okay." She giggles lightly. "I wouldn't want to be a demanding, controlling person, like someone I know…" She giggles harder.

"Babe, you can control me all you want. But no one else, dammit. Only me. But yeah, we'll call him in a bit and let him know. I need to lay down some ground rules for him too."

"We need to ask, Drake, not tell. You don't need to lay out any freaking rules, either. That's trust, honey," she explains, with a cute smile.

"Fuck, it's not you I don't trust. It's fuckin' Hawkins." Bella cocks an eyebrow. "Fine, I trust you. But I'm still gonna talk to him about your safety."

I feel like a ten-year-old, wanting to throw a tantrum because I can't have my favorite toy. I need to suck it up and earn her trust.

"Now that that's all settled, I have some things to do… or are we going to sit here all night? I was hoping to sleep in your bed, but if you'd rather stay here, that's fine. You make a great pillow." She leans back and crosses her arms, trying not to laugh.

"Alright, Bella, let's go have a panty roast." I open the door but turn back quickly. "I see what you're trying to do, though."

"Hey, Stevens!" I shout, helping Bella from the car. "Go start a fire in the fire pit. Make it a big one. We're having a panty roast!"

The guys freeze and all heads whip towards Bella. She slams her hands on her hips, full of indignation.

"Don't look at me like that! If you think I'm wearing those slimy things again, knowing that sick whack-a-doodle saw me in them, then you're all insane!

"Now, I'm going to steal something of Drake's to wear then I'm bringing down all my underthings to torch. You guys just keep doing what you're doing. I'll be back soon. Don't break anything!"

She turns back to me, "Thank you for understanding that I need time. You mean the world to me, and I want this to work."

She leans up on her toes, wrapping her hand around my neck as I bend down to meet her kiss. When she pulls back, I flash her a smile and a wink.

"Hmm, I wonder if I should wear a pair of your boxers, or just go commando?" She turns around and struts into the house as I check out her luscious ass. Goddamn, it's a work of art.

She pauses and looks over her shoulder at me. "Tell Brenden this freaking boot is a life saver! I don't even feel any pain while wearing it."

Then it hits me. Fuck, she's thinking of going commando! I rearrange Henry at that thought.

Bella notices the guys still haven't moved, as she pauses by the door. I think they're all still in shock at her mention of a panty roast. Bella's sass comes out, making me even harder.

"Hop to, guys. I need all my stuff inside so that I can get everything together. You guys act like you've never been to a panty roast! Sheesh!" Bella stomps into the house, her head held high.

Stevens shouts, "Power to the panty roast!"

"Fuck yeah, panty roast!" Jackson chimes in.

"Hey, can we roast marshmallows too?" Clay asks.

"Can I get some to take home before she burns them all?" Carpenter requests.

"Listen up, you fucker. Stop thinking about my woman's panties! It all burns tonight. I will kick your ass if I have to, but this is what Bella does, she burns shit when she's done."

The next few weeks are gonna be hell on my self-control. This isn't gonna be easy. But if it's the last damn thing I do, I will prove to her that she can trust me.

CHAPTER TWENTY

FITZ: TEASING CAN GO BOTH WAYS

*B*y the time we finished Bella's panty roast last night, her girlie shop was closed. Honestly, I was relieved. It allowed me to get her in my bed all the more quickly. I promised her I'd take her shopping in the morning, then hauled my girl away from the fire.

She was so fucking responsive yesterday morning, so goddamn eager with everything I did to her that I was in a bit of a rush for a repeat. I was pretty creative last night, trying to push away the ugliness of her day. I wanted her to have a good night's sleep after a crazy twenty-four hours.

Waking up for the second morning with Bella in my arms is a test of patience. Henry's rock fuckin' hard, which comes as no surprise. It's as if I didn't come at all last night. Bella's draped over me, much like yesterday morning. Fuck, I want to wake up like this every day for the rest of my life.

Bella's dressed only in my shirt. After making her

come twice last night, I refused to give her a pair of my boxers to wear. I wanted to feel her pussy sliding along my leg as she slept. Besides, I've got plans for her this morning.

Slipping my hand under her shirt, I run my hand over her sweet ass and give it a squeeze. She moans in her sleep, causing my cock to jerk. Bella's on her side, her leg hitched and entwined with mine. I stretch my arm and slide my hand down further past her ass and between her legs. Damn, she's already wet.

Her breath catches as I slide my fingers through her wet folds. With my fingers covered in her wetness, I slip my middle finger into her tight canal while searching for her clit with my index finger. Bella's back arches and her core clenches, drawing my finger in deeper.

"Dray," she whispers as her eyes flutter open.

"Good morning, babe."

"Oh... oh God... that's not enough," Bella cries out.

"Sit up, babe," I command, removing my hand from between her legs. "I want you comfortable for this."

Bella complies, and I attack the buttons on my shirt she's wearing. Once I've got the shirt hanging open, I lay her on her back and push the sides of the shirt open, exposing her to my eyes. Henry's pissed, demanding access to the hottest pussy I've ever felt. Fuck him though. This is about Bella's pleasure, not mine.

I kneel between her legs, spreading them wide. Parting her strawberry blonde curls, I find her clit with my thumb as I slide my index finger into her pussy. I slowly thrust my finger in and out of her. Her head falls back into the pillows.

With my free hand, I cup her breast, feeling its fullness. Pulling back, I lick my fingers, moistening them. Returning to her breast, I capture her nipple with my fingertips. I pluck and play and twist, watching it pucker and harden under my hot gaze.

Bella's magnificent. Her cream skin is flushed and her breasts heave with her every breath as her hands clench the sheets, searching for an anchor. I don't want her anchored, though. I want her to soar to the heavens.

Leaning forward, my tongue travels from her belly button to between her breasts, and finally to her neck. I slide my tongue along her jaw, searching for her ear.

"Are you ready to come for me?" I whisper into her ear.

"Uhh," she moans in response.

"You're fucking gorgeous, all spread out for me to worship."

"Dray... Oh God..."

I increase the speed of my finger, pumping a little faster, watching her body for cues and listen to her breathing. Her hand releases the sheet as she grabs my hair, her nails scraping my scalp. So, fucking hot, damn.

"Babe, are you ready to fly?"

"Please, Dray, oh God!"

"What do you need, Bella?" I ask, licking her earlobe.

"Oh," she moans. "Faster, please..."

Goddamn, I didn't expect her breathy request to turn me on that much. Holy shit. I follow her direction, increasing the pace, thrusting faster and deeper. Rubbing back and forth over her clit with my thumb, a new wave of wetness greets my hand. Her core clenches, telling me she's fuckin' close.

Sinking my finger deep, I curl it into a 'come here' motion, searching for her G-spot. Bella sucks in a breath and freezes. *Oh yeah, that's it.* My finger explores her wall, memorizing what feels good to her. I tap a rhythm, listening to her quick gasps. Almost there…

With a final flick of my thumb, she screams as she reaches the stars in ecstasy. I lift my head, watching her. Bella's face is exquisite, eyes closed, cheeks flushed and red. I slow my thrusts, bringing my girl back down to earth. Shit, I'll never forget the sight of her breaking apart for me.

Slowly her eyes flutter open, taking my cue to remove my hand from between her legs so she can witness how I lift my fingers to my mouth, ready to devour the taste of her. It's fucking amazing, and Henry agrees too. I cannot wait to feast on her, trace her folds with my tongue.

Bella stretches, her eyes glazed. Kissing her passionately, I gather her in my arms and lift her from the bed into my lap. On a breathy sigh, she breaks the kiss and snuggles into my neck. Her breaths whisper across my neck, causing shivers to course across my skin. Henry, the demanding prick jerks at the nearness of Bella's pussy.

"Oh, gosh, Dray," Bella says, feeling Henry's reaction to her. "What about you?"

"Nope, babe. This was all for you. Now," I say swatting her ass, "time to get ready. I'm gonna hit the shower in my office, then I'm taking you shopping for sexy shit."

"But, Dray…"

My response is to smack her ass harder as I push her back into the bed. If I don't get some space, I'm probably going to do something I regret, like sink my cock into her.

"Drake, what's with the smacking of my rear?" she asks, rubbing her left cheek.

"Oh, woman. I adore your ass. One day, I'm going to turn it pink and watch you fly from my hand on your ass."

Bella's mouth falls open, and I reach out and close it for her.

"You don't think I can make you come like that? I guess we could reschedule our day and I could show you."

"Uhh, no. No, that's okay. I just don't see how that could happen. Let's save that for another day, though. I don't want too many firsts all at once. I want to cherish the ones you've already given me."

"Alright, go get ready. I'll take Mojo out, then hit the shower," I say as I pull on some shorts.

She climbs from the bed, pulling my shirt closed around her. As she passes me, I smack her ass a third time. Bella jumps and squeals.

"Owie!" she cries. "That stings! You're gonna pay for that Drake. Just you wait." She slams the door to the bathroom in a huff.

"Come on Mojo, time for breakfast, potty and a visit with Uncle Stevens. Mommy needs some sexy as hell underthings, which I'm hoping she'll model for me." Mojo responds with a grunt.

Leaving the room with the beast, I wonder just how Bella's going to get me back. *This should be fun*, I chuckle.

Isabella

WHY IN THE world Drake insisted on taking the Lincoln Navigator is beyond me. I know I need to replenish my underthings, but I'd much rather have taken the slick looking cream car, but Drake said there wouldn't be enough room for our, yes, *our*, purchases.

I can't wait to show him my favorite shop, Nancy's Naughty Underthings. I discovered this place a few months after my return from New York. As a 32DD, it's hard to find bras that not only fit but look pretty too. The best part is that they aren't just a bra shop. They also have a beautiful assortment of lingerie.

Hoping Drake isn't embarrassed to be seen in a 'girlie' shop, I formulate a little plan to shock him. As soon as Drake parked the car, I hop out, feeling excitement course through me.

"Let's go, come on," I squeal.

"Hold your britches, babe. I wouldn't miss this for the world."

Gah, he's so swoony when he says things like that. But little does he know, I don't have any britches under my short skirt. I *cannot* wait to tease him.

After a bit of browsing, I've collected a little pile of necessities.

"Hey, babe," Drake calls, "I really like this one." He holds up a little red silk spaghetti strap negligée.

"Hold on to it. I can try it on, so you can tell me if I should get it."

Drake swallows hard, and I stifle a giggle.

"No need for that. I already know I'll like it." Drake replies.

"If you think so, just add it to my pile on the counter then," I tell him, trying to keep the amusement out of my voice.

I check out the store, making sure no one can see me. There's two older ladies shopping, but they're on the other side of the store near the practical section. When Drake turns towards me, I slowly bend at the waist to pick up the panties I accidentally-on-purpose dropped seconds ago. My skirt rides up, exposing the lower half of my naked behind.

"Fuck," Drake growls as I feel his heat hit my legs. Standing up, I twirl the panties on my finger.

"What do you think about these, honey?" I ask, trying to sound innocent. "There's a gorgeous bra they have that would match."

"Umm, yeah, babe. Those are hot." He takes them from my hand and holds them in front of me, his chest pressing against my back. He turns them, revealing the string back. Drake's hips jerk as he presses his erection against my behind. Good Lord, this might backfire on me.

"I'd love to toy with this string," he growls in my ear. *Oh boy.*

Trying to recover, I grab a bra in front of me and

turn to face him, holding it to my chest. This one's a satin bralette with black lace covering the teal half cups, which would leave my nipples exposed.

"What about this one?" I ask, trying to show him how much would be exposed in this tiny bra. Because my nipples are hard from his teasing, I know he can tell just what the purpose of this bra is.

"Yeah, you're fuckin' getting that one, and a matching thong. Shit, I cannot wait to see your creamy breasts next to that color. Babe, I'm real glad you like this shit. Otherwise, I'd be filling your closet by myself."

He grabs me, pulling me close. Drake's hand slides from my hip to my thigh. His warm hand glides up my leg and under my skirt. He grips my bum, then his questing fingers roam my backside.

"Fuck, woman. Tell me you're wearing underwear."

"Honey, you watched me burn every pair of panties I owned last night. Where would I have gotten underwear?" I ask, batting my lashes at him.

"Are you doing this on purpose to tease me?" Drake's voice is rough. Oh man, that is so freaking hot.

"Who, me?" I ask, smiling innocently. "It's a matter of practicality, Drake. I couldn't fit a pair of your boxers under this skirt, it would look weird."

"I think you're doing this on purpose, trying to test me and make Henry uncomfortable," he whispers in my ear, then he gives my neck a quick nibble. Shivers wrack my body. Yup, I'm in trouble with this man.

Turning away from him, I nab a black, crotchless catsuit. A giggle peals from me as Drake mumbles and swears under his breath behind me. Grabbing me from behind, he grinds his massive erection along the crease of my rear. Lordy, he has no idea how much I crave him.

"You're playing with fire, babe. Don't you feel how hard I am?" Drake's voice is low and gruff in my ear. His tongue flicks my earlobe before he sucks on it. My core clenches as I rub my legs together.

Trying to regain control, I reach behind him and smack the globe of his bum.

"Drake, behave yourself. We're in public," I joke.

"Babe, you started this, showing me nighties and thongs and teasing me with bras that leave your nipples exposed." His voice lowers, as he says, "And by not wearing panties." Shivers slide through my body as he sucks and nibbles on my ear again.

"Well, how have you been, Isabella?" Nancy, the wonderful woman who owns this shop asks, shocking me back into reality. My cheeks heat with embarrassment.

"Oh, I'm great, Nancy! This Neanderthal who doesn't know how to behave in public is Drake." They both chuckle at my smart remark.

"That's great. Nice to meet you, Drake. I see you found all the matching sets in your size. A little shopping spree for your new man? Is there anything else you might need?" Nancy starts to ring up my selections.

"No thanks, I think I'm set for a while," I say, looking down. I've been hoping that Drake is mine, but we haven't fully defined our relationship yet. I hope he's not mad at her presumption.

"Well, we did add a new line since your last visit. We now carry Love Lotion, massage oils, and a few vibrators in various types and sizes."

"Oh, uhh," I stammer, "that's okay, Nancy. But thanks for telling me." My face is hot with the blush spreading across my cheeks. Drake's massive chest rumbles against my back as he chuckles low.

"Oh, I disagree, babe. I'd *love* to take a look at those toys. I might like to purchase something."

"What?!" I squeal. "Drake!" I can't believe what he just said. I'm mortified. Oh my God. Does he really want to look at toys?

"Relax, babe. We're just a couple of adults, checking out some toys. There might be some fun stuff here." He wiggles his eyebrows and shoots me a wink.

"Oh, they're right over here, in this case. Let's go have a look see," Nancy says casually.

Drake grabs my hand and drags me over. I keep my eyes on the carpet wondering how in the world my teasing backfired this badly. Nancy shows Drake the cabinet, pointing out various items while my embarrassment grows by the second.

"Oh, I like that one," Drake says, causing me to snap my head up. *What?* I find Drake pointing at something as Nancy pulls it from the cabinet.

She places a pink box on the counter. "Oh, this finger vibrator is fun. It's waterproof so that you can take it in the bath. The fingertip is ribbed, and the button is on the back of your finger."

Oh, God. I just want to crawl into a hole.

"Isabella, you lucky bitch!" I recognize the voice of my realtor, Dee Waters. "You never told me you upgraded! I'm so glad you got rid of that asshat Paul and traded him in for this Greek god!"

Heavens to Betsy, can this get any more embarrassing? Drake turns his head, greeting the newest arrival to my embarrassment party.

"Hi Dee," I mumble. "This is my friend, Drake."

"Boyfriend," Drake interjects, extending his hand. "Nice to meet you." *Oh, my God, he said boyfriend!*

"Oh, girl," Dee sighs. "I cannot wait for our meeting tomorrow. I know we're supposed to talk about selling your house, but I want *all* the details about this hottie."

"Oh, I guess," I mumble again, this time praying she's oblivious of Nancy holding a little lavender vibrator in her hand.

"Just so you know, Dee, the house is already empty." Drake pulls a card from his wallet and hands it to her. "If you call Samuel Carpenter at Camelot Construction, you can advise him of what colors to paint the walls for the best return. They're planning to start tomorrow morning, but they can start with the priming if you have a color aside from white in mind." *What is happening right now?*

"Umm Drake, why are the guys going to paint my house? Why wasn't I informed of this?" I ask indignantly.

"Babe, you made it very clear you couldn't stay in your house ever again. It's best to sell it, and my place is bigger anyway. Carpenter said he'd take care of making sure it's ready to sell when I gave him the heads up."

Drake shrugs, throwing an arm around my shoulders. He kisses me quickly and tucks me to his side. I'm flabbergasted at how quickly Drake's moved, taking care of the little things so I don't have to worry. Well, fiddlesticks. I keep my mouth shut because I'd look like a witch with a capital B if I said anything.

"Nancy! My favorite woman in the whole wide world!" Dee cries, stepping up to the cabinet. "I love that rotating rabbit you sold me. God, it hits my g-spot perfectly. But, do you have any thrusting vibrators? I need something that has some oomph behind it. You got anything for me?"

My mouth falls open. *Have I traveled to another dimension?* I cannot believe she just said that and in front of Drake. Dee turns back to me and winks.

"Girl, I have that finger vibrator in my purse at all times. Never know when you'll need it." Her eyes trail over Drake at my side. "I don't know why you'd need it with a hunk like that, but more power to you."

My mouth gapes, reminiscent of a fish out of water. *Did she honest to God just say that?* Drake's chuckle in my ear confirms that my hearing is in proper working order.

"I like your friend," he whispers in my ear.

"I've got this awesome thruster," Nancy says, handing a big box to Dee. "Let me finish up with Isabella and Drake, and I'll be right back to answer any questions." Dee grabs it with excitement, lifting the flap cover to reveal a dark purple vibrator. *Holy cow, that looks intense.*

God, please, I pray, *I know sinkholes aren't common in California, but, please… please open one up and swallow me whole right now.*

Dee, noting my flame-colored face, grabs my arm. "Oh, honey. There's no need to be embarrassed. It's fantastic that your man is helping you take care of your needs when he can't. I only wish I could find a man who wasn't jealous of all of my toys."

My only response is a giggle. I'm at a loss for words. Drake just chuckles and gives me a squeeze. I dig my elbow into his ribs.

"This was Drake's idea. I only came for panties and bras." I announce, trying to throw Drake under the bus.

"Dayum, girlie! That's even better. A man who will help you play. You're so effin' lucky!" She returns her attention to the box, reading the description.

"Is there anything else I can help you with?" Nancy questions.

"Erm, that's, uh, that's okay. I think we're, uh, set for now," I stammer, wanting to run from the store.

"Drake, are you sure? I've got all sorts of lubes; heated, flavored, even some that can numb, or the lotions or massage oils."

"Actually," Drake chuckles, "could you grab a gentle, water-based lube? Then we're set. Thanks."

"Hey, Isabella," Dee calls. "If Drake's a traveler and leaves you on your own, you might want to look at the rabbit I have. It's great, works that g-spot real good."

A mortified giggle breaks free. *How is this happening?* I cannot believe I'm discussing sex toys with my Realtor while standing next to my boyfriend... boyfriend, *squeal!*

"Thanks, Dee," Drake replies before I can find my voice. "But I'm not a traveler. I know right where Bella's buttons are and love watching her soar. But I'll keep the rabbit in mind for later. It was great meeting you. I'm sure we'll see each other again soon."

"Geez'um Drake," I cry, punching his shoulder.

Drake just smiles as he steers us toward the checkout counter.

After paying for our things, we load the six bags into the back of the Navigator. Drake helps me into my seat, then returns to the hatch and sifts through the bags. What is he doing?

Finally, he climbs into the drivers' seat. A mischievous look spans his face, eyes crinkling at the corners. Drake buckles his seat belt and pulls out into traffic.

He places his hand on my crossed legs, pulling the top one off then gives it a squeeze.

"What are you doing, Drake? You're driving."

"That I am," he says cryptically.

Drake's hand slides up my leg, pulling them further apart. His finger finds my clit. Shock slams through me at the vibration that hits me.

"Dray—," I gasp. "What are, uh, are you doing? You, uh, need to, uh, pay attention."

"Oh, trust me, babe. I'm paying very close attention. You were a bad girl. For teasing me, going commando and flashing me in public, you need to be punished."

Oh, God, it feels so good. The vibrations against my core cause it to clench.

"I'm using your new finger vibrator to bring you to the edge. And then I'll stop. Two can play at the teasing game. You aren't allowed to come until I say so."

Holy crap-a-doodle. I'm in so much trouble.

CHAPTER TWENTY ONE

ISABELLA: THE ROSE

onday morning finds me at my desk, trying to focus on the schedule for the next two weeks. It's difficult because I'm reliving Saturday night and all the things Drake did to me Sunday. My thighs feel like I've run a marathon, and I'm a bit sore.

He's incredible and is everything I've ever dreamed of and more. I cannot believe everything we've done in the past seventy-two hours. I pinch myself just to prove I'm not dreaming. *Ouch*! Guess I pinched a little too hard.

This weekend was, by far, officially at the top of my all-time favorite memories. Just the thought of everything Drake did excites me. He has a sexual power over me, knowing all the things that will send me into the stratosphere. The way he can tease and toy with me, there were quite a few times I wanted to beg him to keep going but I held my tongue.

Every time I detonated, Drake was right there with me. It made me feel closer to him, sharing my pleasure with him. He played my body so well, making me come so many times I lost count. Lordy, I'm in trouble.

Years ago, I vowed not to sleep with someone before three months of dating. A woman has to have standards. Faithfulness is my first priority in a relationship, and I figured three months was a good amount of time to get to know someone. In five years, no one had ever made it to that mark. Every single one of them had cheated on me. But here I am, ready to throw my standards out the window and give myself to Drake barely three days in.

Saturday was such a stressful day but going to sleep in Drake's arms after both of us touched the stars was incredible. That alone almost helped me to put the police station out of my mind, not once but twice. I never fell asleep so quickly.

But then again, it's pretty wonderful to wake up with Drake's mouth on my breast while his fingers explore areas no man but him has ever touched before. I never realized I could reach so many climaxes, and that it would leave muscles I never knew I had sore.

When Drake walked in at a quarter to seven, I was still rushing to finish getting ready. He chuckled, told me I looked amazing, *swoon*, and grabbed me. After a too-quick kiss, he hauled me down to my van so I wouldn't be late for work. When he goes all Viking and hauls me around, I have to admit, even just to myself, I get a little flutter in my core. Lordy, he's just too hot.

My twenty-fourth birthday is exactly two months after Drake's. I hope I can make it that long because that's what I want for my birthday. I want to make love with him. Setting that as my goal will hopefully help me be strong enough to make it until then. Oh God, I hope I don't turn into a total hussy and beg him to take me before then.

I'm still chuckling to myself when Tory enters my office. Her adorable son is on her hip, thumb in his mouth.

"Hey Isabella, JayJay's being a little crab monster today. I called my mom to come get him. I think he's teething and doesn't want to leave my hip. It's pretty much a good thing because Mom's always complaining she doesn't get enough time with her little man. I'd take him home, but I need the hours. I just wanted to let you know."

Getting up, I walk around my desk and poke JayJay in his little portly belly.

"Are you giving your mama a hard time there, little man?"

Pretending to pull his hand, I declare, "I want a taste of that thumb. It looks so yummy! Will you share with me?"

JayJay giggles around his hand and shakes his head. I turn my attention to Tory.

"Sweetie, that's perfectly fine. If you need the hours, you can close tonight. I'm cooking dinner for my friends and Drake."

"Gosh, please don't tell me it's another one of the Camelot Brothers. You're so flipping lucky. If it weren't for JayJay here, I'd be calling you all sorts of names."

While we're laughing, Tory's mom comes in.

"Aren't you supposed to be working, Victoria dear? I'll take my handsome little man so you can get back to it. Come to Grandma, JayJay. Grandma will take you home and get you ice cream for that mean, owie tooth."

JayJay reaches for his Grandma, and Tory kisses his cheek. "You be a good little man, and Mommy will see you after work. Thanks again, Mom. He's been taking too much of my time this morning." Tory leaves.

Her mom turns to me, her face sincere. "Isabella, I've been wanting to thank you for all you've done for Victoria and for allowing JayJay to come to work with her. The socializing is good for him. Your program is incredible. You're a saint."

"Mrs. Cummings, it's my pleasure. Tory is invaluable to me. She works so hard, I would be lost without her. I'm glad she can put her degree to good use. JayJay's a great little dude, he's welcome anytime."

"I'm so sorry about what you're going through with Paul Edwards, hopefully soon-to-be ex Assistant DA. Did you hear the DA put him on administrative leave pending the outcome of the trial? I hope they lock him up for a long time. And what that evil woman tried to say about you? I didn't believe a word of those filthy lies spewing from her ugly mouth. I want you to know, neither my husband nor I voted for Senator Edwards. Hopefully, this will ruin his political career. He's a two-faced liar who only wants to line his pockets. He tells you one thing but votes for his corporate cronies."

"Well," I muse, "I'm just thankful the Brothers of Camelot have stepped in and helped me out. They're great guys, not at all like what Mrs. Edwards described. I can only pray that I'll never have to see Paul again."

I run my fingers through JayJay's curly blonde locks, looking into his big dark brown eyes. "See you tomorrow, little man. I hope you feel better." Planting a quick kiss on his cherubic cheek, I return my attention to Mrs. Cummings.

"Let me walk you out, Mrs. Cummings," I suggest as my phone suddenly peals.

"No, no, you've got work to do. I can handle my handsome little grandson," she replies.

Returning to my desk, I check the caller ID. I don't recognize the number, so it takes me a second to decide if I want to answer it. Thinking it might be a parent, I decide what the heck?

"Hello?"

"*Hello, Ms. Anderson. This is Detective Jerkins. I'd like to know if my partner and I can come by your office to pick up those letters and cards, as well as the timeline you told us about at Fitz's?*"

"Oh, yes. That's fine."

"*We also have a few more questions. We'll try to keep it brief.*"

"Well, if you're going to be asking questions, I'd like Spencer to be here. I'll have to check with him about his schedule."

"*Let him know we'll be there in an hour. We can wait for the questions, but we would like to get that evidence as soon as possible.*"

Detective Jerkins hangs up without saying goodbye. Well, that was rude. I thump my head on my desk. Ugh, this is going to be so much fun. I'd better warn Tory. She told me they'd followed up with her yesterday to get her statement. I'm grateful she wasn't mad at me, just super ticked at Paul. I'm hoping the cops keep her name out of the media, I don't want to lose her mom's trust.

I pop off a quick text to Spencer, asking if he wants to be here. Tory shouts from the other room, a smile in her voice.

"Have I told you recently how much I hate you?" she cries.

Looking up from my phone, I see Tory standing in the door. Holding a slender, long stem, yellow vase tied with a delicate red ribbon, she shoots me a fake glare. In the vase, my favorite flower, a solitary yellow rose, with edges of the petals tinged in red. Elation suffuses my soul.

"Oh my God," I sigh in joy. "Drake remembered. Tory, I love him so much! Do you know how many guys I've dated who I've repeatedly told *not* to give me red roses, that I'd rather get wildflowers? Red roses are just so common, there's no thought behind choosing them. But this one, the Circus rose, has been my favorite flower since I saw them for the first time with Drake ages ago. I must have gone on and on for hours about how much I loved them, how beautiful they are and how I could never find them anywhere. He'd just rolled his eyes, smiling at me. Two weeks later, I walked into my bedroom and found one lying on my pillow."

"That's adorable, Isabella," Tory sighs.

"He never admitted it was him, but who else could it

have been? Drake never gave them to me on my birthday. No, he'd just leave them for me randomly."

Taking the vase from her hands, I bring the rose to my nose and inhale deeply. The smell alone brings back so many memories.

"Thank you, Tory."

Anxious to open the card, I grab it from the little stick. Before settling back in my chair, I carefully arrange the vase right next to my monitor, so I'll see it while working. Opening the envelope, I find the sweetest words.

My Bella,

Remembering the first time you saw this rose, how you lit up, how much you love it inspired me as much as the meaning behind the colors. The Circus rose describes our journey, from friendship to a perfect romance, full of love and adoration.

You are the only one for me.

Guess who…

Smiling like a loon, I clasp the card to my chest.

"Do you know how much I hate you right now?" Tory jokes. "God, who would have thought any of those Camelot guys would have had a romantic bone in their bodies? But seriously, girl. Congratulations. After months of dealing with that whack job, I'm thrilled to see you smiling again. I'm going to get back to work while you float on cloud nine."

Tory leaves while I grab my phone to take a close-up

picture of the rose. Not only for my memory, but I also need to send it to Drake. I still can't believe he remembered.

Me: *You remembered…*

    Drake: *Naturally*

    Me: *A man of many words.*

    Drake: *LOL, working. Can't wait till tonight. I got plans for that body.*

    Me: *Remember that I'm staying with Hawkins!*

    Drake: *That won't stop me from checking out your bedroom & giving you something to miss when you make me leave.*

    Me: *Who said you could come into my bedroom?*

    Drake: *Babe, I'm in your bedroom until you kick me out. And Bella, I can't wait to taste you.*

SHOCKED, I stare at my phone, rereading his last text. *"I can't wait to taste you."* Oh, goodness. There he goes again, going all Viking and causing flutters. How do I respond? Well, I'm not. Let him stew. Smiling, I set my phone down and get back to work. I've got to clear some stuff before the detectives arrive.

A LITTLE LESS THAN an hour later, Spencer saunters in, looking like he's right off the cover of one of my billionaire romance novels. I can't help it, a giggle escapes me at the thought.

"What's so funny?" he asks. "Please tell me that rose isn't from the dick-less asshole who's now rotting in a jail cell." Spencer's scowl deepens as he swipes the card from my desk. I reach to stop him, but I miss.

"Hey!" I cry. "That's my card. You didn't ask to read it. Please give it back, or I'll have to mess you up. I'd hate to ruin that *I'm a big shot lawyer* getup you're rocking."

He rolls his eyes, handing the card back *after* reading it. "First, I always dress this way." He smirks, adding, "Second, I would've never guessed our little *one and done* man whore had the ability to be such a romantic sap. He's full of surprises. Shit, wait till the Brothers hear about this!" Spencer guffaws.

"You know, you don't have to say anything. Drake's always been a sweetheart to me. You see, the side he shows you is his tough as nails persona. I cherish his romantic side. Don't you go teasing him about it either! I'll come after you if I lose that side of him," I warn sternly.

Chuckling, Spencer acknowledges my point. "You're right. None of the Brothers would believe that our kick ass fighter, the one who could snap a guy's arm in half and not think twice, would do something so corny. I wouldn't want the guys to think he's given up his man card and turned into this pansy."

"What in the heck do you mean 'snap a guy's arm and think nothing of it'? How does one even do that? That can't be true."

Before Spencer can respond, Detective Jerkins and Franks interrupt with a light knock on my door frame.

"Good afternoon, Ms. Anderson. Please tell me Paul Edwards hasn't already violated his restraining order from jail." Detective Jerkins nods towards the rose on my desk and looks like he's swallowed a lemon at the thought. Maybe it's the idea of more paperwork.

"No, no, I'm happy to have received this one. It's from Drake. Isn't it beautiful?" I ask, taking another chance to smell my rose.

"Uh, I guess so," Jerkins says, looking unsure.

Geez, does no one understand the art of romance anymore? *Well, Drake does.* I sigh.

"Ms. Anderson, we need to get that file from you, but we also have an update that might upset you," Detective Franks says, getting to the point.

My eyes fly to Spencer, concern etched on my face. What bad news could they have? Paul's in jail, and there's a mountain of irrefutable evidence against him. I open my desk drawer and pull out the file containing all the notes, letters, and cards as well as the timeline of the things Paul had sent to me since I dumped him. I lay it down on my desk, still looking at Spencer, a bit worried.

"Explain, please. You're causing Isabella and myself undue stress," Spencer demands.

"Ms. Anderson," Detective Jerkins starts.

"It's Isabella," I say dejectedly.

"We believe that even if the judge sets Edwards' bail high, which is unlikely because he doesn't have a record of any kind, that his parents will be able to bail him out until the trial. We also discovered a dossier in his office.

It's a timeline for his senate run. He wanted someone to look good on his arm for it. He had his eye on you for a few months prior to your relationship, stalking you and taking pictures."

"I thought that scum would be locked up until he's convicted. This insane dossier isn't enough to prove he's a nut job?" I question.

"Ma'am," Detective Franks starts, ignoring me, "Edwards will have to comply with the restraining order that covers you, your work, and the Camelot locations. If he violates that in any way, we can pick him up for that and he'll remain in jail until trial."

"Sadly, bail will have to be set shortly," Jerkins adds. "He could be out within 48 to 72 hours. We will notify you, Ms. Anderson, if that happens. If he contacts you in any way, phone, email, text, gifts *anything*, you let us know immediately. Your restraining order is an emergency protective order, and due to the nature of his offenses, it's very encompassing. You just have to keep us informed."

"Seriously, I'm not afraid of Paul. He may be a pervert, but he's harmless. I never want to see him ever again. Believe me. If he contacts me, you'll know." I move to stand beside Spencer, who places a hand on my shoulder.

Detective Franks scowls at Spencer. "I hope you Camelot boys can talk some sense into this young lady. Paul Edwards is a sick motherfucker. Please excuse my language, Ms. Anderson—"

"Isabella, *please*," I remind him.

"I've spent the entire weekend going through the

evidence from our computer specialists. I know what I'm talking about. Edwards could very quickly become a dangerous individual. He's about to lose his job and has lost any hope for a political career, and now his father's political career is in jeopardy too. He could very easily blame you and snap."

Detective Jerkins interrupts, his attention on Spencer. "You boys need to talk some sense into Ms. Anderson," he says, his face grim.

"Look," I say, rolling my eyes. "Paul is one of those all talk, no action kind of guys. I don't think he's ever even been in a real fight. Pampered and coddled his whole life by Mommy and Daddy, he's a man-child. Believe me."

"Isabella, you need to take this seriously. He sees you and you alone, as the one that destroyed his life," he returns.

"I understand and appreciate your concern, but the guys are protecting me. They won't even allow me to stay with friends. Until I get the all clear, I'm splitting my time between Hawkins and Drake. I can handle Paul, don't worry about that. I've done it before and will do it again if I have to," I inform them, crossing my arms.

Spencer stiffens at the reminder of me having to defend myself with Paul when he got too aggressive. Jerkins shrugs.

"We wish you boys the best of luck with this one. She's a hand full," Franks announces.

"Now, about that file?" Jerkins reminds me.

Going around my desk, I pick up the original file folder. I'd made copies earlier for my own records, not wanting to risk losing all of my evidence against Paul. I hand the file to Jerkins, praying it will help in the case.

"Thank you, Isabella. Be smart, and listen to these guys," he says with a gentle voice as he takes the file from my hand.

"Alright," I say, turning to Spencer once the Detectives leave, "what did you mean by snapping arms? You're not getting out of answering that."

"Isabella, Fitz works at Camelot Security. He's got skills needed for the job. Any further questions need to be answered by him." he says, pointedly. "Now, the detectives made a very valid point. You do *not* go anywhere or do anything without our knowledge. Do you understand me? This is for your safety. Fitz and Hawkins will be informed of this latest update shortly."

"Sir, yes, sir," I snap with a mock salute.

"You wait and see. As soon as Fitz finds out, he's going to be unbearable for you. I can't wait to see how you react to his demands." Spencer chuckles as he leaves my office.

Well, poop. Falling into my chair, I find myself wishing I'd never met that jerk-face Paul Edwards. He's ruining my dreams that are finally come true.

CHAPTER TWENTY TWO

FITZ: SHOWING BELLA WHO'S BOSS

S tanding in Hawkins' driveway, I'm surrounded by Spencer, Clausen and my brother. They'd heard Bella was cooking dinner and were playing the family card. Well, except Spencer. He'd just finished reading me the riot act, emphasizing the need to make sure I lay down the law for Bella, making sure that I impress upon her how dangerous that dickhead Paul really is.

Fuck yeah I'll be setting Bella straight on who's the boss in this relationship. Not in front of the Brothers, but in the bedroom. I'll make sure she gets the message loud and clear or her sweet little ass will be red and sore. Damn, Henry stirs at the thought of her ass warm and red from my touch. I hope she argues about this so I can spank her ass.

I shake my head, returning to the conversation before Henry gets out of control. Nodding, I act like I wasn't just thinking dirty thoughts about my girl. I didn't miss much though. Spencer's still prattling on about how Bella's in denial and doesn't understand the seriousness of the situation.

"Dude, she just rolled her eyes when Jerkins and Franks tried to tell her to be safe. Rolled her fuckin' eyes! She thinks Edwards is a pansy, that she can handle him. She doesn't understand that he's as dangerous as a wounded animal. I've already talked to Riggs and Stevens. They're both down to keep an eye on her when she's not here or with you." Spencer finishes.

"Thanks for that," I comment. "And don't worry. I'll make sure she understands just how dangerous Edwards is. From now on, she needs to text me when she goes anywhere. I need to know where she is and who she's with at all times. But I like the idea of her having a tail. She's damn stubborn."

"I agree," Clausen puts in. "She's a little spitfire, has no fear and is way too trusting. I wish you the best of luck, Fitz. Our dad spoiled her rotten, she was his little princess. I know I've only been a part of her life for almost seven years, but she can be a spoiled brat."

"Clausen, I accept that challenge. Remember, Bella's been mine for a long ass time. I've got this," I retort, the confidence strong in my voice.

"Dude, you're in for a bumpy ride. After all the shit she's been through, she's tougher and more stubborn than when I first found out about her at the reading of Dad's will, along with his three other families. I loved him, but he couldn't keep it in his pants.

"Look, I'm sorry I didn't tell you all about the drama my dad stuck us with. She went from that pudgy little girl who followed Drake around like a puppy to someone you all would want to get in bed. Can you blame me?"

"You refer to Bella as a pudgy little girl one more time, and I'll kick your sorry ass," I threaten. "I can only imagine how this screws with your head. I don't know what to think. Part of me wants to kick your ass for never telling us more about your family. One of us would have figured it out."

"Whoa, dude," Clausen replies, holding his hands up. "I think I've already been beaten up as punishment enough this week. Hawkins fuckin' sucker punched me as soon as I answered his summons last week. I didn't want to believe it until *my* half-sister popped out of that cake with puppy-dog eyes for you."

We all crack up, knowing Hawkins would have easily put two and two together, then administer some Camelot justice on Clausen for not telling us about his family shit.

"I guess you're right about wanting to protect your sister," I sympathize. "I'm relieved Brit's never really shown an interest in any of you, beyond a pre-teen crush on Riggs and Stevens. Neither of them would violate the code."

"I agree," Brenden chimes in, slapping Clausen on the back. "I wouldn't want Brit involved with any of you fuckers either. But come on, dude. Fitz and Bella are real. You gotta deal. Now that you know their story, you know it's gonna happen. Time to suck it up."

"I get it, kind of," Clausen starts. "But you have to see it from my point of view though. The greatest man whore of all time is gonna fucking change? He's even got a t-shirt that says One & Done and wears it with pride at parties for cryin' out loud!'"

"Dude, I'm a different man when it comes to Bella." Placing my hand on his shoulder, I give him my full attention. "Your sister makes me a different man. I vow right here, right now, that I don't want to touch another woman. I don't even *see* them. Bella's it for me."

The crunching sounds of tires rolling up Hawkins' gravel driveway have our heads turning. My heart soars at the sight of Bella's cute little minivan pulling to a stop. Fuck, I've got to get her into something I'm willing to be seen in. I'm already calling a minivan cute, but she's fucking adorable in that thing.

Bella's jaw drops as she takes in Hawkins' place. Chuckling, I recall my first visit after he finally finished all the renovations. I think my jaw fell open just like hers. Hawkins went a little over the top with his love of all things Camelot.

After all the shit he went through, and because of his PTSD, he built himself a castle fortress, a place where he feels safe. He spent years getting all the details just right, complete with a moat and draw-bridge. After getting past his outer wall and gate, it's like going back in time to the Middle Ages. It's still hard to believe this place is minutes from Santa Monica. It feels like it belongs in sixteenth century England.

Hawkins insisted on realism in his castle. The stone façade was aged to look like it's hundreds of years old. He had an artist paint moss on some of the fake stones. The inside is just as amazing. No detail was overlooked, and he even included hidden passageways. It's true to who Hawkins is.

Approaching Bella's car, I reach out and open her door. Bella jumps out and resumes her inspection of the castle.

"Why didn't you warn me about this?! It looks so real. It's absolutely stunning!"

"I wanted to see your face." I chuckle at her. "But, yeah, that was his goal. Don't worry though. It has all the modern conveniences. No cooking dinner in a fire pit or having to use a massive fire oven. He's got all the newest kitchen gadgets."

Overcoming her shock, she throws her arms around my neck, and I try to catch her hips.

"How was your day, honey? Mine was spectacular. I have an amazing man in my life who sent me my favorite flower and wrote me the most beautiful card!"

"Hmm, he sounds like a real pussy to me," I joke, copping a feel of her fantastic ass.

"I kind of have a thing for wusses who do sweet things like that," she whispers.

Surprising me, she jumps up and wraps her legs around my waist and kisses me, her tongue sliding along my lips. Groaning, I wrap my arms tighter around her, deepening the kiss. I cup her ass, lifting her so I can line Henry up with Heaven on Earth. I take two steps away from the van door, pushing her against the side of her rainbow and unicorn covered vehicle. Our mouths jostle for dominance, my tongue dueling with hers.

"Fuck, Fitz!" Clausen exclaims. "I *do not* need to see you practically fucking my sister in front of me."

Pulling away, I shove my face in Bella's neck and try to catch my breath. Damn, she makes me forget everything around me.

"We're continuing this after dinner, in your bedroom."

Bella giggles, trying to hide from the glare I feel Clausen sending us. She slowly slides her legs from my hips, and I lower her to the ground.

Once she collects herself, she bellows, "Well, if you looky-loos want dinner, I recommend you stop your gawking and get your buns in gear! I have a big Crock Pot in my car that's been cooking my marinara sauce all day. Be careful though, because it's still probably hot. I wouldn't want one of you pansies who have never seen a woman kiss her man hello before, getting an owie by burning your weak little fingers."

Goddamn, her sass and sarcasm have Henry taking notice, *again*.

"The rest of you losers can help with the other groceries and my suitcases. Now, where the heck is Nicholas? Shouldn't he be greeting me? Since I'm staying in his castle and all? I'm dying to see him in person again."

The guys scramble to help her while Clausen runs to the back of the van. "Dude, she withholds food at the slightest provocation. Believe me, she withheld the peanut butter chocolate chip brownies she made me when I was an hour late to help with one of her daycare events. She refused to give me the very thing she bribed me with. While she gave two-fuckin'-dozen to the kids, I only got *one* measly brownie, and those snot nosed boogers ate them all while teasing me."

Clausen whines, grabbing the two big suitcases out of Bella's van. She slams a hand on her hip and points at him.

"Oh, you're a liar, liar, pants on fire, Asher. You were two hours late and I was lucky that some of the parents stayed to help me set up. You were lucky to have gotten one at all. Now, stop your whining and get your butt moving. What are you guys doing here, anyway? I thought I was cooking dinner for Drake and Nicholas."

Brenden gives Bella his best wounded look. "Girlie, when Clausen and I heard you were cooking dinner for Fitz and Hawkins, I thought you'd forgotten about us. I mean, we *are* family. We deserve to be included. And Spencer," he adds with a smirk, "is here to tattle-tale on you. He told Drake *all* about how you refused to listen to the detectives today. If anyone deserves to get turned away from your amazing marinara sauce, it's that asshole." Brenden grabs armloads of bags and heads toward the front door.

"Hey, fucker! If this shit didn't smell so heavenly, I'd chuck it at your head, but I'm ensuring this Crock Pot full of sauce fit for the gods makes it to the house safely. I've got the most important job here. I deserve to be fed after all my efforts."

Spencer looks like an idiot, holding the Crock Pot with his arms fully extended, taking shuffle-steps to avoid spillage. It wouldn't do for him to spill it on his designer jeans or crisp white shirt.

Bella giggles as she watches Spencer shuffle step his

way into the house. Slinging an arm around her, I lead her to the house. We're barely in the front door when Bella spots Hawkins coming towards us. Squealing, she runs and launches herself into his arms.

"Nicholas! Oh, my God! You look great!" Her voice is higher than normal, betraying her excitement at seeing him again.

A huge smile graces his face, he's happier than I've seen him in a long time. But the sight of him wrapping his arms around my woman and whispering in her ear boils my blood. Huh. This must be jealousy. Fuck, I don't like this shit at all. Nor do I like the way they're looking at each other, talking with low voices.

"Okay, *Nicholas,* time to put *my* woman down and behave yourself." The threat underlying my words is clear. *Do it now before I break you.*

"Ha!" Clausen calls out on his way to the kitchen. "Is that jealousy, Fitz? What, you don't trust my sister with your friend? Time to deal, Brother. She's staying at his house tonight while you go home all alone. You aren't worried, are you?" The dumbass's laughter can be heard from the kitchen. I really don't like all this teasing with Bella.

Everyone starts chuckling along with Clausen. Hawkins finally lowers my woman to her feet, still smiling like a fucking dork.

Turning his attention to me, he reassures me, "Fitz, Brother. You can trust me. What's with the Nicholas shit, *Drake?*" he asks, slinging an arm around Bella, and she does the same to him. I approach, not taking my eyes off of Hawkins and Bella, both of them with huge, radiant smiles.

Bella sidles up to me, wrapping her other arm around me. Her eyes bounce from my face to Hawkins, reading the tension between us.

"Drake, Nicholas. You two knock this crap off. I have dinner to cook, and I don't have time to referee your peeing contest." She smacks us both on the ass, causing Hawkins to jump.

"Now, Nicholas, lead me to this kitchen of yours. I love your house. I cannot wait for the tour after dinner. Do you have fish in that moat? It's just freaking awesome with all the over-grown trees, ivy and wisteria growing up the side of the castle. Does my bedroom have a balcony?"

Both Hawkins and I bust up at her fifty questions. She's always babbled when she was excited. It's so fuckin' cute.

I'll let Hawkins have this week to fill in Bella about all the shit that he's been through. If he hasn't done it by the weekend, I'll have to do it myself. I'm not looking forward to that conversation at all. I just hope Bella can keep it together if he does, for Hawkins' sake.

DAMN, my woman can cook. The chicken parmesan she whipped up in no time was in-fucking-credible. If I don't watch it, I could easily start packing on some weight. The entire time she chatted away, talking about some kid or one of her girls at her daycare center, and not measuring a damn thing. Once she popped the chicken in the oven, she whipped up some brownies from memory. She never missed a beat, not in the cooking or in our conversation. Damn, she's amazing.

When Hawkins took her on a tour after dinner, the first thing he did was get her added to the security system. She was in awe of the eye scanner and the full hand sensor, as well as all the various security measures Hawkins installed. He's a fuckin' badass when it comes to this computer shit.

"Now you've got full access to not just the house, but most of Camelot Security and Camelot Bar & Club. You don't have to get buzzed in when you come to visit us."

Hawkins gave Bella a complete tour, all except for his own bedroom suite. No one's allowed in there. He showed her the wing he lives in, and where the Brothers sleep when they stay with him. When he finally gets to her room, Hawkins explains how the scanner is programmed to allow only Bella and me entry. Relief flows through me, knowing she'll be safe.

I'm shocked when Hawkins takes Bella to his office, showing her the bank of monitors with views of Camelot Security, our offices, and the club. I think he was showing off when, with a few clicks of his keyboard, he switched to the various cameras focused on the Brothers' homes. Yeah, Hawkins has ourshit locked down and keeps us safe.

"Bella, can I have a new security system installed at your daycare centers? I'm pretty sure the one you've got now is shit. This one will not only be linked directly to the police and fire departments, but also to us. Our response time is usually quicker," Hawkins jokes with her.

"Uh, yeah sure. This stuff looks so sophisticated that I'm sure you guys are much more capable than some schmucks in a sea of cubicles when it comes to my safety and that of my kids."

On our way back to the kitchen, where everyone else stayed while we toured the house, Hawkins throws me under the bus.

"Isabella, Fitz has something special he'd like to give you," he announces.

"What the fuck, man?" I question, a little pissed he's spoiling my surprise. "What if I wanted to give it to her when we were alone, and not in front of all you dicks?"

Hawkins shakes his head. "Look, this shit is too important. Isabella needs to know the bigger meaning behind this gift. She's a part of us now. As the first Camelot Wench, she needs to realize we protect our own. We're here as a backup just in case she loses her shit when you tell her what the gift really is."

"What? What gift are you talking about? Why wouldn't I adore a gift from you, Dray?" Bella throws her hands up in exasperation. "I'm lost!"

Fuck, why couldn't Hawkins leave this shit to me? My blood starts boiling the moment we enter the living room, and I find Stevens, Riggs, and Jackson have joined is in what was supposed to be an intimate dinner. Damn, now there's fuckin' eight of us. What the fuck! My Brothers have hijacked my quiet night with Bella in her room.

Well, damn. I guess Hawkins is legitimately

concerned that Bella won't take this as seriously as she needs to, but calling more than half of the Brothers seems a bit extreme though. Shit, this could go either way, especially with Bella being the object of scrutiny.

"Dray, what in the world is Nicholas yakking on about?" She turns, probably to ask Hawkins the same thing, but her head stopped when she notices the new arrivals.

"Oh, hi Noah... and Grayson... and Gabe. What's everyone doing here? Did you smell the brownies and come running?"

"Well, Isabella," Jackson says from his spot at the bar. That fucker has already raided the brownies, the delicious brownies I was hoping to have for breakfast tomorrow. "I'm here a lot, and now that I know you'll be here cooking, I'll be here even more. Hawkins' leftover chick parm was the bomb."

"Asshole," Hawkins mutters while everyone laughs. That's what he gets for thinking I couldn't handle this by myself.

Stevens and Riggs have taken the high back leather chairs on either side of the massive fireplace. The thing is so big Bella could probably stand upright inside of it.

"Well, I guess I need to plan on cooking for an army, knowing you freeloaders will just show up anyway. You all need to keep your grubby hands-off Mojo's serving though!" she warns.

I lead Bella to the matching loveseat and practically pull her into my lap. Everyone stares like they're waiting for a show. Fuck. Mojo gets up from where he was sleeping next to Stevens and trundles over to lie at Bella's feet. That's my buddy, knows where he belongs.

Well, shit. Might as well get this over with. These assholes are probably hoping to screw with my chances of fooling around with Bella later tonight. I'm gonna be pissed if that happens. I take in the faces staring at us, the people I thought were my friends, my Brothers. Rolling my eyes, I turn to my woman.

"Babe, I'll be back in two minutes. I gotta go grab something. These assholes want to make sure you understand what I'm giving you." Leaning over, I allow myself a quick taste of her lips.

"Dray, what the heck is going on?" Bella asks, concern etched on her face as she pets Mojo's head nervously.

"Babe, just a minute," I urge. As I leave the room, I flip off the Brothers. Jogging to her room, I'm hoping they haven't ruined what I'd hoped would be a gift Bella would be so grateful for, she'd give me a passionate thank you in return. Now, I don't know what'll happen.

"Damn, you're impatient," Stevens is saying as I descend the stairs. "Give *Magic Fingers* a second. He'll be back." That fucker, making fun of what Bella said when she broke her foot.

"Goddamn, you all know how to ruin something that's special, don't you?" I complain, walking into the living room.

"Hey," Jackson shoots back. "Clay, Carpenter, Hunter and Bishop send their support."

"Support for what?" Bella inquires.

My fists clench with the need to punch something as

I cross the expansive room to the couch. I cannot believe they think I'd need backup for this.

"Babe, these idiots don't think you'll go along with what I'm about to ask. They think they're helping to back me up, to help convince you."

Chewing her lip, she leans into me as I settle next to her.

"What are you going to ask me?" Her tone is unsure, and I don't like that one fucking bit.

"Earlier today, we had a meeting. Everyone in this room knows how important you are to me. Well, I officially claimed you, you could say. Made you mine."

"Oh!" Stevens' shouts, throwing something at Bella, "I got you something special and sparkly to make it all official. Chicks like sparkly."

Bella picks up the black fabric that landed in her lap. She unfolds it, holding it up in front of her. Oh shit, no he didn't! Sitting back, I prepare to watch my smart mouthed woman tear into Stevens.

"Wench?!" she yells. "Is this some stupid joke? I'm not a wench!"

"Isabella," Stevens says, looking a tad frightened, "it doesn't mean anything bad."

"It means prostitute! Which I most certainly am not!" Bella screams at him.

Oh, God. This is classic. It's about damn time Stevens gets in trouble for his love of having shirts made up.

"No, I looked it up. It means girl or young woman, usually a servant," Stevens argues.

"Servant?! You think I'm a servant?" Bella's tone

turns from angry to dejected. "I didn't think you thought so low of me." Stevens better fix this before I break his face.

"No, no! It's not like that at all, Isabella," Stevens coaxes, trying to fix his mess.

"It means you belong to Camelot. You're the only woman who's ever been entered into our security system. It means we've all claimed you." Jackson adds.

"It means you're one of us. And we protect what's ours," Hawkins confirms.

Her eyes moisten, and she blinks like she's trying to hold back tears.

"Are you guys serious?" Bella asks in a small voice.

"Yeah, babe," I confirm. "They're serious. You're mine, which means you're one of us."

Her head crashes into my chest as she sniffles. I give her a quick hug, sitting her upright again. There's more I've got to get through.

"The gift I have is better. Remember how Grandma gave me all of my Ma's jewelry?"

"Of course," she declares, her smile lighting the room. "I still have every piece you gave me. I wear them all the time."

"Well, I have a few more for you. But there's something different about these." I scrub my hand down my face. "Hear me out, okay?"

"Naturally, Dray. What's going on?"

"Hawkins added something to the pieces I'm giving to you. He, uhh," I struggle to find the words… "added a tracking chip to it."

Bella shifts back, crossing her arms across her

glorious rack, the very rack I'd rather be playing with right now instead of having this conversation.

"Uh huh," she scoffs.

"Now, hold on a second. Before you get mad, let me explain," I plead.

"Look, if this is because of Paul, Nicholas needs to remove those trackers before I accept anything. You've got to be kidding me right now!" Bella retorts.

"I warned you, Brother." Clausen gloats, chuckling. "I gotta go make some popcorn for this."

I discreetly flip him off before turning back to Bella.

"Babe, it's not just that fucker. It's more about protecting you."

Riggs holds up his hand, interrupting me. "Fitz, let me see if I can help her see the light. This has to do with you being five foot what? You're just a little thing. Anyone could grab you, force you to go somewhere with them, and you couldn't do jack shit about it."

Brenden chimes in, "For your information, Sarah, Brit, Brenda and even Carpenters' little sister wear trackers. Almost all the women related to us wear stud earrings Hawkins can track. Even the moms."

"And no," he continues, "we don't track their every movement. But if we haven't heard from them or need to know where they are in a hurry and they aren't answering phone calls or texts quick enough, we damn well will pull up their location and find out where the fuck they are."

"Remember when Brit graduated?" Spencer asks. "That crazy girl flew up to Tahoe and partied for two days straight, then she almost married some asshole she didn't even know."

"Goddamn," Brenden confirms, "those diamond studs we gave her proved their worth a million times over. Thank God we got to her in time and stopped that shit."

"Diamonds?" Bella inquires, uncrossing her arms.

Guffaws sound as Stevens shouts, "See, I told you assholes, chicks like sparkly things!"

"Probably should have led with the jewelry," Riggs deadpans.

Fuckers, I think, pulling the box from beside me. Bella's eyes widen at the sight of the dark green velvet box. Slowly, I open it, watching her face. Her hand flies to her throat on a gasp when I reveal the pieces I chose for her.

Bella's chocolate eyes flick to mine then back to the jewelry. "Are those, um, yellow diamonds?" she breathes.

"Yeah, babe. They're yellow diamonds. I had the ring resized, and Hawkins already installed the micro-tracking chips in all the whole three-piece set."

"I don't care if these have trackers. They're beautiful," she breathes.

There's a few scattered chuckles as Bella extends her hand and lightly touches the ring I've always known would be hers.

I pluck the ring from the box and cradle her right hand with my left. She gasps, her eyes flying to mine, tears sparkling in her eyes. Slowly, I slide the ring onto her finger, a hidden promise behind it that she will be my wife, and soon.

"Dray," her voice is brittle with emotion, "it's the most beautiful ring I've ever seen." She holds her hand out and inspects the ring sparkling atop her finger.

"Thank you, honey," Bella whispers. Leaning over, she kisses me. Not willing to let her get away that easy, I grab the back of her neck. Holding her still, I deepen the kiss.

"Damn it, get off my sister!" Clausen yells.

"There's a perfectly good room upstairs you can put to use later. This is not the place for a make-out session," Hawkins adds. "Right now, we need to finish this discussion."

Pulling away, I watch a beautiful blush spread across Bella's creamy skin.

"Asher, don't you be a butt-head. I'm a grown woman."

Clausen grumbles as Bella points at Hawkins as she continues.

"Nicholas, don't be crass. That was just a thank you kiss for these gorgeous diamonds. Someone obviously hasn't made out with a girl in a long time if that's his idea of a make-out session."

"Oh sweet, innocent Isabella," Hawkins fires back, laughing. "There's no lack of female companionship here."

I can't help it, I crack up along with everyone else. Riggs puts us back on track though.

"Alright, enough. Isabella, you need to wear the ring and the earrings at all times. You can wear the necklace when you like because that's the easiest thing someone can remove. But if we see you without the ring or earrings, you'll catch hell from all of us."

Bella clutches her hand to her chest. "I'd have to be unconscious or dead before this ring leaves my finger."

Oh yeah, she loves my present. I'm definitely gettin' some lovin' before I leave her tonight. Maybe I should officially introduce Bella to Henry. A vision of Bella's small hand caressing my cock makes me rock hard.

"Brothers," Spencer calls, interrupting my naughty daydream. "Bella doesn't understand just how dangerous Paul is. She's under the impression that he's 'all talk and no action.'"

Bella shakes her head slowly, that sassy smirk I usually adore on her face.

"Babe, fuck, seriously, I do not want you anywhere near that dick-less motherfucker. You don't talk to him. You don't text him. If you see him, you call us and get the fuck out of there pronto. I'm being straight, no games, no jokes. I will tan your little ass and you won't be able to sit for a week if you don't do as I say when it comes to that demented fuck. Do you understand me? I'm dead fucking serious right now."

Halfway through my rant, Bella's shoulders start to shake as her eyes crinkle in glee. When I finish, she loses it, laughing loudly.

"Oh, Dray," she laughs, wiping a tear from her eye. "Paul is a total wussy. When I kneed him in the family jewels, he dropped to the floor and *cried* like a baby. I'm not scared of Paul Edwards in the slightest. But, if it'll make you 'big, bad, 'tough guys' feel better," she teases, using finger quotes, her voice heavy with sarcasm, "I'll turn tail and run like a scared little girl if I see him, and then call you immediately. Does that make you feel better?"

Oh, fuck no. "This is not a game." Pulling her into my arms and swat her ass pretty hard, then I give it a good squeeze. "Stop being a smart ass. We're completely serious."

"Owie," Bella giggles. "That stings. Why do you keep spanking me? I will smack your butt in return if you keep it up, Mister!"

"Bring it on, babe. Just know that I *will* smack your ass just as hard as you smack mine."

"Shit, enough flirting already," Hawkins complains. "You need to *hear* me, Isabella. You need to listen to me. This is very serious! When I hacked into that fucker's computer, I found a lot of sick and twisted shit on there. He is whacked in the head and has some serious fucked up ideas about sex." His voice rises in volume with each word out of his mouth.

Getting up, Hawkins paces his living room and runs his hands through his hair. "If you don't fucking start taking this threat seriously Bella, I will show you just how depraved and twisted that asshole is. Until that mother-fucker is behind fucking bars and you're fucking safe, you need to listen to us and take this situation very seriously."

Hawkins reaction is a little too much. He knows something that he hasn't shared yet, which pisses me off. If he knows something about my woman and hasn't told me, I'm going to kick his ass.

"Fine, fine," Bella relents. "No more jokes about

wimpy Paul. I'll be a good girl, promise. And I'll always wear the ring and earrings."

"Nicholas," she calls, stopping Hawkins' attempt to wear a hole in his wood floor. "Paul's in jail right now and I'm safe here surrounded by what, eight strong guys."

Bella's words seem to pacify Hawkins, for which I'm grateful. He was getting close to losing it. I've always known that Hawkins has harbored feelings for my woman, but I know, deep down, even when my jealousy gets the best of me, that he'd never cross that line with her, but his reaction to Bella ignoring the threat of Paul is too much. I'm gonna have to get him to fill me in without triggering him. Fuck, PTSD is a bitch.

Spencer pulls out his phone and checks the screen. "Fuck," he mutters, and all heads swing to look at him.

"Just got a text from my sheriff buddy downtown. Edwards was released on bail twenty minutes ago."

"Lockdown starts right now, Isabella," Riggs instructs. "You will stay with either Hawkins or Fitz and communicate your plans. You will go nowhere without first communicating your intentions, texting when you arrive, how long you intend to be there and when you leave."

In silent acknowledgment, Bella removes the earrings she has on. She pulls the much larger ones I've given her from the box and puts them in her ears. After handing me the necklace, she turns and lifts her hair for me to put it on her.

When I'm finished latching the necklace, I look at Hawkins. "We've got this covered, Brother. Nothing will happen to Bella. Feel free to monitor as you need to, okay?"

Hawkins nods as the others pick up on the stress that is radiating off him in waves.

Jackson gets up and stands next to Hawkins, careful to keep a bit of space between them.

"Bella, we need to hear your verbal agreement that you understand what Spencer has said, and that you will abide by the rules."

"I promise," Bella swears. "I won't go anywhere without sending a text to both Nicholas and Drake. But, you guys, Paul's parents will have him on a short leash. Relax a little."

The confidence in Bella's voice is strong. I just hope she's right.

"Hey, I need a smoke. You wanna join me, Hawk?" Jackson asks, gently touching Hawkins' arm, testing to see how far gone he is.

"Yeah." Hawkins nods numbly, his gaze still on Bella.

"Wait for me!" Stevens calls out. "If Hawkins is providing the smokes, then I need one too." He follows after them.

"Isabella, you might want to put on your wench shirt and get into the kitchen to make some munchies. If they're smoking Hawkins' stash, then they're gonna raid it in a few hours." Riggs jokes, pouring himself a whiskey.

CHAPTER TWENTY THREE

ISABELLA: SEXUALLY DISCOVERING AND PREPARING

I'm currently hiding in my bathroom at Hawkins' house. This bathroom is just as phenomenal as the rest of the house. A massive, white clawfoot tub is in the center of the room, and I can't wait to climb in there with some bubbles and a good book.

Less than ten minutes ago, Drake swatted my bum, *again*, and told me to hurry my butt up, only he didn't say 'butt'. The short glimpse I had of the room was extraordinary. I've already finished brushing my teeth and hair and am dressed in Drake's dress shirt, my preferred pajamas. It smells like him and makes me feel safe.

What am I even waiting for? It's Drake, for heaven's sake. I want him with every fiber of my being. There's no reason for the butterflies in my belly. He loves me, and I love him. Time to get my man.

Slowly, I crack open the door to spy on Drake. He's

reclining on the bed, shirtless, surrounded by a mountain of burgundy and gold pillows. He's dimmed the lights, and, oh gosh, he's started a fire in the small stone fireplace, setting off a romantic vibe.

The bed itself is a work of art, a massive, four-pillar frame with burgundy and gold sheers tied at the corners. There's steps leading up to the mattress, it's so high. I might just have to steal this bed. Maybe Drake and Asher will help me.

Taking a deep breath, I pull open the door and lean against the frame. Drake's head turns to me, and his eyes widen. I feel his gaze roam my body, like a physical touch along my skin. He licks his lips then pats the bed.

"Don't keep me waiting any longer, woman. Get that fine little ass over here before I feel the urge to spank it again."

Giggling, I sprint-hobble to the bed. At least I don't have to sleep in that stupid boot. Gosh, how unsexy this must look. Climbing in, I get a close up look of Drake's glorious chest and abs. God, the dips and valleys... I want to trace them with my tongue. Reaching out, I trace the edge of our tattoo.

"Drake, this house is amazing. It's a perfect recreation of a castle from the days of Camelot. And this bed! Can you and Asher help me steal it?" I tease, looking at Drake through my lashes.

Reaching out, he grabs my arm and pulls me on top of him.

"I don't care about the house, or the bed. I only care about the beautiful woman in it. *My* beautiful woman, who I've been craving a taste of all fuckin' day."

The butterflies I felt in the bathroom return, running riot in my belly. Drake flips me onto my back. He gently sweeps my hair from my face, his gaze locked on mine. Those dark green eyes are the window to his soul. They show the love he has for me, and the desire. Oh, God, the desire is intense.

Drake lowers his head, his lips meeting mine. My hands lift of their own accord, finding his hair. He groans at my touch, deepening the kiss. When I softly tug his hair, his hips thrust against my leg, pressing his erection into my hip.

"Damn, babe," Drake groans into my neck. "You have no idea how badly I want to take you right now, to make you mine."

Shivers wrack my body at the need in his voice. He trails kisses along my neck, causing me to moan his name.

Drake shifts us and moves into the cradle of my hips. I spread my legs, allowing him access to me. He presses his hips against mine, grinding into me, but he's still wearing his dang'um jeans.

"Dray, honey," I moan. "Why are you still wearing your pants? I want to feel more of you, take them off, but leave your boxers on."

His frame freezes for a split second before he lifts his head and studies my face. Liking what he sees, Drake flies into motion, popping the buttons of his fly before shoving his jeans to his knees and wriggling out of them.

"You're a demanding little thing, aren't you?" Drake prods, kneeling between my legs. My eyes are glued to the massive erection hidden behind his boxers. Knowing he's watching me watch him, he slides his hand under the waistband and grips his very erect penis, stroking himself firmly.

Releasing himself, he grips my ankles, being gentle with my hurt toes. He pushes them up, bending my knees, sliding his hands up my legs, parting my knees further, causing them to fall to the bed.

Watching his eyes as he takes in my most private area, lightly tracing the top of my white lace bikini panties. Drake inhales a deep breath, his eyes following the path of his finger.

"Babe, I'm going to take your panties off. These are mine now."

Oh, God. His dirty words fire my core, making me feel empty.

Sliding his finger under one side, he tugs it down. His gaze moves to my other hip as he rips, *yes, rips*, them from my body. My surprised gasp echoes throughout the room. He pulls my panties from my body and tosses them to the side.

"Dray, kiss me," I request urgently, needing him close. "I need your mouth. I need to kiss you again."

He places an elbow on the bed and leans forward, complying with my request. His other hand unbuttons my shirt, pushing it open as he goes. When he reaches the bottom button, his hand slides up my belly to my breasts. His rough fingertips twist and pinch one of my nipples, as I moan in response to his ministrations.

Releasing my mouth, he moves to my ear, sucking and nibbling my lobe, sending goosebumps across my skin. Drake glides his tongue down along my neck, pausing to bite and nip as my breath hitches in response. He then kisses a path down my cleavage and turns his head, my nipple captured between his warm lips.

"Dray—" I moan, throwing my head back and clenching the blanket beneath me.

The man is torturing me with his talented mouth. His hand finds my neglected breast while his fingers mimic what his mouth is doing. Oh, God. What is he doing to me? Pinching both nipples, one with his teeth, the other with his fingers, he gently tugs and twists them, causing lightning to flash behind my closed eyes.

"Dray, oh God," I cry out, my hands flying to his hair. My back arches, my breathing heavy. Lord above, I'm close to detonating.

When he abandons my breasts, my hands clench in his hair as I try to keep his head in place. Drake chuckles and grabs my hands. Opening my eyes, I find him staring at me with a satisfied smile. Slowly, he slides my arms above my head.

"Leave them there," he growls. Goodness, that is so freaking hot.

Lifting my head, I watch as he returns to his mission. His mouth returns to my belly, trailing kisses lower and lower. His hands, firm and determined, slide along my sides to my hips.

Oh, sweet Jesus. Drake's eyes watch my face as he presses a kiss to my pubic bone. My thighs clench, my core flutters.

Hooking his hands behind my knees, he lifts them, throwing them over his shoulders. He takes a deep breath before he slides his mouth lower still.

"Oh, Dray… You, uh, you don't have to do, uh *that*, Dray… Oh, God, Drake…" I gasp as his mouth makes contact with my mound.

"I'm gonna fuck you with my tongue until you come," he murmurs against my folds. The vibrations against my core cause me to squirm against his mouth.

Gasping, I call out his name as I fist my hands in the pillows. His tongue explores me, tracing my folds. When he reaches my clit, Drake flicks his tongue on that oh-so-sensitive spot, driving me wild with need.

"Dray, Dray—" I cry. "Oh, God, what are you doing to me? I can't… I can't take it…" I moan. Forgetting his direction, my hands fly to his hair. I'm not sure if it's to pull him away or keep him there. I'm losing my mind with all this pleasure.

Drake moves his mouth lower, to my core. His talented finger takes over the torture on my clit. He slides his tongue inside of me and my hips buck. Sparks of pleasure radiate from the focus of his attention and my back arches.

"Dray… Oh, Dray—" I cry, my voice is husky, deeper than I've ever heard. "I'm gonna… I'm going to come!"

His tongue slides in and out of me, and I push my heels into his shoulders. My hips lift from the bed as he grabs my butt and groans. My thighs squeeze against his head.

Drake increases the pace of his tongue, his fingers on my clit keeping pace. *It's happening.* My core flutters, a wave of pleasure cresting higher and higher.

And I break, flying to the heavens. Oh my God, oh

my god! I shake as sparks light across my body. Drake lowers my relaxed body to the bed.

"Honey," I murmur dreamily, my eyes still closed. My hand searches for his.

He finds my hand as his chest presses against mine, his mouth near my ear.

"Babe... that was the most beautiful experience of my life. Your taste, the smell of you, your moans and the way your breath would hitch. Fuck, babe."

"I want to return the favor, Dray," I whisper, shyly.

Drake's body goes solid. Even his breathing has stopped. I thought I'd have gotten a curse out of him with that request.

"What? Cat got your tongue?" I tease, my energy returning.

"Babe, are you, uh, saying what I hope you're saying?" he asks.

"I want to satisfy you the way you did to me. I, uhh," I trail off, unsure of myself.

"You 'uhh' what, babe? I need you to be clear."

"I, umm... You have to help me. I've never done this before." I rush out.

Fitz

Oʜ, fuck yeah. My woman wants to suck my cock. I'm so down with that. I sit back on my knees, and she follows me. Her gorgeous hair falls over her shoulder, covering her beautiful breasts.

Henry's not small by any stretch of the imagination, so I need to figure out the best way for Bella to do this. Grabbing a pillow, I place it on the steps at the side of the bed. All the while, a litany of things runs through my brain, like trying not to come like some horny little boy at the thought of Bella's mouth on my cock. The old librarian from high school, football stats, getting kicked in the nuts are all thoughts I'm trying to hold on to, to make this last as long as I can. Grabbing Bella by the waist, I pull her over and set her on my lap. Her face is shy, and a little scared. Pushing her hair over her shoulder, I cup her jaw.

"I, uh, think it might be easier..." I start, but my voice cracks, betraying how eager I am to feel her lips on Henry. Clearing my throat, I continue, "Easier if you kneel here on the steps between my legs."

"Okay," Bella whispers. Her timidity is fucking hot.

Bella carefully slides between my knees, kneeling on the pillow. Her face is just a little higher than my groin, just as I'd hoped.

Hesitantly, she traces Henry with the tip of her finger, causing him to jerk behind the constricting fabric of my boxers.

"You're really big, Dray." Damn, her breathy voice further ratchets up my arousal.

"I like to think so," I reply, my mouth dry in anticipation.

Slowly, her fingers move to the waistband of my boxers. As she begins to tug them down, I push up on my heels to help her along. Henry pops free, pointing straight at her mouth. Her eyes widen as she gets her first glimpse of my cock.

Bella swallows then licks her lips in trepid anticipation. Holy fuck, that's goddamn hot. I run through my list of things to calm Henry down again. This time, though, it's pointless. My body shakes as my hands grip the side of the bed.

"Can I touch you, Dray?" Her raspy voice tells me this is affecting her almost as much as it is me.

"God, yes," I practically yell. "Henry's waited for this a long time."

In my head, I start singing 'Ring Around the Rosie,' attempting to distract myself, but it backfires because 'Rosie' makes me think of Bella's pink folds, and how wet she was for me. Fuck.

Bella's cool hand lightly brushes Henry, causing him to jerk.

"It's so hard, but your skin… It's so soft and warm, so different than I thought." Her hand continues to explore me as my breath stutters in my lungs.

Bella wraps her hand around my cock and runs her thumb over the tip. A bit of precum escapes, lubricating the movement of her thumb. With her hand lightly wrapped around my shaft, she slowly glides her hand up and down.

It's not enough for me, so reaching down, I grab her hand and bring it to my mouth. I lick her palm, getting it nice and wet. Returning her hand to my cock, I wrap her fingers around it, covering hers with my hand. Squeezing tighter and showing her how tight to grip me,

I make her stroke me. When I show her the wrist twist as she nears my tip, my hips buck.

Watching her explore me as she learns how to touch me is fucking hot. My head falls back on my shoulders as my eyes close. Goddamn, she's a natural.

"Babe, in a few seconds, speed it up a bit. Keep your grip tight... Oh, shit babe. Fuck, that feels so damn good. Don't stop," I instruct her. I'm not going to last long like this.

"Holy fuckin' shit," I shout in surprise as Bella's mouth captures the tip of my cock. Looking down, her hair is blocking my view. I grab it in my fist and hold it out of the way. My thighs flex and tighten as her mouth works in tandem with her hand.

Bella's fantastic tits bounce and sway with every bob of her head. Good God, she's got me holding on by a thread. Her hot, wet mouth is incredible. Her tongue swirls the tip of my cock every time she pulls up. She twists her head, matching the movements of her hand. Fuck.

"Babe, I'm not gonna last long. Babe... Fuuucck," I groan.

Her eyes open and there's a sparkle in those almond shaped eyes. Bella's proud of herself. Oh, that little minx.

Speeding up, she takes my cock deeper into her mouth. Sucking and licking, I'm seconds from blowing.

"Bella, fuck," I plead. "Slow down, babe. I'm gonna blow."

She pays no heed to my words. They have the opposite effect, and Bella speeds up yet again.

"Fuck, babe," I groan, my thighs shaking. "I'm coming…" As I climax, my woman takes every drop of my cum and swallows it. She licks my cock clean, sending shivers through my body.

I pull her up from between my quivering legs and kiss her passionately. The salty taste in her mouth makes it even hotter. Rolling her to the side, I lay half on her. My hands roam her body.

"Damn, woman." I declare, looking into her eyes. "That was in-fucking-credible. Better than I'd ever dreamed. Fuck, Bella."

"That wasn't as yucky as I thought it'd be. I liked it. Can I do it again soon?" she asks with a smile.

"Oh, fuck yeah, babe," I laugh pulling her into my arms. "Anytime you want to suck my cock, you just say so."

She giggles softly, and I watch her eyes slowly blink. I can tell I've worn her out, and she's close to falling to sleep. Lightly caressing her hair, I whisper, "Go to sleep, babe. I'll leave when you're safely dreaming, I promise."

Kissing the top of her head, I continue playing with her hair. God, I've missed her hair so much. Feeling it spread across my chest is amazing. I'll do anything for this woman, including lay down my life for her.

After about fifteen minutes of feeling Bella pressed against me and playing with her hair, I know she's completely out. Her soft, little snores are fucking adorable. I never thought I'd experience anything like this peace, this contentment. But here it is, and I'm one lucky son of a bitch to have it.

Knowing I need to get up before I fall asleep, I carefully slide out from under Bella. She grumbles a bit but snuggles right into the warm spot I just vacated. Quickly dressing, I snatch Bella's panties from the floor and shove them in my pocket. Damn straight these are going home with me.

Sneaking downstairs via Hawkins' hidden passages to avoid the Brothers and head to the wine fridge in the kitchen. I grab the two Circus roses I stashed there earlier. Knowing how much she loves them, I plan to surprise her with them regularly. We've shared so many great memories with these roses when we were teens. I didn't understand then, but I do now. The variegated colors of these roses truly represent our journey from friends to lovers.

Sneaking back up to her room, I mentally thank the florist today who told me about the meaning behind the number of roses you give someone. She pulled out a chart and showed me what the numbers represented. One means 'I love you' and two means 'we are in love and deeply committed to each other.' Thankfully, the woman gave me a copy of her little chart. I'm gonna need it later.

Quietly, I place the two roses on my pillow. Grabbing the blanket from the footboard I cover my Bella and tuck her in. Before I leave, I pull the florist card from my pocket and scribble out a quick note.

LOVING YOU NOW AND ALWAYS.
Missing you more than you imagine.
~Guess Who

I SET the card on top of the stems of the roses, knowing it'll be the first thing she sees when she wakes up. I smile, recalling how we always signed our notes with 'Guess Who.'

Unable to delay any longer, I lean down and give her a quick kiss. She's so beautiful, her strawberry blonde hair surrounding her like a halo. She looks so peaceful, fast asleep and completely satisfied.

"I love you, Isabella Anderson," I whisper in her ear. "Goodnight, my love. It won't be long until you're in my arms forever."

Forcing myself to leave is hard, but I do it. I need to prove she can trust me. Damn, it's so fucking hard to leave her. As I walk out the door, pain pierces my chest. Fuck, this hurts so damn bad.

I really hope I don't have to wait three whole months, I pray silently.

CHAPTER TWENTY FOUR

FITZ: COVER STORY

*I*t's been four weeks, a full month since Bella came back to me. It's by far, the greatest month of my life. I've accepted her rules, understanding why she needs them. Being ruled by my dick, not by my heart, tainted the beauty she freely offered. Now I need to prove myself worthy of her and her trust.

Thank fucking God Bella's okay with doing everything else but having full-blown sex with me. I'd lose my mind if I couldn't explore her fantastic body, show her how much I love her. Even without that, I'd still want to be with her though. She's the best part of my day. I see her every day, sometimes for dates, but mostly we're just relaxing after work. There may have been a few nights where I've 'accidentally' on purpose fallen asleep with her in my arms, but I'd never admit it to her.

I'm hoping once this shit with Paul is cleared up, she'll be mine completely. Thank God she hasn't figured out that she's under guard 24/7. That fucker ain't getting anywhere near her. I'm beginning to plan our future, and I've already gotten a jeweler started on her engagement ring. It's going to look incredible when it's done and sitting on her finger. I just need to wait for her to be ready.

About two hours ago, Hawkins put out a call for a mandatory meeting requested by Jackson. We're all gathered around the round table in our private conference room at Camelot Security, and have been waiting for Jackson to show for about twenty minutes now. Yeah, sure, it's great to catch up with everyone and shoot the shit, but I've got a late lunch date with Bella in about thirty minutes.

I have to say, Camelot Security office is the shit. From the dark wood paneling and accents and high ceilings with exposed beams, to the suit of armor standing by the door, it feels like we've been thrust back into the days of King Arthur and his Knights. Shit, we even nicknamed the suit of armor standing by the door. I always greet Lance with a pat on the shoulder whenever I enter the room.

All our important meetings are held in this office, with all of us gathered around this roundtable. With the push of a button, the wall parts to reveal a bank of monitors where we can check on any camera we need to. There are hidden exits and a safe room in here as well. Hell, there's even a passageway to our holding cells, in case we ever need them.

Hawkins decked out this room with every high-tech

gadget imaginable. He's constantly upgrading it as new things come on the market, even designing some things himself. The room is completely soundproof to the point that even if someone was at the door with their ear pressed up against it, they wouldn't be able to hear a gun was being fired. Testing that was a fun day. Riggs built a bullet box so we could fire guns without worrying about ricochets. Hawkins knows his shit. He has the same soundproofing in our indoor shooting booths downstairs.

Getting restless waiting, I ask Hawkins, "Dude, what the hell? Where the fuck is Jackson?"

"Calm your tits," Hawkins retorts. "He'll be here soon."

It's rare that Hawkins is out of his house. His attending this meeting in person tells me something big is going down. I'm hoping it doesn't have something to do with Bella, but it probably does. Hawkins doesn't leave his house for just anyone.

Jackson bursts into the room from one of the secret exits, breathing like he ran here from his house. What in the fuck?

"Sorry I'm late," he apologizes, shaking his hand. "I had to sneak back into town, make sure I wasn't followed."

"Why are you shaking your hand, Jackson?" Carpenter asks.

"I may have, uh, punched someone. A few times. In the face, and the vibration of my Harley didn't help."

"Jackson!" Riggs bellows. "We've discussed you getting into fights. And I *know* I've taught you better than using your fists. Elbows, knees, and *the heel of your palm,* dumbass."

"I couldn't help it. I beat the shit outta Paul Edwards early this morning... And the cops are probably on their way here now."

Silence blankets the room.

"Explain," Riggs demands. His face is hard like he wants to beat the shit out of Jackson.

"So, I'm hanging out with my Pops at Cuddle's Pussycat Club, you know the one Hell's Fury co-owns? Anyway, Edwards walks in, drunk off his ass, yelling about Isabella and saying she ruined his life, calling her all sorts of shit. I saw red, but Pops held me back, telling me to wait. He handed me a bandana and a hat, so the asshole couldn't identify me. Then the fucker starts demanding to see the whores. Pops' doesn't allow fuckers to call the girls whores. They're his moneymakers, and he wants them to be happy. But Pops held his tongue too. Guess he wanted this guy to dig his own grave.

"Anyway, Edwards says he wants a hard and dirty fuck, with someone who has 'strawberry blonde hair and huge tits,' and that he'd pay big bucks for it. Rosy, the chick who co-owns it with Hell's Fury has a huge rack, fake but huge, and red hair. She told him she was the closest he'd get to his request. He looked her over and said, 'Get your old, sorry ass away from me. I want someone young, or at least a pussy with some tightness to it. Eh, maybe you'll do. I'll just fuck your ass.'

"Only a moron would walk into a strip club under biker protection with a dozen bikes in the parking lot at nine in the morning while they're eating their breakfast and start insulting the merchandise. Cuddle Bear, the bartender, told him to get the fuck out of the club. No one messes with Cuddles, he's six foot five and 300 pounds, and loves to squeeze the life outta people. But Edwards, being drunk off his ass, felt like a big man. He announced he wasn't leaving till he fucked the redhead up the ass and slapped her around a bit. Well, I snapped, and Pops lost his grip on me."

"Please tell me you didn't use only your fists." Riggs bites out.

"At first, yeah. All I could think about was he wanted to do that to Isabella. I grabbed him by the back of the shirt and pulled it up over his head to make sure he couldn't see me. I clocked him in the jaw, then the heel of my palm to his nose. He fell like the pussy he is. Once he was down, I landed some good kicks to his ribs. Straight up, I beat the ever-loving shit out of him. Literally. As in, he shit his pants when I kicked him in the balls. My dad had to pull me off him and told me to get the hell out of there and back to Camelot.

"I had to take the back roads and fields, which took a couple of hours, to make sure no cameras caught me. I called Hawkins to let him know what was up and to get all of you here. I need plenty of witnesses and a damn good cover story, just in case anyone can place me there."

I look at his hands again. They don't look too bad. "How badly did you beat him? I mean is there a chance he could die?" I'm hoping there is a chance of that happening.

"I don't know man, someone called the cops. When I hit the first field not more than a mile down the road, I heard sirens coming my way. I had to get the hell out of there and needed to make sure I wasn't seen. I don't have any idea how he is doing."

Jackson goes over to the wet bar and washes his hands. A shudder runs through him as he pulls his shirt off. Adrenaline crashes suck balls. He grabs a clean Brothers of Camelot shirt from under the bar where we keep them in case anyone needs one.

"Edwards is alive and just came out of surgery," Hawkins announces, looking up from his laptop. He probably hacked into the hospital computers. "Seems like he's going to live, but you did some major damage to his balls. They had to knock him out and put them back in place. According to this, it could be weeks or possibly months before he will know if they're fully functional again.

"His other injuries include a broken nose, several broken ribs, a few stitches, and a lot of bruising. Aside from you dislocating his balls, he made out pretty good. They're keeping him for at least forty-eight hours."

I walk over to Jackson and shake his hand. "Thank you, Brother. Maybe he'll learn something and get the hell out of town."

"That fucker is obsessed with Isabella. He's bitter and angry. I'm afraid I only made matters worse. I'm glad we have a 24-hour watch on her. I honestly don't think this'll stop the motherfucker. Isabella is a tiny little thing. Even if Edwards is a flat-out pussy, he's still a man, close to six feet tall. He could take her."

"Cops are on their way," Hawkins calls out. "Seems like someone named you and two other guys as possible suspects. They'll be here in about ten to fifteen minutes to question you."

"Alright, Stevens, Fitz, Clay, Carpenter, Hunter and Jackson, we're hitting the gym," Riggs instructs. "Gotta have a reason why your knuckles are red. Spencer, Gregory, Bishop, go inform the rest of the staff. They know the drill, but we've been here all night. Come to the gym when you're done."

"Um, that's a nope for me. Gotta lunch date with Bella," I inform Riggs.

"Pussy-whipped," Stevens coughs into his hand.

"Fuck you, asshole. I will always choose Bella before any of you losers," I fire back.

"Fitz, I need to talk to you anyway," Hawkins says.

The Brothers scatter as they were told. I approach Hawkins and take the chair next to him.

"What's going down now?" I have a sick feeling that I'm not going to like what he's about to tell me.

"Isabella's gonna be fine, Fitz. We're rotating three guys on her watch. She doesn't take a piss at Starbucks without one of the boys knowing if she washes her hands. Which she does, you clean freak."

A small grin cracks. Hawkins just wants to give me peace, to get me to relax.

"Thanks for that, Brother. But I've known for years that she's a pretty tidy woman, except for leaving her shoes everywhere. Once she's home where she belongs, I'll work on the shoe issue, believe me."

Hawkins laughs before changing the subject.

"I'm glad she's back here with all of us, and for you most of all. It's been great having her stay with me while the two of you get to know each other again. As she tells it, I also know you told her about my family. Come on bro, did you really think she wouldn't break down in front of me about it? She's Isabella.

"I talked with her briefly about what happened, but I was able to keep my shit together. I didn't go into much detail, just explained my issues. I wanted her to understand why I don't leave the house, even though I want to. I think she got me.

"Thank you, though, for giving her a heads up. It made it easier to tell her what I did. I didn't have the balls to tell her everything, not now at least. It's been great this last month, feeling normal around her. We've talked just like old times. She doesn't even act like there's something wrong with me. It's nice, even when she complains about her mom and shit. You're a lucky son of a bitch to have her as your own."

"Dude, you're her old buddy, *Nicholas*... Or should I call you *Nicky*?"

I laugh, and Hawkins reaches out and slugs me in the shoulder.

"Knock off the *Nicky, Nicholas* bullshit right now, dick wad. Only Isabella can get away with that, but you sure as shit can't."

"But seriously, now that she knows, she'll never treat you any differently. To her, you're the same person she left when she was fifteen. More importantly, thank you.

Thank you for finding her for me. God only knows where she'd be if we weren't there with all this Edwards shit happening." I shudder at the thought of what that sick fuck would have done to her. "I owe you my life for that, Brother. Without her, I don't have a life worth living."

Grasping his hand, I pull him in for a manly bro hug and pound his back.

"Alright, enough with the mushy feelings shit. I gotta go, or I'm gonna be late for my date with Bella. You know she wants me to take her on real fucking dates."

"Pussy-whipped," Hawkins coughs into his hand, just like Stevens.

"Fuck you. I'm proving to her I don't need any other pussy. I can control Henry and keep him in my pants. It's been over a month since I've had sex with anyone. I deserve a fucking medal for that shit. I haven't gone that long since before I first had sex."

"Well," Hawkins laughs, "I guess that means no one's won the pot yet. Damn, I'd have thought you'd have tapped that by now. I just lost a hundred bucks on you. I thought that you wouldn't have lasted two weeks. Damn. You think she'll make you wait for her three-month rule?"

Hawkins finds the thought fuckin' hilarious. He throws his head back and laughs, a full hearty laugh, one I haven't heard in a long time. It feels good, feels right.

"Fuck you very much for laughing at my pain. I sure as fuck hope I don't have to wait two more months. But it's up to her. By the way, jackass, we're doing everything else. And I mean *every*thing else. It's *damn* good too. If I have to wait for my woman, so be it. Now, I have a date, and I'm not going to be late."

Hawkins closes his laptop, still chuckling. "Congrats again, I'm really glad you got her back. I believe in you. You aren't going to screw this up and fuck someone else. No way in hell are you that much of a dumbass. Because if you do, every single one of us Brothers will move in on her faster than a jackrabbit in front of a prairie fire."

Reaching over, I punch him in the shoulder.

"Come on, Brother. That teasing shit's not funny." I don't think any of the Brothers would really move in on her. Would they?

"Not teasing you, Brother. I'm headed to the gym. I need a workout. Say hi to Isabella for me and enjoy your lunch. I'm sure I'll see you at dinner tonight."

Hawkins jogs out of the room, using the back way to the gym. I turn to leave the room and down our private hallway. This exit leads toward the security door that separates our conference room and our secure sleeping quarters from the rest of the building. Thank God for these quarters, they're like an apartment with four bedrooms. I've used them when things are hectic with a case, or just to take a power nap.

Hawkins uses it the most. It's one of the places he feels safe and most like himself. When he ventures out, he has all the comforts of home. Sometimes he stays for days and there are times he doesn't come here for months. With Hawkins, we've just learned to go with his flow.

At the end of the hallway in the corner of this 'L' shaped building is an elevator, which leads to the lobby, gym, and the parking garage. Few people know we have a full medical room and holding cells in what used to be an underground parking garage. Sometimes we need a bit of patching up if anything goes wrong when we're on a security mission and we don't want to deal with police asking questions. Brenden stocked his domain with everything we might need for minor surgeries, keeping it all off the record.

Access to this area requires a full hand scan. Only one other person aside from the twelve of us is allowed in here, and that's Tiffany. Well, now two. Bella has access but doesn't know it.

Tiffany's our office manager and a damned good one. She doesn't put up with our shit, having known us since she was a teen. Her dad was a cop and served in the military with Stevens' dad. When her dad died in the line of duty, he left her an eight-unit apartment but little money. We needed someone to corral the crazy, she fit the bill, and she needed the money. We've given her full access because she's earned our trust. I wish she'd take us up on the offer to help her out, but the stubborn woman 'doesn't need a handout.'

As I step out of the elevator and enter the main lobby, I find Detectives Jerkins and Franks talking with Tiffany. Their heads turn to me as Tiffany talks, hands gesturing.

"What brings you gentleman here today?" I inquire as I approach Tiffany's massive, round desk and lean over the high counter. No one gets past this counter unless Tiffany buzzes them in.

"You're not on your way out, are you Fitz? We need to talk to you for a minute," Jerkins informs me.

"I'm about to meet Bella for a late lunch. If you make it quick, I got a few. Don't want to keep my woman waiting."

"Who's here at the moment?" Detective Jerkins asks.

"I think everyone, still, we just had a meeting. Now why the third degree? Why are you taking a head count on our whereabouts?"

"Paul Edwards was assaulted early this morning at Cuddle's Pussycat Club,"

"Well, fuck me," I interrupt. "They fucked him up? Any permanent damage? You know the asshole had it coming. I'm fuckin hoping he's breathing through a tube."

"And," Jerkins continues as if I hadn't said anything, "We know Jackson's father is the head of Hell's Fury and hangs out there a lot. One of the women said the guy who beat the shit out of Edwards kind of looked like Jackson because he was so big. Naturally, we have to follow up and talk to him." Franks takes notes.

"Look, if that's what brings you boys here, I can clear the air now," Tiffany interjects. "You know me. You live in my building. Was I home last night? Nope. I was freaking here, corralling the monkeys, ordering drinks from the bar and getting snacks. Hell, I even had to do a run for those nasty, menthol cancer sticks for Jackson. Yuck. But I'm the only one who'll put up with them.

"Most everyone was here all night. Loverboy here,"

she jerks a thumb at me, "showed around eleven last night. They're probably in the gym now, which is their usual routine post meeting. I just don't understand why they want to beat the crap out of each other. Would you like me to show you the way to the gym, so you can talk to them? I have to warn you though, it's not pretty in there."

A weird half smile spreads on Franks' face. I've never seen him smile at all.

"Please, Tiffany. I'd love for you to show me the way."

Franks spoke quickly, his voice excited. Fuck, I hope he isn't interested in Tiff. She's so far out of his league it isn't even funny. Jerkins looks a bit pissed at Franks' reaction to Tiffany, probably noticing that he used the singular 'I' instead of 'we.' Well, shit, do *both* these dickheads have a thing for her? I'll have to have a talk with her about this real soon. They live in her fucking building.

"Jerkins, you never answered my question about Edwards. How bad is he, could he die?" I need to hear it from them.

Jerkins chuckles. "No, sorry he'll live. He got his balls kicked up into his stomach, something I didn't know was even possible. But yeah, he'll live. He may not be able to have kids, though. Everything else will heal in time. I'm sure you're happy about that."

"Fuck, no. I'd rather he's breathing through a tube for the rest of his worthless life. I wish I was the one to put him in the hospital and fucked up his junk. I hope you don't find the hero that did me a favor though," I answer. "Tiffany can show you to the gym so you can go harass my Brothers. Have a good day, boys."

Before exiting the lobby, I turn back and watch as both fuckers jockey for the spot next to Tiffany. She's clueless, walking with efficient steps ahead of them toward the gym. Yeah, I'll definitely be talking to her about those dickheads. She needs to wake the fuck up and shut that shit down immediately.

CHAPTER TWENTY FIVE

ISABELLA: HOW THE BEST DAY BECAME THE WORST

*L*ying on Drake's chest after just waking up from one of the most incredible nights of my life, I inspect his chest. Over the last two months, Drake and I've gotten closer than ever, even more so than when we were kids. I've explored him, learning how to please him. It's not that hard, he loves anything I do to him and that feels amazing. He's taken me to levels of ecstasy and pleasure I'd never dreamed possible.

Last night, I'd decided I couldn't live another night without Drake next to me. He's been so patient and understanding of my need to trust him completely. He didn't push me to come stay with him or give me any trouble about staying with Hawkins. I know he's truly mine and has fully earned my trust.

Today is Friday, two months after our reunion. It's also my twenty-fourth birthday. I can't believe I made it this long without giving in to my desire for Drake. But, tonight's the night. I'm ready to give all of myself to him.

To surprise Drake and inform him of my decision, I came to his house last night. He was working late, so I lay on his bed, clad only in black satin panties and a smile. When he walked in, his steps faltered. A hot, sensual smile graced his lips.

"I can't spend another night without you," I'd said.

Drake's answer wasn't verbal. He flew into motion, stripping the clothes from his body. Watching Drake reveal his fabulous body made me want to do what Clay had suggested many times, and that was for me to 'ride Drake like a pony'. I almost gave in but held back the urge. That doesn't mean the night wasn't amazing. It was.

I continue inspecting his incredible chest, my fingers tracing his sculpted abs. Slowly, I slide down his body, admiring every dip and curve. When his massive erection comes into view, nervousness hits, and I wonder how that's actually going to fit inside of me.

Drake's been preparing me, stretching my core to take him. I've woken up sore from his ministrations, but I didn't tell him that. It's a good sore, the kind that reminds me throughout the day of Drake's talents the night before. I'm hoping that's how it is when we finally make love tonight. A little soreness, but no pain. Turning my face towards Drake's penis, I whisper to him.

"Good morning Henry, you fine sir. I'm about to wake up your master in the best way."

Drake moans from my warm breath teasing him.

Slowly, I run my tongue around the head. It jerks towards my mouth. Flattening my tongue, I lick the top.

"Fuck, Bella. What a way to wake a man up," Drake groans.

His hands slide into my hair, gripping tight.

"Come on, babe. Open your mouth wide. Henry wants a good sucking."

Giggling, I do as he instructs. I slide my mouth down his shaft as far as I can take him.

"Holy fucking shit," Drake groans. "Damn, that's so good. Don't stop, babe."

Encouraged by his words, I wrap a hand around the base of his shaft, squeezing and stroking as Drake showed me. With his hand in my hair, he controls my head, moving my mouth up and down. His hips thrust and flex, pushing himself deeper.

"Oh, fuck babe, this is going to end fast." Drake's voice is gravelly, turning me on even more. A second later, the thick vein on his erection pulses as he reaches his climax.

"Holy fucking shit! Damn!" he repeats. I love those words, he uses them when he loses control.

I lick him clean, then crawl up his body, kissing a path up his abs and chest. Drake tries to catch his breath as he pulls me up. Once I'm in his arms, he reaches down and squeezes my bum firmly while kissing me gently.

"Good morning, Dray," I sigh, pulling away. "I hope you liked your wake-up call."

"Fuck, babe, best goddamn wake up ever. Feel free to wake me up that way anytime."

Drake's face turns serious as he studies mine.

"I love you more than the air I breathe, babe. I don't want to spend another night without you by my side. Move in with me. Live with me until you're ready to marry me. That's our next step."

Marriage? I blink in surprise. I know we've loved each other forever, but this is the first time he's actually said that. I climb on top of him, kissing every inch of his face. Pulling away, I stare into the gorgeous green eyes I never have to live without again.

"*YES!*" I yell. "Yes, I'll move in with you, and I'll be here with you every night. I feel the same way. I can't survive another day without you. I love you, Drake Allen Gregory-Fitzpatrick, with all my heart and soul, my very being. I am *yours.*"

As he rolls me onto my back, Drake's kiss consumes me. Our passion and love for each other drives our frantic movements, touching, squeezing, caressing as if we're starving for one another. He tears his lips from mine, resting his forehead against mine.

"As much as I want to make love to you right now, we'll wait until tonight. When we make love for the first time, I want it to be perfect, no interruptions. I hear Mojo, Brenden, and Clausen downstairs right now. Join me for a shower before we have to face the day. I know we're running late for work, but I've been dying to do this."

"You're right, now is not the time. But tonight, we're leaving my birthday dinner as soon as we're done eating. I want you so much. I don't want to wait another day to be yours completely." I press a quick kiss to his lips.

"Tonight, we'll make sweet, passionate love. But all weekend, your ass is in this bed, and I will fuck you in all the ways I've dreamed. I'll plan everything out, don't worry. I'll have food delivered so you can maintain your energy. Now, shower time," Drake says, cocking an eyebrow.

I blink slowly, nodding my head. He smiles at me and pulls me to standing. After pressing a quick kiss to my lips, he grabs my hand and tugs me into the bathroom.

~

MY LEGS ARE STILL WOBBLY from my shower with Drake. The things he did to me leave me in a daze. I can't even remember if I've brushed my teeth already, so I reach for my toothbrush. He made me come not once, but twice. Holy cow that was amazing, I think while brushing my teeth.

Tonight is the night I'm giving myself wholly to Drake. Handing in my V-card. I can't wait to spend the next two days locked in his, *our*, room. He said we would "christen every square inch of our room." When I told him I'm leaving work early, the smile that spread across his face was freaking hot. I'm not even nervous, but that might change as the day goes on.

My mind continually wanders back to our mind-blowing shower as I get dressed. I'm really the luckiest woman in the world. I've captured my childhood sweetheart. Drake truly loves me. We're on the verge of skipping off into the sunset. All of my dreams are close to coming true, a wedding, children, and a life together. Nothing can ruin this for us now. As a bonus, I even have all of my friends back too. Life is wonderful.

Pulling my Rainbows and Unicorns T-shirt on and slide my feet into my favorite flats. My black skorts are perfect for work, in case I need to help out with the kiddos. I twist my hair into a messy bun and use two hair sticks to hold it in place. Tory's little boy, JayJay, loves to pull them out and watch my hair fall down. It's cute seeing his face light up every time he sees my hair like this. He's getting so big, the little bugger.

Skipping down the stairs, I check my iWatch when it vibrates, showing a text from Tory. "Need snacks, running low. Delivery tomorrow," it reads. I need to let Drake know that I have to stop at the store before I leave.

I bounce into the kitchen and find Drake, Brenden, and Asher drinking coffee and eating the cinnamon rolls I made yesterday.

"I hope those aren't too stale. I'm running late this morning and didn't have time to make anything fresh."

Drake looks up from his laptop, some frosting on his lip. Gah, I just want to lick it off his lip. Mmmm, frosting and the taste of Drake. His tongue peeks out, sliding along the path I want to take. Oh, man... Here comes the hot and bothered feeling. I'm not accomplishing *anything* today.

"Sorry, babe. They were delicious. Your brother wouldn't save you one, even though I asked. Would you like me to pour you a travel mug of coffee before you go?"

"Damn, Fitz, *you* were the one who took the last one," Asher says.

"Nope, Clausen," Brenden mumbles, his mouth still full. "That was you, asshole."

"I can't believe you ate twenty-four of those in one day. I guess that's how you all stay so big. Thanks, honey, but I gotta run. I need to stop and get some treats for the kids on my way to work, so I'll just swing by Connie's Coffee House on the way."

Stepping up to Drake, I kiss him goodbye. I take a quick peek at his screen and see he's ordering dinner for tomorrow from my favorite restaurant. I act oblivious of his plans, but man, I love him so much. I kiss him one more time, then wave goodbye to Brenden and Asher.

As I drive to work, I'm focused on tonight. I can't wait for Drake to see the navy silk nighty I bought just for tonight. It's perfect. It has a slight push up bra and ties in the center of my chest, making my cleavage look fantastic.

Suddenly, I'm cut off by a newer white Honda. Slamming on my brakes, I startle as my heart races at the near miss. That idiot!

"Okay Isabella, keep your mind on the road. You want to live to see tonight," I mumble to myself, still shaking.

Looking closer at the Honda, I realize I've seen it around several times over the last week or so. The car pulls into the parking lot of Connie's Coffee House. Well, they must not be too bad since they like their coffee from here.

I order my usual lite chocolate latte and a chocolate

croissant in the drive-thru. There's a new server at the window this morning, and he's taking forever. I tap my fingers to the beat of my music, waiting for him.

"Good morning," I greet him as soon as he opens the window. "You're new, you'll be seeing a lot of me. I stop here daily on my way to work."

I hand him my phone for Apple pay.

"Oh, no," he smiles. "Your boyfriend already paid. Said to say he can't wait to see you again."

"Aww, Drake's so sweet. I have the sweetest boyfriend in the world. Thank you."

"No, thank you for being patient with me on my first day going solo at the window. I'm still learning, but so far so good. Have a wonderful day, and I'll see you tomorrow," he says handing me my coffee and croissant.

Taking my coffee and the bag, I smile at him. Pulling forward a bit, I take a big sip before getting back on the road. I really do have the best boyfriend, but how did he manage to pay for my drink from the house? As I continue drinking my coffee, I think there must be a new barista too. The latte tastes weird, like it's a little salty.

Turning the cup in my hands, I see a heart drawn in red marker, and "See you soon, Isa." Wait, Isa? Drake calls me Bella. Why would the barista write Isa, anyway? I didn't tell him my name.

Bringing myself back to the task at hand, I turn into the store parking lot for the treats Tory needs. The white Honda turns into the next entrance. How strange, it's like he's following me from in front of me.

After parking, I grab my chocolate croissant and pull it out of the bag. Oh, man. It's a plain one. Well, I'll just have to add jelly to this one at the office. I'll let the new barista know tomorrow, it's *always* a chocolate croissant. I might be nibbling on the kid's crackers, my stomachs been a little upset the past few days.

~

FIFTEEN MINUTES later I'm back in the van, leaving the parking lot. I'm suddenly dizzy and woozy. It hits so quickly, I wonder if I'm coming down with the flu or something. I look in the rearview mirror to check out my face. My eyes blink slowly, but I notice the white Honda following me. A strange feeling comes over me. I push the call button on my steering wheel.

"Call Drahhh."

The car beeps, telling me to give it a voice command. My voice is too slurred for it to understand me. I fish in my purse for my phone while trying to focus on the road. Finding it, I slide my finger across the screen and hit Drake's name. It rings five times before going to voicemail.

"Dray— Somfing wong. I dizzy. Have to shtop da van. Like I drunk. Only had the cobbee you got me. Somfing very wong." I look around for somewhere safe to park, but the white Honda is still following me. Then I see the driver, and my heart starts racing as I recognize Paul in my rear-view mirror. "Dray— I wuv you. Paul behind me... Come get me, need wou..."

I manage to jump the curb of a bank parking lot. My van stops when it crashes against the light pole, under the cameras. My hands are shaking, and I'm sweating as I try to lock my doors.

"Wuv you, Dray. Wuv you," I repeat in an attempt to stay awake.

I blink slowly, each time it's harder and harder to keep my eyes open. My body isn't responding and my head pounds, my stomach starts to churn badly. I hear a weird noise, my eyes flutter as I try to open them again. Paul's voice filters through the door, then it opens. Something cold presses against my iWatch. Oh God, is it a knife? It falls off me. What is Paul doing? I hear his voice by my ear.

"I'll teach you, you bitch, for destroying my fucking life."

My arm is tugged, and I'm lifted from my seat. I flop, falling into Paul's arms. I struggle with myself, trying to move to push him away, but I can't. He lifts me up, but all the movement makes me nauseous. Suddenly, I'm falling, and a sharp pain strikes my head. Everything goes dark.

CHAPTER TWENTY SIX

FITZ: THE WORST DAY OF MY LIFE

I've finally completed all my planning for the weekend. I've called three florists and the one hundred and one Circus roses will be delivered by two o'clock, before Bella gets home from work. The handy-dandy chart the florist gave me says that one hundred roses means *you're my one and only*. One of the florists had some broken stems and offered to give them to me so that I could spread petals over the bed.

The meals for this weekend are planned. Unfortunately, Mom's planned a birthday dinner for Bella. We're leaving right after dinner, I don't care how much Mom begs us to stay. Tomorrow's dinner is prime rib with all the sides from Bella's favorite restaurant. I even ordered her a white cake with cream cheese frosting. I know how much she loves her sweets, and I love feeding them to her just as much.

Closing my laptop, I look up to see Brenden and Clausen staring at me like I've grown a second head.

Fuck. I told them this was for our two-month anniversary and Bella's birthday, but I don't know if they're buying it. There's no way I'm telling them the real reason for my actions.

"You gonna go all out like this for every damn month-aversary? I never figured you'd be so pussy-whipped," Brenden comments.

"Just you wait until you're in love. You'd be surprised at what you'd do just to see her smile. Don't forget, this pussy can still kick your ass, big brother, so watch it."

"I still have issues with this. She's my little sister," Clausen says, his face serious.

"Look, bro. I get it. But you're gonna have to deal with it. I love her, and we're together. Forever. You're going to be the uncle to our kids one day. As soon as she's ready, I'm going to ask her to marry me. She's not just some fling to me. She is my life, my breath. Call me a pussy, but I don't give a fuck. She. Is. My. Life," I tell Clausen, emphatically.

"Shit," Clausen mutters. "Ivy's gonna have a shit fit," he laughs.

"Fuck, I forgot about that snotty bitch. How the hell is Bella so different from her mom?" I ask on a sigh.

Brenden's got a shit-eating grin on his face. "Proud of you, brother. You couldn't have picked a better woman. We all knew you loved her. She fits with you, and with us. I'll enjoy being your best man."

I chuckle in response. "Yeah, you're gonna throw one hell of a bachelor party."

"Ha," Clausen adds, a mischievous grin on his face. "I just realized you need to suck up to me. I'm the one you have to ask for Isabella's hand. I'm the one who will be walking her down the aisle and giving her away. It's not Ivy you have to worry about. It's me, big boy."

Relief spreads through me because it seems Clausen is accepting that we'll be brothers-in-law.

"Oh, so that's how you're gonna play this?" I joke. "I'll show you, big boy."

All of our phones ring in unison. Oh, shit, it has to be Hawkins. I dive for my phone, knowing something is wrong for him to call us all at once.

Before I can even ask, Hawkins is already speaking.

"Have you heard from Isabella?" His voice is stressed. *"Her van is in a bank parking lot, with her phone and watch. You were the last person she called. She didn't hang up, but your voice-mail disconnected her because it reached the time limit. She's not with her van now. Find out what you can, I'm trying to locate her. Call you back."*

"Wait!" I scream into the phone. "What the *FUCK*?! She called me about fifteen minutes ago, but I was on the phone. I haven't checked the message yet. I'll listen to it now, but we're heading out. Call us back."

"Brenden," I yell, "you drive us to the bank! Bella's van is there, but Hawkins doesn't think she's in it. She didn't tell us she needed to stop at the bank. He's going to call us back when he finds out more, and I have to listen to that message she left."

We take off running to Brenden's BMW. I climb in the back seat, shaking so bad I can barely slide my finger across the screen of my phone. I put it on speaker, praying. *Dear God. Please let Bella be safe. Let her be okay. Let me find her.*

"Dra Somfing wong. I dizzy. Have to shtop da van. Like I drunk. Only had the cobbee you got me. Somfing very wong. Dra, I wuv you… Paul behind me. Come get me, need wou…"

She mumbles something over and over, there's an odd noise, then we hear Paul's muffled voice.

"I'll teach you, you bitch, for destroying my fucking life."

"Oh, shit!" I punch the back of the passenger headrest in front of me. *"Fuck. Fuck! FUCK!* That bastard has her! Who the fuck was watching her?"

Brenden is speeding, weaving in and out through cars, running red lights. My phone rings and I snatch it up.

"Hawkins, where in the *fuck* is she?" I growl into the phone. I'm close to breaking. "He drugged her somehow. He has her. She sounded drunk, her words were slurred. I think she passed out. She said she only had her coffee. She said she was going to hit the Connie's Coffee House drive-thru. She goes there every day. Then she needed to pick up snacks for the kids."

"Calm down, dude. The cops are at the bank. A security camera has the perfect angle. Find out what it picked up. Give your phone to the cops, so they have the message from Isabella. Her ring GPS shows she's on the freeway headed north. I'll call you back in five unless they stop."

Before I can respond, we pull into the bank. My breath is coming in pants, as my mind is racing. Why the fuck are we stopping? We need to be chasing after my girl!

Brenden throws the car into park and bolts without shutting it off. I follow behind him, running to Detectives Franks and Jerkins.

I notice a yellow evidence tag near what looks like blood. Holy shit.

"What the fuck is this?" I ask Jerkins, pointing to the spot on the ground.

"Fitz, keep it together. We'll find her, okay?" Jerkins says.

"Fuck that shit, Jerkins. *We* will find her. So, help me God, if he's touched her or hurt her in any way, he's a dead man. You understand me? Now, what the fuck is this on the ground?"

"We just watched the tape. He had a Slim Jim and broke into her car. She drove into the parking lot, crashed into the pole, and we think she then passed out.

"This pole has the security cameras on it. Edwards pulled up behind her in a rented white Honda. He proceeded to try to pull her out of her van and heft her over his shoulder. He failed, throwing Isabella over his shoulder instead and dropping her on her head. We also found her iWatch in the van with her iPhone, making sure we couldn't trace her."

"I guess he's still too injured from his beating to do any lifting," Franks interrupts.

"Once she hit the ground," Jerkins continues, "Edwards grabbed her under the arms and dragged her to his rental and threw her into the front seat. We've put out an APB. You just need to keep your shit, Fitz."

I pull up the message from Bella and hand him the phone.

"Fuck that stay calm shit. That pervert the courts let go free has my woman. Bella is tracked. We're outta here, and I'm gonna hunt her down my own damn self. We'll call you once we have her."

"No!" Franks and Jerkins shout. "No fucking way. We're following you."

Jerkins shouts at the officers on scene as I book it back to the BMW. Clausen and Brenden are right behind me.

Peeling out of the parking lot, Clausen calls Hawkins for directions. Brenden heads for the freeway.

My heart is pounding so hard I can hear it reverberating in my ears. I've never wanted to kill someone in my life, but right now I want to rip Edwards limb from limb. I take a few deep breaths as Brenden flies down the freeway.

"*Fitz, are you in the car too?*" Hawkins asks from the phone.

"I gave my phone to the detectives, so they could listen to Bella's message. They're following. Where are they, Hawkins?" The desperation is evident in my voice.

"*They just arrived at the Waterson Plaza Hotel seven minutes ago. He somehow got her into a room. I can only give you an approximate location in the hotel. I'm trying to hack into the hotel's security cameras. She hasn't moved for the last ninety-five seconds.*

"*I installed an app on Brenden's phone remotely that will help you track her down, you just need to restart the phone. It'll beep faster the closer you get to her, like the hot and cold game. Do you understand me?*"

"Yeah, man," Clausen says. "We're about eight minutes from the hotel, but with the way Brenden's driving we should be there in half that."

"*Fitz, she's going to be okay, Brother. I've called an ambulance and notified both the police and the hotel. If the cops aren't there, hotel security will be waiting for you. He had to have drugged her coffee. There's no other answer. I'm sending some guys to find out what happened to her guard. He isn't answering my calls, but his car is still in the grocery store parking lot. Keep me posted."* Hawkins hangs up.

"I will kill the fucker with my bare hands," I force out between clenched teeth. "I swear to fuckin God, he is a dead man walking."

"Only if I don't shoot the motherfucker first," Clausen growls. He pulls his gun out, checking that it's loaded.

"Brenden, give Clausen your phone so he can reboot it. We're close to the hotel," I instruct him.

Clausen is all over the rebooting shit. I close my eyes to pray, but Bella's beautiful face is all I see on my closed lids. My prayer is incoherent with thoughts of keeping Bella safe, nothing harming her, for her to be okay all jumbled together. I've never prayed so much or so hard in my life, but I feel useless just sitting here.

Pulling into the Waterman, Brenden bypasses the waiting valet and stops in front of the doors. We jump out as one and race into the lobby. Brenden has his phone in one hand and his California Medical Association card in the other.

"There's a medical emergency in one of your rooms. Where's the nearest elevator?" Brenden asks the bellman.

"This way, sir," he says, leading us around the corner.

"Check with the front desk and security, we're going

to find her with the tracker," Clausen calls to Franks and Jerkins when they enter the lobby.

I'm too wound up, too consumed with worry to speak. As the elevator doors open, several more officers flow into the lobby.

Brenden holds his phone out, his hand shaking. He has his medical bag slung over his shoulder, Clausen carries one too. When the hell did they grab those?

The phone beeps a steady pace as the elevator climbs the floors. Fuck, this is taking for-fuckin'-ever. As we near the fifth floor, the pace increases, and we punch the button to stop there. When the doors part, we follow the phone as it beeps.

Moving down the hall, the beeping goes wild as we pass the fourth door on the left. The door is partially open.

Clausen draws his weapon, but I rush through the door, murder my only thought. The sight that greets me wipes that from my mind.

My beautiful Bella is laid on a bed, her body stripped of her clothes. She's not moving, and I run to the bed.

"*Fitz!*" Brenden yells. "Don't touch her."

My eyes plead with him. I need to touch her, to know Bella's okay.

"Let me check her for a head or neck injury," he answers my non-verbal plea.

I sit on the edge of the bed and gratefully accept the towel Clausen brings me to cover her with. I slide my fingers along her cheek, feeling her warmth. The fist holding my heart hostage loosens a touch.

"Bella, babe. Can you hear me? I'm here, babe.

Brenden's checking you out, you're going to be okay," I say, fervently hoping I'm right.

"The fucker isn't in here. Room's clear," Clausen growls, holstering his weapon. "What can I do to help? Is she going to be okay?"

"She's alive. Give me a minute to check her out." Brenden opens his bags, pulling things out.

"Bella," I plead, taking her hand. "If you can hear me, squeeze my hand. Please, babe, squeeze my hand." There's no response. I look her over, seeing a baseball-sized lump on her head. A trickle of blood runs into her hair.

"Brenden, she's bleeding. Give me something to clean it up," I request.

Brenden finishes listening to her heart and taking her pulse, then stands, leaning over to check the wound.

"Here," he says, handing me a towel wrapped in plastic. "Get this wet with hot water, and you can gently clean it."

I run to the bathroom and turn the faucet too high, causing water to splash everywhere. It takes a fuckin' eternity to heat up. Once it's wet, I rush back to the bed. I realize that Brenden was trying to get me out of the way.

He's listening to her lungs, checking her pupil reactions and looks concerned. He checks the automatic blood pressure cuff on her arm, and his face falls.

"What the fuck, Brenden? What's going on? She's okay, right? Don't keep anything from me!" I demand.

"I'm not. I'm not as concerned about her head wound right now. Her blood pressure and respiration are

very low. She needs a hospital, STAT. We need to minimize her movement."

"Where the fuck is that asshole?" Clausen's voice
whips across the quiet room. "How the fuck did he get
away? I called Jerkins, they're sending the EMTs up right
now. Brenden, is Isabella going to be okay?" His voice
cracks on the question.

The similarity between Clausen and Bella hits me.
They both have a habit of babbling when they're
nervous, spewing questions and statements, not waiting
for a reply. Clausen's voice is shaky as he paces the room.

"I'm working on it," Brenden says quietly. He slowly
pulls the towel back and looks at her arm.

"Don't touch anything in here. Leave it for the cops.
Maybe the shit head left something behind."

Bella's skin is pasty, sickly looking. A gurgling sound
comes from her.

"Brenden, what's happening to her? It's like she's
throwing up!" I cry.

"Alright, we need to carefully roll her to her side,
toward me, in a smooth movement. Use the sheet under
her to help you. Clausen, when we get her to her side,
bend her knees carefully."

Brenden pulls a bulb syringe from his bag. As soon as
we get her on her side, liquids flow from Bella's mouth,
followed by a white, foamy substance. My fear hits a new
high. This looks like an overdose or an allergic reaction.
Oh, fuck.

Brenden pushes her hair back from her face.

"That's it, Bella, we're gonna get you to the hospital,
and pump this shit out of your stomach. You hang in

there, girlie. We're gonna take good care of you, I promise. You fight this and hang on, you got me?"

The paramedics, as well as both detectives, barrel
into the room. Brenden takes charge.

"Twenty-four-year-old female, severe head injury.
Unconscious. Possible overdose or allergic reaction.
Needs a neck brace. She just vomited fluids, then white
foam. Respiration and blood pressure low. I want to start
an IV STAT and push fluids," Brenden states to
the EMTs.

The EMT's move fast, coming to my side of the bed.
I move to Bella's feet, giving them room to work. My
eyes remain glued to Bella, praying there's some sort of
response. One of the EMTs moves the towel on her.

"Keep her covered!" I shout. "I don't want her
exposed in front of everyone!"

"He's her fiancé," Brenden explains when the EMT
sends him a questioning look. The EMT nods, understanding lighting his face.

Jerkins and Franks move around the room with
gloves on their hands, looking for evidence. Jerkins lifts
Bella's Rainbows and Unicorns shirt on the floor with a
pencil. There's a straight cut up the center of her shirt.
That fucker cut it off her. That asshole cut off all her
clothes. I didn't even check her for cuts. Fuck.

"Order a rape kit, just in case," Franks says to
the room.

Bile rises in my throat. I take a shaky breath to keep
it down. My hands tremble in rage. If that fucking
asshole raped her, I will shred him with my bare hands.
Slowly.

"Fitz," Clausen says gently as he lays a hand on my back. "We gotta believe she'll be okay. You with me, Brother?"

My only response is a nod, my eyes on Bella's still form in the bed.

"On my count," Brenden says. "One, two, three."

They lift the backboard Bella's strapped to. Carefully, they transfer her to the gurney and cover her with a blanket after fastening her to it. When they push her toward the door, I follow them, my heart pounding hard in my chest.

Once we're in the elevator, my hand snakes under the blanket and I take her hand. Her fingers are cold. Fear tightens my throat.

When the doors open to the lobby, Riggs, Stevens, Jackson, and Carpenter snap to attention and move quickly toward us.

"Riggs, take Fitz and Clausen to the hospital. Meet us there," Brenden directs.

"Fuck that shit," I croak. "I'm not letting her go."

Brenden nods as Clausen opens his mouth.

"No, Clausen. There's no room for you. It'll be tight with me, the EMT and Fitz. Go with Riggs. Meet us there and trust me to take care of her," Brenden says.

We move to the ambulance and load Bella in. I climb in after her, and Brenden follows. He and the EMT hook her up to the monitoring equipment. Brenden hands me something, telling me to put it on her index finger of the hand I refuse to let go of. They place sticky pads on her chest, and the EMT starts an IV.

Brenden's speaking into a two-way radio, probably

communicating with the hospital. His words sound distorted, as if I'm underwater. My brain can't focus on anything but Bella.

I hold her hand in mine, bringing it to my lips. Trying to warm her ice-cold fingers, I blow warm breath across her hand, kissing it while talking to her.

"Bella, babe. I'm here. You're going to be okay. Fight this, babe. Be strong. I love you. Babe, you're the only one for me. Be strong."

CHAPTER TWENTY SEVEN

FITZ: THE NIGHTMARE CONTINUES

*W*e pull up to the ambulance bay at the hospital. When the back doors open, there's a crowd of nurses and doctors waiting, and Mom is among them. My focus is solely on my woman, who looks lifeless. Oh, God. She has to be okay.

Brenden tries to pry my hand from Bella's frozen one. I fight him, trying to maintain my connection to her.

"Mom, help me out here. I need to take her back for tests and get her stabilized." Brenden's voice is muffled.

"Drake, honey. You need to let go. Let the doctors fix her up."

"No, I need to be with her, Mom. She won't want to be alone. I need to be there when she opens her eyes." Tears fill my eyes, and I hold them back by sheer force of will.

Mom pries my hand from Bella's, making me release it. The doctors take off, taking Bella away from me, into the trauma room. I watch her until she's out of sight and Mom wraps her arms around me, holding me back.

I fall to my knees, crying for the first time in over twenty years. Mom follows me to the ground, holding me tight. I hold onto her just as hard.

"I can't lose her, Mom," I whisper.

"You won't, honey. Isabella's a fighter."

"She's my breath, Mom. My heart, my life."

"Drake, honey, she loves you just as much, always has. That little spitfire won't let go of her dream come true so easily."

"Mom, it hurts so bad."

"I know, sweetie."

"Fitz," Riggs calls quietly, sliding his hands under my arms. "Come on, up off the floor. Isabella's the strongest chick I know. Keep the faith. We're here for you, and her."

My nod is wobbly. I can't catch my breath, and my heart is racing.

"Grayson," Mom calls, "help me move him to the private waiting room. We can wait in there, out of the way."

With Mom on my right and Riggs on my left, they lead me down the hall. I barely manage to make out Stevens holding a door open for us, through my tears. They place me on a couch, and I collapse in on myself, wrapping my arms around my stomach trying to hold myself together.

"Bella's going to be okay," Hawkins says. I vaguely recognize the importance of him being here, away from his safety net.

"Did she have her ring on?"

"Huh?" I ask. "Ring?" I blink my eyes, trying to remember. "She had it on when she left."

"No," Clausen pipes in. "She didn't have it on in the hotel room."

"Got the fucker!" Hawkins suddenly says, with a smile in his voice. "Riggs, give me your phone."

Hawkins gets to work on his computer mumbo jumbo, keys clicking on his keyboard.

"Any updates?" Jerkins asks, from the doorway.

"Get your ass over here, Jerkins," Hawkins calls. "I already know where the asshole is. He stole Bella's ring, but little does he know it has a tracker in it. He's headed east. Riggs, Jackson, and Stevens are about to go after him. You can follow them if you want, if you can keep up."

"I'm fucking going!" Clausen says, through clenched teeth.

"You sure you don't want to stay here with Drake? We got this, brother. Isabella's your sister. We know you'd rather be here for her." Riggs tries to give Clausen an out.

"Drake, I trust you with Isabella. I know you'll keep me posted. I need to go, you understand me?"

"Clausen, I wish I could go and handle the fucker myself," I choke out. "But I won't leave Bella. I can't, not until I know she's okay. I totally understand, Brother. Go and get the motherfucker for me." I'm glad Clausen's going. It'll keep him busy and hopefully get his mind off Bella. One of us losing our shit is enough.

Clausen leans down and half hugs me, "Thanks, Brother. I'll update you once we get the fucker."

"Any updates on Isabella?" Franks asks, looking at Mom.

"I'm about to go see what I can find out." Then she turns to me, speaking softly, "Drake, I need you to take nice, long deep breaths. I don't need you to pass out by hyperventilating and have you hit your head too. Okay? I'll be right back."

She gives me a quick kiss on my head then leaves the room. The door closes, and I look up to find everyone staring at me.

Scrubbing my hands down my face, I take a couple of deep breaths.

"Okay, go and find this fucker. I'm not leaving this spot until I can see Bella. I'm depending on you guys to handle this. I don't trust the cops to do this on their own."

"We're standing right here, Fitz," Jerkins says. "We'd like to follow you, Riggs. We don't have the surveillance on this dickwad as you do. Let's go get him."

"I'll lead," Jackson says. "You follow behind Riggs in the SUV, but we're not leaving until we get an update on Isabella. Hawkins, send us hourly updates once we hit the road."

Hawkins nods as he continues typing and programming their phones.

We wait in silence. I'm lost in my thoughts, wondering where we went wrong. How did we miss this? Bella was supposed to be safe. How could this have happened? How did this sick fucker get his hands on my woman?

The door opens, revealing Mom dressed in scrubs.

"They just pumped Isabella's stomach and sent out for blood work. They're giving her medication to counteract what they think is GHB. She's breathing easier, and her blood pressure is rising. She's better, but not yet stable," Mom announces, like the professional she is.

"Dr. Diana Riggs has examined her. She was not raped, thank God." A collective sigh of relief sounds throughout the room.

"She shows no trauma, but she does have bruising on her breasts. There are no other signs of any other form of sexual assault."

My head pounds with the need to slaughter the asshole for even touching her. Mom sits beside me and grabs my hand. My rage subsides a bit at her touch.

"Isabella has a serious head injury. She'll be taken for a CT and MRI shortly. We're confident she has a concussion from the fall, but the scans will show us if there are any other injuries. She hasn't woken up yet, so we're a little concerned about that.

"There are several abrasions and bruises on her head, buttocks and the backs of her legs, confirming she was dragged across the asphalt. There are a few small lacerations, we assume those are from her clothes being cut off. They're all minor and do not require stitches. They've been cleaned and a simple bandage has been applied. The laceration on her head required three stitches. From the size of the hematoma, there is concern that there may be some swelling on her brain. They're monitoring her vitals, pumping fluids and have her on oxygen. Okay, update done. Now, go get this asshole, boys. I'll personally text updates as I share them here. Now, get your asses moving."

Some of the guys chuckle at Mom's swearing. It's not something they're used to, but they know she means business.

Jackson squats in front of me. "We're gonna get this mother fucking asshole for you. When Isabella wakes up, you tell her my exact words so she can add it to my swear jar tab."

"I'll do that. Go get the fucker," I say, my voice lifeless.

Jackson pulls my forehead to his with a hand behind my head. "We got this. If he puts up a fight, I'll put a bullet in him myself."

"Be safe," I mutter.

"Come on, Riggs, Clausen, Stevens. I'm outta here. Keep up, cuz I'm more scared of Mom Gregory than Fitz right now. I'm in the wind."

Riggs and Stevens give me chin lifts, vowing silently that they won't let Edwards escape their wrath, before leaving with Jackson.

Clausen leans down and whispers, "If I get the chance, I'm putting a bullet into the fucker myself. Give my sister a kiss for me."

Once my Brothers and the detectives leave, Mom puts her arm around me and tugs me close. I feel like a child again, needing the comfort she offers.

"Drake, I promise you, Bella is getting the best care possible. You have to believe she'll be okay. I'm going down the hall to check with Diana and Barbara. Both of them are waiting for Isabella to be brought back to the room after her tests. I want to see if they have any updates yet."

"Okay, Mom. I'm just gonna sit here and try to keep my shit together."

"Okay, sweetie. If you need anything, have one of the Brothers come get me." Mom rubs my back for a second before kissing my cheek, then leaves to talk with Riggs' and Stevens' moms. They've been friends since before college and all work here with Brenden.

I place my elbows on my knees and stare at the floor. The memory of Bella's cold hand in mine flashes through my brain. Fuck, she was so still. I can't accept her not being okay. Fresh tears fall to the floor, splashing silently. Black, wing tipped shoes stop in front of me, then move to the side. My father sits next to me, and I close my eyes. Fuck, I don't need this right now.

I feel my father's hand hesitantly rubbing my back.

"Son, it's going to be okay," he says, his voice wavering. "That young lady loves you, always has. She'll not give up on her love, or on having you back. It's a dream come true for her. Her face lights up at just the thought of you. I've seen it myself over the years. She's a strong woman. She will not give up. You need to believe that. You need to be strong for her.

"I'm sorry for keeping you apart, and not telling you she was back home. I was wrong. I should have stepped up years ago and given you her messages. I'm truly sorry, son."

My ears are ringing in the silence. Did my father

really just apologize? Did he say he was wrong? He continues to rub my back, giving affection freely. More tears flow at this new experience, the first sign of affection that my father has ever given me.

"Drake," he starts, then clears his throat. "I'm... I'm sorry for being an asshole to you for all these years. I don't even know why myself. I need you to know I'm proud of you and what you boys have accomplished. I love you."

Turning, I collapse into my father. He wraps his arms around me as I cry harder. Emotions bombard me, and my breath hitches. I can't get control, and I'm lost in a sea of feelings.

"I can't lose her," I breathe out.

"It's going to be okay, son," he vows. "Your mom and brother won't let anything happen. She'll pull through. Isabella's a tough cookie."

A few minutes later, I pull myself together and stop the tears. My breathing is still jumpy, but I'm composed enough to pull away from my father, who keeps an arm around me.

"Oh, *noooo*!" Brit's scream is blood curdling. She rushes to me, sliding on the floor and kneels between my legs.

"Oh my God, she can't be dead! Don't tell me that bastard killed her," she cries, throwing her arms around my waist.

Brenda, Sarah, and Tiffany follow behind her, their faces white with fear.

"Britney Rose Gregory," my father scolds, "don't say

such things. We're waiting for an update from your mother. Isabella is alive, and she'll be fine."

Brit lifts her head from my lap, her face confused.

"But… Erm … You were hugging Drake. I've never seen you touch him."

Brit wipes the tears from her face, and I pull her onto the couch next to me, throwing an arm around her.

"Brit, it's okay," I whisper. "I lost my shit and Dad was just trying to help me keep it together. I'm okay for now." Brit nods into my chest. Realization hits me that for the first time in my life, I just called my father, Dad.

Mom enters the room, a small smile spreads across her face at the sight of my dad and I, side by side.

"Okay, Isabella's in ICU, in a private room. We just got her MRI and CT scans and blood work back."

Brenden walks up behind Mom and puts his arm around her.

"I'll take it from here, Mom," he whispers to her. "Okay, good news. Isabella doesn't have any bleeding in her brain from when the asshole dropped her. She does have a concussion, and there is a bit of swelling as I suspected. It's not too bad, and she should recover just fine.

"She's not yet regained consciousness, so we're monitoring her and pushing some medications to speed the healing. Due to the concussion and swelling, it may be a day or two before she wakes up. She can have visitors, two at a time. You need to understand that she doesn't look so hot right now as she's hooked up to monitors and has a few IVs. Everything considered, she's stable but critical. We're hoping she'll only get better from here on out."

I shoot up from my seat, abandoning Brit.

"Take me to her. Now. Please, Brenden," I beg.

"Alright, alright. Drake can stay by her side, and you all will have to rotate. Is that okay with you, Brother?"

"Yes. Now get your ass moving and take me to Bella. I need to see her."

Brit hooks her arm through mine.

"I'll take Brit and Fitz now, and then you all have to rotate every ten minutes until visiting hours are over."

Brenden leads us down a long corridor to the ICU. There's an officer posted at the door.

"I've requested two twenty-four-hour guards for her until that asshole is found. There's one here and one outside of her room," Brenden explains, at my questioning glance. I nod as he leads us through the doors and into a room surrounding a circular nurse's station. Encircling the large, round area are eight sliding glass doors, the lights dim behind sliding curtains.

Brit gasps when we enter Bella's room. My heart sinks at the sight of her. Bella's skin is whiter than normal, and the color has drained from her cheeks.

I step up to the bed and take her hand in mine. I'm relieved to find the warmth has returned to her skin.

"Can I kiss her?" I ask, looking at Brenden.

"Quickly, and make sure you replace the oxygen mask. It'll help her heal faster," Brenden answers.

Carefully, I lift the mask and press a quick kiss to her pale lips, then replace it.

"I'm here now, babe. You're going to be okay. I love

you," I whisper into her ear.

I hook the chair by the bed with my foot to pull it closer and take a seat. I'm not moving from this spot until Bella can come home.

Brit comes to my side and places a hand on Bella's leg.

"Isabella," she says quietly. "We're all here for you, girlie. You be strong and sleep as long as you need to. Just get better. Fitz needs you. And we'll celebrate your birthday once you get out of here. Love you, sis."

Brit's voice cracks a little at the end, betraying her emotion at seeing Bella in this state. She leans in and kisses Bella on the cheek.

"Drake, if you need anything, text me. I'm going to send the girls in first, then we can get back to your place and take care of Mojo and Stevens' critters. We left Rachel, Sam, err, Carpenter's sister, watching them. I don't want to leave her there by herself too long. She asked what to do with the flowers you ordered." Brit kisses my cheek.

"Thanks, Brit, I'm staying right here until Bella can come home with me. I'll see if they'll allow some of the flowers here. Tell Rachel thanks for me, too. There'll be food delivered too, either eat it or feed it to Mojo. I'll re-order it when Bella and I come home."

She just smiles and nods, then leaves the room.

Holding Bella's hand, I listen to the machines beep, telling me she's very much alive. I study her face. She looks beautiful, almost peaceful. I kiss her hand.

"I'm not leaving your side, we go home together. You hear me, babe? I love you."

CHAPTER TWENTY EIGHT

FITZ: LONGEST NIGHT OF MY LIFE

*P*eople filter in and out of Bella's room, saying a few words of encouragement, kissing her cheek and then leaving to send the next one in. Throughout it all, I hold her hand against my cheek and let people have their moment with my woman.

When Dad came in, he stood in the doorway before taking a deep breath and finally making his way to the bed.

"I'm so sorry, Isabella," he whispered. "Be the strong woman I know you are and get better for my son." He pressed a gentle kiss to her forehead, then her cheek.

A few minutes after Dad left, Hawkins appears in the doorway. He, too, hovers for a moment before approaching the bed. He takes Bella's hand and kisses it, then runs his fingers along her cheek. I know how much her friendship means to him.

"Alright, Isabella. Seems I drew the short straw and I'm here to keep an eye on your basket case of a boyfriend. He's lost his shit more than once today. He even broke down and cried, girl. I know, I know. Shocked the shit outta me too! But, the man loves you so we understand. We all love you." He leans down and kisses her on the cheek.

As Hawkins leaves her side he grabs the chair in the corner. He pulls it up next to me. Once he's settled, he grabs his laptop out of the satchel he always carries.

"Okay, Brother, tough question for you. Do you want to call her mom, or should one of us do it? She needs to know what's going on. Ivy is Isabella's next of kin. The story hasn't hit the news yet because Edwards is still on the loose. I'd hate for her to find out through the news."

"Fuck. Yeah, I hear you. I'll call Bella's mom. Are Mom and Dad still here?"

"Yeah, everyone but the girls are in the waiting room. Dude, the Brothers' families are showing up, even some of Hell's Fury. They're just waiting for an update and chatting. Hunter called in for pizzas right before I came in here. Fuck, I had to get outta there, that's why I'm here. Jackson's parents kept sneaking looks at each other, they haven't been in the same room in years. His dad's probably gonna bail soon. He kept mumbling something about hunting down Edwards himself. You know he'd deliver righteous justice."

"Dude, did you track that fucker down yet? It's been a few hours," I ask.

"Oh, yeah. Looks like he's heading toward the mountains. His parents own a cabin in Big Bear. I sent the boys in that direction. Because they don't know if he's armed, the cops are following the guys. They'd rather avoid a chase, and they're about a mile behind Edwards. They'll close in when they get closer to the bottom of the mountain. Jackson's sped ahead a few times to make sure he's in the car alone. He's clueless that he's being followed. I'll keep you posted as soon as I find out. Now," he says, taking a deep breath, "stop avoiding it. Do you want me to stay with Isabella while you call her mom? I swear I will call for you if she so much as twitches."

"Yeah, thanks, Brother," I say scrubbing my hands over my face. "I'll send someone in while I make the call. Do me a favor, talk to her, let her know she's not alone and we're here."

Standing, I remove the oxygen mask and give her a quick kiss, then replace it.

"Babe, I'm gonna call your mom. I'll be right back, promise. I love you, Bella. Hawkins will be right here with you."

I turn to Hawkins, "I'll be right back. Thanks, man."

Knowing I'm leaving my heart in the room, I look back as I cross the threshold. The left side of Bella's face is swollen, and her eye is blue and purple. That shiner is gonna hurt like a bitch when she wakes up.

Bella's hair is in a messy bun on top of her head, courtesy of Mom. Other than the damage to her face, the IV and monitors, she looks like she's taking a nap. Brenden keeps reassuring me that the oxygen will help get the swelling on her brain down, and that she's breathing on her own. Fuck, I'm glad he's here to take care of my Bella.

Finally, I turn to the waiting room, knowing what I

have to do. When I walk in, everyone's head snaps up, and Carpenter jumps to his feet.

"Is she okay? Did something happen?" he pleads.

"No, nothing's changed. I realized I need to call Ivy. Mom, can I borrow your phone? The police still have mine. And if Ivy gives me any trouble, can you and Dad help me with her? You know how she is."

Dad and Mom come to my side. As Mom is handing me her phone, Dad starts talking,

"Yes son, call her. She needs to know what's going on with her daughter. If Ivy gives you any trouble, you hand the phone to your mom. I'll call the New York office and get the plane ready. Tell Ivy a driver will pick her up within the hour, and she'll be here in a less than six hours."

"Thanks, Dad." I look around the room, "If someone would like to go and visit with Bella while I handle this phone call, now's a perfect time."

"I'll go in there, Drake. I'd like to check with Hawkins and get an update on everything as well," Bishop says.

"Thanks, I'll be back shortly," I announce.

Taking a deep breath, I move to the balcony door, open it and walk through. I'm hoping Ivy hasn't changed her number since the last time Mom called her. It rings twice before she answers.

"*Hello, Monica. I was wondering when you were going to call me.*"

"Hello, Ms. Anderson. It's not Monica, it's me, Drake. I was hoping to catch you before you heard."

"What are you talking about? I thought Monica would be calling to chat about you and Isabella. What's going on?"

"I'm sorry to be the bearer of bad news, but Paul Edwards kidnapped Bella earlier today." Ivy gasps into the phone, but I continue. "We rescued her before he was able to do anything, but during the kidnapping, the scumbag asshole, uh, excuse my language. I'm trying here."

"No, no, he is a scumbag asshole!" she interrupts. *"Please, tell me Isabella is okay. Why isn't she calling me?"*

"Ma'am, during the kidnapping he tried to throw her over his shoulder, but the fucker dropped her. She's sustained a serious head injury. Somehow, he drugged her, possibly her coffee. Details are still sketchy, but we do know she's been unconscious since the time he took her. There's some swelling on Bella's brain. She's in the ICU. The doctors think she'll wake up when she's ready," I finish.

"Oh, Lord Jesus. I have to get there." There's a rustling noise, like Ivy's tearing through her closet. *"I have to pack, book a flight. I'll be there as soon as possible. Oh, God. My baby! How did this happen?"*

"Ivy, ma'am. We have that covered. My dad called the New York office of his law firm, and a car will pick you up within the hour. The plane is waiting for you at the airport."

"That is not *happening. I will* not *accept any help from that bastard. I want nothing to do with him, or his law firm."*

"Mrs. Anderson," I plead, raising my voice. "Look, you can take his help and be here in six hours, or you can take the risk and end up here sometime tomorrow afternoon. Dad has changed, let him help you get to your daughter."

"*Forget that, Drake. She wouldn't be lying in a hospital right now if she'd stayed away from you.*"

Oh, this bitch. Fuck.

"You know that's not true. I had nothing to do with this. It was all Paul Edwards and his sick obsession with your daughter. We had her under twenty-four-hour guard, but Edwards must have done something to the man we had on her!" I yell into the phone.

"I love her more than my life. I would give anything to trade places with her right now. Don't you dare put this shit on me!"

The door opens behind me, and Mom joins me. She pulls the phone from my hand.

"Ivy, listen to me right now. Do not be a bitch to my son. Your daughter is in critical but stable condition. Get that goddamned stick out of your ass and get over it. It happened years ago, and Allen is trying to help. Drake is barely keeping it together. I'm not about to let you give him any shit. Do you understand me?"

Ivy responds. I can hear her bitching, but I can't make out the words.

"No, you and Allen are one and the same. You've both been messing with these two long enough, keeping them apart. They're meant to be, and *no one* is getting in their way, or I'll kick your ass myself, Ivy. Now, get your shit packed and your ass in gear. The driver will be there in forty-five minutes. Accept the fucking help. Do you hear me?"

Mom falls silent as Ivy replies. She nods, and uh-huh's a few times.

"Honey, it'll be okay," she says, her voice soothing. "Brenden is a brilliant trauma doctor. He's been with Isabella since they found her…"

"Okay, I love you too…"

"It's alright…"

"We'll get through this…"

"See you soon, Ivy."

Mom hangs up then hands me her phone.

"Ivy's on board. She'll take your dad's help. Don't you worry, I'll make sure she treats both you and Isabella with respect. Now, you get back to your girl and tell her that her mom's coming."

"Thanks, Mom," I smile, appreciating her badass side. "She was trying to blame me for this shit because Bella and I are together. Fuck that shit."

I pull her into a hug, needing the comfort. Fuck, this is damn hard. I take a deep breath, trying to keep my shit together.

Mom returns my hug, laughing gently.

"Sweetheart, none of this is your fault. And no, you're not a pussy. You're a real man, one with feelings. I know, hard to believe. But you're in love, and some-times things like this can take you to your breaking point, and that's okay. It doesn't make you a pussy. Now, I'm going to sit with your dad, and you get back to Isabella."

"Okay. Thanks for your help."

I take a few deep breaths of fresh air to compose myself before heading back into the waiting room. Once again, when I enter, all eyes come to me as everyone falls silent. I give them a half-smile.

"Look, guys. I'm okay. You don't have to walk on eggshells around me. I'm going back in with Bella. Feel free to rotate in and out with Hawkins. Thanks for being here and supporting us. Ivy will be here in about six hours, so get your visits in before then."

Carpenter stops me as I leave the room, concern etched on his face.

"Fitz, can I get you something to eat or drink? I doubt you've had anything since this morning."

"I had coffee and some cinnamon rolls this morning, but I want to get back to Bella. I'll take a Coke, though," I reply, grabbing one from the table.

I sneak a peek at Jackson's parents. His mom is as beautiful as ever, and her navy pencil skirt and floral blouse show her class. She's sipping a diet Dr. Pepper, chatting with Stevens' and Carpenter's moms. Glancing at Jackson's dad, he's openly checking her out. He's wearing his signature biker gear of boots, t-shirt, and leather vest. His black leather jacket is slung over the back of his chair.

Yeah, I'll never understand how those two hooked up. They're night and day.

As I enter Bella's room, Hawkins stands to leave.

"I'm going to find someone to go wait for Bella's brother and sister. Arielle texted me because Clausen called her on his way to look for Edwards. Ashton's driving them here. They both want to see her."

"Oh, shit. I forgot about them. Yeah, okay. You do that," I respond.

I approach my chair as Hawkins leaves the room. Leaning down, I give Bella a quick kiss before sitting.

"Hey, babe," I say, taking my seat and picking up her hand. "I'm back. Your mom's on her way. She'll be here in about six hours. I missed you while I was gone."

I caress her arm, careful of the IVs. She's gonna freak when she wakes up. My woman hates needles.

"Hawkins told me the Brothers should be in Big Bear soon. This will be over fast, hopefully." Bishop says, pulling me from my thoughts.

"Did he find out what happened to the guy that was guarding Bella?" I question him.

"Yeah, the cops found Eddie. He was in his car at the grocery store, it looks like he was jabbed in the neck with a good size dose of Ketamine. He was still knocked out when the police found him. He was brought here for observation, but he'll be fine. He'll probably be sent home later tonight."

"The cops have added attempted murder to the list of charges on Edwards. Edwards' parents are flipping out. Spencer has been handling this, and Eddie's family too. He just turned twenty-one but thank God he'll be okay."

"Fuck, that dickwad! I knew something had to have happened. Our crew is well trained and none of them would have let Bella be taken like that. Let him know I'll visit him once Bella's awake. Tell Spencer to cover all medical costs and any hotel costs if his family needs it."

Goddamn, that fucking asshole. If I ever see that prick again, I'll rip him apart with my bare hands.

❧

This has been the longest day and night of my life. Mom came in about an hour ago and demanded that I eat something, threatening to have the Brother's force feed me if I didn't. I tried to tell her I wasn't hungry, but she wasn't hearing it. Once I smelled the green bean chicken from my favorite Chinese restaurant, my stomach let out a growl that I'm sure they heard in the waiting room. Mom sat beside Bella, holding her hand while I devoured my food. Damn, when Mom's right, she's right.

Feeling a bit better after my meal, I inform Mom, Dad, and Brenden that there is no way in hell anyone is prying me from Bella until she can leave with me. Brenden and Mom pulled some strings to allow me to stay with my girl.

When I finish eating, Mom finally leaves. Ashton, Bella's little brother, enters and I'm shocked at how much they look alike. Their hair and noses are so similar they could be carbon copies of each other. It makes me wonder what his mom looks like. He's a good kid, and it's obvious how much he loves his sister.

"Look," Ashton says. "I don't know you, only what Asher's said, but you seem devoted to my sister."

"I am," I respond, trying to keep the smile off of my face. Is this little shit gonna try to get me away from Bella?

"Arielle and I are gonna stay at Asher's place. If anything changes with Bella, I need you to call me immediately. Otherwise, we'll be back in the morning."

"Will do."

Shortly after Ashton left, Arielle cautiously comes in. She's folded in on herself. At her first sob, I'm out of my chair and pulling her into my arms. She cries, shaking in my arms. I know the feeling, having been in this same state a few hours ago.

"Arielle, Bella is going to be okay," I reassure her. A sniff is her only response.

She gathers herself up and pulls back. Her eyes search mine, and I give her a small smile. Damn, her eyes are the same blue as Clausen's, and she's tall for a chick. Bella's father's genes must have been strong. Same hair and nose for Bella and Ashton while Clausen and Arielle got his eyes and height.

Arielle spends some time with Bella, whispering to her while holding her hand. When she's ready to leave, I call a nurse to escort her to the waiting room. She looks lost and devastated.

Since normal visiting hours ended when Arielle left two hours ago, my only interruptions have been the ICU nurses checking on Bella every hour. They adjust her oxygen and administer medicine through her IV. They all give me a small smile but never say a word. I sit and hold her hand, occasionally caressing her arm.

My phone buzzes and I pull it from my pocket.

HAWKINS: *The guys have Edwards in a standoff at his cabin. Will update when more info is received.*

RELIEF FLOODS ME. I kiss Bella's hand, saying a prayer of thanks.

"They got him, babe. That fucker isn't getting away this time. You rest, my love. I'll be here when you wake up. I love you, Bella."

I'm so drained from this damn stressful day, my eyes get heavy. Laying my head on the bed next to Bella's hip, I angle my face toward hers. I just need to rest my eyes until I get an update from Hawkins.

CHAPTER TWENTY NINE

FITZ: IVY AND BELLA

*L*oud voices from the hallway wake me up from a much-needed snooze. Kissing Bella's hand, my eyes lift to her monitors. I'm not sure what they all mean, except for the blood pressure. I gain comfort in seeing that it's in a safe zone.

Lifting my head, I see Hawkins out of the corner of my eye. He's typing away on his laptop as usual. It makes me happy that he's hanging here with me.

The voices come closer as their volume increases. What the fuck? This is a damn hospital and the fuckin' ICU. They need to calm their shit before I calm it for them.

Bella's door slides open and Ivy, her mom, enters. Dressed in designer clothes, she takes one look at Bella, and the hysterics begin.

"Oh my God!" she wails. "Look at my poor baby's face!"

She runs to the side of the bed and lightly touches

Bella's face. Ignoring Hawkins and me, she turns to the foot of the bed where Mom and Brenden stand. Some dorky looking pansy hovers behind them. He's got wire framed glasses, thinning hair, and he's not even five ten. I shoot a glare at Brenden for letting all these people in while Hawkins and I are here. He shrugs.

Fuck, Hurricane Ivy has arrived.

"Look at my poor little girl! Is she breathing on her own? Brenden, why is she in such a small room? She needs a room appropriate to her status. I don't care about the cost. My baby deserves the best care. I want her moved ASAP!"

Ivy turns to the dorky fuck and points at him.

"Stanley, make the calls to make this happen. If they need a donation, do it. This matter needs to be handled without delay."

"Ms. Anderson," Brenden calls. "The ICU is the best place for Bella to get the care she needs. This is where all the equipment is, and where the best nurses and doctors are. We are not moving her for your whims."

Mom shakes her head, knowing her friend's eccentricities.

"Brenden, this is my only daughter, my baby. And I frankly don't give a damn what you think. I know that if she was the president or a movie star, she wouldn't be in this pathetic room like a common person. I want her moved now to a private room, big enough for everyone to be comfortable."

She turns to mom. "Monica, isn't Barbara Stevens a nurse? I'll pay her double whatever this hospital is paying. I want only people you or I know personally caring for Isabella. I don't want any strangers touching her. She needs to feel the love of friends and family." She turns her demands to Brenden. "Brenden, why are you not moving to get this done? Must I do everything? I'd rather not go over your head but, believe me, I will. Now move it."

Hawkins looks like he's on the verge of cracking up, and Brenden looks as exasperated as Mom.

Glancing at Bella's monitors again, I see her pulse and blood pressure numbers are rising, and that scares the shit out of me. This fuckin' temper tantrum needs to stop right fuckin' now. Still holding Bella's hand, I stand up.

"Ivy, glad you could grace us with your sunshine," I growl. "However, you need to take this discussion somewhere else. All this yelling is stressing out Bella, making her blood pressure go up. Look." I point to the monitors.

Ivy's mouth snaps shut as her head swivels to the monitors. Brenden comes to my side and adjusts a few of them. Betty, my favorite nurse, comes with her hands on her hips.

"Alright, everyone out except for Drake and whom he chooses," she announces, her voice stern. "Dr. Gregory, I'm shocked you've allowed this mess to happen. I watched her stats rise at the station. You know better," she chides him.

"You beat me to it, Betty. I was just going to escort Isabella's mom and her friend to the waiting room," Brenden replies, his voice strong.

"Yes sir, Dr. Gregory. I'd appreciate the room being cleared so I can take care of my patient properly."

"Now, I'm not asking, I'm telling," Brenden says to Ivy and that dork, "Ivy, let's move this to the waiting room. Hopefully, Fitz can calm down Isabella because I will not allow you back in this room until her vitals are stable. Do I make myself clear?"

"Looks like you grew up to be as crass and rude as your father. Monica, let's discuss this elsewhere. I'm no longer speaking to Brenden. He completely ignored my request to get Bella into a suitable room."

Mom clears her throat. "Okay, Ivy. Let's go talk about this ridiculous notion of yours. By the way, you're being a bit of a bitch. I assure you, the ICU team here is stellar. I know them all personally. This is the best place for Bella. I'd have moved her myself if it wasn't."

Ivy gasps at my mom's forthrightness, and turns, hooking her arm with Stanley's and prances from the room. Mom and Brenden trail behind them, leaving Hawkins and me blessedly alone with Bella again.

"Now that was some funny shit," Hawkins chuckles. "I'd have never put that MILF with the likes of *Stanley*. That pansy-ass was following her around like a trained dog. She's so out of his league. Huh, wonder if Isabella knows about him?"

"I agree, he's gotta be mega rich. But dude, MILF? That's just wrong. Did you see the way she bossed him around? I wouldn't put up with that shit for a nanosecond. But whatever makes that bitch happy, the less she'll bother Bella and me."

Removing Bella's oxygen mask, I kiss her lightly before replacing it and sitting again.

"So, Hurricane Ivy's arrived, babe. She's issuing

orders like she's the fucking Queen of England. I see why you came back home."

As I stroke her hair and talk to her, Bella's numbers slowly even out. Thank fuck, that scared the shit outta me.

"That's it, my beautiful Bella. You calm down. I'm here with you, and no one, not even your mom, is making me leave your side. My mom will handle Ivy for us, okay? You just get better."

Hawkins' phone beeps, and it hits me. Hawkins has been here with me the whole time. In the flesh, not on an iPad screen. In a very busy, public hospital. That just confirms how much Bella means to him. There aren't many people Hawkins would venture out to be here for. Bella's definitely a full member of Camelot.

Hawkins picks up his phone, looking at the screen.

"Shit," he mutters. Turning to his laptop, he types like a person possessed.

"What? Did they capture Edwards?"

"They did more than capture him. Edwards is dead. He shot Jerkins, and the Brothers took him out. They're being questioned at the sheriff's station now. Thank God Edwards wanted a clear view of the lake. They took Jerkins around back to the massive lawn and airlifted him to a hospital. Riggs had to use the XStat."

Peace rolls over me. I shudder and let out along sigh. It's fuckin' over. My girl never has to deal with that fuck again.

"Can't wait to hear the details," I tell him. "Let them know it's appreciated."

Hawkins nods as he continues typing. I stand and

lean over Bella, staring at her beautiful, peaceful face. My poor woman has a huge black eye, a good size lump in her hairline and stitches on her forehead.

Pulling her mask off, I give a lingering kiss before whispering in her ear.

"Babe, they got him. He can never touch you again. You're completely safe. I love you, babe. Once you're home where you belong, I'm asking you to marry me. I never want to be apart from you again."

CHAPTER THIRTY

ISABELLA: CONSCIOUSNESS

Feeling pressure on my lips, I know it's Drake. I want to respond, but my body doesn't feel like my own. I can't move anything. I try to return his kiss, to open my eyes, anything, but my body refuses to comply.

The pressure leaves my lips, and Drake speaks in my ear. I feel his breath against my skin, but his voice sounds far away, or as if I'm underwater. But he's here, wherever I am. I can smell him, hear him, feel him, and I know I'm not dreaming.

He tells me I'm safe. Safe from what? What happened? 'Go home'? What does he mean? I don't understand.

Wait, what did he just say? Marry me? Oh. My. God. Oh, heck yeah! I want that so bad. Of course, I'll move in with him tonight. I never want to be apart from him again.

I want to hug him, pull him to me. Why can't I move? Why can't I open my eyes? What in the world happened?

Think, think. What is the last thing that happened? Oh my, the shower with Drake. Coffee run, snack shopping… then… Oh man, think, think, think. I was feeling nauseous, the coffee tasted weird. Driving to work but getting dizzy. Seeing Paul behind me, needing help, crashing into a pole at the bank.

I'm so tired, all this thinking is making me really sleepy.

Listening hard, I focus on the noises around me. There's a rhythmic beeping noise. I have to be in a hospital. Oh, poor Drake, he has to be so worried.

"Bella!" His voice is louder, excited. "Can you hear me? Hawkins! Look at her eyes. They're fluttering like crazy. Babe, I'm here with you. Come on, open those gorgeous eyes. I'm not leaving your side until you can come home with me."

I try. I try so hard to do what Drake asks. My body just doesn't want to work.

"That's it, Isabella," Hawkins says.

What? Hawkins is here? He never goes anywhere. Am I at his house? "You keep fighting, gorgeous. Brenden's taking care of you, and your boyfriend is glued to your side. He's a bit of basket case, but don't worry. I'm here to take care of him," he jokes.

I want to smile at Hawkins' humor, but I'm so tired. So, exhausted. Blissfully, everything goes dark as I'm dragged under.

~

Fitz

BRENDEN FLIES INTO THE ROOM, along with Nurse Betty.

"What's going on, Drake? You pushed Bella's call button," Brenden asks, looking frazzled.

"Look! Her eyes are moving like she's trying to open them!" I'm so fucking excited. This has to be a good sign.

"How were they moving? Were her eyes just moving around, or was she trying to open them?" Brenden questions, lifting her eyelids one at a time and shining his penlight in them. He checks her machines.

"Hawkins saw it too, I didn't imagine it. They were moving towards me, behind her eyelids, like she was trying to look at me. They weren't shaking, just moving around."

"I believe you Drake, that's good. She's trying to come out of it. Her body has gone through a lot. Give her some more time, she'll wake up soon. Has she moved her hand or squeezed your hand yet?"

"No, not yet. Is that bad?" Fuck, now I'm worried.

"Brenden, I saw it too," Hawkins chimes in. "They were moving, her blood pressure went up a bit too, but once we started talking to her, it went back down."

"That's good, Hawkins. She's fighting like we knew she would. This is all a very good sign. She needs time to heal. Isabella's trying to come out of it. It won't be tonight, and maybe not for a day or two, but she will wake up, I promise."

"Thanks, Brenden, that's good news. But I'm still not leaving her."

"Neither am I. I'm here as long as they are," Hawkins announces. Both Brenden and I look at him, jaws hanging open in astonishment.

"What the hell are you two assholes looking at? I have spoken, I'm not leaving. If Ivy can throw her weight around, then so the fuck can I. I'm not going anywhere."

"Okay, Hawkins, you can stay at the hospital. But I'm sure Drake will make you leave the room when we have to examine her, unless you want to face the corner."

"I can do that. But I'm not leaving this hospital. Dude, I can always make myself comfy in your office," Hawkins smirks.

"It's okay, Hawkins. No one is big enough to kick either of our asses out of here," I reassure him. It's a huge step for him to even be here in the first place, but I understand why he needs to be here.

"It'll be fine, feel free to roam the hospital. I'm sure Ivy will try her very best to control everything. Consider yourselves warned," Brenden says, as he walks to the door. Brenden stops and turns to me. "By the way, Isabella filled out an Advanced Health Care Directive weeks ago. She named you as her agent, Fitz. You're in charge here. Watch out for Ivy."

"I know. And I'm not scared of Ivy, she'll have to deal with it. Bella and I are together now. Neither of us are teenagers anymore. Ivy can kiss my ass if she tries to cause trouble."

Feeling a million tons lighter, I count my blessings. Edwards is dead, and Bella's trying to wake up. I finally feel like she's going to be okay. I just have to be patient. She's fighting, she wants to come back to me again. I'm the luckiest bastard alive.

CHAPTER THIRTY ONE

ISABELLA: WAKING UP

The sweet heady scent of roses fills my nose. I struggle to open my eyes. My eyelids flutter, a sea of red and yellow color hits my eyes in the dim light. My eyes are so heavy, it's like climbing Mt. Everest to keep them open. Finally, I'm able to open them fully. Looking around, I'm surrounded by my favorite roses, every available surface is covered in beautiful arrangements. There have to be a hundred Circus roses in here! A smile spreads across my face.

Oh gosh, I'm in a hospital bed! What happened? I look down to find Drake's head lying by my hip. My hand feels like it weighs ten pounds as I lift it to touch Drake's black hair. Running my hand along his cheek, his eyes flutter and he shoots up in his seat, his eyes bulging in an almost comical way.

"Babe! You're awake!" He quickly stands and leans over me. He tries to kiss me through my oxygen mask, and we laugh.

"Sorry, I'm just too relieved to see your eyes again," Drake murmurs. "Let's try that again, shall we?" I nod as Drake pulls the mask from my face. He leans down again and presses his lips to mine. A feeling of peace and my love for him wash over me, and I want more.

As Drake pulls away, he says, "You scared the ever-loving shit out of me, Bella." Still cupping my face, I stare into his jade green eyes. "I'm so glad you're back with us. You've been asleep for two and a half days."

My voice is weak and sounds breathy even to me, as I ask, "Two and a half days? What happened? I remember realizing I'd been drugged, but how?" I try to demand.

"Here babe, try an ice cube, let it melt in your mouth." Drake reaches over to the side table and runs an ice cube over my lips. It feels amazing. I take the ice cube and let it slowly melt in my mouth... oh, that's the best thing ever. He continues to explain.

"Edwards told the barista he was your boyfriend and wanted to pay for your order. He asked to write some-thing on your cup, too. Because the dude was new, he gave him your coffee, which gave the fucker the opportu-nity to drug it when he wrote a message on the cup. You had an allergic reaction to it. When the asshole pulled you out of the van, he tried to throw you over his shoul-der. Due to the epic beat-down he got a few days before, he was too injured and ended up throwing you way over his shoulder, and you landed on your head. That fuck gave you a major concussion, and some brain swelling."

"You are freaking kidding me!" My voice lacks the volume I want it to have. "That jerk face dog turd. He's in jail, right? He didn't do anything else to me, did he?" My speech is slow and slurred. I need to know every detail, but I'm getting tired already.

"No, babe, he didn't do anything else. You got sick, and the dumb ass thought he killed you and split. I'm not going over the last two fucking days right now. That can wait. I need to know how you're feeling. Does anything hurt?"

"Drake, I've got a slight headache and I'm very queasy. My mouth is dry, and I'd love more ice. My whole body just feels so heavy, it's hard to move. I'm so sleepy." A yawn escapes me. "My throat hurts too, but I'm fine. I missed you and wanted to be with you. I could hear you talking to me, but I couldn't respond."

Hawkins pops up from a rollaway bed I hadn't noticed. He practically runs to the side of my bed.

"Isabella, you're awake! Thank fuck. Jesus woman, you scared the shit out of us. Don't do that again."

Both Drake and I chuckle as I try to whisper, "Okay Nicholas, I promise never to get kidnapped again. I'm glad you're here. Thanks for coming, and for taking care of Drake."

"You heard me? So, it's true, when you're out like that you can still hear us?" Hawkins asks.

"I heard bits and pieces. I kept trying to open my eyes to look, but nothing worked."

Stevens' mom comes in and gasps.

"Drake Allen Gregory-Fitzpatrick," she points at him, "were you not told to buzz me if she woke up?"

"Hi, Mom Stevens. I didn't give him a chance." I defend Drake, my voice sluggish.

"Well, that's no excuse. How are you feeling, sweetie? Any pain?" she asks, pushing Hawkins away and replacing my oxygen mask. Mom Stevens checks the machines I'm attached to, then pulls out a penlight to check my eyes.

"I'll text Brenden, I know he had the 5 AM shift. I'm sure he'll be here shortly. Now, Isabella, you didn't answer my question. How are you feeling? Any pain?"

"I'm just really sleepy, my head hurts a little and..."

Brenden interrupts me when he bursts into the room.

"And how are you, Isabella? See Fitz, I told you she'd wake up."

I lift my hand with the IV and gingerly wiggle my fingers at him.

"I just knew you wanted to poke me full of more needles. One IV wasn't enough for you?" Everyone chuckles, as I continue. "As I was just telling Mom Stevens, I'm super sleepy and every part of my body feels heavy. My head does hurt a little, and I'm super nauseous. Like, if I move at all, I'll barf."

"All normal due to the concussion and brain swelling. It'll take a while for you to regain your full strength. If you're in pain, just push this button," Brenden says, handing me a cylindrical thing, a button on one end and the other attached to a box near my IV stand. "It will administer a dose of pain medicine. It will only give medicine within prescribed limits so you can't get too much. But remember, it's some heavy stuff so you'll probably fall asleep. The nausea might be from the concussion, or maybe something else. We'll talk later about it." Brenden smiles big, then winks at me. He's being weird. What is that about? Why won't he tell me now?

I'm having a hard time keeping my eyes open, they're so heavy. With each blink, it's harder to keep them open.

"Mom Stevens, please give Isabella some Zofran to help with the nausea," Brenden instructs her.

"I'll go get that right now," she replies, and I hear her Dansko clogs walking away.

"I'll be okay, I just won't move. I don't want a shot. I have enough needles in me," I mumble, desperately trying to open my eyes.

"See, even with her eyes closed she can hear you. She hates needles," Hawkins jokes.

"No shots, Isabella. We'll use the IV port. You won't feel a thing, I promise," Brenden explains.

Trying to reopen my eyes, I nod. I turn my head to Drake, admiring the nice beard he's got growing in. I like the look and wonder if it's soft. Gosh, it'd be nice to just cuddle up with Drake. I know I'd get better faster if he could just hold me. He's the best form of medicine.

"Fitz, she's falling back asleep. That's okay, she'll need a lot of sleep to recover. You should go home and shower, shave, maybe have a nap. Mom will be here soon," Brenden tells Drake.

"No shave," I mumble. Drake chuckles and squeezes my hand.

"There you go. My woman doesn't want me to shave. Besides, I've got this wonderfully comfortable chair to keep warm," Drake says.

Their voices start fading as I fall deeper into sleep. I

don't want Drake to leave. I want to listen to him talk and feel his hand holding mine. Giving it my all, I squeeze his hand and try to pull him closer.

"Look, she just squeezed my hand. Dude, I'm not going anywhere. I'm fine in this chair. I've even had a couple of naps on that rollaway."

"Whatever, man. Have you texted Ivy yet to let her know she woke up? You'd better, or she'll have your ass. She'll be here at eight I'm sure, ready to bark orders. I have to admit, you're handling her a lot better than I thought you would. Try to keep it up."

"What the hell is that supposed to mean?"

"Nothing, nothing, just let her know. I don't want her chewing my ass out again. And if I text her, I can only imagine what she'll do to you, knowing you didn't text her first."

"I'll text her. Damn it, she's a pain in the ass."

I try to smile. Only my mom. She is a pain in the patootie. I hope she's on her best behavior with Drake, or I'll have some choice words for her.

"Hey Brenden," Drake calls, "what else could be causing Bella to be nauseous? If it isn't the concussion, could it be from the drugs that asshole gave her?"

"No, she threw up in Edwards' car, and on the bed at the hotel. The first thing we did was pump her stomach. I'm confident the Rohypnol has nothing to do with this. We'll talk later about it. It's nothing to worry about. I'll be back in a bit, I have to do my rounds."

"You sure, Brother?" Drake sounds worried.

"Yes, Fitz. I'm sure. At least take a shower, dude. You look like shit and you haven't shaved in three days."

"I'm not shaving with the shit razors you have here. I'll be fine. Brit brought me a change of clothes, and since Bella's not clutching my hand, I'm pretty sure she is asleep again. I'll take a quick shower. I don't want to smell like ass when she wakes up again."

Feeling like I'm sinking, I decide maybe I should rest as their voices fade away. Maybe I'll have more energy after some sleep. Hearing Brenden's voice again in my head, telling Drake that I need lots of sleep to get better, I give in to the desire and fall back into a deep sleep.

CHAPTER THIRTY TWO

ISABELLA: THE BIGGEST SURPRISE OF OUR LIVES

I've been awake for about an hour. I feel a dull pressure in my head, but not too bad. I don't want to take pain meds because I'm afraid it'll put me back to sleep. When I fell asleep the last time, Brenden had them remove one of my IVs, leaving just the one in my left hand. I'm glad they did it when I was passed out and unable to remember the trauma of seeing a needle slide out of my flesh.

Getting to the bathroom was an ordeal. Drake helped me, to my utter embarrassment. I was so weak, clutching his arm for what felt like a three-mile hike. Drake was wonderful, saying he wanted to be the one to help me. *Swoon.* After using the toilet, I pulled myself up and stood in front of the mirror, horrified by my face. Drake tried to warn me, but I didn't expect this.

My cheek is scraped from Paul dragging me, but it's the massive black eye I'm sporting that almost crumpled me. There's only a little residual swelling, but it's the most disgusting thing I've ever seen. My whole eye is black, my cheek is covered in splotchy red and purple bruises as well. How can Drake even stand to look at me? I feel gross and would love a shower, but I lack the energy.

Mom arrives shortly after my trip to the bathroom. She hovers and fusses, crying over me. She has high standards and wants me to have the best care. I reassure her over and over that Drake is taking great care of me and Nicholas is being a gentleman and leaving when necessary. She's freaking exhausting.

Stanley, Mom's boyfriend, was a shock. She never mentioned him. He's nothing like I would expect her to choose, but he seems to adore her. Heck, if he can put up with her for three years, then that's less pressure I'd get from her. Thank God they left a bit ago for lunch. Mom promised to bring me crackers and a 7-Up because I'm still nauseous.

After Mom and Stanley left, Drake and Hawkins finally tell me everything that happened. I owe so many people a huge thank you for helping rescue me. Poor Eddie, getting dosed with enough Ketamine to paralyze him temporarily.

Drake told me that they had a tail on me since the day after Paul's arrest. He didn't want to take any chances. Camelot Security must train their boys well because I never saw anyone following me. I told Drake we'd be having Eddie over for dinner to thank him once I'm a little better.

I'm so glad Detective Jerkins pulled through too. Paul almost killed him, and if it wasn't for Grayson's and

Noah's quick thinking and the training they got in the military, he probably wouldn't have survived. Detective Franks came by and asked what I remembered. He told me that it'd be a while before Jerkins is back at work, but the doctor says he'll be okay. I told Drake I wanted to visit him once I'm better myself. Jerkins will be in the hospital a lot longer than I.

I'm shocked at the things Paul did. He's not the person I thought he was. The reality that Paul is dead is overwhelming. He was obsessed, sick in the head. I never really loved him, but I did care about him. I hated what he did to my friends and me, but he didn't need to die. I hope his parents can find some form of peace somehow, even if it is by hating me. I feel sorry for them. No one ever needs to lose a child, and certainly not like this.

Staring at Drake as he talks with Hawkins, all I want to do is cuddle with him. That'll make me feel so much better. I can't handle him sitting in that uncomfortable chair any longer. I try to slowly slide over to the edge of the bed, to make room for him to join me. My movements draw his attention.

"Babe, be careful. What do you need? I'll get it. Do you need to go to the bathroom again?" Drake asks, coming to my side.

"Don't move me, Drake," I demand as he tries to pull me back to the center of the bed. "I'm making room for you. This bed is plenty big. I want you to hold me. That's what I need, it'll make me feel better. I need to have you close to me. You can at least sit up here with me and let me lean up against you and feel your closeness."

"Bella, I don't want to hurt you. I'm fine sitting beside you in my lovely hospital chair," Drake replies with a chuckle.

"No, join me." Pulling back the sheet, I pat the bed.

With a smirk on his face, he kicks off his shoes and climbs into bed with me. Drake pulls me into his arms, lying on his side, facing me. Shifting, I burrow into him, finding my peace, my safety. Drake's arms wrap around me, and my eyes fall closed as I inhale all that is him.

"Okay, that's my cue to sneak out of here and give you two a few minutes of privacy. I'll go hang out in Gregory's office, make some phone calls and order us some decent food. Want anything special?" Hawkins asks, grabbing his satchel. He grabs his baseball hat and slaps it on his head, pulling the brim down to hide behind.

"Nicholas, you don't have to leave, you can do that from here. It isn't like I'm going to jump Drake right here," I joke, trying to make him feel comfortable.

"Nah Isabella, that's okay. Have your reunion while I make some Camelot Security calls." Nicholas slips out the door.

Once the door is closed, I look up and into Drake's gorgeous jade eyes. Drake pushes my hair out of my face, careful not to touch my stitches. His eyes dart from mine to my lips and back again.

"Kiss me, Drake. I want you just as bad," I plead, answering the unspoken desire in his eyes.

He doesn't hesitate. His lips are on mine as I lift my hand slowly, placing it on his chest. The feel of his muscles flexing under my hand excites me. I slip my tongue along the crease of his lips, teasing him. With a moan, his lips part and our kiss soars to exhilarating heights. This is what I needed.

"You know, this is what got you two in this mess in the first place, right?" Mom Riggs announces as she walks into my room.

Drake pulls away, blushing a bit as he sits up and starts to slide from the bed.

"Drake, just stay there. That is if you think you can control yourself for a few minutes," Mom Riggs jokes, her voice betraying her amusement.

"Uh, Bella wanted me to hold her, and I couldn't deny her," Drake defends, like a teenager getting caught making out.

"Well, that looked a bit more than holding, but that's okay. I need to talk to the two of you and tell you what's going on."

"Oh God, NO! Please tell me I wasn't raped?" I beg the fear in my voice is evident. After all, she is the doctor who did my rape kit.

"No, sweetheart, you weren't raped. All we know for sure is that Paul cut your clothes off, leaving a few nicks, none of which will scar. He did squeeze your left breast, leaving finger sized bruising. But, no, he didn't rape you. There was no sign of trauma. With that said, there is a very small remnant of your hymen intact. That would not be the case if you were raped, or if you had had intercourse. Rest assured, rape didn't happen."

She tilts her head to the side, raising one eyebrow and spearing Drake with a look.

"Drake, do you remember the sex talk we had when you were a young boy with your mom?"

I tune out her words, feeling violated and disgusted at the thought of Paul seeing my naked body, of him touching me. Drake clears his throat, drawing my attention. He gives Mom Riggs an embarrassed smile. In all the years I've known him, he's never been embarrassed. What is this about?

"Yeah, I remember. Why are you bringing this up? We had sex talks with you several times growing up. No need to worry, I got this handled."

"Well, you must not have heard what I said *many* times. I might need to sit all you boys down and explain how things work again. But I'll use you as a great example of what not to do. It's too late for you."

Drake chuckles, and I'm completely lost in their conversation and wondering where this is going. The door opens again, and Mom Gregory comes in.

"Have you told them yet?" Mom Gregory asks, a glorious smile on her face.

"Wait a minute, Monica, I'm getting there. I'm waiting for Brenden to bring in some equipment." Mom Riggs sits on the foot of my bed as Mom Gregory takes Drake's chair. I'm so confused, what the heck is going on? Sitting up a bit, Drake's arms wrap around me, and I lean into him.

"Drake, do you remember when you were five and Grayson and Noah were seven? Noah asked me how a woman gets a baby in her tummy?" Mom Riggs asks.

"Lord. Yeah, I remember that. Why, what does this

have to do with anything?" Drake returns, with an embarrassed chuckle.

"I don't think you were listening. I told you boys that sperm are like little fishes, in search of a warm stream to swim in. They search to find the eggs that a woman has deep inside of her vagina. And once that fishy catches that egg, a baby is created inside of the woman." A huge smile spreads across her face as she stares at Drake.

My head swivels, looking between the three of them. Mom Gregory's ecstatic smile, Mom Riggs' knowing one and Drake's confused face. His confusion clears, and his face lights with joy. Drake's hand slides to my stomach in a possessive touch.

"What? What's going on?" I demand.

"You have got to be shitting me! How do you know? Are you sure?" Drake questions, his voice thick.

"Drake, I've been an OBGYN for longer than you've been alive. I think I know how to read blood work and an ultrasound," Mom Riggs retorts, laughing.

Mom Gregory squeals, standing up to hug Drake. He squeezes me from behind, lightly caressing my stomach.

My dull headache is making it impossible to figure out what is going on. Confusion rides me hard. The door opens, and Brenden pushes a sonogram cart into the room.

"Okay, what the hay is going on? Someone tell me, please!" I beg, needing to know.

"Babe, we're pregnant," Drake answers me, kissing my neck, giving me another gentle squeeze.

"What? I can't be! We haven't even had sex yet!

How?!" Mom Riggs and Mom Gregory both smile like loons.

"Isabella, you and Drake have done everything short of penetration. At some point, he ejaculated somewhere very close to your vagina. You don't have to actually have intercourse in order to get pregnant. It happens every year with kids messing around who are a lot younger than you two." Mom Riggs kindly says, getting up to give me a hug. "Congratulations Isabella, you and Drake are going to be parents in about seven months."

My mouth drops open in shock. I can't be pregnant. It's not possible! How did this happen? This isn't happening.

"Congratulations sweetie!" Mom Gregory says, hugging me. "I couldn't be happier for both of you. I know this is a shock for you and a bit early, but it's true."

"I can't be pregnant!" I wail. "My mom… my mom will have a cow. Literally, she will have a cow, right here in this room."

My heart is racing. My breathing is picking up pace, and I'm beginning to panic. As if it couldn't get any worse, Mom and Stanley return with my crackers and 7-Up. Oh God, no. This is going to be a disaster.

"What's going on? Is Isabella alright?" Mom asks, noticing all the people and equipment.

I pray silently that no one says anything.

"We were just congratulating the kids and about to show them their baby with a sonogram," Mom Riggs informs my mom proudly. Obviously, God is too busy to answer my prayers.

"Pregnant! No, no, no, Isabella is *not* pregnant. She

can't be, she wouldn't be. She knows better than that! You would've had to tell me that when I got here. I asked for a full update! I'm her next of kin, I'm her mother," Mom rants, looking between Mom Riggs and Brenden.

I'm silently freaking out. My headache gets worse, and my temples are pounding now. My heart is thundering in my chest so hard, I'm afraid Drake can hear it.

"No, Ivy, Isabella declared Drake her medical agent in case she was unable to make decisions. She filled out an Advanced Health Care Directive when she filled out the paperwork and scheduled an appointment for her well-woman check with Diana. HIPAA laws prevented us from telling you anything," Brenden informs Mom.

"Is that true, Isabella? Did you give Drake that right? And you're already pregnant? Without any plans of getting married? You've been sleeping with Drake already? How can you trust him? Don't you remember how he treated you in high school? He was fucking around right in front of your face, with NO respect for you at all! At least your father hid it from me." Mom's voice rises with each word out of her mouth becoming more shrill and biting.

I begin to shake from anger and shock at her vile words about Drake. I'm blown away that she cursed. That was the reason I left New York. She heard me say someone could 'kiss my butt' and tried to make me eat soap.

"Ivy, shut the fuck up!" Drake yells, pulling me from my thoughts. "I'll call security and have you removed if you don't. Bella is *my* responsibility now. You're upsetting her. Shut your mouth or leave." He pulls me into his chest protectively.

"Drake, put her oxygen mask back on. I don't want her hyperventilating. Isabella, look at me," Brenden instructs.

Dutifully, Drake replaces my mask, and I slowly turn to face Brenden.

"Isabella, breathe slowly, okay? We don't want your blood pressure getting high. That could be dangerous for you and the baby, okay girlie?" Nodding, I breathe slowly as instructed.

Mom sputters behind Brenden, gearing up for another go around. Mom Gregory jumps in to yell at Mom.

"Ivy, Drake doesn't have to do a damn thing. I'll personally remove you from this room and have your self-righteous ass banned from this hospital. You are not messing with these kids' lives again. You ripped Isabella out of Drake's arms eight years ago, breaking both of their hearts. And by God, I will *not* allow you to hurt either of them again. Do I make myself clear?

"Not only will I protect both of them from you, but I'll also protect *our* grandbaby. You can either get on board now or walk the fuck out that door. You do not have another option," Mom Gregory finishes, pointing toward the door.

"Okay, let's lighten the mood. Isabella, Drake, would you like to see your baby? I'm sure both grandmas would," Mom Riggs asks, breaking the tension. Mom and Stanley move to the back of the room.

"Can we? I'd love to see him!" I gasp excitedly, smiling up at Drake.

"A boy, huh? I think it's too soon to find out, but I'd love to know once we can." Drake gives me a quick hug then kisses the top of my head.

Brenden sets up the machine, and Mom Riggs pulls my night shirt up over my stomach, making sure the blanket covers my lower half. Just as she's putting gel on my tummy, Mr. Gregory and Hawkins enter the room.

Mom Gregory reaches for her husband, saying "Get over here, Grandpa. We're about to see our grandbaby for the first time."

Drake's dad wraps his arm around her, shocking me. He's got the biggest smile on his face, telling me he already knew. When Mr. Gregory squeezes Drake's shoulder in congratulations, I'm bowled over in surprise. Drake gives me a wink when I send him a questioning look.

"What the fuck, a baby?" Hawkins exclaims. "You lying dick! You've already had sex, and Isabella's pregnant? Congrats Brother, I can't wait to see him. You don't mind, do you, Isabella?"

"No, it's okay. I'm glad you made it back in time." I barely finish before being interrupted by Mom.

"Well Nicholas, I never knew you to have such a foul mouth," Mom states, scowling at him.

"Excuse me, I didn't know you were standing here. But I've always had this mouth, I was just careful not to use it in front of you." Nicholas gives Mom a wink.

Mom Riggs pulls out a wand, and pushes it firmly against my stomach, sliding it through the gel. Drake and I stare at the monitor. He lays beside me on the bed, his cheek pressed to mine. A sudden *whomping* sound fills the room. Tears spring into my eyes as Drake presses closer to me.

"Is that the baby's heartbeat?" he asks, awe evident in his voice.

"Yes! Drake, meet the next generation of Gregory-Fitzpatrick. That's what we have been calling him," Mom Riggs answers.

Drake removes my oxygen mask again and kisses me tenderly. Looking me in the eyes, he vows, "You're the only one, Mama. I love you."

"Fine, I can tell when I'm not wanted or needed. Stanley, let's go," Mom pouts, breaking the tender moment between Drake and me.

I sigh as they leave the room, knowing she'll be back. She loves me desperately but needs to get her way. When she doesn't get her way, she pouts like a kid who got her toy taken away, but she always comes back. We were due for one of her tantrums, anyway.

Mom Gregory sighs, then turns to Drake.

"I assume you're going to make an honest woman of Isabella, young man."

"Damn straight I'm gonna marry her. If it were up to me, the moment Bella is released we'd fly to Tahoe and get married."

I gasp as Mom Gregory shouts "No!"

"No trip to Tahoe, or Vegas," Mr. Gregory says. "You need a fairy-tale wedding for your girl."

"I haven't even officially asked Bella yet. Fuck, none of you are ruining this moment for us. We'll let you know after we get out of the hospital," Drake admonishes.

Pulling my oxygen mask down, I kiss him quickly.

Drake puts his hand on the side of my face and smiles. "I love you, Bella. We're going to have a baby! I hope you are as happy as I am," he whispers.

"Oh, yes, I'm so full of all kinds of emotions right now, excitement, joy, fear." A horrifying thought hits me.

"Could the drugs Pervert Paul gave me hurt our baby?" I ask.

"No Isabella, you had an allergic reaction to them and immediately threw up. It could have even been the pregnancy protecting you. *And* your stomach was pumped," Mom Riggs answers. Once I examined you and discovered you were pregnant, we made sure every drug you've been given is safe for you and the baby," she adds.

"Brenden, you and Mom knew all this time?! And neither of you told me?" Drake scowls at them.

"Dude, you were a fucking basket case. We decided to tell you both together. Deal with it, you would've just been freaking out more," Brenden tells him.

"I love you, Drake. You're going to be a daddy. We're having a baby." I smile.

The door slams open and Stevens and Riggs walk in, Jackson and Asher following behind them. They all freeze by the door, listening to the whomping noise.

"Dayum Fitz, you lying ass," Stevens says. "You crashed the custard truck and knocked Isabella up? When? How far along? Who won the bet?"

"Fuck, how many of you assholes are going to

squeeze into this room and give me shit?" Drake calls out.

"Fuck you, this room is one of the biggest in the hospital. There's plenty of room, you lying piece of shit," Jackson adds as they continue filing in.

"Are you really pregnant, Isabella?" Asher asks, walking around everyone to get a closer look at the monitor.

"Yup, apparently I am." I return Asher's smile.

"Congrats to the both of you. It looks like I'll be waiting for you to ask me for her hand in marriage. You are marrying her, Fitz. Now I get to kick your ass for knocking my sister up before you married her," Clausen asserts. Drake laughs in response.

"Everyone be quiet and look at the monitor," Mom Riggs points at the little screen. "See that? The little flutter?"

The room goes quiet, all eyes glued to the screen.

"That's your baby's heart beating. It's got a nice, strong heartbeat. And here we have the head. Now, that's a good size, and measuring somewhere between… seven and nine weeks."

"Oh my God, Drake, do you see that? I really have our baby growing inside of me." Wonder and awe fill me as tears flood my eyes.

"Stevens, order me a huge fucking roll of Bubble Wrap. Bella needs to be wrapped up in it for the next seven months," Drake calls out.

"Well, I guess Hunter is the lucky bastard to win the pot. Damn. There was a good size wad of cash in there," Jackson says.

"What are you talking about, Gabe?" Mom Riggs asks him.

"You know us, Mom Riggs, we bet on everything. And since Drake has been lying about doing the nasty with Isabella, the pot had gotten pretty damn big. The lying piece of shit kept telling us he hadn't taken that dive yet," Jackson answers with a smile.

"Well then. Drake has *not* been lying. They have not had sex. That pot is still intact, just like Isabella's virtue," Mom Riggs jokes with a wink to Drake and me.

Oh, my gosh! She did not just say that. I can't believe she threw us under the bus like that. My face flushes with embarrassment, and I cower behind my hands. Drake's deep laughter rumbles from his chest beside me. Mom Riggs cleans off my belly and hands me a small black and white picture of our baby taken from the ultrasound.

I ignore everyone in the room, staring at the picture in my hands. Drake leans in close. I rub my tummy and smile.

"Don't you worry little peanut, Mama is going to take real good care of you," I murmur to my tummy.

"Are you messing with us, Mom Riggs?" Jackson asks as she hands Mom Gregory two copies of the ultrasound pictures. Drake's dad leans in close to examine the picture in his wife's hand. He's smiling and nodding as she explains the picture. Something big must have happened when I was unconscious.

"No, Gabe, I've never lied to you boys. Actually, now is the perfect time for a refresher course. The only safe sex is no sex. That means not letting your penis near any vagina. Drake and Isabella are the perfect example that pregnancy can happen without penetration. It happens hundreds of times a year."

"Congrats to you, sweetie." She reaches down to hug me. "I didn't mean to embarrass you. I've always talked openly with these boys about sex. I'll come back when there isn't a room full of Camelot Brothers and talk to you and Drake. But you and the baby are doing great. Talk soon." Mom Riggs kisses my cheek and leaves my room.

"Congratulations, darling girl," Mom Gregory says, leaning down to hug me. "I'm going to give your mom a copy of the ultrasound picture, and to ream her a new one."

"She'll be back. This happens occasionally," I reply.

"Oh yeah," she scoffs. "I know, Isabella. I've been friends with Ivy since we were younger than you are now ." Drake's mom leaves with his dad, holding hands. It's cute to see.

My head's beginning to hurt, it's hard to keep my eyes open. I push my button for pain meds and lean into Drakes' chest as all the Brothers tease and congratulate him at the same time. It's a struggle to keep my eyes open.

Resting my eyes, I think about all I've been blessed with. Reuniting with Drake, the precious baby in my tummy. *I'm hoping for a boy with his daddy's green eyes,* and *squeal!* We're getting married! All of my dreams are coming true. Nothing and no one can stop us.

Now I just have to heal up, so I can leave this stupid hospital and *finally* make love to my man.

CHAPTER THIRTY THREE

FITZ: GOING HOME

*L*ying on the bed with Bella in my arms is heaven. I'm beyond relieved that she's going to be okay. I was finally able to get a solid five hours of sleep last night with her cuddled up on my side. We've been here for five long-ass days, and I just want to take my girl home. To OUR home.

After Mom Riggs told her what that fucking pervert did to her, she was on the verge of losing it. Bella insisted on a shower, which I helped her with after everyone left. Seeing the bruises and small cuts that asshole left on her skin made my blood boil. I wish I could have been the one to end his miserable existence, but I couldn't, and wouldn't, leave her side.

My mind keeps running back to the fact that we're having a baby. Shit, fooling around like we were, I was careless. I didn't even think she *could* get pregnant that way, but I'm damn thrilled she is. It helps me speed up my plan to make her mine forever.

Gazing down at her sleeping face, I hope it's a girl with her mama's big dark chocolate eyes, but it'll be another couple of months or so to find out the baby's gender.

Bella stirs, and does her little cat stretches, telling me she's almost fully awake. Her eyes flutter as she lifts her head, a huge smile spreading across her face.

"Good morning Mr. Wonderful. I hope you were able to get a little sleep." Bella reaches her arms up and does a full body stretch.

"Yeah babe, I always sleep better with you in my arms. I love you." I pull her to me, so I can claim her mouth.

"Excuse me, you two. But this is still a hospital with an open-door policy. How is our patient doing this morning?" Mom Riggs asks as she approaches the bed.

Pulling away from the kiss, I find that I can't sit up due to Henry's excited state without them noticing. I'd much rather keep him hidden until he relaxes some.

"She just woke up, and you could always knock before barging in, you know." I flash a quick smile to Mom Riggs to let her know I'm only joking.

"Yeah, but that would take half the fun out of busting you two making out at 7:30 in the morning. Now, how are you feeling this morning? Besides being frustrated by my interruption."

"Erm," Bella groans, trying to sit up. "My headache is gone, but now that I'm sitting up, the nausea is coming back, and strong." She rubs her stomach gently.

"Well, the nausea doesn't have anything to do with your head injury. I think it's just plain ol' morning sickness. I'll have Barbara give you some nausea medicine in your IV. I'll also write you a prescription to get filled on your way home. You'll need to take it first thing in the morning with some crackers and juice, or whatever sounds good. I'm signing off for you to be discharged today, pregnancy-wise. We just have to wait for Brenden to sign off about your injuries."

Bella squeals and cuddles up to me. "We get to go home!"

"I know, babe. I cannot wait to have you in our bed." I give her a kiss on top of her head.

"Make an appointment to see me in one month unless you have spotting or anything concerning. I don't see any reason you should though, you have an all clear from me. That 'little peanut' as you've been calling it is a strong little bugger. And if he's hung on through what you've been through the last few days, he'll be just fine. Once the morning sickness passes in a few weeks, it should be smooth sailing. Do you have any questions?"

Looking down at Bella, as her face blushes, and she stutters through her next question.

"Emm, emm, does 'all clear,' uh… Does that mean… you know… can we…"

"Are you asking if you can make love? Yes, and I wholeheartedly encourage the two of you to do just that if you feel up to it, Isabella. Enjoy it. The first couple of times could be a bit uncomfortable, you're still very much a virgin. But trust me, it will get better. I highly recommend you two enjoy this next step in your relationship. Just relax and trust Drake."

Bella smiles and curls into me again. She seems as

excited at the news as I am. Fuck, I'll probably be stuck with a permanent hard on with Henry knowing we have the all clear. Hot damn, I can't wait! Fuck. I just hope Bella's stomach starts feeling better by tonight.

"One last thing, the baby you're carrying is already large for its age. I'm predicting a big healthy baby in seven-ish months. With your small build, you might want to enjoy this newly found sex life you're about to embark on. You're going to need to be prepared and stretched for the birthing process. We'll talk more about that in the coming months."

Holy fuck! Stretching Bella? Goddamn! Gotta change the subject before I fuckin' come in my pants.

"Any questions from you, Drake?"

I clear my throat, trying to empty my mind of the dirty, naughty thoughts I'm having about Bella right now.

"No, I think I'm good. We'll make an appointment for next month."

Now, to begin making up for the fact that she missed her birthday. I've got big plans for us this weekend. I just need to convince everyone not to visit without tipping my hand on making love with Bella.

"One last thing, wait at least till Monday to return to work, Isabella. It'll give you two a little extra quality time. That is if you can figure out how to keep the rest of the Brothers away." She sniggers at her joke. "I'll see you two soon, good luck." Mom Riggs finally leaves, still laughing.

Damn, she knows my Brothers. I need to figure a

way to get them to stay away. Fuck, this is not going to be easy.

"Sweetie, we've got this. Don't you worry about the Brothers ruining our time," Bella reassures me with a wink, as the door opens again revealing Brenden.

"I hear you two are planning your escape? I want to do one more blood test, and if it all comes back good, you're out of here before dinner tonight."

Mom Stevens enters with a needle in hand, and Bella gasps. I hug her a bit tighter.

"I see the look of terror in your eyes, honey. This goes in your IV. If it takes away that nausea, we have a winner. I'll check back in about two hours and see how you're feeling," Mom Stevens says, swiping an alcohol wipe over the port to Bella's IV.

"Mom Stevens, I'll need you to take blood too. If everything comes back as good as yesterday, I'm releasing these lovebirds," Brenden instructs her.

"Bella, I'm confident you'll be going home today. But, if you develop a bad headache that doesn't go away with the meds I'm sending home with you, I want you to call me immediately. Drake, I expect you to keep an eye on her. We both know she'll probably lie about her pain level."

"Brother, you have nothing to worry about there. I can tell when my girl is lying. She's never been able to pull that one off."

"Hey, I'm not that readable," Bella objects. "But I don't like pain, Brenden. If I'm hurting and the meds aren't working, I'll be calling you to complain."

We both laugh, knowing she's not kidding. As Mom

Stevens finishes taking Bella's blood sample, Ivy saunters in the room, Stanley following after her like the puppy dog he is.

"Uh," Brenden stutters, looking at me. I give him a subtle nod. "We'll give you guys a few minutes."

"Hi, Mom," Bella acknowledges, sitting up.

I get up from the bed and move to greet Stanley. His handshake is limp, probably like the rest of him.

"Isabella, darling," Ivy croons, holding a binder, pages and sticky notes sticking out here and there. "We simply must discuss your wedding. I've been talking with Monica. We only have about six weeks before you start really showing, and I don't want a baby bump to ruin your pictures."

Rolling my eyes, as Bella shoots me a grin.

"Alright, Mom. Let's see what you and Mom Gregory have come up with," she responds. "If Drake and I like it, we'll give it sincere consideration."

"Babe, I thought that maybe we could get married at Hawkins' estate," I put in before Ivy can say anything.

"Honey, that's an ah-maz-ing idea! Oh, Mom, you have to see Nicholas's home. It's a castle! Here in California!"

"Drake, both Monica and I have already checked out the churches and talked with the country club about hosting the reception. Deposits have been made. We've even already spoken to the minister. We have all this handled for you," Ivy announces.

It looks like I'm going to have to set my mom straight on this later.

"Ivy, I was trying to be nice. Now I'm telling you.

We're getting married at Hawkins' place. You and mom can deal with that. Or we can always go to Tahoe and send you pictures. Your call."

"Drake, I'm sure Nicholas' house, or castle, is just wonderful. But Isabella will be married in a church, with a man of God performing the service. I'm sure Monica agrees. And we have over six hundred guests coming as well. The country club is a must for the reception," Ivy argues, looking at Bella and hoping she'll agree with her.

"Ivy, if it has to be a church, we'll have one built, and a reception hall too. Hawkins' estate has plenty of room, he'd probably love it. We'll need them in the future, anyway. I'll get a hold of Hawkins, Carpenter, and Clay and get them on it. That pushes the wedding back three months from today, which will give them time to build both structures. If you and Mom can't accept that, then we'll head to Tahoe tonight. This is our wedding, not yours. Also, start cutting the number down to no more than three hundred total. One hundred and fifty each."

Ivy's mouth hangs open at my announcement. I walk back to Bella, bending down to kiss her on top of her head. Seeing the sparkle in her eyes pleases me.

"Doesn't that sound just perfect, babe?"

Bella smiles at me, the joy evident in her beautiful eyes. She turns to Ivy.

"Mom, it really does sound wonderful. Especially since I want a Camelot themed wedding. I'll have a beautiful old fashioned fairytale wedding dress, with the full skirt. That way, if I have a bit of a baby bump, the dress will hide it. It's settled. Drake and I are having a

Camelot wedding, at Hawkins' castle three months from today. You and Mom Gregory 'just have to deal,' as Drake says. You two have a lot of planning to do, now that you know what we want." Bella's smile is radiant. I love it, this'll be perfect.

Ivy just nods, reluctantly accepting our plan. Bella smiles up at her mom as they continue talking about colors and flowers, food and fabrics. I tune it all out. I already know what I'm wearing, full on formal Camelot gear. The Brothers are going to love it. Interrupting Bella and Ivy, I give my girl a quick kiss.

"Babe, I'm gonna call Stevens and check on Mojo. Remember, no expense spared on our dream wedding."

"Oh Drake, that's sweet, but I've had a wedding fund for Isabella since she was two. I'm paying for this. It's my right."

"Alright Ivy, I'll give you that. I'll get that church and reception hall built," I tell her.

Bella giggles as I leave the room.

Now, to get a hold of the Brothers and get this shit knocked out. I've got more important things to work on. I need to figure out how to get a hundred and one of Bella's favorite roses to my house before she's released. I checked the list the florist gave me, and 101 means *You're my one and only*. I have my one and only and I need to show her how much I love her.

BRENDEN FINALLY SIGNS the discharge order, and we're going home. Everyone has been by to visit, to watch

Bella sleep on and off. I texted everyone telling them not to overwhelm us once we get home. I'm sure Hawkins will be there waiting, but I'm hoping the rest of the Brothers will steer clear for a while.

"Okay, the SUV is parked downstairs, just waiting for Isabella," Stevens informs us, walking into the room.

"Aren't you supposed to be with the SUV? And I'm supposed to wait for a text?" I ask him.

"Well, Clausen and Carpenter are with it to make sure no one tickets it. Are you going to wheel her out or just pick her up and make an escape?" Stevens jokes.

"What the hell? I told you guys Bella needs time, she still isn't a hundred percent. Look at her, she's still asleep." I whisper loudly.

"Hey, we're here to support you, Brother. We don't want you going crazy while staring at her sleeping. We can keep you company. You and Hawkins have been watching her for five days. Hawkins went home in the wee hours this morning. He's called a half a dozen times to check on Isabella, to see if she's home yet. You two are gonna lose it if you don't get a break," he asserts, concern in his voice.

"Brother, I'm fine. I'm just dog tired. Once I get Bella home and tucked into bed, I'll take a fucking shower in my own bathroom, and climb into bed with her and sleep for eight fucking hours. Once we get to the house, you, Clausen and Carpenter need to go over to the guest house and play cards or whatever the fuck it is you do. And take Mojo with you, I don't want to get up early in the morning to let him out to piss. No one is coming into my house until tomorrow morning. Do I make myself clear?" I'm not allowing them to mess up my night with Bella.

"Chill Brother, fine. You really are a bit crabby, not getting your beauty sleep," Stevens jokes on a chuckle.

Walking back to the side of Bella's bed I push the hair out of her face. "Babe, you wanna wake up? I'm calling Mom Stevens so I can take you home."

Her eyes flutter open, and she smiles. "Finally, I get to go home," she mumbles, followed by a big cat-like stretch.

"Okay Isabella, here is your last dose of your anti-nausea medication. On your way home, Noah can go through the pharmacy drive through and pick up your prescription. Don't forget to take them the moment you wake up, and give them about thirty minutes to kick in before moving around, okay?" Mom Stevens explains to Bella as she injects the medicine into her IV.

Knowing what's about to happen, I sit down beside Bella and turn her head to me, looking into her eyes.

"I love you, Bella." I kiss her passionately to distract her from the fact that Mom Stevens is removing her IV.

"Okay, you're ready to go home, to continue *that* without all of us barging in on you. Now you only have to worry about the Brothers," she snickers as she walks towards the door.

"That's not going to happen. If it does, you might be stitching them up or setting some broken bones. I've already told them to give Bella a couple more days to get stronger," I vow, making myself clear.

"You tricked me with that kiss," Bella accuses,

rubbing her hand where the IV was, now covered with a bandage. "But it worked, I didn't feel a thing."

A young male nurse walks in pushing a wheelchair. "Your chariot awaits, Ms. Isabella."

I scoop Bella up, and she throws her arms around my neck, cuddling into me. Fuck that chair, I'm carrying her to the SUV.

"You can follow pushing the wheelchair with her stuff in it, but I'm carrying her. Stevens, grab my bag and help put some of the flowers and gifts people brought in the wheelchair. When I pushed her in that thing to have lunch with Eddie, she got an upset stomach by the movement. She's not getting in the chair again," I instruct them.

"But sir, it's hospital policy that I push her out," the orderly kid says in a nervous voice.

"Kid, do you think you can physically take her from me? That's the only way she's getting in that chair."

"Be nice, Sir Grumpy." Bella slaps my chest feebly. "You definitely need a nap when we get home, because I will not listen to Mr. Crabby Pants," she says with a smile and lays her head back under my chin.

Before lunch, I changed her into a blousy, loose dress her mom brought for her to wear home. I packed all the pajamas my mom had bought for her in my bag too. I wanted to get the hell out of here as soon as they said we could leave.

I walk out the door the orderly had propped open to bring in the wheelchair. With Bella snuggled into me, I couldn't be happier. I don't want to see another hospital until the baby is born. Bella reaches out to push the down button for the elevator. Stevens' arms are full of Bella's gifts, and the kid is pushing an overfilled wheelchair, following behind us.

Bella whispers, "Watch this." We enter the elevator, and I'm wondering what she's up to. "Drake, I think I might barf. My stomach is really turning."

"Oh, shit. Drake, you should have told me to grab a fucking garbage can," Stevens says nervously.

Once the elevator stops, Bella lets out a sound like a dry heave.

"You okay, babe? You want me to go back? You sure you're ready to leave?"

"Drake, please take me home. I promise I'll be fine once I get in bed and can go back to sleep." Bella whispers loud enough for everyone to hear.

"Okay babe, we're going home. Stevens, why don't you grab a bag, for safety's sake, from the gift shop?" I order, hurrying to the SUV.

When the hospital's automatic sliding doors part, Carpenter opens the back door of the SUV for us. I carefully place Bella in the back seat and climb in beside her, pulling her partially into my lap. Carpenter gets in the driver's seat, with Clausen riding shotgun. Stevens loads the back with our stuff and slams the hatch. We're finally on our way home.

I'm beginning to get nervous. While Bella was often nauseous in the hospital, she didn't actually throw up. Not once. But for the last fifteen minutes, she's held that bag to her mouth and heaved. I just rub her back, hoping to soothe her.

Stevens looks a little green, occasionally gagging

himself. I never knew he was such a pussy. Everyone else is quiet.

I'm hoping it's just the car ride causing this. The meds that Mom Stevens gave Bella before we left usually only takes a few minutes to calm her stomach, but they don't seem to be helping now. Once I get her into bed, I'm calling Brenden to ream him out.

When the car stops in front of the house, Stevens practically jumps from the SUV.

"We'll bring the stuff in and then head to the guest house and let you two get some sleep," he calls out.

"Yeah, if you two need anything, just text, we'll run out and get it for you," Carpenter adds as he opens my door for me.

"Hope you feel better real soon, Bella. It looks like that baby is kicking your ass. I'm calling it now. It's a boy. Fitz Jr.'s giving you hell," Clausen announces. Carpenter and Stevens chuckle their agreement.

"Okay, thanks, Brothers. I'll give you a holler in the morning. I'm getting Bella to bed, then taking a shower before crashing hard myself."

Bella pulls her barf bag from her mouth mumbling, "Thanks guys, good night. I just want to go to bed. I'm sure it's just the car ride."

They all call out goodnight to Bella as I walk through the door.

"Hey Buddy," Stevens calls out to Mojo. "Mommy's sick. Wanna go for a ride in the big SUV and get a hamburger? We can get your big ass in the back seat, and you can hang your head out the window like you love to do, then you can hang out with us tonight."

A loud yawn escapes me before I can stop it. I'm relieved to have Bella home, finally. Now I just need to get Bella settled in bed. With Bella still in my arms, I head toward our room.

"Now," I say, laying her down gently, "you relax while I shower. I'll be back in a few minutes."

Bella catches me off guard, grabbing me and pulling me toward her. I stumble, landing on her. She kisses me with a fervor I've not seen before. Pulling away, I inspect her face. She wears a playful smile.

"I told you I'd handle the Brothers. A little fake heaving and they run for the hills. They'll call everyone else and tell them I was throwing up all the way home. None of them will think we made love tonight. We have the whole night to ourselves. We win."

"Babe… that was all a performance? Damn, woman, you had me worried!" Holy fuck, she fooled us all. "You're honestly feeling okay? Not sick to your stomach at all?"

"The medicine worked great. And it isn't upset enough for me not to get my birthday present. Make love to me, Drake. Tonight, I want you."

Holy fucking shit. I grab Bella and kiss her passionately.

I pull away and inform her, "First, we shower. Then we make love. All night."

CHAPTER THIRTY FOUR

FITZ: MAKING LOVE

*C*arrying Bella into our bathroom, I set her on the stool. I'm trying to maintain control, knowing tonight is the night I've dreamed about for over a decade. I'm making love to Bella, claiming her as mine forever. I'm the luckiest bastard alive.

Reaching in and turning on the shower, I turn around as Bella stands up. I grab the hem of her dress and lift it over her head, taking a minute to admire her beautiful body, her perfect tits, the flair of her hips. I'm so damn glad she's not wearing a bra.

"I love you so much. You're so fucking beautiful, and all mine. I want this night to last forever. I have to take care of Henry because you've got me so hot, I'm about to explode already."

"Dray, it's not your place to take care of him anymore. That's my job. I get to make you come first. I was planning on it, anyway. I want us to bathe each other, explore and start our flight to the stars right here."

Her voice is sensual as she reaches for the fly of my pants. She slowly pops each button, watching as Henry slowly reveals his head from the top of my boxers.

"Babe, he's not used to waiting, and it's been five long days since I've come. That's a fucking record for me. He won't last long, especially with you talking like that."

Bella's smile is so damn sexy as she watches me pull off my shirt. She slides her panties down her legs, standing before me completely nude, her hair in a sexy-as-hell messy bun. Quickly kissing the small scar on her forehead, I stare into those dark chocolate eyes. I grab and kiss her with all the passion that's been pent up for the last week.

Stepping away, I try to catch my breath. As I watch her face, I get my boxers off in record time. I grab her hand and pull her into the warm shower, allowing it to rain down me, blocking the water from her so as not to let her hair get wet.

"Drake, let's wash each other first. I want to feel clean and touch every part of you."

"Fuck babe, you can't talk like that. I don't know how long I'll last. Henry's painfully hard for you." She looks down at my cock, and Henry jerks at her attention.

"Okay, big guy. Let's take care of you first then. I think the shower will go smoother after that."

She takes my hand, turning me to face her. She then takes a seat on the built-in bench. Shaking in anticipation of what is about to happen, I cradle her cheek in my hand. My cock is in her face, inches from her beautiful lips. Shit, I'm not going to last long.

"Let's first get you good and clean, shall we Henry?"
Fuck, she's talking to my cock!

Bella reaches for the liquid soap, squeezing some into
her hand. She lathers up before placing her hands on my
pelvis. I lean back, letting the warm water cascade over
my body. Damn, maybe I should make the spray colder
to help me maintain control. I spread my legs, giving
Bella access to all of Henry.

Avoiding my cock, she reaches between my legs and
gently washes my balls. My hands hit the tile behind
Bella with a *smack*.

"Fuck babe, you're killing me here," I groan.

"Lean back, Drake. Time to wash this soap off, so I
can take care of you," Bella instructs.

Closing my eyes, I do as I'm told. The water rushes
down my chest as Bella's hand glides over Henry.
Praying I don't shoot my load in her face, I try to
remember my football stats.

My eyes shoot open when I feel Bella shift. Placing
my hands on the wall again, I look down at her through
my arms. She peeks up at me with a mischievous smile.
Henry jerks in her hand when she licks her lips.

Bella lowers her head, licking the tip of my cock.
Goddamn. She's so fucking beautiful.

My breaths come faster as I'm mesmerized by the
sight of my woman between my legs. She hums against
the tip, sending vibrations along the shaft. Fuck, she's so
good at this.

"Mmm, Henry, you taste so yummy," she tells my
cock, threatening to take my knees out from under me.
She runs her tongue around the head, announcing,

"Now, I'm going to take good care of you. This time, I want to watch YOU come."

Holy. Shit.

Bella firmly slides her hand up and down, continuing to press her full lips to the head of my cock. Her lips slowly part as her mouth covers the head of Henry, and she rotates her wrist then finally sucks my cock halfway into her mouth. My eyes threaten to close in pleasure, but I want to watch her.

Her head bobs up and down on my cock, pushing me closer to coming.

"Holy fuck, Bella," I moan. "That feels incredible. I won't last long."

Her cheeks hollow as she sucks hard on my cock. Lights flash in my eyes. With a pop, she pulls her mouth from Henry.

"So, you like it?" she asks, her eyes hooded.

"Fuck yeah, I like it. Get that beautiful mouth back on my cock," I demand, biting my lip. The need to find my release rides me hard.

"Ooo, I like it when you get a little demanding and needy. Is this what you want?" Keeping her eyes on mine, Bella bends forward and sucks my cock to the back of her throat.

"Goddamn, Bella. Baby, I mean it, I'm going to come if you keep doing that." I continue watching her suck and work my cock, her hand twisting up and down my shaft. Unable to fight it, my eyes close and I throw my head back. My hips rock of their own accord, fucking her mouth.

Bella opens her throat, and I feel her swallow around

the head. Fuck, that's so damn good. My body ignites, throwing me into the abyss when her other hand finds my balls and cradles them gently.

"Bella... I'm coming," I ground out. Every muscle in my body contracts as I let go.

"Holy. Fucking. Shit."

Opening my eyes, I look down at Bella. She releases my cock with a loud *pop*. She licks her lips, her eyes find mine as she slowly works my cock from base to tip. My body shakes as I find my release, watching my cum coat her glorious tits.

"Goddamn, that's fucking beautiful," I moan. Bella looks down at my cock, sticking out her tongue to catch the last bit of cum shooting out of my cock. Fuck, she's beyond perfection. She owns me, there's nothing I wouldn't do for her. If she wants the moon, I'd move Heaven and Earth to get it for her.

Reaching down, I pull her into my arms and capture her mouth, tasting myself on her tongue. She wraps her arms around me and ideas race through my mind of how to make her come.

"Bella, you blew my mind. That was amazing. I felt that, Bella, down to my fucking toes. Now, I need to return the favor, babe. Take the position."

I turn Bella around to face the shower wall I was just leaning against, slowly sliding my hands down her arms, taking her hands in mine. I place both of her hands on the cold tile, causing her to bend over more than I was. I slide my hands down her sides, over her hips, and down each leg. Bending beside her I slowly spread her legs.

Grabbing her body wash, I stand back up behind her

as I squirt it down the center of her back. Bella arches her back, a soft moan escaping her lips. After lathering her back up really well, I move down to her gorgeous legs. Finally, I reach her sweet ass, giving it the attention it deserves.

"Oh God, Drake, this is unbelievably hot. Standing like this makes me needy. I need you to touch me. I need more. Please Drake, I feel so empty," she pleads.

"Holy shit, Bella, you're already getting me hard again. I'll take care of you, babe. Just breathe, be patient. It'll be worth it," I growl into her ear. Shivers race down her spine, and she whimpers.

Fuck, she's goddamn beautiful in this state. Admiring her ass again, I press myself against her back. Reaching around her, I wash those luscious tits, pulling and plucking her nipples. Henry has come back to life at the feel of Bella's ass, and the thought of fucking her from behind causes him to jerk.

Grabbing one of the many portable shower heads from the wall, I turn the dial to pulsating and rinse her body. With her legs spread for me, I aim the spray right between her folds, knowing it'll hit her clit. A deep moan from Bella makes me thrust my hips against her.

"Oh, Lordy that feels good. Oh, God, I can come just from this," Bella murmurs, causing me to groan.

"No way in hell am I letting you come like that. I've got a lot more in store for that pussy before I let you come." Standing up, I return the shower head to its home. I run my hand up and down her spine then slide my arms around to play with her swaying breasts. As I pluck and twist her nipples, she bucks and moans beneath me.

"Dray, please... please touch me. I need you... to touch me," Bella begs.

"I got you, babe. Are you ready for me to lick you now? I want to taste you before I fuck you with my fingers."

"Oh God," Bella moans. "Yes, please... please... I can't wait any longer."

"Okay Bella, after I let you come, I'm carrying you to bed and making love to you, showing you how to really soar."

Sliding my hand down over her ass, Bella moans again. Sitting on the floor of the shower, I twist so that my back is to the bench, and I can look up into Bella's face. Pressing my tongue firmly on her clit, her legs shake with need. I flatten my tongue and lick across her core, feeling her contract. She's fucking close to her release.

Bella lets out a deep moan, "Dray, oh God, that feels so good. I need more."

With one hand, I caress her shapely ass. Moving my tongue to her clit, I slide two fingers inside that tight little pussy of hers. The walls of her tight canal contract around my fingers, sucking them deeper. Bella rocks her hips towards my hand, needy and responsive.

"Oh God, Drake. That's it. Oh, honey that feels amazing. Don't stop."

"I won't. I can't wait to feel that tight pussy of yours wrapped around my cock." Her pussy flutters at my dirty words.

"Oh, damn, babe. Your body's telling me you like me talking like this." Her pussy contracts around my fingers again.

"Ooh Drake," she pants. "It's not enough, I need more."

Pulling my fingers from her hot channel, I add a third finger. Slowly, I push my fingers as deep as I can get them. Bella loudly moans.

"Oh God, that's it, faster Dray, faster."

"Fuck," I mutter, watching my hand move faster, seeing her wetness coat my fingers. Henry is rock hard, demanding I pull my fingers out and ram into her. He bounces against my stomach. My other hand smacks her ass, causing her to rock her hips faster on my fingers.

My free hand finds the crease of her ass, and I slide one finger down to her tight hole. I tap it to the same rhythm of my fingers in her pussy.

Bella goes wild, her hips thrusting madly as she moans deeper than I've ever heard.

"Dray," she cries. "I can't take it. I can't... it feels so good. So good. I want you, I need you now. Make love to me now. Please! I have to feel *all* of you."

"Holy fucking shit. Okay babe, I got you." I pull my fingers out and scramble to standing. Shutting off the shower, I grab a bath towel and wrap it around Bella. Grabbing a second towel and I wrap it around myself before picking her up. I practically sprint to our bed.

"No way in fuck am I making love to you for the first time in a shower." I capture her mouth like the starving man I am. I lay Bella down on our bed and remove our towels. Lying beside her, I squeeze her breast firmly. With my knee, I spread her legs, sliding between them.

Bella quickly bends her knees, spreading herself for me. Goddamn, she's hot. Fuck, I hope I can go slow for her. Gotta make sure she's still ready for me. I slide two fingers back into her and fuck her with them for a second. Her pussy contracts and she rocks her hips even faster.

"Dray, please make love to me now," she pleads.

"I love you, babe. Tonight, I'm claiming you as mine in every way. I've dreamt of this moment for so long." Removing my fingers, I lick them, her taste revving me higher. Leaning forward, I kiss her passionately, aggressively. Pushing up with a hand near her head, I line my cock up with her hot, wet pussy. I slowly push the head of my cock into her tight entry. Shivers race down my spine. Bella's pussy tightens around the head of my cock as she moans loudly.

"Drake, I love you. I need more of you."

"Oh fuck, baby I don't want to hurt you. Let me take my time. I promise I'll get you there," I vow.

Bella wraps a leg around my back, trying to pull me closer. She's so wet, I slide deeper into her. I've never felt anything so incredible in all my life. My eyes roll back in my head.

"Drake, it hurts," Bella moans, "but feels so good. I need more. Please, Dray, make love to me," she demands again.

In one swift move, I thrust all the way in. A deep gasp escapes Bella, causing me to freeze. Her lips part, her eyes squeezed closed. A solitary tear rolls from the side of her eye, down into her hair, breaking my heart.

"Oh, fuck Bella, I'm sorry I hurt you. I love you, babe." I don't move, her tight-as-hell pussy squeezing my cock. My body trembles with the need to move, but I won't till she does.

Bella reaches up, capturing my head. She pulls me into a hungry kiss. Our tongues battle for control and my cock swells even further. Keeping my body still is the most difficult thing I've ever had to do. Bella falls back to the pillow, breaking our kiss. My breath is shaky as I wipe the tears from Bella's face.

"I love you so much Drake. I've dreamt of this moment for so long. I'm yours, and you're mine, forever. You're my one and only. Please make love to me. I need you to move."

"Oh babe, you're mine, now and always."

Testing her, I slowly shuttle my hips. She moans, her back arching. Bella's so wet, so tight around my cock, I know I've found paradise. Picking up the pace, I watch as Bella looks into the mirror above us.

Reaching over to my side of the bed, I grab some pillows. Without pulling my cock from paradise, I lift Bella's hips and shove the pillows underneath her ass. Looking down at where our bodies are joined, I watch my cock coated in her wetness, slide in and out of her pussy.

Sitting up on my knees, I growl, "Watch me take you, Bella. Watch my cock take you. You're mine, forever." I look up into the mirror, making sure she can see us. Pulling almost completely out, I slowly push back into her, inch by inch. Bella arches her back further off the bed, her hips rocking in time to mine.

Her moans and cries come faster and louder with each slow thrust of my hips. Bella's skin flushes with her mounting desire.

"Damn baby, you're so fuckin' hot. Tell me what you want. I want you to soar."

"Faster, Drake. Faster," she begs.

Falling forward, I kiss her, pouring my need into her. My hips pump faster, matching her pace. With every thrust forward, I grind my pelvis against her, putting pressure on her clit. My body trembles, I feel myself building. I'm on the verge of losing all control. I've never felt such pleasure, such passion, such need. Bella widens her legs again, planting her feet on the bed. She lifts her hips off the bed, trying to fuck me faster.

"Oh, God Drake, faster, harder. I'm so close," Bella cries.

Fuck it. I lose control at her plea. Grabbing her hips and holding her up, I thrust faster. Bella's whimpers drive me wild. The sound of our flesh slapping together echoes through the room.

"Dray... Dray... I'm going to come. Dray now, now," Bella screams.

With one last thrust, Bella's pussy contracts, squeezing every bit of cum out of me.

"I love you!" she cries as her orgasm consumes her.

Falling forward, I roll us over so Bella is laying on top of me. Panting, we try to catch our breath. Bella places little kisses on my chest. Holy fuck, that was unbelievable. I'm never letting her go. Running my fingers through her hair, I kiss the top of Bella's head.

"Babe, I've finally discovered what real and true love is with you. I'm never letting you go. You're forever mine. I love you, from the depths of my heart and soul. You're my everything."

CHAPTER THIRTY FIVE

ISABELLA: ENJOYING HIS NASTY

*L*ifting my head off Drake's chest as my eyes slowly open, I smile up at him.

"Drake, you've always been my *one and only*. There never has and never will be any other for me. I love you, and only you." I vow, staring deep into his jade eyes.

Stretching, I inhale deeply. The scent of roses tickles my nose, causing me to take in our room for the first time. Arrangements of Circus roses cover every surface, the nightstands, the dresser, the armoire hiding the TV, even the floor. My head snaps around, my mouth hanging open. "Oh my God! How, when? How did you do this? You've been with me every second." I question him.

"Remember when I made those calls? Brit set it up."

"I wanted you so badly when you carried me in here, I didn't even notice them."

"Do you know how many there are?" Drake asks, flashing an impish smile.

"There has to be close to a hundred in here," I answer after taking another look around the room. "Brit did a beautiful job arranging them."

"There are exactly a hundred and one roses in here Bella, my love."

"Oh my God, you know what that means?" I gasp. "How did you know it means *you're my one and only?*" I don't give him a chance to answer, leaning down to kiss him sensuously. My core hums as his penis jerks inside me. Henry hardens, filling me again. I'm slightly sore, but I don't care. I want him again, now. He cradles my face, pulling me away and ending our kiss. He rests our heads forehead to forehead as we slow our breathing again.

"Babe, I was going to do the whole get on my knee shit and ask you to marry me, but I think this is so much better, still connected with you." My head snaps up as I search those gorgeous, heart stopping, jade green eyes.

"What! What are you saying, Drake?"

Rolling us over, still connected, my girlie parts flutter around his ever-growing erection. Drake reaches over to the nightstand and pulls open the drawer. In his hand is a small red velvet box. He snaps it open with one hand and turns it to me.

My jaw drops at the massive rose cut yellow diamond. Small rubies run along the posts holding the diamond in place, trailing to a gold band. It looks just like the roses surrounding us here. My heart races as my breathing stutters at the gorgeous ring. My core contracts, fluttering around Drake again.

"Babe, I've imagined dozens of ways of asking you this, but this is the perfect moment.

You know I love you. Will you marry me, and be mine forever? I never want to spend another moment without you by my side. Will you make me the luckiest man in the world by becoming my wife, my lover and forever best friend?"

"Oh God YES... YES... YES! Now put the beautiful ring on my finger and kiss me, Drake, before I implode from excitement!" I squeal.

Shoving my hand in his face, Drake chuckles. He takes my hand and slides the ring onto my finger and kisses my knuckles. He presses his lips to mine, kissing me like a man starved. Rolling us again until I'm lying across his chest, I bend my knees, so they're tucked against his sides.

Drake's big hands grab my bum and squeeze. I lift my hands and release my hair from its messy bun, knowing how much he loves my hair.

"Goddamn woman, you unman me," He growls as my hair falls around my shoulders. "You're so fucking beautiful, and that hair. I can't wait to pull it as I fuck you from behind and slap that ass."

"Drake, oh gosh, your nasty mouth is making me hot again. I can't wait to feel you take me from behind either."

"Holy fucking shit. Oh babe, you gotta stop teasing me like this. You have to be sore."

God, I really want to feel him take me from behind,

the image of him doing that races through my brain. Lifting off of Drake's lap, I force the next words from my mouth.

"Drake, I want that. I want to feel you take me from behind. Break me in, so I can get used to you faster. It's crazy, but that's what I want. I like the sting. I can handle it, if it gets to be too much, I'll let you know. Claim me, make me yours."

"Holy fuck, woman."

Crawling over him, I get on my hands and knees and look over my shoulder at him. Drake blinks slowly and licks his lips.

"Woman, I'm in charge now. This is how I want you, I want you so fucking horny for me, until you're thinking of swearing for the first time, demanding I fuck you, and hard," he growls, smacking the side of my bum.

A loud moan escapes me. I can't keep still, squirming and rocking my hips. My core squeezes around the finger he slides into me. This is so freaking hot, I can't handle it. I need him inside of me, *now*.

Drake then runs his hand up my back. He shoves a pillow under my chest.

"Trust me, baby. Lay your head and chest down on these pillows. Keep that spectacular ass up in the air like this. Turn your head to the side. That's it. If it gets too much, or you can't handle it, tell me to stop, and I'll slow down and not go as deep.

"You told me to break you in, fuck, that's every man's fantasy. Unless you tell me to stop, I'm going to fuck you hard. I'm so fucking turned on right now I don't know how long I'll last. Babe, I need to hear you say the words, that if it's too much, you'll stop me?"

My voice shakes with excitement when I answer him. "Okay, honey. I'll say stop if it's too much. But right now, I need you to fill me. Please."

"You got it, babe. I'm going to take care of that now. Hold on to the blanket, babe."

He removes his finger and his hard erection slowly fills me. This angle stretches me more, fills me differently. He feels much deeper than before. I try to breathe through the sting as he pulls out a bit and slides back in until his hips touch my bum. He stays planted to the root, pumping his hips forward and grinding into me, pulling me back with both hands on my hips.

My legs quiver with a bit of discomfort and new sensations. It hurts but feels dang good. He pulls out again, still going slow and slides back in. I whimper at the feel of his penis sliding along the sensitive nerves. After a few more strokes, the pain dissipates and it feels un-freaking-believable. My muscles relax, and I fall into a rhythm with Drake.

"That's it baby, relax that pussy and take my big cock. I wanna touch this tight little ass hole of yours while fucking you and see how responsive it is."

Gasping, I wonder what the hay. Drake slides a finger around our tight connection. His wet finger slides to my back opening as I tighten up.

"Relax baby, trust me. I just want to make you soar to heights you've never reached."

"Okay Dray, I trust you."

With his wet finger, he slowly taps my back opening.

His thrusts pick up speed. My every nerve-ending fires in ecstasy. My hips rock back into him.

"Oh, Dray… Oh, Dray, I can't control it, I need it now. I'm so close."

"FUCK!" Drake cries out, one hand firmly gripping my hip as he slams into me. He pulls almost completely out before slamming back in, in quick succession. The scent of our sweat and sex tickle my nose, and his grunts and the slapping of our bodies connecting makes me even hotter.

Drake's tapping finger slowly breaches my backside. My climax consumes me, and I scream and moan. Shivers and heat dance along my skin, lights flash in my eyes as my legs turn to Jell-O, unable to hold me any longer.

"Goddamn, that's fucking hot!" Drakes calls out as I collapse completely onto the pillows. Drake thrusts into me once, twice more and then pushes all the way in as I feel him reach his own release. A few seconds later I feel him slowly slide out of me.

Lying on my stomach, I try to catch my breath and regain the feeling in my body. Shivers continue to race along my skin.

"I love you, babe. That was un-fucking-believable," Drake whispers, feathering kisses along my back and neck. "Don't move, I'll be right back."

"Don't worry, I can't," I mumble into the pillow. My eyes feel heavy and threaten to close. That was ahhh-maz-ing. Oh, man, I can't believe everything that just happened. I snuggle into the pillows and rest my eyes, absorbing every single moment from the shower till now.

Drake leaves the bed as I lay spread out, unable to even pull my sore legs together. Heh, I'll be lucky if I can make it to the bathroom tomorrow, but God, it was so worth it.

Drake's heavy footsteps return from the bathroom. He joins me on the bed, and I jerk when he runs a warm washcloth between my legs. Oh, that feels so soothing. My back arches as he tenderly kisses the dip in my spine.

"So gorgeous," he mumbles before leaving the bed again. The air conditioning kicks on, sending cool air over my hot skin. Oh, gosh. Slowly, I gather my waning strength and roll to my side to await Drake's return.

"Babe, I want to tell you something," he says, climbing back into bed and pulling me onto his chest. "Tonight, was a first for me in many ways, too. Beside it being, by far, the best fucking orgasm of my life, it was the first time I've ever made love, and it's the first time Henry's ever felt a real pussy wrapped around him. I've always suited up, and never had sex once without a condom, including my first time."

"Really? So, in one way, you can say I was Henry's first?"

"Yeah babe, you can," Drake answers, chuckling. "Now go to sleep baby, knowing I love you, soon-to-be Mrs. Drake Allen Gregory-Fitzpatrick. You ready to share my long-ass fucking name?"

While admiring my stunning four-carat yellow rose cut diamond, I reply, "I've been dreaming about marrying you since I was four years old. You're dang right, I'm ready to have your name. I've been practicing writing it forever," I admit, giggling.

"I told you the day we met that we were going to get married. You remember, I'm sure. I've wanted to marry you forever and to have green eyed babies."

I take his hand in mine and place it on my tummy.

"You've made all my dreams and wishes come true. Our son, little peanut here, growing in my tummy, is going to look just like his daddy."

"And what if I want it to be a beautiful baby girl, who looks just like her mommy? A princess I can protect from all boys until she's thirty?" he inquires.

"Dray, neither of us are anywhere near thirty. We can't have a double standard already for our daughter," I giggle.

"I don't give a fuck. She's my daughter. You're right, though. It might be best if it's a boy. He can be the oldest of the new generation of Brothers. One day, my wild-ass Brothers will find love and start families, too. Our little peanut won't be alone for long."

"You do know our moms are going to go crazy with this, don't you? I'm sure they've secretly been planning this since we were kids. Are you ready for that? As much as I'd love to run away to Vegas tonight, we can't do that to them."

"FUCK, I'd love to run away with you. How mad do you think they'd be? I'm sure they think its tux time. But how fucking nutty do you think they'll go with the other bullshit they'll want us to do?"

"Yeah, an old-fashioned wedding dress, perfect for your wench," I say playfully. "And I agree, no tuxes. The Brothers need to be in their Camelot gear. But you'll have to tell them no bare chests. They must be fully clothed. I put my foot down on that one. It may look hot in your portrait, but not for our wedding pictures."

"We're getting married at Hawkins' castle. The pictures will be badass. We don't have to worry about security, and Hawkins can be there for the whole event without freaking out." Drake adds.

Laughing I cuddle into him, still feeling sore. "I'll love you, for the rest of my life and beyond."

"I'll love you even longer. Now go to sleep, babe." he says, kissing the top of my head.

Beyond exhausted, I cuddle into him and let my mind wander to the wedding and all I've dreamt of for years. I'll be counting down the days. But for now, I get to enjoy the next five days learning the passions of sex and making love, like a pre-honeymoon. A smile spreads across my face as I fall into a blissful sleep.

EPILOGUE

COFFEE AND A MYSTERY

2 Weeks Later …

"*T*hose pills Mom Riggs gave me for the morning sickness work like a charm. I still can't eat breakfast, but by lunchtime, I'm completely fine. How long before you think Grayson shows up? I thought you said he got coffee here every Friday after work." Questioning Drake, I'm doing one of my favorite things, people watching at our favorite Starbucks.

"Chill babe, I promise he's already texted and said he'd be here in just a minute."

Sipping on my chai tea, I glance at the counter and notice a very beautiful, petite girl bopping up to it. She has a cute big brimmed baseball cap on, with her long black loose-curled ponytail pulled through the back of the hat. She's wearing huge, dark sunglasses like she doesn't want anyone to see her face.

She approaches the counter and motions over a

barista, then leans over and whispers something to her. She lowers her sunglasses, revealing the most incredible light blue eyes I'd ever seen before. Wow, she's truly breathtaking. I wonder what she's whispering about. With those sunglasses she could be famous, but I don't recognize her.

"Drake, look at the petite girl at the counter. She has the lightest blue eyes I've ever seen in my life. They're beautiful and eerie at the same time. There's just something about her, something mysterious."

Looking up from his phone, he glances toward the counter. "Wow, I've never seen anyone with eyes that color either. I bet they really stand out when she has her hair down and not covered up with that hat," Drake adds as we continue to observe her.

"Dray, did you see that? She just handed the barista a fifty-dollar bill but didn't get a coffee. What was that for? I didn't see a drug exchange or anything." I'm still worried from Pervert Paul's attack. "She was leaning over the counter whispering to the barista just a minute ago. Strange, don't you think?"

"Babe, I didn't see anything. Do you want me to check with the barista when the chick leaves?" Drake asks, concerned.

"I just think it's odd. I love her Lululemon outfit, those black leggings with the cutouts down the sides of her legs are the bomb. Dang, I wish I had a bum like she does and that tiny waist... She's a lucky little thing. I bet she's shorter than me. Did you notice it? I mean it was a perfect bubble bum." I'm rambling, but the girl is striking.

"Emm, no babe, I wasn't looking at her ass. And for your information, I love your cute little ass, all the better for swatting and biting," Drake replies chuckling, as he nibbles on my neck.

"You sir, have a one-track mind." Giggling, I try to pull away from his teasing.

Returning my attention to the girl at the counter, I watch as she smiles and waves goodbye to the barista. She puts the big dark sunglasses back in place again and pulls the rim of her baseball cap down. She definitely doesn't want anyone to see her face. Everything about her is exquisite, from her eyes down to her long black and auburn highlighted ponytail that falls down passed her shoulders in big curls. That has to be natural.

My eyes follow her as I ponder her story. I lose her in the crowded mass of people. The door opens, drawing my attention again. Grayson enters with a smile.

"Hi Isabella, Fitz. Do either of you want anything?" he asks.

"Thanks Brother, but we already have ours. Bella said she's feeding Peanut a chocolate croissant," Drake divulges, kissing me on the forehead.

"I can't help it. Peanut is going to have a chocolate tooth like Mommy. You can't expect him to crave protein shakes, can you?" I deliver a teasing elbow to Drake's stomach.

The same barista who talked to the girl makes Grayson's coffee. When he tries to pay, she refuses his money. That's odd, I'll have to ask him about it. Finally, Grayson shakes his head, throwing his money in the tip jar.

"What was that all about?" I ask when he reaches our table. "How did you get a free coffee? Is that barista picking up on you?" I demand, curious.

"No, it's the strangest thing. This is about the fifth time I've come in here to get my coffee, and the barista tells me it was already paid for by an old friend. But fuck if I know who it is. They tell me it's a petite, shapely girl, but they refuse to tell me anything more. Not even her hair or eye color, so I can't figure this shit out. They always tell me *they've probably told me too much.*"

"Really? Drake, I wonder if it was that girl with those clear blue eyes. Grayson, you should have seen them. They were the clearest blue we've ever seen. She did have on a killer Lululemon workout outfit."

"Bella, are you trying to play investigator now?" Drake chuckles at me again.

"Isabella, what did you say about this girl's eyes?" Grayson asks fervently, sitting down with his brow wrinkled. His eyes are intense, curious.

"Emm, Drake saw her too. I mean she was probably shorter than me and really beautiful. But her eyes, *wow*, they were just gorgeous. They were such a clear blue, it was almost eerie. Weren't they, Drake?"

"Yeah, Brother. What I saw of her, she was very pretty and had incredible eyes. Her hair was pulled through the back of a baseball cap, you know like girls do with their ponytails. Why she covers those eyes up with big sunglass is beyond me."

"Fuck, are you shitting me?" Grayson growls looking between the two of us, and to the door. "What door did she go out of and how long ago?"

"Riggs, we're not shitting you. Isabella demanded I look at her because she'd never seen eyes like hers before. She was a little thing, I mean short. But she had curves, even Bella was envious. Why bro, you think you know her?"

"Fuck, you're describing Aless. But if it's Aless, why hasn't she said something to me? Or left a number on the cup? What the fuck?" Grayson looks distressed, still staring at the door I pointed to.

"Really, the girl you met years ago, the one you told Drake and me about before? Your one and only? You think that it's her?"

"I don't know, but it sure the fuck sounds like her. I've had such a strange feeling for the last couple of months. Like someone's watching me, and with these random coffees, it makes me wonder. Is fate going to bring her back to me, really?

"There's also some chick who watches me jog on the beach almost every week, but she's covered with a hat and big... Holy shit, the same chick's been watching me. But if it is Aless, why the fuck hasn't she said something?"

"Oh, that's so romantic," I swoon. "What was her name, Alice? She doesn't look like an Alice."

"No, it's Aless," Grayson mumbles, lost in thought.

"Maybe she is planning a surprise or something, letting fate takes it course," I suggest, elated at the romantic thought.

"Excuse her Riggs, she's been talking wedding stuff all week," Drake says with a sweet smile.

"Fuck, from your lips to God's ears, I hope it is her.

I'm going to have to confront that girl who watches me jog. I'm ready to give fate a helping hand. But shit, now you have me really wondering. I have to figure this out, that's for damn sure."

"Isabella, one last question, why would you think it was the girl with the clear blue eyes that paid for my coffee? I only know one girl with clear blue eyes, and that's Aless."

"Well... I like to people watch. She came in and went straight to the barista and whispered something to her. I couldn't hear her from here, but she gave her a fifty-dollar bill and walked out minutes later without a coffee. And it was the same barista that gave you the free coffee."

"Fuck, I think that barista just got off work, too. I'll have to come back tomorrow and see if I can get any more information out of her. Maybe if I give her a hundred, she'll talk. If it really is her, it'll be worth it."

"Riggs, you think it might be your girl? If I see her again, I'll make sure to call you. You deserve to get your woman back and be as happy as we are." Drake pulls me closer to him, kissing the top of my head as I finish the last bite of my croissant.

"Okay, enough about me and my shit. I'll get to the bottom of it real soon. I hear your moms are trying to plan your wedding. All I have to say is if that is my Aless playing games with me, after I tan her hide, I'll be bringing a fuckin' date. I just have to find her first."

"Really hoping it's her, Brother. But when it comes to our moms, I laid down the law. It's a Camelot wedding at Hawkins place. They've already broke ground, and the buildings are going up. Our moms just have to deal."

We all laugh, knowing the moms are having a blast, driving us nuts over this. Grayson keeps looking out the doors, looking for his Aless. I hope it is her, and whatever she's up to, I hope she talks to him soon. Grayson deserves a good woman, and she's beautiful. But dang, Drake is a foot taller than me. Grayson has to have at least fifteen inches on her.

My gaze slides to the front door, pondering what she could be up to. I watch the crowd of people and spot her. She's the still figure among the moving throng. Lifting my arm to tap Grayson and point her out, she notices me watching her and takes off running.

"Grayson, I think that's her! She took off running when she saw me watching her. She ran towards the beach. She's wearing a cute pink baseball hat and black leggings with cutouts on the lower leg, and a track jacket, with a little black backpack."

"Fuck!" he shouts. "See you tomorrow!" Grayson yells, bolting from his chair and out the door, leaving his coffee behind.

"I hope it's her. Grayson put his trust in fate over eight years ago, hoping to see her again. That would be fucking awesome for him. He's a great guy and deserves the woman of his dreams. Let's get the fuck out of here. I have things I want to do to you now that you've had your chocolate fix and energy boost." Drake pulls me out of the booth, giving my bum a squeeze.

"Drake, we're in public," I protest.

"I don't give a fuck. We're done having coffee with a

friend, and you better move that cute little ass of yours before I show the world a lot more than you want me to."

Giggling, I take off out the door, keeping just out of his reach. He'll catch me in a matter of seconds.

Book 2 in the Brothers of Camelot Series
Prelude: Almost Caught

Holy shit, Isabella saw me. I've got to get out of here and fast. Thank God I still have on my gym shoes. I make a mad dash towards the penthouse hoping not to be seen by Grayson in the crowd. I don't want to bump into him for the first time in over eight years, in leggings and looking a mess.

"Aless!" Grayson's voice calls out from behind me.

Crap, crap, crap. Up ahead I spot the fire hydrant near the corner of the alley by my penthouse, my legs pump harder. I just hope the dumpster lid is closed so that I can get a good leap up to there. Oh, how I pray these large trees hide my trip up to the balcony as well.

"Is that you, Aless?!" he calls again. My heart aches to answer, but not yet. I'm not ready.

Swiftly turning the corner, I leap up placing my foot on the top of the hydrant and push off. My silent prayer that the lid of the dumpster is closed is answered when my foot connects with it. Thank you, Mother Mary and all that is holy.

I tug my collapsible grappling hook from the side of my backpack with a push of a button it opens completely. I toss it onto our balcony. Giving it a little tug to make sure it's secure, I scramble up the rope, hoping not to be seen. Once I reach the top, I swing my leg over and fall on to the safety of my balcony.

"Holy fuckin shit balls, woman!" Anissa yells, walking out of the sliding door. "Lexy, what the fuck? You scared the ever-loving shit out of me with your ninja shit. You're supposed to warn us when you're doing that shit!" She stops at my feet, looking at me lying on the floor.

"Sshhh! Grayson followed me home. I had too." I whisper, trying to catch my breath.

"Fuck, girl. Why didn't you tell me?" Reaching back into the penthouse, she grabs a pair of binoculars, the ones she regularly uses to check out the guys on the beach and boardwalk across the street. "Yup, there he is. He just a block down the road headed our way. Want to see?" she offers but never stops looking into the binoculars, nor does she hand them to me.

"Damn, girl. He's looking around, obviously for you. He's even stopping and asking people. Shit, he's hot as hell and *huge*. I've seen pictures of him on Facebook, but damn, they *do not* do him justice."

I slowly sit up and peek through the cutout cloverleaf in the stucco.

"Yeah, I believe he's even bigger now than he was that last time we were together. He's let his hair grow out a bit." I informed her, in a trance just staring at him.

"Goddamn, that man must do squats every day. Mmm-mm, that bubble butt, I bet you could rest your drink on it. Your poor children are going to have ass issues with that two-seater swing you have in your own backyard. Mixed with his ass, yeah, your children surely won't lack in that department."

"Anissa, stop looking at Grayson's ass." Slapping at her legs, I move to stand up and take the binoculars from her. Grayson's still looking for me, but at least he's walking away from us. Damn, that's one mighty fine view.

"Yes, he's one gorgeous man." I sigh. "I can't wait to be in those arms again." Lowering the binoculars, I turn to my bestie. "Nissa, this proves one thing to me. He hasn't forgotten me, either. He was calling out my name. It's time to put the wheels in motion and get back into his life."

"It's about damn time. I just hope your little game of cat and mouse doesn't piss him off." Anissa says as we both watch him walk away, almost out of sight.

"It won't, it can't. This just has to work. I do believe in the fate he talked about years ago, I just need to help it along a bit."

FOLLOW ME ON SOCIAL MEDIA

If you want more, follow me on Facebook at Author Necie Navone and Twitter @NecieNavone.

I'm hoping to not only share Grayson's story with you very soon, but also a 3-book series of Aless' Life ('My Hidden Life', 'My Tragic Life', 'My Free Life') Don't worry: I hate cliffhangers too. So, all three books will be released within a week of each other.

Thank you, and I hope you come along with me on my journey with the Brothers of Camelot.

www.ingramcontent.com/pod-product-compliance
Lightning Source LLC
Chambersburg PA
CBHW051511250626
47156CB00001B/46

* 9 780999 723500 *